PENGUIN BOOKS

THE CUT

Daniel Blythe was born in Maidstone in 1969 and read modern languages at St John's College, Oxford. He now teaches adult learners and is completing a Ph.D. on the supernatural in German Romanticism. He has contributed two sci-fi novels to a bestselling series, has had stories published in magazines and anthologies, and has been a prize-winner at the Kent Literature Festival. Daniel Blythe lives in South Yorkshire.

DANIEL BLYTHE

The Cut

PENGUIN BOOKS

PENGUIN BOOKS

Published by the Penguin Group
Penguin Books Ltd, 27 Wrights Lane, London w8 5tz, England
Penguin Books USA Inc., 375 Hudson Street, New York, New York 10014, USA
Penguin Books Australia Ltd, Ringwood, Victoria, Australia
Penguin Books Canada Ltd, 10 Alcorn Avenue, Toronto, Ontario, Canada m4v 3b2
Penguin Books (NZ) Ltd, 182–190 Wairau Road, Auckland 10, New Zealand

Penguin Books Ltd, Registered Offices: Harmondsworth, Middlesex, England

First published 1998

10 9 8 7 6 5 4 3 2 1

Typeset in 10/13.5 pt Adobe Janson Text
Typeset by Intype London Ltd
Printed in England by Intype

1 *End of the World Song*

Hi, I'm Bel. I'm waiting. I can taste the rain, the petrol-smoky town and the sea. I've got a knife in my pocket.

I'm standing in the rain, and it's all round me, but I'm in this magic ring under my umbrella so I'm all right. The water clatters around me. It makes the reflections fizz like on a bad TV channel.

I'm waiting. In the rain. With a knife in my pocket.

People hurry by. There's a couple under one huge multi-coloured umbrella. They're in matching raincoats – even the drip-patterns match.

We must think about installing cable TV, he says. I know, she says, but it's hardly a priority, and there's that wedding present for mumble-mumble.

Now they're swallowed by a taxi which disappears with a vroom and a swish down the High Street – heading for the suburbs, probably, Beston Well and Beckford and High Down. Places where there are still houses like ours. Houses that don't touch.

There's movement in the doorway of the video shop. I've been watching the people and now they're leaving. The video shop gleams big and yellow like a spacecraft in the night. Down the dark street, other spacecraft are parked. Red-white takeaways, one club doorway drawn in blue neon. There isn't much else. This is the edge of the world. The wind blows in from the Arctic, here, 'cos there's nothing further up the country to stop it. Nothing between Kent and the North Pole. You carry on down the street two hundred yards, you get to the sea wall and the stacks of boarding-houses, gawping out to sea.

There's nobody in the video shop now, just the old guy behind the counter, so I'm going to give it a go. I'm testing myself now. I'm seeing how far I can take it.

I fold my umbrella down, leave it at the door. Water drips on the mat. The door creaks. The lights in the shop are buzzing, hospital-white, and three screens are playing, all showing the cartoon-bright uniforms of a *Star Trek: The Next Generation* episode. The old guy looks up over his newspaper for just a second, then goes back to reading it.

I can feel my face getting hot with annoyance. It's as if he doesn't think I present a threat, doesn't think I'm worth bothering with. We'll see. I stroll up the New Releases aisle, my coat dripping water on the carpet. Staining it dark. There's box after box with Sharon Stone's eyes and Schwarzenegger's pecs and Hugh Grant's grin and Kurt Russell looking moody.

I stroll under the flickering screens, affecting casual interest. But my heart's battering away. Thud. Thud. One hand in my raincoat pocket, on the smoothness of the folded knife. Above me, on the screens, Captain Picard tells Mr Riker to go to Red Alert. I rummage through the Previously Viewed. There are boxes and boxes of outdated stuff. I can't do it with one hand and so I let the knife nestle in my pocket for now. The plastic on the video cases feels clammy, alive, as if other hands have just been here. My palms are sweaty. I can smell them, pungent as kebabs, and it almost makes me feel ill.

Thud. Thud. Got to keep calm.

He's still reading his paper. He turns the page, seemingly unaware of me at the moment.

I push my hair back, let it tumble forward as I look up and down the comedy section. I pick up a video box. Newman and Baddiel. It's empty, of course, they're all empty, the boxes are just tokens, in case anyone takes a vid off the shelves and runs off with it. It would be bizarre if other shops did the same. Supermarkets with dummy bean cans, empty cereal boxes, plastic turkeys, cardboard cheese. You take them all to the checkout where they exchange them for the real thing. Sometimes they don't exchange them, and you don't notice.

I take Newman and Baddiel to the counter. I'm still trailing water.

My hair's sticking to my forehead. His paper comes down as I approach, and I see a wrinkled brown head, big grey-black moustache.

'All right, love,' he says. 'Nasty night out, innit?'

'Yeah, not too good,' I reply. 'This, please.' I hold it up, the big plastic token.

'Right – oh, you'll like that.' His head gleams under the lights. He's got a halo. The three screens zoom in on Lieutenant Worf zapping something. 'Our Tammy liked that one when she saw it.'

He's rummaging under the counter. I go hot and cold. Maybe he's triggering an alarm. He knows something's up, he can see I'm bad news. I tell myself he can't, I look respectable enough, I've done nothing yet. My fingers close over the knife. I imagine the greasy prints, the thrust. I see the blood.

'Course, she liked them before they were famous, thinks they're not as good now.' He's grinning at me under his moustache, so I have to grin back. He's saying, 'That's two pound fifty please, love. Have you got your card?'

Oh, yes, my card.

In my pocket. It's not my card in my pocket, it's my knife. My knife is my card. I want to make it my calling-card.

He's holding the vid in one hand, in its new, anonymous case with the shop's yellow logo on. He's holding out the other hand for my card and my money.

He said something about his Tammy. He's got a family. Wife and a daughter, probably. This is stupid. This is ridiculous. My head's spinning now because it all seems so idiotic, so unmotivated.

It would be wasted here, the Cut. I can't get angry about him, can I? Just another victim in the town at the end of the world?

I can't get angry, but I'm meant to be pushing myself. That's what it's all about. Seeing how far I can go.

My hand comes up fast on to the counter and it's there – bright, sharp, thin. Incongruous between my fingers.

It's my video membership card.

I pay for the video. He smiles. We say good night and I leave, picking up my brolly on the way.

*

The sea air's cold. Tastes of fish and chips. I hurry along the promenade, where life used to be. Dark ghosts of the funfair watch me from the beach. Cliffs of hotels and guest-houses loom on my left. I walk on. Click, click. The sea washes the beach, hissing quietly to itself. The only thing that couldn't be stopped in this dead town.

The flick-knife sits in my pocket, still unopened. It's warm, now, like a lover.

I wonder if I will find the right home for it.

2 *Communion*

I trace the knife slowly over the photo of Kate. I'm cutting jigsaw pieces out.

Broad, clean and sharp. I keep it sharp. There's a man, for keeping it sharp, comes round once in a while. It has to be a man. He does it between his legs. Hooks up his bike to this contraption and shoves whatever blade it is into the works – garden shears, knives, spades. Brings them back with the best edge. One day, I'll show him how well he does my knife.

Kate's gone to pieces. Kate is now fragments, each piece of her like a little coloured jewel on my black carpet.

Kate married my father just eight months ago. They got married in church, on the altar I desecrated, that Saturday night, ten weeks ago. I remember. I cut her up now, and remember.

The church door feels damp under my hand, and it creaks like coffin-wood. I'm pulling him in behind me. As we step over the threshold, I must be nervous 'cos I feel the drink resurging inside me, acid and warm. I gulp it down.

It's not totally dark. They've left candles burning. Very thoughtful. It smells of candle and cold, fusty air and old hassocks. There are pamphlets in a rack and a font with a frilly edge like a giant grey shell. Over in the corner, dim in the orange light, a rocking-horse and blotchy, impressionist paintings on paper. Playgroup stuff. In a church? Well, who am I to argue?

I let go of his hand, as he's not important for the moment.

*

I met him in Domingo. Want to know how?

It's a warm night and I'm looking round Domingo for a pair of eyes. There are plenty looking at me, none of them the right sort. Domingo is full of eyes on a Saturday night. Hunters' eyes, bright in the shadows, peering from the red smoke like lecherous demons. I'm not exactly inconspicuous. My hair, black and long and straight, is brushed to a gloss and falls to meet a scarlet crushed-velvet top, set off by a silver skirt. My silver and red earrings wink in the whirling lights.

I am not subtle tonight. It's my eighteenth birthday.

I'm walking up the aisle, pirouetting, conscious of my mouth open, gaping up at the squinches and pilasters and colonnades. A month before I wouldn't have known they were called squinches and pilasters and colonnades, but I remember an article on architecture. I remember things these days.

The altar is draped in virginal white, crowned by the two candles. They look like something Wiccan, like horns. My first thrill of blasphemy.

He's shuffling, hands in pockets.

'Can we go?' he says awkwardly. 'I don't like it here.'

I smile and slide towards him, put my arms round his neck and kiss his mouth. I can't taste much, my own mouth's pretty numb. It just feels slippery. He doesn't seem to respond at first. But he knows what I'm doing when I slide my hands down his shirt and start caressing his jeans.

His eyes open wide in disbelief. Or unbelief. Anti-belief.

It's what we're about to do.

Acts of unbelievers.

It's almost boring, the way I chose him. It could have been any of them.

So I'm in Domingo, perched on a bar stool, like some farty sculpture on a spindly stand. I can feel the music in my body, as if it's rushing into my blood without even passing through my ears. The barmaid has huge Romany ringlets and blue lipstick, and clatters with metalwork as

6

she polishes the glasses. She's got a gigantic cleavage, constrained by a thin yellow top, through which I can see her nipples standing up. I wonder what she's excited about.

He lurches up next to me. Black hair, I remember that much, and a warm, male smell like an animal. Dark jacket, white trousers. Pale skin. I recall his arms. Smooth, almost hairless. He's holding out a tenner, waving it under the barmaid's nose.

'Bloody Mary!' he's shouting. 'Bloody bloody Mary, Mary, now!' and he shoves the tenner at her ample bust. I don't know if it's a demand for a drink, or if he's swearing at her, or both. Is the bejewelled creature called Mary? That would make sense. She pours his drink with bad grace and slams it down next to him. Some of it sloshes over the edge and splatters his finger, as if he's cut himself. He sucks the finger with meaningful anger, before slamming the crumpled note into the warm wet circles on the bar.

I'm watching in amusement, and he turns glittery eyes to me.

'What's funny?' he says, but it doesn't sound aggressive. He's got a proper, almost feminine roundness to his voice.

'Nothing.' I smile quietly to myself, shifting position so as to reveal more thigh.

He opens his mouth. He's drooling slightly.

'What's your name?' he asks.

I open my eyes wide at him.

'Tequila Sunrise.'

Mary slams his change down, pieces of silver. It trickles over the edge of the bar and falls in his lap.

I grin and lead him to the altar. The first and only time. There's no wedding march except the wind and the rain shaking the place. The watching ghosts. With my hands on his neck and my legs round his, I'm on top of the altar. He's falling, rolling on top of me, seems not to care where we are any more. That's good, if it works for him. Me, I want to remember where we are. I always want to remember this. *Take and eat this body in remembrance of me.*

'The candles,' he says, almost in panic.

I snuff them out with swift pinches. *Let there be darkness*.

His mouth is exploring mine. I'm conscious of the heat, the liquid, but my mouth's quite numb. No taste of anything. My teeth have gone all tingly as if from electricity. I can feel the stone walls listening, soaking up our lust. His hands grip my legs and part them. He grabs my knickers by the waist and pulls them down. I've just pulled his shirt open and I've bitten his shoulder, hard.

It's soft meat, like chicken, and it feels good under my teeth. They rake across his shoulder to his neck. I lick, up to his mouth, where a strand of saliva links us. *Take, drink*. He's breathing hard as he fumbles to get inside me. Up in the rafters, pigeons are twittering.

The candlelight flickers against the cool, impassive faces of saints. My eyes are closed in ecstasy, and I can feel my hair loosening, then my head lolling off the edge of the altar. He finishes in remarkable speed, with lots of gasping, but little else, and pulls out of me as if I am now contaminated.

My body turning to jelly, I hoist myself up, kneeling on the white cloth, all sense of decorum lost. My loins feel liquid. Fluid splatters from between my legs. A runny, pinkish mixture of blood and juice. He's pulling his trousers up, red-faced, and staggers against a pew, looking very furtive. I can't help bursting out laughing as I adjust my underwear, and it echoes round the vaults like the laughter of saints.

'Yeah,' he mutters. 'Funny.' He slumps into a pew.

So after I choose him I mutter the suggestion in his ear and he seems keen, so I slide off my bar stool, allowing myself to leave on his arm, and we're oozing through the sweaty people until we get into the harshness of the night air.

He starts off in one direction, then suddenly stops and turns to me.

'Where can we go?' he asks in desperation.

'You haven't even got a car, then?' This is turning out worse than I'd thought.

He shrugs again. I want to tell him to stop it because he hasn't got enough shoulder to shrug with, he's too spindly and spiky. He looks like a pneumatic drill, going up and down and up and down. If he shrugs again, he'll spike himself right through the pavement.

I stand there, hands on hips, glowering at him.

'Church is open,' I say to him.

He goes a bit pale. I think so, anyway. It all looks orange under these lights.

'We can't do it in the church!'

'Why not? No one's using it now.'

I grab him by the hand and pull him, protesting, down Guild Street towards Union Square and the Church of All Saints.

Oh, his name was JJ, by the way.

Joshua James McCann, 'Call me JJ'. I wouldn't have remembered, it's just that he's scrawled it on the torn-out title page of a hymn-book which he must have pressed on me just after my little service.

I wonder if it's 'Call me JJ', or 'Call Me! – JJ'.

There is a number on the other side. The latter, then.

JJ wanted to clean up the cloth – he wanted to get some soap and actually wash it. I kicked him in the shins and said let them find it tomorrow, probably think it's Christ's blood or some other sort of wondrous sign. When actually, it's my slightly menstrual love-juice.

In the Ladies off Guild Street, I take a hard, hot piss which practically tears me apart. The stream hurtles into the bowl, and I can feel it scouring the porcelain as if it's going to take the surface off.

I read all the graffiti again. The usual crap – some lesbian stuff, bits of cod advice about boyfriends. One long outpouring in blue and black goes on over most of a wall. Ms Blue, to judge from her complaints, is spineless, and Ms Black is an over-sympathetic do-gooder. I get out my lipstick and scrawl DUMP HIM in horror-letters over the whole of this closet correspondence.

Then I shove some sheets of bog-roll down my knickers to stop leakage, snap my bag shut, hoist it on my shoulder and go home, ready to kill Kate.

I don't, though.

3   *Knowing Me . . .*

I can hear Kate. I suppose I will have to talk to her in a minute, and pretend to like her. It's a bit more complicated than that, though. Bear with me.

I wish I was a better girl sometimes, because I do love Jesus.

No, really. When I did it with JJ on that altar it wasn't just token blasphemy, and it certainly wasn't a random place. As far as he was concerned it could have been in the multi-storey or down on the beach or in one of the burnt-out cars by the Undercliff. But I chose the place.

I've had this dream, ever since I first read the Bible and went to church, about screwing on a cross, a cruci-fixation, you might call it. From shagging JJ to shagging JC.

Course, it isn't really Christ, it's a young acolyte of some incense-heady church, one of those I don't frequent. He tells me I must give my virginity to Jesus. Together we go to the centre of town where the wooden Easter cross is proudly standing by the war memorial. Under the spring stars we push the cross and heave at it together in a parody of the new settlers at some colony raising the sign of their God.

It crashes to the ground. I lie down on the cross, my arms and legs extended, and I am bound, the rope chafing. I can see the stars. I can see the moon. My hands and feet are numb and I can feel my legs gaping open like a big mouth, ready to receive. I'm totally in control. Get down on me, I tell him. Do it now.

When he enters me I am closing my eyes, thinking of Jesus being hammered to his cross, gouts of blood spurting up and splattering his flesh. I come, straining at my bonds. Powerful, beautiful pain. There are flowers opening in my mind, bright and blood-red, Easter flowers of renewal, blood-giving, life-giving. I've cut the vein and there's the erection and the life, spurting inside my ready, bready body.

Kate has come in. I can hear her clattering around downstairs. I gather up the bits of her face into an envelope and slam them into a drawer.

So the video shop was yesterday, right? All that stuff with JJ, that was ten weeks ago on my eighteenth birthday. And Kate's been married to my father for eight months now.

I've wanted to kill her fifteen times since then, each time for a particular, precise reason. I haven't done it, yet. Obviously I haven't really wanted to. When I really want to, I will.

She knocks. I'm lying on my bed, reading.

'Yeah?'

She puts her styled blonde head around the door and gives me a glittery smile.

'Would you like a cup of tea?'

No, I'd like you to put your head down the toilet. Of course, this isn't what I say.

'No, thanks.'

I give Kate the sincere smile that I have perfected over the past year. The great thing about deceiving Kate is that it's a deception based on total truth. I don't like her. I have never liked her. But I've allowed her to believe that I have put aside my dislike. That I've buried the hatchet. That I'm making an effort. I don't have to pretend that I really like her, I just have to pretend that I'm being polite.

Whereas really, I am plotting her death.

You see, no one gets in my way. That's been my philosophy for a long time.

Kate says, 'Can we talk?'

I sigh, fold my book up and put it to one side.

'The Cowbitch wanted to talk,' I tell JJ. I'm out of breath, I've been running. 'So where are we going?'

He grins, leaning against the bollard in Promenade Avenue. 'Not much choice in this dump, is there?'

'Yeah,' I say thoughtfully, and he's lit the cigarette I've flipped out before I even realize it. 'Makes you wonder where people go in this town. Real people, I mean.'

We are not real people. We are from what's euphemistically called Middle England. People in council-tax bands E and F. Our parents have gravel on their drives, are nearing the end of the mortgage payments and could just have afforded to send some of us to public school, if they made economies. Some of them have swimming-pools and time-shares in France.

Sickening, isn't it?

No, not really. I rather like having money. Gives me the chance to do all the things I need to do. Just another year, and I'll be out of this dead-end town, and I've got to make sure I've rounded myself before I get off to college. I've always had and done what I wanted, and I see no reason to stop now. I've never wanted to do any of the things that were arranged for me – cookery classes, music lessons, the church. I want to drink, dance and screw, and there's not much else to do. Got it?

I'm off with JJ down the street, arm in arm and out for fun.

Kate's sitting on my bed. She's wearing a red pullover with bumpy patterns like cake icing, and swirly black and white yin-yang leggings. They're the kind of leggings you wear when you are eighteen. And you need to get laid that night. And you haven't got big rumply cellulite. None of these, I have to say, applies to Kate.

'I need to ask you something,' she says, smiling sweetly.

Her foundation almost splits. Her pink lipstick doesn't quite mask the fact that her lips are cracking. She obviously doesn't know about running a toothbrush over them now and then, to help your pouting and smoothness. I know all these tricks, but I'm not telling Kate anything.

'Do you . . . intend to do anything this summer?' she inquires, with her cake-icing face sweet and demure. I'd love to plunge a knife right into it.

'What do you mean?' I've drawn my knees up, clasped my hands around them.

'Your father and I were just wondering if you were planning to stay in town, or if you were . . . going away anywhere. And if you're staying, whether you were planning to . . . get a job of any sort.'

A *job*?

Is she kidding?

Let me put it this way. My father's annual income is something in the region of ninety K after tax. Kate, as far as I'm aware, has always been a professional housewife. Oh, sorry, am I meant to say 'Domestic Incarceration Survivor' these days? You'll have to excuse me, I've never been in the PFC brigade.

Anyway, that all went horribly wrong the first time round – messy marriage, all the usual stuff. Want to know how it went? In three words: antinomy, acrimony, alimony. Marriage might be grand, but divorce is ten grand.

As soon as she was a free woman, moneyed for nothing (and her kicks for free) off she went in search of another saccharine-daddy, another income to take out. She found my father at some industry ball, which she was attending with a couple of her many men. One on each arm. (Some people are detached when it comes to relationships. Others are what you might call semi-detached. Kate, I have learnt, was always what you might call terraced.)

She had the whole house done out by an interior designer as soon as she moved in. Except my bedroom. No one was touching that. She still goes on about it sometimes, about 'co-ordinating' the furniture, whatever that means. I chose the furniture in this room specially not to co-ordinate. She had the lounge done in powder-blue and navy, with shell-shaped dishes on blue marble tables, an eggshell-blue carpet, thick navy velvet curtains tied back with gold and aquamarine tassels. She had matching high-backed wooden chairs put in the dining-room, and went through all the cutlery and crockery making sure it matched her new selection of tablecloths (mustard yellow and kiwi green).

Then she started asking round about gardeners, and had one in to transform the three acres of scraggy countryside into a *Good House-keeping* showpiece. Green-jelly smoothness. Chocolate trees. Flowers in aniseed-ball red and sherbet yellow and peppermint white. All we needed was a gingerbread roof and I could feel justified in shoving her in the oven.

My father was delighted. At last, someone who would take control of all those fiddly, fussy things like décor and entertaining and the garden. I mean, I can see how it happened. I was all for having someone in to look after the house, because, fuck it, I'm not doing my own dirty washing. So having a Woman Who Does was appealing. But she did too much. There was no need for him to marry the cow.

Someone weaker, stupider maybe, would have hated him for it. Felt betrayed. But that would have been too easy, and she'd have loved it. As far as I'm concerned, he's just to be pitied. It's her I hate, this woman who stepped into our life and made my father think there was a need for things like drinks parties, landscaped gardens and elaborately folded napkins. People create these needs in society to give themselves sinecures – what use, otherwise, would there be in jobs like style consultants and catering-service managers and interior designers?

So what I say is, 'I hadn't really thought about it.'

Meaning – if a stupid bitch like you can sponge off my dad, there's no way you're telling me that I can't.

Kate sighs, and has a little smile to herself, as if to say, *How can I tell her? Maybe she'll understand when she's older*, and places her hands in her lap.

'And also,' she says, 'as you are intending to stay here over the summer, your father and I aren't really happy with the company you keep. We wonder whether it might be better for you to find some friends who are more . . . well, who are more suited to you. A better class of people.'

I have to gulp down my rage, like bile. I can almost see it, spreading reddish-black across my face. And don't you just hate people who talk in the plural? We wonder, we think, we feel. I force myself to look unperturbed.

'I'm quite happy with the friends I have, thank you.'

'Well,' Kate says, strolling over to my bookshelf, and before I know it the bitch has actually started rearranging things on top of it. In a designer format, no doubt. Is that what you've learnt from *Bookcase Monthly*, Kate? The spring look for paperweights is Edge, while note-blocks should be set at a thirty-degree angle to pot-pourri? 'Let's see,' she says. 'Maybe things will work out.'

So I think, yeah, maybe they will. Meaning, work out my way. And she's no doubt thinking she's got it her way, too. I have to bite the inside of my lip – so soft and slippery, like fish – to let her have the satisfaction. For now.

4 *Nightcrawlers*

The bright glass rushes towards us, the size of a postcard in the dark, the size of a book – with the engine screaming – the size of the whole windscreen, the size of a fucking great shop window made of plate glass and full, brim-a-chock-a-block full, chock-a-block-a-noodle-doo-what-you-do-to-me full – of CRASH.

OK, so it's fifty minutes before. I'm holding on to JJ, and Damien and Marcie are marching on ahead there, in the orange-blotched darkness, as we stagger down this warehouse-bordered backstreet, through the neon puddles, under the big girdery walkways. The sea glitters, there, through a crack. Kids are throwing stones down on the beach.

Marcie's leaping up and down and laughing. She rolls over the bonnet of this car, a Vauxhall Nova. She's being a photo-model. The alarm screams, like an alien bird, and Marcie, staggering up from the other side of the car, shrieks with delight and does the alarm noise herself from her grit-smeared face.

'It's callin' out to me!' she shrieks, opening wide panda-eyes to me. Marcie's mascara dribbles down her face, carving channels in the icing-sugar of her make-up.

'Who's gonna drive?' I ask, looking at JJ. I remember that he is clean tonight. He was going to drive us home. Right? But he doesn't seem steady on his feet. Those dark eyes look haunted. What the hell's the matter with him?

Earlier, in the pub, JJ's hand rests on my thigh.

'Bel thinks she's clever,' he says airily, leaning back in the green leather seat. The pub burbles and wobbles around us. 'She's got three A levels and wants to go to university, so she thinks she knows it all.'

'What university?' It's Marcie, a ghoul behind her haze of smoke and a wedding cake of glasses that she is building. She asks the question but doesn't look at me. Probably because the answers wouldn't mean much to her, and she knows it. She's more interested in her glasses, anyway. Her hand's trembling.

'Western England, probably.'

'Bristol fucking Poly,' says Damien with a snigger, teeth snagging on his lip again the way they always do. I shoot him a murderous look.

Marcie has a base of eight Guinness glasses – I don't know where they came from – and on top of that a second layer of six lager glasses, which don't form such a stable unit on account of their vase-shaped curves. Then, four wineglasses on top of that. She's leaning over her shoulder now. Looking for small ones, from someone who's been high in spirits.

Damien, laughing contemptuously, flicks ash on the glasses and pretends to give them a push, then grins as if inviting the rest of us to admire his daring. Damien always looks self-satisfied. He's got the face for it – a big, broad face, scrubbed and smooth, with a second chin just beginning to grow. He's not fat; just contented-looking, well-fed. His hair's collar-length and tucked behind his ears in a couple of sleek little curls. His face sometimes has an uncanny resemblance to that of those lipsticked slappers squeezed into black Lycra who sip their bilious-looking drinks on the techno floor at Luigi's in Herne Bay. His teeth are unfortunate, and so are the hairs poking up above his collar. And the leather necklace is just tragic.

'Wha's fuckin' pointa university?' asks Marcie idly, as she balances another glass on top of her sculpture.

I can't help feeling that she's secretly sniggering at me. 'Lots of things,' I snap at her, irritatedly crossing my legs. 'It's not just about academic work. You learn how to meet people, get on with people from all sorts of backgrounds.'

'Oh, yeah,' says Marcie, her fingers slowly loosening their grip on her penultimate spirits glass. She gazes into the pyramid, her expression intent. Her thickly outlined eyes bulge with glassy distortion. 'I went to the University of Life,' she says casually.

'Yeah,' I retort, 'but you got a Third.'

Marcie balances her final glass. I expect she is still working out that last remark and isn't aware that it's an insult.

Damien starts to snigger very loudly and obviously. His snigger becomes a snort. Marcie rounds on him, letting go of her final glass just that little bit too early. It wobbles, sending impulses through the entire structure.

Only JJ and I have the sense to leap up as the pyramid collapses, smashing in a hundred pieces over the table and the floor.

So the Nova's alarm goes off and Damien's standing there smoking and trying to look cool, right? He's a big long shadow in his coat, with a floating orange speck and a ghoul-face.

And JJ's restless and edgy, kicking puddles into shimmery rags, occasionally staring into the darkness as if he can see something a layer beyond the rest of us.

Marcie slumps down by the wheel, knees up, eyes down, one hand dangling over her stockings like a limp fish. On a fishnet. Just a second ago she was rotating across the bonnet, now she's totally gone. Came down with a thump on her arse, too.

Something grabs me from inside. We have got to move one way or the other. We can't stand here gawping at this shrieky car, with the kids from the beach looking over at us.

Marcie's face floats up at me. I have a sudden fear that I'm not holding on to reality, but then there's the crisp blue siren of a police car from deep in the town, shrieking along with the car alarm, and before I know what I'm doing I've opened the door and people are bundling in after me.

Marcie, with a big muddy stain on her yellow dress, somehow gets shoved in the passenger seat, and the two guys are behind, laughing. For some reason, Damien is blowing a raspberry. His fag-end is close to my neck. The Nova smells of heat, beer, smoke and oil.

'If that touches me, you're a dead man,' I tell him. 'JJ, got your knife?'

JJ's multi-purpose penknife, special import from America, flips over and lands in my lap. My own, you see, is my secret.

I dig out some electrics and start getting the wires together. Marcie gurgles alarmingly and tries to lift her head up to see what I'm doing. She's strapped in, and the belt's all that stops her from lolling on to the dashboard. I don't remember doing her up. Must have been JJ. One step ahead.

'Marcie's lost it,' JJ points out, in that strangely calm, polite way of his. I suddenly get the idea that he will object morally to Marcie being in the car with us. He's quite proper sometimes, like when he didn't want to do it in the church. You wouldn't have guessed it from those first words I heard him say – *Bloody bloody Mary, Mary!* – but he's looser when he's had a lot to drink, and tonight he's only had a bit. I'm glad I got to know him, or I could have got totally the wrong impression.

I glance behind me. They look so different. Damien, with his brownish-red face, nodding and laughing – or leering, I suppose – at me. And JJ, sitting there with his hands folded in his lap, gazing out at the orange lights and the sea as if he isn't really concerned with any of this. Bastard.

A few more jiggles, and the engine coughs into life. We lose the alarm at the same moment, which is funny.

'Hey!' says Damien in delight. 'Party time!'

It's as if I'm not here, now. Someone called Belinda Archard has taken control of everything like a teacher on a school trip. Belinda checks her mirrors, for Christ's sake, she even checks her mirrors and Marcie's belt. Right, then. Belinda's in charge here. She almost feels like checking if everyone's got their packed lunches, and taking a register.

She giggles – no, she doesn't. Belinda's in charge, see, she's the one who knows what she's doing. She doesn't giggle. She depresses the clutch, gets into gear, and hits the accelerator.

The car jerks into action, and Marcie is in serious trouble now.

Belinda swings the car round the warehouses so that the run up to the shoreline is dead ahead. She's thinking about the route down to the beach, but she can see Damien laughing away in the back, that squawking laugh. The sea wall is ahead. They swing round and they're whizzing past the ranks of spectral hotels. She can't see JJ but she reckons he's got a smug smile. Her mouth tastes of old beer, that dry-cask taste, and her eyes have gone suddenly heavy.

She stops. Slams the brakes. Marcie lolls and shrieks, JJ swears quietly.

Why did she stop? She got frightened. I got frightened.

The town's still. All we can hear is the water crashing on to the beach, and the engine purring, and my harsh breath. It sounds as bad as it feels, acid in my lungs.

'So we fuckin' sightseeing, Bel, or what?' Damien demands. 'Top of a bus job. On your right, the industry. Damp old guest-houses full of smelly old people.'

'On your left,' JJ adds softly, 'the edge of the world.'

For a brief moment Damien and I are united as we turn to look at him with the same quelling, contemptuous expression.

My heartbeat has slowed. It sounds quiet all around.

'All right,' I say to them. 'The beach.'

So I'm taking the car at about forty, right, on the cool and empty beach, on the edge of the water, shredding the sea.

And we kick along with the moonlight sparkling. We're carving our mark in the sand, when Marcie sits bolt upright and chooses that moment to do it.

She opens her mouth wide, as if in complete astonishment, and vomits a steaming, pungent trail of beer into her lap.

So we've got the Nova with its doors open full like it's about to fly or something, the air's sharp with sea salt, old beer and Dettol, and Damien's lighting a fire with the car manual.

JJ, amazing as usual, got this bottle of Dettol from a twenty-four-hour chemist. He just disappeared into the night when we stopped the car down by the water's edge, and I was cursing him, but he came back ten minutes later, coat flapping, carrying this fucking massive plastic bottle. I thought for a minute he'd found some miracle all-night off-licence in the town, and then Damien snatches it and glowers at the label and says disappointedly that he thought it might be meths. He's got the cap off and he's given it a sniff before JJ snatches it back without another word. Then he's pouring it neat all over the seat and the floor, and he says to Marcie, who's lying in a stinking heap on the sand, 'Get your dress off, Marce.'

That's JJ, you see, thinking about the after-effects and the side-effects again. Me, I just live for the moment, but he likes to have things tidy. Like that time in the church when he wanted to clean up. He can take control when he wants to. He's like me in that sense, except my way of taking control would be to kick stupid Marcie out of sight behind some rocks and let her wake up, sandy-mouthed and reeking, in the morning sun.

Marcie's sitting up, looking a right state, and JJ squats beside her and says, 'Marce, you've already looked stupid. So getting undressed in front of us isn't going to make it worse, is it?'

Damien stifles a giggle, and turns away, biting on his cigarette.

I'm watching JJ – his voice is still soft, and he's got his big eyes open wide, beseeching, like he was before I half undressed him in the church. He's fascinating, sometimes.

And so Marcie's sitting up, breathing heavily. She pulls off her stockings and dumps them in a pile of netting on the sand. Now her dress comes off over her head, peeling, a lemon-skin, and underneath she's got scarlet knickers, wet with beer and mud.

'Them, too,' says JJ languidly, tossing the soiled dress over his arm like a waiter's cloth. Marcie, forgoing all dignity, pulls them down and chucks them on the sand, then she hugs herself and curls up against the rocks and seaweed.

She belches loudly, and I turn and give her a hard stare. For a minute I think she's going to let it all out again, but she's puffing her cheeks and she must have swallowed it back. She's wrapped her arms tight around herself, squashing her tennis-ball tits. Her eyes – a victim's eyes, coaly, thumped-looking with black mascara – beg me from a face thick with crunchy layers of foundation. She's suddenly made me angry with that casual, animal noise, as if she hasn't even got the decency to behave now she's sobered up a bit.

'Don't you dare,' I snarl, leaning over her and poking my finger at the air five inches from her wafery, waif-thin face. 'JJ's fucking well putting himself out for you, bitch, so you just fucking stay there and shut the fuck up, all right?'

'It's OK, Bel,' JJ murmurs. 'It's OK, leave her.'

I swing round and face him. 'No, it's not OK! She's ruined my evening.' I'm conscious of my voice being louder than I'd want, and there's a buzzing in my ears that I don't like very much. I can feel the air and the sea in a white-noise rush in and around my head, and for a moment I almost fall over. But then, I recover myself, and I shrug, flap my arms and go over to Damien's fire. JJ heads off to wash the clothes in the sea.

Damien wanders – or staggers – over to me. He stands there nodding at some private joke for a moment. He has an annoying habit of doing that, as if you've just said something that he agrees fervently with, and you're trying to recall what it was. He drinks from his cigarette, too, as usual. He always tips them right back, makes the end glow firework-bright and puckers his lips as if he's sucking as much badness as he can get out of them.

We watch JJ, disappearing towards the water's edge with a filmy yellow dress and the scarlet pants of a scarlet woman flapping soggily in his left hand.

'Good lad,' Damien offers. 'Eh?'

I nod, watching JJ rubbing furiously at the cloth as the foamy water washes over his arms. 'Yeah. He's all right.'

I've known Damien since school, and never especially liked him much, but most people I know have moved away from this shit-hole – good for them – and so we seem to end up going out. Marcie is more his friend than mine, and she's a recent addition. She's really got no fucking excuse, 'cos she wasn't even born here, she moved here.

I couldn't get my head round that when I first heard it. Someone actually *came* here from somewhere else.

I've heard bits and pieces from Damien about the whole sorry tale, and I've put together the rest of Marcie's story from other bits of gossip, sewn in a quilt of many colours and held together by threads of truth.

Marcie's mum used to have a little enterprise going in Southampton, employing foreign students to fulfil a local demand. (I report Damien's phrase without comment: the Bettinas and Conchitas were short of cash, and the sailors and engineering students were short of gash.) This had been going on since Marcie herself was mewling and puking in Mummy's arms. As opposed to in our stolen cars, then.

Then, Madam Hales found out that a few of the girls, miffed at the cut she was taking, had decided to miss out the middlewoman. They pooled some earnings and bought a flat to use just for business purposes, taking clients there on an individual basis without Madam needing to know at all. This sliced a third off the selling price and bumped up the girls' wages by about as much again. It didn't make them popular. Old Mother Hales, who was a formidable character, planned her revenge over five years. When Marce was fifteen, she got her tarted up and pretending to be on the game, just to infiltrate the girls – they didn't know her, you see, or rather they didn't know what she had become. Last time they'd seen little Marcella, she'd been a dimply thing with a chocolate mouth and a flowery dress. Now, she was a woman with cheekbones and 'attitude', whatever that was. From what I've seen of 'attitude', it seems to mean poncing about as if you own the world and treating people like shit.

Marce got their trust over time, and one day in August she acted on Mummy's paid instructions, did the business in the flat. She fed the dog its favourite meal, mashed up with a bar or two of laxative chocolate. She tipped all the girls' perfumes down the sink and poured in the sardine oil she'd brought with her in tablet-bottles. And to top it all, she called up the phone-sex lines all through the night when the girls were out. Next day, Marcie legged it back to Mum – leaving the girls to a distressed dog treading its turds into the carpet, to their putrid scent bottles and, a month later, to a phone bill from hell.

I say Marcie went back to Mum – that was the idea. She went back to a house which had been pretty much cleared out, top to bottom. Marcie's own stuff was packed into two tea chests, sitting on their own on the bare kitchen tiles, under the empty light socket. She found out later – months later, I think – that her mum had gone up North with Derek the Haulage Management Executive, telling him and all his mates that her daughter had gone off the rails, and she didn't want to be associated with her any more.

So Marcie took out all the money she had. She got the train to the end of the network, to the edge of the world. To this town looking out on the cold, cold sea, the spattered window on the glittering North. And when she got here, after two nights in a B&B, she realized that her mum had always done the shopping, and that now she had to do it herself. She went on down to Safeway and piled a trolley high with stuff. Ridiculous stuff. Family packets of frozen sausages and pink surgical slabs of chicken and great froths of broccoli, because that was what she'd always seen her mum buy, and it made sense. When she got to the checkout, she did what her mum had always done: she handed over a card. Marcie had her own card, but it did a funny bleep when it was put through the first time, and the second time. And the checkout girl asked her if she had any cash, and Marcie looked at her like she was stupid.

So she had to leave it all there, all those economy packs harvested from the ice. She stood on the other side of the glass door and watched a spiky-haired boy, who had a blue overall and red scurvy, trundle it all away to be dealt with. Shame it wasn't all empty boxes like those videos.

Then what did she do? Stories differ. I think she went to the bank, at least tried to get some cash out of the hole in the wall, 'cos I don't think Marcie's thick or anything. No joy at the bank, so I think it was then she nicked the chocolate from Mr Pounj and got away with it. That was the worst thing that could happen, because it put the idea into Marcie's head that it was easy to get things and not pay. If Mr P had caught her – well, I know him, he'd have given her a hell of a bollocking, but he'd have wanted to know why, he'd have found out she didn't have anywhere to live or any money, he'd have tried to help. As it was, she got caught by the professional store detective in Woolworths that afternoon. I know her, too. She's a bitch.

And Marcie ended up with a criminal record. Eventually, she rented a room the only way she knew how. She let a sweaty businessman pork her for thirty quid in the Seaview Hotel.

And Marcie became meat. Steak to be pummelled with a hammer, until it was red and soft. Bacon, crunchy to bite. Mince. Some days, she would come out furtively to the newsagent's in dark, wrap-around shades to hide a black eye from an over-enthusiastic punter. And there were the times she got raped, when she didn't report it, because she had decided what the police attitude would be. (So you didn't get paid. So what? You had a punter who nicked it rather than paying for it. Shoplifted his meat.)

She was one of the lucky ones, eventually, one of those who got out in time before she became part of the whole process. Before the alien sperm crusted on her for good and made her one of them, perpetually smelling of lubricated rubber, carbolic soap and cheap scent. Something, I don't know what, grabbed her by the neck and told her there could be more. She got a job at the leisure centre, cleaning the bogs. And after a few months, they put her on the more salubrious task of cleaning the offices, which led to the better-paid cleaning job at the insurance building. There, she met Babs, who'd just signed on for a WEA course and got Marcie to come along as well.

Just one year after arriving at the end of the line, Marcie's points had changed and she was leaving the old goods behind her. Except for the men who recognized her in the street and in the pubs, who took the fact that she was out and about, being seen, as an indication that she now did it all for free and willingly. You don't lose an image overnight.

And that's pretty much where we are. Marce, who now has her Office Skills, does drudge work where she can get it, and keeps her shagging to the status of a committed hobby. Her other hobbies

– shared with mine – are drink and spliffs, although she doesn't read books the way I do. The best of my non-sexual fantasies is to be locked deep in the library vaults with a year's supply of food and booze. And, you know, a bed and a bath and all that. Goes without saying.

'Here. Wear it.'

With a sea-salty slap, Marcie's dress hits her in the face, and JJ folds his arms and exchanges satisfied looks with the pair of us. He's done his good deed for the day, I think, giving him a sulky look, but at the same time I don't begrudge him it, 'cos I know he means it, which is more than I would. He doesn't want Marcie to be uncomfortable, he'd just rather she went home with a sea-wet dress than a puke-soaked one. And that's JJ all over.

I start to feel a bit guilty, as it's not really Marcie's fault, and it's not as if she was sick over any of us or anything. It's almost as if JJ's highlighting my callousness.

Damien sighs, kicks over the fire. 'Come on. Let's go.'

JJ's moving back to the car as well. He doesn't seem to want to talk to me tonight.

Marcie's head pops through the hole, and her mermaid's dress is on. She still looks sullen and dazed. She pulls at it around her cleavage without much enthusiasm.

'It's bloody wet,' she points out, opening her victim-black eyes wide at me as if to accuse me.

'Not much gets past you, does it?' Bugger it, I feel sorry for her now, don't I? Bitch. I give her my hand. She hesitates for a moment, then she reaches up, grasps it.

Her wrist and hand feel cold and spindly as I pull her up, and the way she slops in the dress, together with her big eyes, makes me think I'm hauling in some fish-woman from the depths of the ocean. Her gaze meets mine and she gives me a wobbly smile, which makes me go cold. I don't know why – maybe a chilly flux, mushy and seaweedy from her aqua-world, has pumped down her arm and into my blood.

I let go of her, suddenly overwhelmed by it, and wanting to distance myself with surliness again. 'You can fucking walk, come on. Fucking walk.'

The Nova bucks and swivels, getting started in the sand. I crunch the gears and try to ignore the smell of Dettol.

'When did you pass your test, Bel?' Damien snarls.

I glare at him in the rear-view mirror. 'Sometime soon, I expect. All right?'

The car growls in anger, and we're off, kicking along the beach, leaving it behind us and heading for the bank. I tell them all to hold on tight, 'cos the concrete slope's studded with raised squares designed to prevent people from doing exactly this. For a few seconds, we're the lentils in one of those jars Mrs Beck would use to show us Brownian Motion. Then I've made the accelerator sing and scream and I've hauled us back on to the road, with a thump. Great suspension, these Novas.

It's two-thirty and the roads are dead empty. They're all up for a bit of a laugh, now – sloppy wet Marcie, Mr Ironic-distance JJ, and Mr Who-gives-a-toss Damien. We rush the lights at Western Promenade – they're ghost lights anyway, red and green phantoms in the night. No one to see what we do or where we go.

'Red for dead, green for a queen!' It's Damien, with an old one from school days. The boys used to have to put these bands over their T-shirts at primary school to make themselves into two teams. Someone coined that stupid phrase and from that day on they'd tear each other's flesh scrabbling for the red bands. Red for dead, green for a queen.

'What's amber, then?' I force the wheel and we thump over a traffic island, doing a U-turn fit for a politician.

'Uh?' Damien responds. It's just me and him – Marcie's still too dazed and JJ's too cool.

'Amber? What's it rhyme with?'

'Fuck-all. Hang on. Bamber.'

'Yeah!' I shriek with delight. 'Amber for Bamber. Starter for ten!' I drive the car up Alexandra Avenue, round the back sides of the hotels with their choking bins. The sound booms round the whole town – I want the hovercraft to hear it. I'm suddenly consumed with the desire to be heard, to be seen, to be felt, just so as to escape from the stupidity of watching Marcie spew her guts and of being down on the beach and pouring Dettol into a car. Let's be *felt*.

'I hate this town!' I shout, stepping on the pedal.

'Easy, Bel.'

It's J J. Being proper and fussy again! My God, I've got him worried, have I? Well, then.

At the end of the street is the still twenties tableau of Goodmans' Clothes, stiff human parodies adorned with bobs and monocles and necklaces.

Closer. It's total fantasy, *Great Gatsby* stuff, like it's laughing at us for being stuck in the Town at the End of the World, where there's no British dream, let alone the American one. Useless.

So I don't slow down. I take us right through it.

Good place to cut.

5   Blame Game

Kate says: 'I thought we might all go out together.'

I realize I've got to say something. My toast is poised halfway to my mouth, and the bit I'm chewing on suddenly goes all flavourless and hard to swallow. A globule of marmalade drips from the edge of my toast, down on to the paper, where it gives John Prescott a runny and magnified nose.

Kate's face, round and red and powdery. My father's, hawklike, with sharp-looking glasses. I think he wears them because they look like filters of truth.

This morning, the police were busy picking a Vauxhall Nova (slightly damaged) out of a town-centre shop-window (wrecked). Bodies lay all over the place. There were severed heads, arms, legs, fragments of hair. One torso was right under the front of the car and took the full impact. The police were collecting the amputees and the bits and putting them into black plastic bin-liners. One of the younger ones laughed as he picked up one of the severed heads, a woman, and turned it around towards his mate, making like it was going to snog him. I was watching, and I thought, looks like all those dummies failed the crash test, then. And Goodmans will have to buy some more to model their obnoxious clothes.

I lounged against a lamppost in the morning light, smoking quietly, listening to the sea breathing in and out, to the gulls whooping overhead, calling out my name to the cops who were too ignorant to hear.

A guy with a manky, mangy dog went past just before. It was

straining on its leash – well, string – barking my name at the clean-up squad, and they ignored that, too! *Bellen*, means to bark in German. I know that because I'm intelligent, and the police don't because they're stupid, that's all there is to it. Anyway, it was hauled away, still barking, as I watched. Ugly, crazed-looking animal with tangled hair, coat ripped in three places, nails all in need of a good scrub. And his filthy mutt was almost as bad.

I suppose what they'll find inside the car is a strong smell of Dettol, maybe an empty bottle, but even if it has JJ's prints on it, they won't be able to match them up with anything. (He's – what is it Damien says? – cleaner than a virgin's cunt. These little Damien-phrases keep slipping into my mind, and I feel I have to get them out.) What else? Maybe a bit of sand. They'll go for a stroll down to the beach and maybe find the remains of our fire. It's a bit hard to dust for prints on ashes.

Basically, they don't care. They know these things happen in town, and they know it's 'the kids', and no one thinks it's us. The middle-class, respectable kids. They kind of accept that it must be a gang or two from the Fallowdale estate. The Fallies.

It's a huge, sprawling monstrosity high above the town. There's this joke Damien told me when we first drove through Fallowdale, and I've used it time and again. 'I can never remember,' he'd say. 'What do you call those little boxes that you always get behind satellite dishes?' And the one who hadn't heard it before would be frowning and saying, transformers, is it? Transceivers? 'Nope,' he says. 'I remember. It's council houses.'

There are parts of Fallowdale where even the police don't go, little sub-cultures left to their own devices. So no one suspects us, the nice kids from the big houses on the roads towards Canterbury and Maidstone. They know it must be Fallowdale. After all, they practically invented joyriding up there, and we know all the jokes in school.

Like these.

What do you call a Fally in a suit? The accused.

Why's a Fally girl like a Kit-Kat? You get four fingers for twenty-five pence.

Why doesn't Fallowdale have any election posters up? 'Cos they peel them off and sniff the backs.

What do you call a Fally in a three-bedroom house? A burglar.

You get the idea.

Marcie, of course, would have been a Fally girl when she first came to town. I think she had a flat, just on the edge. After she started temping she got herself a one-bedder in Churchill Row, near the town centre, and got in with us. She's got cracks, Marce, and they've been painted over. If anyone gives us away it might be her, stupid cow.

Maybe I ought to see her.

If I need a pretext, I want to see how she is, don't I? 'Cos I'm a caring, sharing type, and I like to look after my friends. (Right, and the Pope does ads for Durex.)

'I want to – see Marcie,' I say tentatively to Kate, and I'm aware that my voice has tailed away at the end, not sounding quite convincing. Even Kate knows that seeing Marcie is something I do, unavoidably, when I want to go out with Damien and J J. It's not usually a desire.

She puts her blue-glass plates away in the cupboard with a strained lightness of touch.

'Do you really like that girl, Berlinda?' she asks. She always gives me that stupid pronunciation of my name, when she can be bothered with a name at all. So I'm Berlinda. (I straddle two worlds and I've had my wall knocked down. Yeah, right.)

I push my lower lip out in that way people do when they are thinking about something, when they are trying to give a diplomatic answer. I never just do, you see. I watch, think and do. It's possible to give someone an entirely misleading impression, if you really bother to study human behaviour properly. If you hate someone and want to kill them, then the worst thing you can do is to show it.

'I feel I can really *do* something for her, Kate,' I say earnestly, trying to sound as much as possible like one of Kate's morning-coffee companions. 'She's been *such* an unfortunate girl, and she needs people of more class around her to help pull her up.'

Steady, Bel, steady. This is like riding a bob-sleigh. You've got to keep it going, without flagging, but without taking it over too far and crashing.

In the end, I don't go round to see Marcie. I head for JJ's first, to ask him what he thinks.

Yeah, it's his own place. He didn't want to tell me about this when we first got off in Domingo. I asked him if he had a car, and he didn't, so that was true enough. Didn't mention he had a fucking basement flat, did he? Would have been useful. His Aunt Imelda bought it for him, as his parents are dead. Calls it his 'own space'.

Technically, he lives with her, with Aunt Imelda. She's a dead-fit-looking thirty-fiver, all rich brown limbs, designer clothes and jet-black kd lang hair. Lesbian, I think. Doesn't bother me. She's got a big place out towards Canterbury, and she got him this place at the Edge of the World because it was going cheap. I've only had one visit, and this is about to be my second.

I kick along the seafront. A mist hangs over the grey sea, defining the borders of our world. I shiver slightly as I pass the dead fairground. It's like some great castle of metal, adorned with lights for a forgotten carnival. Shops on my right, some open, others just ghosts with yellow boards over the windows. Funny how these dead names leave their imprints. Almost as if they're whispering at you from the walls, to remind you of what once was.

I huddle into my coat and hurry on through the petroly, salty air. Great slabs of lorries thunder past on my right, huge names like Norbert Dentressangle and Christian Bergansson. You probably need a bloody great articulated truck to trundle a name like that around Europe.

JJ's flat is in the basement. He could have had a higher one, but he wanted a basement. I know why. He looks up women's skirts through the grille in the ceiling.

As I come in, he's looking up through the binocs, while lying back on his therapy couch. That's what he calls it. I wanted to make him a sign for it, done on the computer in nice block capitals. THERAPY COUCH. But I thought it might be misleading if the subconscious were to place a gap after 'the', to turn it into a place where JJ took girls to deflower them. I don't think he does that. He's actually very shy. He'd rather look up a skirt than get up one, any day.

'Hello,' I say to him, and he waves absently in response. He's concentrating on the binocs, with a steady hand.

The floor creaks as I step towards him. The floorboards are of stripped, varnished pine, but not too new, it would appear. I wonder if there is a cellar underneath. I settle myself in his leather wing-chair, cross my legs (my attire today is a burgundy skirt with a matching jacket) and spin round, sighing with contentment and breathing in the aroma of the flat. It's varnishy, woody, slightly un-looked-after, a bit like a library smell. I know library smells; I used to hide myself away between the bookshelves and read while Mum went shopping, sometimes for hours on end.

'You know that's fucking disgusting,' I tell him, but I know I sound vague, uncommitted. I flip out a cigarette and light it, drawing in its sharp taste with relief.

'So's that,' he says, without unsticking his eyes from the binocs.

Three metres up, on the grating, feet thump and clatter, garments swish, no doubt caressing thighs, whether smooth as eggs or orange-peel-puckery with cellulite. JJ isn't really bothered, I've discovered. To him, the flash of anything is entrancing, even if it's just the dullest underwear of corn-plaster texture.

He told me a story. He read about some old guy who was going round the libraries with a mirror stuck to his toecap, looking up skirts. JJ thought this was a great idea, and spent ages at the vice trying to glue a vanity mirror to one of his rugby boots. When he eventually tried to put it on, it made him hobble, and he got kicked off the bus too.

I should be appalled by him, I should throw him out of my life for it, but I don't want to. You see, he's kind to me, always looks after me and conducts our relationship on a totally equal footing. He agrees with me about all the usual issues – women's rights at work, sterilizing rapists, legalizing prostitution. It's just that – totally separate from it

33

all – he likes to look at bits of strangers which he wouldn't otherwise see. I find what he does fascinating, in a way, which makes me a kind of voyeur of voyeurism. No problem with that. He does it in a really clinical way, too, experimental even, as if what he's really doing is peeling back realities that we wouldn't otherwise find. I mean, how often do you get to see strangers' knickers? It's the same as the mentality which makes people look in at lit windows when they pass them, or make appointments to look round houses that they've got no intention of buying, or buy things from boot fairs.

I still have to have a go at him about it, though. Sisters, and all that. I blow a stream of smoke up into the room. 'Are you going to start complaining about passive smoking? When you're there doing your active leching?'

'Yes,' he answers absently.

I laugh, and blow more smoke in his general direction. 'Whose sin is the worse, dickbrain? Don't know why people are so hung up on this passive smoking business, I mean, I have to put up with passive God knows what other kind of shit, don't I? What about loudmouths sounding off on buses? Don't I have to put up with their passive bollocks-talking? And passive poor grammar, every time I pass one of those signs with the apostrophe in the wrong place?'

This is a personal bugbear. I saw one last week – Jone's Stationers was what it said. Now, I don't have too much of a problem with the second word, because it could just mean they're plural, and not that the shop is a place for purchasing stationery. You with me so far? But either he's called Mr Jone, or the sign was done by a thick wanker. I think I know which option I would go for.

And then there's one of my fave expressions, 'Jesus shit' – that's another problem. Is it the genitive – the excrement of Jesus? (No doubt prized above the Holy Grail – I mean, what did the Last Supper turn into?) Or is it the imperative, in which case it would be quite right to leave the apostrophe off? Or simply an adjective, as in Jesus sandals? Room for debate. Get the church on to it right away.

JJ isn't really listening. He's lost in his own personal reality of glimpsed gussets.

After a few minutes, he puts down the binocs and turns towards me with a welcoming smile.

I don't meet his eye, and I deliberately stub out my cigarette in the abandoned teacup next to me. 'You can go and relieve yourself if you want. Don't mind me.'

'What?' He rolls over on one elbow, and he looks faintly shocked.

'You know, toss the caber. I won't watch.'

JJ wrinkles his nose as if at a bad smell. 'Excuse me, but I don't do that.'

This is news to me! I thought all boys did. I always thought it must be terrible being the parents of a teenage boy, pretending not to know about masturbation and nocturnal emissions. I mean, you know that if he's anything like normal, he's at it most nights, tugging away, and yet you can't really say anything. And here's JJ, claiming he's the exception.

'Catholic priests don't, either,' he points out, looking somewhat pained. 'It doesn't do them much harm.'

'Shit, no, except the odd bout of prostate cancer. You've got that to look forward to.' I make a rueful face. 'Well, you would have, if you weren't shagging me. How useful of me.'

I don't think that the irony goes over his head – it rarely does – but, as he often does, he makes a show of ignoring it. 'Yes, I'd say you were pretty useful.'

I spread my hands, open my eyes almost accusingly at him. 'But why? I mean – isn't it normal? Healthy?'

Awkwardly, he scratches where his eyebrows almost meet. 'Suppose so. People go out running in the morning, though, don't they, because it's healthy? And eat muesli and stuff?'

I agree, as I must, that there are some strange souls on this earth who find pleasure in doing such things.

'Well, then. I can't say I find that very appealing, either.'

'Yeah, but – ' I slam the arm of the chair in frustration. 'This is *wanking*, JJ, the favourite occupation of every randy male in the country. I mean, what do you do when you're, I dunno, looking through a fashion magazine, and there's some model posing in the latest designer PVC underwear? What do you think?' I'm practically leaping out of the chair, and probably filling the air with saliva. I don't care, I want to hear his answer.

He contemplates it for a moment. 'I tend to think,' he offers, 'that she must have had to pose like that for a long time, and that it must be uncomfortable having to wear that kind of stuff.'

I sigh, slump melodramatically into the seat. 'I give up. You're a space alien.'

I should have guessed it, actually. I mean, doesn't this just confirm what I was saying? There's really no sexual element in his peeping at all, it's just childlike curiosity.

With a ridge of faint freckles across his dainty nose, he looks like a summery schoolgirl from a teenage romance. Maybe that explains a lot of it.

'Did you come here,' he says languidly, flicking the TV on with the remote, 'to give me a crash course in masturbation? Or did you want something?'

'You should know me. I always want something.'

He hops through the channels. He's even got cable here. There's reruns of mid-eighties episodes of *The Bill*, with lots of familiar faces running round in uniform. There's sad Yank wankers in killer tank-tops doing ads for laser-sharp knives – these mainly involve sticking the knife face up and throwing tomatoes at it to be sliced cleanly in half, like in some circus act. It has a horrible fascination. I used to shudder at tomatoes, for a good reason.

'I wanted to ask you about Marcie. How she's coping.'

'Coping?' JJ glances at me briefly, his dark eyes perhaps rather troubled. He doesn't seem to like the word.

'I don't think she really goes with us, JJ. I don't think she fits in. We should drop her.'

I realize that I have said it now, that there can be no going back. Even if I deny the truth of it, divorce myself from the intention, it can't ever be un-enunciated.

JJ rubs his finger over one ear, tracing its whorls and crevices. He flops back on to The Rapy Couch and has a think, with his hands folded, deathlike, over his chest.

'What do we drop her into?' he argues after a while. 'People like Marcie – '

'No, they don't,' I argue.

'You didn't let me finish. I was going to say, people like Marcie don't float. They sink. Into nothingness. Unless you shove buoys under them.'

I snigger, and it comes out as a splutter from my nose, a harsh snort of snot and smoke. 'Sorry,' I tell him, shaking with giggles. 'I was just thinking about all the boys who've been shoved under Marcie.' I sigh, close my eyes. 'I know what you mean, but we're not socially responsible for the stupid little slut, are we?'

JJ smiles indulgently. 'Look,' he says. 'You know that shop window?'

I'm cross at him for mentioning it. 'What about it?'

'Marcie wants to take the blame for breaking it.'

For a moment or two, I'm convinced he's telling me another joke, building up to something. I'm waiting. I'm watching my smoke and the dust dancing in the air. I listen to the distant sounds above us. Clatter-clatter of feet, quite near, and the boom of distant voyages out on the water. Seagulls cry like babies high above the town. But it's all strangely looped-sounding, as if my time has been suspended for me to accommodate this extraordinary fact. I try to articulate a response.

'Why?'

It's not very good, but it's the best I can manage.

'I'll only tell you if you're interested in letting her do it.' JJ gives me a grin, big and broad and white under his floppy fringe. It says that he knows more than me.

So I'm unsettled. I'm thinking of the embarrassed way we got dressed after shagging on the altar, of how I felt totally in control of him, how I'd enjoyed pulling him to me and enveloping him in my flesh and scent, and how he'd responded like a little boy, like a teenager being given his baptism of love-juice. I enjoyed it, being the teacher, being experienced Bel, mothering this toyboy. Even if he's only a few weeks younger than me. And now, he's pulled the carpet from under me, he's rolling me up in it.

What does he know about Marcie? Why's he been talking to her without me?

'All right, so I might be interested. Tell me.'

'It's just that, I was talking to Damien,' he explains. 'About what happened.'

This makes sense. JJ and Damien hang out together without me.

'He was saying about how Marcie needs some money. Didn't say what for. But she reckons she might be able to get some from you – in return for saying she was driving the car that night.'

I laugh incredulously. 'Old habits, eh?'

'That's precisely it,' says JJ, and there's that middle-aged, reproving tone in his voice again. 'She doesn't want to go back to the old ways. She could sell herself and get the money this afternoon, couldn't she? Half the guys in town still think she does it, for Christ's sake.'

And he channel-surfs again. Beaming American women showing off chrome-bright saucepans. Barney, the hideous purple dinosaur. Paula Abdul dancing with a cartoon, a video that's over ten years old. And lingering, shadowy close-ups of a woman with cropped dark hair kissing her way up the bronzed, shuddering back of – another woman. JJ's eyes light up and he sits up to watch it.

I groan. Don't tell me he enjoys watching lesbians get it on. What a dull, brickie-type fantasy. But I watch his face, and it's the same as with that gusset-peeping. Not a leer, just genuine, unabashed curiosity. Peep-hole sex doesn't seem to embarrass him, whereas the real thing – a real-life, full-blooded, pungent-juiced, hot, heaving, hands-on practical – really rather leaves him somewhat flustered. That's nice. I like that.

'So what you're saying is,' I venture (idly watching the two women working their way up to each other's mouths with much melodrama and unnecessary quivering), 'that Marcie'll tell someone she did it, if I give her money?'

'That's about the size of it.'

'Oo-er, missus. Why should I be bothered? We haven't been caught before. No one's on to us. What's in it for me? If I let Marcie take the rap, she might just drop us all in it, when we're all fresh-smelling and respectable.'

And it's true. No one suspects kids with decent clothes and trust funds. All those times we've lit fires down on the beach, or bunged up some exhausts just for the hell of it. Or when we got out of our trees on the promontory at sunset (some weird blue shit in a capillary inhaler thing that Damien's brother's mate got hold of in Glasgow). And now that the dares, the after-dark japes, have started to get bigger and better and bolder and more totally fucking irresponsible, the police just put it all down to Fallowdale kids, because some Fally or other steals a car every night and, usually, gets banged up for it. Ha-ha. Best place for them.

'You went too far, Bel,' says JJ almost casually, and flips himself up so that he's sitting on the couch, legs dangling over the edge. He raises his eyebrows as if defying me to contradict him. 'You smashed the car into one of the main shop-windows in town. Pretty soon, someone's going to ask questions about the tyre marks on the beach, the Dettol, all those little clues. There's twenty thousand people in the borough. You know that? It won't take long before they start asking questions about who's always out and about after dark.'

He gets up and starts to make tea. He slams the kettle on to the gas hob, gets the tea out of its tin and gets the teapot down.

Something's made me sit up and listen, something that might give me a clue to why JJ's bothered about all this.

I wind back his speech in my mind. 'The Dettol.' That's it, I'm triumphant. 'You're worried they'll trace it back to you from the Dettol.'

JJ doesn't meet my eye. He's shovelling tea into the pot, with a rather tense and jerky movement.

I smile, and spin the chair round, stretching my legs and kicking off my shoes. 'Ahhh . . . poor JJ! Have I blown your plan? That's it, isn't it? You thought you'd convince me I was in shit and get me to pay Marcie! I'm impressed. Well, I mean – if you weren't my boyfriend and hadn't just done an utterly bastardly thing, I might be impressed.'

He's stirring the tea-leaves into the boiling water, clunking and clunking the teaspoon against the pot. He's looking surly. I laugh, come up behind him and encircle his waist.

'There was one girl in the chemist,' he says at last. 'She was on the night shift.'

'And which chemist, JJ, dear?'

'The one in Eastbroome Rise. Next to the Catholic church. I went in, got the disinfectant off the shelf, paid. We didn't say much. I don't think she really looked up at me. She was blonde, about twenty. I think she smiled. Yeah, she smiled.'

'Had you seen her before?'

'No. She might have gone to your school. Certainly not mine. Didn't really get much of a look at me.'

'Well, then. You can relax.'

'Not really,' he says guiltily.

'Why not?'

He slams the lid down on the teapot. 'I paid by Switch.'

This takes a moment or two to sink in. 'Ah. It'll be on their copy. Your name and number, and what you bought. Brilliant.'

He turns around. His soft, feminine eyelashes are quivering, bless him. The scent of bergamot fills the kitchen area as the Earl Grey releases itself into the water, making me realize how much I need a cup of tea. I lean up and kiss him gently. 'Look, if it makes you feel better, we could find her.' I giggle, press myself up against his body and pout. 'We could threaten to pulp her head if she said anything. I've always wanted to do that.'

'Bel, don't – '

'Or I could kill her for you. I mean, it would make more sense for you to kill her, but then they'd trace it easily. We could swap murders, you kill Cowbitch Kate for me, and I'll do the Pharmacy Girl for you.'

I'm excited by the thought, you know. I realize it's wrong but I'm still thinking about the Cut.

'Don't joke, Bel. We could be in trouble if this gets out. Neither of us would ever go to university. Imelda might disown me, your parents would hit the roof.'

'Does Imelda really care what you get up to?'

He shrugs. 'Maybe.'

I sigh. The options are narrowing.

And what Marcie wants to do is interesting, to say the least. I want to find out what it is the silly little slut really wants.

'Let's talk to Marcie,' I say to JJ.

And why not? I was going to go around there anyway.

On the TV, the camera swoops along flesh, as the two-dimensional Sapphic embrace is carried to a squealy and thumpy conclusion. The frames flicker, distorted, in the bright teapot. I grin, reach up to JJ and kiss him softly but firmly, letting my arms wander around his neck.

In my mind's eye, one of the two girls, the one underneath, is Marcie, and I'm poised above them with a scalding pot of tea.

6 *Garden Zone*

As I said before, Belinda sometimes takes over the story. I feel she is a truly separate person at times.

In 1990, when Belinda was nine, the family moved from suburbia to the big house in the country.

On the day that Belinda first saw the house, she learnt a wonderful word in school. She kept saying it quietly to herself as she trotted around on her nine-year-old legs, behind her mother and father who, a couple of feet higher up, were booming deep and important pronouncements into echoing rooms. It sounded a good word, and it sounded like the thing it described, like the banging of a wooden door in the wind – *ram!* – followed by the skittering of tiles on a roof and the scuttling of insects in the skirting-board – *shackle shackle shackle!*

The house looked as if it had too much space. She couldn't imagine how they were ever going to fill it all. She marvelled at the big windows with their fresh paint and their unmarked glass, and the expanses of scrubbed floors, tree-coloured, full of knots and undulating grain. In a couple of rooms she actually bent down to sniff the wood, and the house smelt like part of Nature, as if it had grown there.

From outside, it looked camouflaged, wrapped in trees, and almost alive, as if it were about to toddle across the garden, spilling soil and tiles, chuckling *ramshackle-ramshackle*. The attic room, with its squinty blind and big, solid gable, seemed to be winking at her, seemed to be saying, come and play.

Once the house started to fill up, it was as if its character had been stifled under layers of carpets, shrink-wrapped in paint, trapped under heavy wooden chests and clocks and vases and giant wickerwork linen baskets. Belinda helped to carry some of these things in, and she couldn't help saying, 'Sorry, house,' every time someone knocked a corner or put something down with unnecessary force.

After a while, the house seemed to stop speaking to her, especially once the weatherboarding had been given its fresh coat of white. For a year, the garden became her sanctuary, her personal playground. Her parents didn't bother much with the garden. Jonathan Archard worked in town, at a property developer's office, and put in hours and hours of overtime, while Emma, who was a freelance illustrator, worked on and off throughout the day, including evenings. She was so preoccupied with getting Nature right in two dimensions – book covers, magazines, the occasional piece of crockery – that she never gave a thought to bending it to her whims in real life.

This suited Belinda very well. It meant she could spend hours crawling through the thick, tall grass at the perimeter, and emerge smelling sweetly of hay. She could observe the comings and goings on the terrace from her clump of goose-grass, and as she watched she would be imagining the tenacious little burrs as her personal armoury, tiny smart bombs studded all over her combat gear (black jeans and 'Sit Down' sweatshirt – unlike most of her classmates, she knew James were far cooler than New Kids). She would drop stones down the crumbling old well, imagining that they were grenades timed to repel the enemy, who lived down there in its dank depths. At least, she did so until Jonathan, worried to discover how deep the well was, had a piece of thick wire mesh put across it.

Belinda was popular, but had little patience with most of the girls she knew at school. They all had dead-end, giggly obsessions with the likes of David Hasselhoff. Some of them even fancied Marc Almond, and when Belinda scornfully pointed him out to her father in a magazine, he laughed and said, 'Him? He plays for the other side, love!' Belinda liked this phrase – although unsure of its meaning, she repeated it in the common room, where it made the third-year girls shriek with laughter at her silly little classmates, and got her some new-found respect among the higher echelons of the school. Not that she wanted it, much.

When she was fourteen, Belinda started smoking, but unlike many of the other girls, she had the intelligence to suck peppermints and wash her hands to keep it a secret from her parents.

With hindsight she can see that, while they would not exactly have approved, their reaction would not have been standard outrage. Jonathan and Emma were young parents. They were twenty-one in 1981, when Bel was born, thanks to some drunken post-finals celebrations on the campus at York. Among the incisive electro-beats of the pre-Aids eighties, they had abandoned caution. They liked to think that they were liberal, and perhaps they were.

The garden remained hers. No other girl ever entered her domain, and her parents would hardly try to make her share her games with others if she didn't want to. She seemed stable, and happy, and she had friends with whom she went to art club and choir and gymnastics, and who sometimes came home to tea.

They couldn't shake the uneasy feeling, though, that Belinda had read up on how little girls were supposed to behave, and that she would often make token gestures just to keep her parents happy. They knew she was intelligent and creative, and because they had the money to indulge her, they did, however strange her desires seemed. Even at the age of ten, she was spurning Malory Towers and the Chalet School in favour of Robert Westall, Point Horror and, a couple of years later, Virginia Andrews. She used words like 'tragic' and 'destiny'.

In 1990, her father found her slumped on the sofa watching *Citizen Kane* on video. This seemed a bit much, even for Bel. If it had been something like *Driller Killer*, even he would have firmly directed her away from it, but he wasn't quite sure what to do about finding his nine-year-old daughter watching a seminal classic of cinema. So he sat and watched the end with her. Good, isn't it? he asked her hopefully. Oh, yes, she said, nodding. I like the documentary technique, but I guessed about Rosebud.

She very rarely wanted to buy tapes – in fact, she listened attentively to stuff from her parents' collection like Pink Floyd, Gary Numan and Gen X – but when she did get something of her own, it was not exactly to be found in the pages of *Smash Hits*. One day in 1992, Emma, sitting in the garden and painting, heard for the fifth time in as many hours the chugging riff of something which, she had discovered, was implausibly called 'Smells Like Teen Spirit'. She remarked to her husband that their daughter had gone punk, either fifteen years too late or five years too early. He smiled and, flicking through his flip-charts, told her not to worry. It was called grunge, and the extent of its rebellion was big boots and tousled hair. He had been reading his *Q* attentively.

The garden got smaller and less forbidding as she grew up. It could no longer be a jungle for the eleven-year-old Bel who listened to Nirvana, but she learned to appreciate it in different ways – the feel of the moss on the stones was sensual, like velvet cushions, and some of the pungent grasses smelt of sex.

It would return to her, that smell, in years to come. Creeping up on her and dragging her back into childhood.

Something else happened in the garden, too, and indirectly, it made her change her life. But that was later.

7 *Topology of a Ghost City*

The house crackles with the negative energy of a drinks party.

Kate organizes drinks parties. It's primarily what she is for. That, and sex, I assume. My father, of course, has to go along with her, because he claims to love her, and if he didn't do what she said, then the cracks might start to show.

She is the sort of person who is especially proud of matching. The serviettes and the cloths. The curtains and the carpet. The clothes and the make-up. All her friends are similarly anal-retentive. They're all masked behind their greasepaint and their designer dresses, 'cos they're all women with things to hide from their pasts, too. Hiding from the buzz of gossip that echoes in the Mzzz of their titles. Hiding from dry-squeezed husbands, from past men who've faded to just a name on a cheque. Maybe this preoccupation with order, with matching pastel shades, is a way of convincing themselves that they've got structure to their lives, and that it's not just an endless round of church fetes and dinner and trips to Harrods, and that little extra from the Child Support Agency for Tommy's school fees.

Look at them. Plastered in cake-icing foundation and cherry-red lipstick, hair spray-sculpted. Maybe they know that the way to a man's cock is through his stomach (so always knife downwards, ha-ha). And they make themselves good enough to eat. They're gingerbread-women, high on E-additives. They're cake decorations made of ersatz icing sugar.

When they're not food, they're puppets. They waggle their glasses of Beaujolais in the air when they want to make a point. They get redder and louder the more they drink of it. I come round, dispensing it with the sweetest of smiles, because I enjoy giving them stupidity ammo.

'I hear your husband's in property,' says one of the darlings, a woman with sponge-blonde hair and sugar earrings. Kate smiles indulgently.

There are only certain types of job you can be 'in', aren't there? No one talks about being 'in' supermarket checkouts or roadsweeping. Nope, you can only have inverted commas if your job's introverted and comatose. Oh, piss off out of here, Bel, you're getting a social conscience again.

Jeff, Damien's father, is 'in' property too. And, like my dad, he's in development, and in employment creation. (Oh, look at Bel! Losing the oh-so-ironic inverted commas! Does this mean she's been absorbed by the establishment, hired by the hierarchy? No, I just take the irony as read, right and true.)

Interesting, being in employment creation. It involves a lot of things, very few of which are to do with putting people to work. Most of them are to do with making money. Fine by me. I like my dad's money. I spend his money. I don't feel guilty. This is a free market. Sure, there are Fallies living in council flats, but they all buy frigging satellite dishes, don't they, and they're always down the pub, and spending ten quid a week on cigs and booze and the lottery, and bringing up kids who think burgers and chips are gourmet food, and reading the fucking *Sun* and believing every word of it, and caring, yes caring, what the hell happens to that bunch of losers on *EastEnders*. So why should I feel guilty for having money?

What was I saying? ... Yeah, interesting, being in employment creation. There are ways of creating employment, quick ways. You create a cycle which needs constant renewal. Like toothpaste. Follow? Toothpaste, that's right. Everyone knows they made the perfect tooth-paste years ago – protect your teeth for life, it would. If it were allowed to go on the market. And it never will, because of the industry. Same with the common cold. Of course they've found a cure, but the research was sponsored by the major pharmaceutical companies whose cold-relief tablets and lemon drinks and lozenges would become obsolete overnight. It's just so frigging obvious that I can't see why no one's said it in public yet.

And another way is to use cheap road surfaces. They have some great stuff in Germany these days, elastic tarmac that expands and contracts without cracking. Mr Henson told us about it in German lessons. One of the few times I listened. And they're quite happy to use it in Germany, because they're not afraid of change. Here, we use stuff that's meant to crack, because if we didn't, we'd have thousands of road-menders on the dole.

You see my point. Employment creation. All makes work for the working man to do.

Anyway, Damien's dad. Jeff. You see, he works with my dad. I found myself with them one evening when they were discussing a new, important project.

I'm getting a lift into town, under protest. We have to go somewhere first. We're in my father's car and I'm huddled into the seat, hiding in my biker's jacket, underneath the lapels and zips. Trying not to be seen. Encased in sticky leather, on the seat and in my jacket.

They take the car past the wasteland in front of the metal skeleton that will become Asda. It's a sea of mud, ringed with cones and fences and clogged by old wrappers and packets.

Now we're climbing high above the town. Jeff is talking about Total Quality Management targets. My own father has slipped effortlessly into his jargon, and they're chattering away happily in their code.

We drive up into brown roads which are bordered by cliffs of pub and kebab shops. Below us, the glass city shines, the hollow towers of the dream still intact. But up here, borders start to be defined not by walls of brick and glass and steel but by shoddy, hastily erected trappings. There are chain-link fences which sieve the landscape. Ranks of cones. Blind, boarded-up shops. A scrawny dog shambles out in front of the car, not seeming to care for its own life. I twist around and see, out of the back window, a boy in shorts running after the dog and sitting in the road to cradle it.

The light is fading, and we're driving into the heart of Fallowdale. We stop the car on a corner. They get out.

My father slips on his sunglasses, as the sun is shooting a last, yellow burst over the town. He stands with hands on hips, nods sagely at the scrubland before us. It falls away towards the town, bile green and burnt brown.

'Ideal,' he says to Jeff.

Jeff unrolls several large sheets of paper which look like architect's plans. He and my father spend the best part of the next half hour consulting, pointing, scribbling, gesturing towards the wasteland. The sun swells with thick vermilion light and sinks ever further towards the horizon.

I sigh, leaning against the car. I can't see what fascinates them so. It's all stuff that I must have seen before but never particularly wanted to look at. There's the wasteground stretching away, and beyond, down in the valley, there's a mess of railway lines and factory buildings. Between those two landscapes, about three hundred yards away from us on the edge of the hills, there's a pair of dead, condemned blocks of flats. They are a dull, yellow colour – wilting cheese with grey holes. Above them, the sky is decorated with those soft clouds that seem to hang upside down, like the acoustic mushrooms in the Albert Hall.

A poet might come up here and expound about the haunted beauty of neglect in the ageing flats, and the way the sunset gives them a crumbling nobility evoking time and shifting patterns of love. Me, I just think they look like fucked-up council flats.

After a while, they nod, and Jeff rolls up the plans. While Jon notes some things on a notepad, Jeff chats to me.

'We've already entered into negotiating stages for the restructuring operation,' says Jeff. He talks to me, gesturing with his clipboard, as if I would be interested.

I shrug. 'It's all ugly,' I point out to him.

'Excellent, great,' says Jeff, and he gives me a bright white grin. 'The ideal end-user observation.'

Behind, in the estate, roads radiate away from us. The culs-de-sac were a town planner's folly, I remember reading. A Fally folly. They were made like spokes in a wheel to foster a caring, neighbourly atmosphere. Instead, they became the perfect nightmare-trap. The designer of one of those combat games on expensive piers couldn't have done it better. Soon, night will fall, and the smells of petrol and dust fill the air as motor bikes tear up and down a ready-made playground. Lone women will scuttle from one street light to the next, sprays in hand, hurrying home to be beaten black and blue by salivating boyfriends.

'You see, Bel,' he continues, 'I've been streamlining our utility acquisition programme.'

'That must have been fun for you.'

He smiles, but not with his eyes. I can see a hint of Damien in him, perhaps – the widely spaced eyes and dark, clearly defined eyebrows, with a flat nose and a knowing face. But Jeff is perhaps more lean, and certainly more stubbly. He hasn't got Damien's sleek, comfortable look.

'You don't take me entirely seriously, do you, Bel?' he asks, moving closer to me. He's lifting his chin in a slightly superior way. I can scent aftershave, the sort that's advertised by telling you it helps you shag women.

I meet his gaze, coolly, the sort of thing that I bet not many women actually do. 'I wouldn't say that,' I assure him. 'But I do wonder if you've learnt to maximize your interpersonal relationship margins.'

He opens his eyes, wide, staring, as if he's about to tell me he hadn't thought about that.

I smile. 'Don't bother. I'm taking the piss.'

Throughout this exchange, my father, as he does at home, has achieved neutrality by non-intervention. He has been leaning on the rickety wall, looking out across the wasteland. He's nodding to himself, as if he has decided something.

I stroll over to him, stretching and yawning.

'This is really boring,' I tell him. 'Did you bring me all this way just to see a load of troggy flats?'

'Take a good look,' he says quietly. 'They're going.'

'Going?'

He nods. 'In three months' time, the demolition order comes through. We've managed to get the go-ahead for the Fallowdale complex.'

I can't help snorting with laughter. 'Don't use words like "complex" round here. Keep it simple.'

But I realize my dad is deadly serious. His face is full of that uncanny brightness which always comes upon him when he's talking property. It's the kind of glassy-eyed zeal which I've otherwise seen only in born-again Christians.

So we stand and look at what is soon to be destroyed. The clouds, as if presaging something, are starting to disintegrate. Hazed with orange edges, they are shifting, fragmenting at the edges, pictures breaking up on a TV screen.

'So the flats have to go, then?'

The sunset is in my father's glasses. He nods vigorously, without even turning to look at me. 'This town needs change. Look at all the dead-ends round here. Dover. Herne Bay. Terrible places. Change. That's what it needs.'

'How do the people in those flats feel about it?' I ask.

There is a long pause, an evening pause, filled by an overlap of sound – seagulls over distant traffic and, perhaps the sea, just at the edge of our hearing as ever.

'They don't know yet,' he says curtly, and then he turns around to head back to the car.

Jeff, his hair blowing in the evening breeze, gives me a grin the size of a mobile phone, and a complicit wink.

I give him a rueful smile back. 'They ain't going to like it.'

Jeff shrugs as he chucks the plans on the back seat. 'They don't have to like it,' he points out. 'They haven't got much choice. Some of them will be rehoused. The council's got this scheme, actually.'

'Oh, yeah? Does it involve execution at all?'

He laughs and rubs his nose. Yeah, I definitely saw a bit of Damien in him just then. 'Not exactly. They want to put the worst ones in specialized housing. You know, strengthened concrete houses with reinforced windows and security cameras. It's a sort of project, monitoring families with background problems. You know, try and understand them a bit better.'

'Right. These houses wouldn't happen to be rent-free, would they? In other words, paid for by normal people?'

Jeff gives me another big grin and a non-committal shrug. 'It's an innovative idea,' he points out. 'The council like innovative ideas.'

'Oh, yeah, as long as they're P C enough.'

This is the same body, I remind myself, which last year announced that it didn't have the money for any new library books, but which somehow found a few thousand to send its councillors on a three-day Sexual Difference Awareness Enhancement course in a four-star hotel in Taunton.

And so this is how it'll work. Many of the law-abiding spend their nights papering over the damp and working out if they can afford to switch on the extra bar on the fire and being crippled by council-tax bills inflated by local government incompetence (and trips to four-star Somerset hotels). And meanwhile, the others – those with noses which are not quite so clean – end up having it all taken care of.

I wonder how long it'll take the Fallies to work out the connection between a bad reputation and a council grant. If they're canny enough, they might start sending their kids out joyriding and robbing, just to get a slice of what's going. Same story all over. Like riots. Nobody gives the inner cities any money until they have a really good riot and smash up their own neighbourhood. It seems that pissing in your own backyard is the only way to get anyone's attention.

JJ gets the biscuits, while I pour more wine.

Kate twitters around us. 'Thank you, Joshua,' she murmurs. 'That's very helpful of you.'

If I know him, he doesn't want to be helpful and he doesn't want to be Joshua. But it is useful to be both, for the moment.

We lean against the wall in the garden and watch the pageant of floating hats and glasses through the patio doors. JJ occasionally sips from a glass of orange juice.

'How did Jon end up with her?' he asks, tilting his glass towards the house. The question is not intended to sound impertinent or critical – JJ has spent the afternoon playing the golden boy, and only some of it was an act. He is Well Brought Up. He's simply curious to know the answer.

'I don't really know.' He stares at me in an oh-come-on sort of way, but I shrug. 'Really. He just came home with her one day. I think she was screwing some business partner or something, and she decided my dad had more money. You know she's been married to three other men? All of them little gold-mines, too. She knows what she's doing.'

'Don't you ever want to kill her?' he asks me casually.

'Often,' I tell him, with feeling. 'Very, very often.'

He shrugs. 'Why don't you do it, then? You'd be doing your father a favour.'

I grin, remembering what I said to him about the girl in the chemist's shop. 'No-one can get away with murder these days. They have DNA fingerprinting, all that stuff.'

The best answer is always the pragmatic one.

Inside, Kate squeals in delight as she embraces another new arrival.

'Easy, from here,' I murmur. '*Pchow, pchow, pchow.*' My finger chops into the crowd, slicing it up with imaginary bullets.

'Could you kill someone?' he asks. 'Just out of interest.'

'People do, just out of interest. Vested interest, and compound interest.' I giggle. 'Never know, Kate might be mixing up the weed-killer for Dad, right now.'

I have avoided the question. JJ just sighs and shoves his hands in his pockets. 'Come on,' he says, 'let's go into town.'

Upstairs on the bus, it smells of piss and sweat, and it rattles with abandoned cans every time we go round a corner. I tell him about my father's and Jeff's plans for the Fally estate.

JJ looks perturbed. He fiddles with his bus ticket and slices a hole in it with his fingernail. 'And no one on Fallowdale knows yet?'

'Nope. I think they're gonna tell them when it's too late to protest.'
I grin ruefully. 'Rather neat, don't you think?'

We don't talk much more about it. Neither of us really cares.

In town, we amble down the main street, kicking a carton between
us until I finally lose patience and send it ricocheting off against a car.
We stop outside one of the well-known chain stores.

'I want a new jacket,' I tell JJ. 'Come on.'

In Ladies' Wear, he hangs around a few feet behind me as if he's
frightened of being thought a transvestite. The leather jackets are all
fixed together with something that looks like a bike chain, so no joy
there. Black denim, though, is a definite option.

'You haven't got any money,' JJ points out.

'Who needs money?' I ask him disgustedly. I select a jacket in size
12 and twist off the label with the bar-code. Then I take it from the
peg and walk off, whistling.

JJ keeps close to me, nervously, as I stride off. I'm dangling the
jacket very obviously by the hanger. 'You're not very discreet,' he
hisses at me, as we jostle our way through the late Saturday crowds.

'You've never done this before, have you?' I shake my head pityingly,
and we stop at a cash desk.

'Hello!' I say with a smile. Instantly, I am well-spoken, upright,
adult. I plonk the jacket down in front of the cashier, who's a middle-
aged woman in wire-framed glasses, like someone's kindly gran. My
smile is returned, which is a good start. 'I wonder if I could possibly
exchange this? I bought it here last week, and it's the wrong
size.'

'I'll do it for you, love,' she says in a quiet, amiable voice, peering
at the collar. 'What size was it you wanted?'

'I'm actually a ten now!' I tell her, remembering to simper slightly.
'Must be the diet. I've been following it regularly.'

And a minute or so later, I'm strolling out of the shop with a green
carrier-bag swinging from my fingers, the proud owner of a size 10
black denim jacket. A bewildered JJ scurries after me.

I have a look up at the sky. 'No rain. Oh, well.'

'Rain?' he asks, baffled.

'Just after it's been raining – always the best time to go lifting. Know why?' We stop at another shop window.

JJ shrugs. 'Tell me.'

'You can spot the store detectives more easily. They're the ones with dry shoes.'

'Any more tricks up your sleeve?' he asks. I'm pulling the jacket on now, and I abandon the carrier bag in a municipal flowerpot.

I grin at him. 'We can try.' I beckon him inside the shop.

It's one of the more hopeful local shops, called Bright. This place has an alarm set-up at the door, one of those barrier things like at an airport, and thick plastic security tags on all the clothes.

Downstairs, they're nearly ready to close, and they're cashing up. Upstairs, there's no one except a stupid bitch with green nails, feet up on the counter, reading a magazine.

I take a little red number into the changing room and start working on the disc. It seems to take an age, but I can feel it coming. Finally, it rips off with what seems to me like a huge noise. The dress is torn, of course, but that's the price you pay, and I can easily fix that at home. I shove it into my pocket and stride confidently out.

JJ, who's been scratching his nose hard enough to take the skin off, seems to have got this idea that he's supposed to do some distracting – probably seen too many police films at school. He's asking the girl about paisley ties. She's giving him a hard stare and saying, 'We don't do men's,' or something like that, but by that time I'm halfway down the stairs with the little silk dress scrunched in my jacket pocket.

Outside, it takes a lot to persuade JJ to have a go, but eventually I do, by letting him go for the easiest option of all – the double-layer manoeuvre. Still so few shops have actually twigged to this one. We try it in a place pounding with techno, called Klobber (yuk!), just off the main square.

I stand outside and watch him take two identical red check shirts in one hand into the changing rooms. Make sure you get the label off, I tell him. They're always tagged, even when they don't seem to be. Luckily, he's got quite a loose shirt of his own on today. He emerges, very red, after about ten minutes – Jesus, we're going to need to get some practice in – and puts his one shirt back on the peg. Now, the key is not to scarper straight away. You stay, look at a few similar things, peer intently at price labels. JJ's not happy about this bit, I can tell. Eventually, we slip out of the shop. He's got his eyes closed as if he expects alarms to blare at any moment.

In the street, I jump up and down, laughing, and kiss him, but he doesn't seem happy. It's only then that I notice the collar of the check shirt sticking out from under his own. And no one even saw.

8   *Unsound Waves*

There are ghosts.

Belinda Archard says there are ghosts.
  My mother's eyes open wide in the hollows of my memory.
  Of her memory.
  She is Belinda Archard. I am Bel. I have to remember that.

There are ghosts here, of course, at the end of the world.
  There are the wraiths of girls who never turned up to their weddings on the marshland churches and now haunt their pewless shells with blue light.
  Then, on the stumps of crumbling stone high above the town, which some wag on the tourist board decided they should call a castle, there's a woman in grey patrolling the ruined walls. I often wonder what she thinks of the town on a darkening September night, when the blackness is dusted with the orange and blue of sodium and mercury, and cars squeal down on the harbour wall, and great steaming clouds of light move across the horizon as the hovercraft thunder towards Dover and Folkestone. I wonder what she makes of the pungent fish-and-chips air and the empty fag packets in the holes between the ruins. The spiky needles. The sloppy, dead condoms.
  JJ told me he knew someone who'd seen her face. He said she had thick, dark glasses with no earpieces, welded to her white face – insect's eyes – and that the grey cloak was actually all shiny, like silver foil. He told me this theory that ghosts can echo back as well as forward in time, and that she could be a ghost from the future, not of the past.

One who'd come to see what her Aids-decimated, post-holocaust world had once been like, recording it all with the dark cameras of her eyes. I sort of tried not to think about that.

This is a renowned place for ending your life. You'd have thought people would want to end it on a high, rather than in the South's biggest shit-hole, but never mind. And there's the cove, out beyond the pier, where nobody goes these days, where the sea water's clogged with decaying cars.

Some are no doubt frightened of the slippery, frog-eyed bodies within the wrecks. Me, I'm more worried about the cars themselves. I imagine those great steel demons, dripping with seaweed, rearing up on their fragments of rubber legs. They bare their metal teeth and flash their green, algae-filled eyes as they lunge at the unwary traveller.

Night. What is it about night that brings out the darkness in us all?

At night, I listen to the radio. Sometimes it makes my ears hurt, the same way that those 3-D pictures – the magic cardboard cut-outs that emerge from a sea of colour – hurt my eyes.

The town lights are lollipop orange and ice blue. They're scattered in a glitter on the slopes between here and the Edge of the World.

Voices jabber away, transmitted from somewhere up beyond the hills, washing over us on their journey to the sea.

'*I saw this programme an' they was talkin' about puttin' the M1 unnerground. That's what they wanna use that Millyum Fund for. Buryin' the motorway unnerground.*'

'I . . . see.'

'*Put loadsa trees and stuff over it they said, and bury it unnerground and no one would know it'd ever been there.*'

'Ah, really. Yes. Kelly, there is a possibility – isn't there – that some irony was at play here?'

'*Irony.*'

'Yes. Yes, that's right.'

'*Wha's irony?*'

'Well, it's when you say something that you don't really mean.

You're keeping a kind of distance from it by being not entirely serious.'

'*Oh, right.*' (Pause, breath.) '*Well, anyway, that wann't what I rang up for, I wanna talk about marriage and that.*'

'And – and what, sorry?'

'*Marriage and that. You don' listen, do yer? Me boyfriend an' me, we was gettin' this flat together, right, but me parents, right, they said we was stupid.*'

'I see – they believe in marriage and, er, that?'

'*Yeah. I said to me dad the other day, you coulda killed summun an' been let out by now.*'

'I'm . . . sorry?'

'*They 'ad their thirtieth weddin' anniversary, an' I said to me dad, you coulda killed summun an' been let out by now.*'

'Light dawns, Kelly. I see what you mean. You're referring to that old adage – marriage isn't a word, it's a sentence.'

'*. . . ?*'

'Kelly?'

'*Yeah. An', well, me parents think we're stupid.*'

'How unkind. And have they offered any kind of substantiating evidence for this claim?'

'*. . . Uh?*'

'Er, why do they say that? About you and your boyfriend?'

'*Dunno. He ain't me boyfriend now. Weren't really me boyfriend, anyway. I dinn't really like him, like. I wanna marry someone rich, me. Rich an' good-lookin', right?*'

'I . . . see. And you're looking around, er, Chatham?'

'*Live in Cha'am, yeah.*'

'I was just trying to suggest, you see, Kelly – I'm sorry, it's this irony thing, really, and maybe it's my fault for not having explained the concept adequately – I was just trying to suggest that you should expand your horizons a little?'

'*Right.*'

'OK, Kelly, good luck with it. Thanks for your call, I'll speak to you soon.'

I'm not really listening. I want to make that clear. The presenter annoys me with his personal approach to censorship. I called them up once, but when the person taking the calls found out that I wanted to advocate castrating paedophiles, they wouldn't let me on the air. Said it would cause too much offence. Well, who decides what causes offence and what doesn't? They let stupid tossers come on and cause offence with their low IQs, don't they? I'm definitely going to start a campaign against passive listening-to-bollocks.

They cut someone off last week who said he supported the BNP. This made him look *important* enough to be censored. If they'd just let him carry on speaking, he'd have shown himself up as a dickhead, with no effort required.

Of course, all the BNP have to do, if they want respectability, is not beat anyone up for say, three months, then declare a 'ceasefire' (without handing over any weapons as such) and within a few weeks they'll be shaking hands with presidents and government ministers. And if the arms fund is a bit low, their new friends will surely oblige.

Anyway, as I say, I'm not listening. I'm thinking about this morning, when I went to see Marcie.

Now, the autumn days seem to be coated with mush, sheened by drizzle. The light has the greyness of eternal twilight. As I hurry through the town, shivering in my coat, cars sweep past, lights scattering in puddles at half-past three in the afternoon. Sunlight is a concept we made up. Days are becoming squashed in the middle by great clouds of blackness as we're squeezed towards winter.

I've heard Marcie is pissed-off. I don't think I've ever seen her properly happy – just drunk. Of course, the American for angry is 'pissed', which no doubt causes a little confusion. ('Gee, you guys, I came home drunk from the high-school prom. My mom was real pissed.')

I digress. They say misery loves company – well, not from where I stand. Not unless the company is fully-privatized, run by a quango and makes home-brew depression kits. Producing whines by fomenting gripes.

No, I wouldn't be here if I didn't have to. I've got other fish to batter. They say 'other cats to whip' in France, did you know that? Gives you some idea what their minds are on.

The metal staircase up to her flat is dusty. Dust hangs in the air, too. The air's got a thick, gritty quality.

Marcie doesn't come to the door straight away. There's a lot of thumping and scratching from the other side of the door, and a pattering like the paws of an animal. I'm curious. I put my ear up to the door, smelling its warm, painty odour. Then the door clicks and I straighten up just in time as it opens.

Those bashed-looking eyes are there, flicking up and down.

'Oh,' she says. 'It's you.'

I shrug. Not much of an answer you can give to that, is there? 'Can I come in, then?'

Marcie's eyes flick over her shoulder for a moment, as if she is checking something inside the flat.

'I can come back later,' I tell her, and my heart is beating faster with the excited thought that I might be able to put off this meeting.

'I'm decorating,' Marcie says. 'Mind the paint.'

I step inside the hall. There is a strong odour of paint and paste. It's a smell of transience, but also a slightly fishy, spermy smell.

There's a patch of pinkish granules on the carpet just inside the hall, next to the bedroom door. I narrowly avoid stepping in it. I realize after a few seconds that it's a pile of salt, soaking up a red-wine stain.

Marcie, in a silver dressing-gown, slinks down the hallway with a cigarette in each hand. There are small flecks of paint on the shimmery surface of the gown. I follow her, tasting the sharpness of her smoke, not quite sure where I'm going.

She lurches up against a door, making me stop short, and lazily says to someone inside the room, 'Amuse yourself. Got a visitor.'

I manage to peer through the door, where the intoxicating smell of paint is stronger than ever. The room's covered in cloths and strewn with great swathes of green wallpaper, like sloughed-off skin, and there's a man, naked, perched on a stepladder.

Or at least, he is until Marcie's words 'Got a visitor' echo round the room, and my inquisitive little head pokes itself round the door. Now, all of a sudden, with a most un-masculine shriek, he's grabbed one of the huge snakeskins of wallpaper. He's wrapping himself up in it, trying not to look at me.

I smile at him. 'Hi.'

He's blushing, trying to blend with the wall.

'Have you got her for free?' I ask him in mock surprise. 'Make the most of it while stocks last.'

The next caller after Kelly is Andy, who served in Northern Ireland. He's talking about gays in the forces. I sharpen my pencil while I listen to him. The fragments make a perfect, thin roll of wood like the peel of some wooden fruit.

'Now, Andy, surely it doesn't matter? You're all in together, comrades in arms and all that. Why should it matter?'

'*Yeah, right, you're all in together, yeah, but you have to trust the other lads. Sometimes it's quite normal, when you're out on trainin' exercises an' that, to huddle together, like, y' know, nothin' funny about it, jus' for warmth and that. At night.*'

'And if someone you huddled up with later confessed to you to being homosexual, you would feel uneasy about this?'

'*Too f-flippin' right I would.*'

'What would you do?'

'*I'd prob'ly punch his lights out.*'

I finish sharpening my pencil. Just for fun, I start digging the point into the flesh of my arm. I wonder if you could do a home-made tattoo in sharp pencil?

Listening to this verbal ping-pong, I suddenly get a picture of JJ's Aunt Imelda in a flak jacket, with a beret over her short back and sides, mud foundation smeared on her perfect alabaster face, lying in a ditch and waiting for her target to come over the hill. Actually, I think she'd look quite good in fatigues.

'*Yeah, but I mean it, right? You 'ave to trust the other blokes.*'

'And you'd feel you couldn't trust someone, simply because they happened to enjoy a different kind of relationship from you? Do you imagine that there haven't been gays in the military in the past? T. E. Lawrence was gay. Did you know that?'

'*Yeah . . . well, he were a f-flippin' perv, weren't he? We did one of them books in school. Obsessed with sex, he was.*'

'Er, yes – Andy, I rather feel you're confusing him with *D. H. Lawrence*, who's another kettle of fish entirely. Well, never mind.'

Is it just me, or is everyone obsessed with it? From the point of view of orientation, I mean? Generally speaking, it's the last thing I need to know about someone when I meet them. Unless I fancy them, that is. Sure, if JJ had preferred blokes it would have made a difference to me, 'cos I wanted him.

But I don't actually need to know what his Aunt Imelda prefers, and yet as soon as I met her, she thought she had to make it clear. (Why? In case I felt like jumping her bones?) Just get on with doing it, that's what I say – don't waste time bragging about it. Otherwise I have this fear that pretty soon, I'm going to feel this perverse need to walk up to a complete stranger at a party and say, 'Hi, I'm Bel. I get off on crucifixion fantasies. Is that a hammer in your pocket, or are you just pleased to see me?'

I get bored with the pencil. It's not as easy to break my skin as I thought.

Anyway, after this morning with Marcie, I've got an important decision to make.

Marcie is in the kitchen. She's pushing her paint-streaked hair back with one hand and shoving the plunger of a cafetière down with the other.

How refreshingly middle-class. Yeah, irony. Marcie, just a year ago, would have made a cup of coffee by turning the hot tap straight on to Happy Shopper granules in a chipped mug. How she's changed. The saddest kind of social climber, isn't it? One who's actually trying to be bourgeois? I've always thought of middle-classness as something you can't really help – like being ginger, or having buck teeth.

Shame the effect's ruined by her two burning ciggies, parked in a lump of putty on the worktop.

She opens the fridge to get the milk and I get a glimpse of something odd. Nestling there among all the butter and beer and cheese and an iceberg lettuce, there's about a dozen stoppered little bottles, all labelled. They look like those bottles of milk that we used in school when we did that pasteurizing experiment. I'm a bit uneasy about home-sterilized milk, but no, the stuff that Marcie's got out is an ordinary supermarket carton. What's all that in the fridge, then? She closes the door. So I have to ask something different.

'Is he . . .?' I venture, waving a hand down the corridor.

She looks up at me, or rather past me. I realize she's tuned-out, this early in the day. 'Fuckin' decorator. Bit of all right. So I thought, what the hell.'

I have a worrying feeling about this. 'This wouldn't have anything to do with payment in lieu, would it?'

She looks up from pouring the coffee. I hate that stoned gaze, looking right through me like blind beggar's eyes.

'Lounge,' she says. 'Not the loo.'

Cascades of thick, brown coffee are trickling across the worktop, down the cupboards and on to the floor. Some of it splashes on Marcie's naked leg, and she doesn't even seem to feel it – but then she shrieks when she sees what she's done. She drops the cafetière and it rolls to the edge of the worktop and smashes. Marcie's mouth opens in a silent scream and she puts her hands to her face.

'It's all right,' I'm saying. 'Don't worry.' I start wiping up with a cloth – would you believe it? I'm clearing up, taking control. I wrap up the bits of glass in an old newspaper and put them in the bin. 'Don't worry,' I keep saying. 'It doesn't matter.'

I have to keep saying that, because I know that when you're stoned it does matter, something like that matters a great deal, unless you think it's hilarious. It's like when you've been seriously weeding all night and you want something to eat, need something to eat, and you go to the bar to buy a pastie or something and it's absolutely vital that you show the barman that you know what you are doing, that you are not a useless stoned idiot, by having the totally correct change. And you fumble through piles and piles of coppers and those trinkety little

64

Mickey Mouse fives and tens, and you start to understand what the old biddies are going on about when they say coins are so fiddly nowadays.

I sit Marcie down at the kitchen table, grip her shoulders and shake her. Blonde hair falls in a scrappy fringe over her deep, dark eyes.

'Listen, Marcie,' I say to her, sounding stern now. I sound like my mother. Jesus H. Christ, on a Harley-Davidson. 'What I mean is – are you letting him shag you to pay for your lounge to be decorated?'

She bites her lip, looks away as if seeking the answer on the wet tiles of the kitchen floor. Then she shrugs. Nods.

I lean back, exhaling deeply. She is such a stupid slut. I've always said so. Why is it up to me to get her out of this mess? I don't even know her properly, for Christ's sake.

Why's Damien not here? I don't want to answer that.

'Tell me about what you want to do.' I realize I've asked her, now, and that there is no going back. 'Tell me about wanting to take the blame for the shop-window.'

She looks up at me with those haunted eyes. 'I need the money, don't I? Need it bad.'

'What do you need the money for, Marcie? You've got a job.'

Silence. She bites her lip, plucks one of the cigarettes out of its putty and draws deeply on it. I watch the ash glowing, hanging on the edge, wondering if it will fall off. I realize what has happened.

'You . . . haven't got a job any more? Have you, Marcie?'

She won't look at me. 'Shit job anyway. Get something better, I will.'

'Yeah. Yeah, sure you will.' I lean back in the chair. Well, that's taken the wind out of my sales pitch. 'What happened, Marcie?'

'I was off. Ill. For a day.' She pushes her hair back, and I see her fingernails, varnished with flecks of white paint. 'Just a day.'

'Ill? When?'

'Well, hung-over. Same as ill, innit? Anyway, they got a temp in.' She reaches for the other cigarette now, smoking double-barrelled. (I'm quite impressed. I've never actually seen anyone desperate enough to do that before.) 'She was this bitch straight out of seccy college in Canterbury. They decided to keep her. Instead of me.'

I am stunned. I really thought Marcie was on the way up, or what she saw as up. Now, in the snakes-and-ladders economy, down she goes.

'What was she so good at?' As I ask, I can imagine a few things. More words per minute, or more adept at the hieroglyphs of shorthand perhaps, or a firebrand in the filing department.

'Telling the truth,' says Marcie absently, leaning back in her chair and not looking at me. She shrugs, scattering two sprays of ash. 'She told them about me. About me past.'

'They . . . didn't know, then?'

'One or two people knew. But they didn't say nothin', 'cos they couldn't prove it. But she didn't care, she just said something outright.' Marcie leans forward, and her breathing is ragged. 'I need the money, Bel. I really need it now.'

'All right, all right.' I hold up my hands. 'Let's think carefully about this. You were too busy getting smashed, so you may not have noticed, but there's nothing at the moment to connect us with putting that car through Goodmans' window. Right?'

'Except JJ an' his Dettol,' she says.

Coolly, she stubs out both her cigarettes together, and the trails of smoke frame her face in a V. I can't believe her, sometimes. Maybe Marcie isn't as stupid as she's always seemed.

'OK. So they find that the car smells of Dettol – because you vommed inside it, I would point out. What do they do then? Go round all the chemists, asking if anyone was seen buying Dettol in the small hours on Saturday night?'

Marcie shrugs. 'Yes,' she says, simply.

'What?' I sound more cross than I intend. Probably because I've realized, with sudden, crashing clarity, that she's right.

She shrugs again. 'I know the police,' she says. 'That's how they work.' She leans forward, looking into my eyes with deep urgency. 'Look, Bel, I ain't totally stupid, right? I'm not goin' to go blabbin' off to people if nothin' comes of it, am I? You pay me for security. If anyone asks any questions, and if they start to link it to us, I'll say I was the driver. For fifty quid.'

'Fifty. Right.' So, she's mentioned a sum, now. That's the price of truth, is it? I briefly wonder – and I have to bite my tongue to stop myself from asking – what it used to buy from Marcie, before. Would it have bought the full job, or what I believe they call 'hand relief'? To be honest, it's not as much as I thought she might have asked for.

'An' the expenses, of course,' she says.

'Expenses?'

'The fine and the costs, if there are any. You agree to pay if it comes to that. It's part of the price of your non-involvement.'

I'm starting to get the picture. 'You wouldn't just say you were driving – you'd leave me and JJ out of the picture totally?'

She shrugs. She fumbles with her lighter. It's a tacky little thing, like a tree decoration or something. Not what I'd call a lighter.

'Yeah,' she says. 'Totally.'

Her eyes flick up to me, down, up again. I'm leaning back in my chair, watching her closely.

'I'm just not sure, Marcie.' Trying to be honest with her.

'Please, Bel,' she says.

I decide it is probably a good time to go, just in case she starts begging with me to give her the money anyway. 'I'll let you know,' I tell her.

On the way out, I poke my head round the lounge door again. 'Get your brush out, mate. Happy pasting.'

Even on the bus, I can't get the smell of paint out of my nostrils.

Behind me, as we pull away from the town, a giant cloud looms over the harbour. It's like a big V-sign at me, written in smoke. As if the Town at the Edge of the World is saying, Stuff You.

And so I listen to the radio, brood, watch the lights, and think. Down far beyond the town, out on the misty sea, a hovercraft booms as it heads out to fall off the edge of the world. I look with my binoculars, but I can only see the lights of the town deep below me.

'*It's terrible, I'm telling you. Far worse than when I was a lad. You're a young man, aren't you?*'

'Well, I don't really see that my age has anything to do with it, but I, and the listeners of Coast FM, would love to hear your views, Alan. In what way is it worse?'

'*All these muggings and vile-ance and riots and stuff. Young people going on the rampage.*'

Oh, great. A miserable old git, stuck beside the radio with nothing better to do than moan about the younger generation. Tell me one thing: if the good old days were so great, how come they didn't last?

'Alan, it's a matter of perception, isn't it? I agree that it does appear rather grim. But it might be that public perception of crime has increased, rather than crime itself.'

'*Eh? You saying it's right, all this mugging?*'

'No, absolutely not. I think perhaps you didn't quite understand me. You see, methods of disseminating information are becoming more sophisticated, and the chances are that nowadays, in the nineties, you're hearing about things of which you would have been in ignorance during your youth. Isn't that so?'

'*You calling me ignorant, young man? I despair, sometimes. When you get to my age, you'll understand.*'

'I see. Maybe you could share your wisdom, Alan, and speed up the process ever so slightly?'

'*You'll find out. When you get to my age. Think you know everything, sitting there in your radio chair and calling people ignorant what have been on Earth for forty year longer than you!*'

I feel suddenly cold. I open my desk drawer. The knife is there, resting on its bed of sliced photographs and tissue-paper.

I wake up out of a strangely thrilling dream, sweating, and damp between my legs.

There were two faceless girls, both pink and fleshy, swimming inside a teapot, their bodies getting coated with the brown liquid and the big flakes the size of autumn leaves. They swam towards each other, laughed, embraced, started to lick the stuff off each other. I somehow knew that one of them could be JJ's Aunt Imelda, and that the other was Marcie with her deep-bruised eyes.

One of them, the one who might be Imelda, starts to pull long, slippery strands of seaweed out of the tea and wind it round the other girl's head. She winds and winds until the chin has disappeared, then the mouth, and then the nose, and the eyes. The girl has a face of seaweed, an alien monster's face. Then, she pushes her under the tea and holds her down.

I sit up in my bed for a moment, shivering. I pull on my red silk dressing-gown – a guilt present from Cowbitch, and I was hardly going to refuse it, was I? Carefully, I patter downstairs. The uplighters are on in the hall, and the carpet, which is swamp-thick, absorbs my footsteps. I'd imagine that my father and Kate are fast asleep.

By the long-case clock in the hall, it's ten past two. Late, but not unreasonable. In the lounge, I lift the phone off its mahogany table and dial a six-figure number. There are thirty-six rings – I count them – before a man answers.

'*Yeah?*'

I am only taken aback for a short moment. 'Well, hello there. Mr Deluxe Gloss, I presume?'

'*Eh? . . . Uh . . . You want Marcie?*'

'Oh, you're too kind.'

There's a kerfuffle at the other end. Marcie comes on, her voice slurred with sleep or dope. '*Mmm, wha'?*'

'You're on,' I tell her. 'Fifty pounds, in cash, tomorrow.'

I put the receiver down. Then I shiver, pull my dressing-gown tighter around me and hurry back to bed.

The next day, after breakfast, I go down to the cashpoint, draw out fifty pounds from my savings, put it in a Jiffy bag and take it round to Marcie's. No one is in. Or at least, no one's answering the door. I assume she's still having a bit of internal decorating done. I drop the envelope through the door and hear it land with a thud, echoing in the hall.

All right, I want to justify it. I have bought peace of mind.

Back home, I switch the radio on again and flop on to the bed. Kev from Sheerness is on the phone-in. He's saying that we need capital punishment because it acts as a detergent. *Sic*.

I fall asleep, thinking of executioners in whiter-than-white hoods.

9 *Shopping List*

'This Saturday,' says Damien, sitting at the table in Dianti's coffee-shop. 'Let's go for it.'

Earlier, he finishes his can and hurls it against the nearest bin. It bounces and clatters to the paving-stones. An old woman with an offensive shopping trolley stops dead outside Dotty-P's and glowers at us. I smile sweetly. JJ shoves his hands deep into his pockets and walks along ahead of us, pretending he isn't with us.

JJ, Damien and I are in the Park Mall. Marcie's not here. I think she is down at the Job Centre.

Park Mall is nowhere near a park, and it's more of an indoor street than a mall. It's another one of the great jokes of this town, actually. A sticking-plaster on the urban cancer. Filled with jumpers and wooden ornaments and greetings cards that I can't imagine any of the Fallies or the other commoners buying. It smells of fresh coffee and flowers, and the shops have smooth, parqueted floors. So unreal, and yet, amazingly, it still exists – while, all around, shops turn into shuttered spaces, burning with lurid graffiti, splashed with pungent piss and beer.

We sit down among the chrome and Formica of Dianti's coffee-shop. JJ has a small black coffee. I think he's being businesslike, today. I go for a cappuccino and a *pain au chocolat*, and Damien, who is obviously feeling frivolous, has a great cone of smoked green glass, filled to the brim with a froth of green and white and huge globes of mint-chocolate ice-cream. He grins in a devilish way as he prepares to scoop into it. His wonky front teeth always make his grins look lecherous.

In fact, he is being a lech. He's watching the two schoolgirls on the next table. JJ's noticed, and he's sipping nervously at his coffee.

You see, that's one of the ways they're different. I've already spoken about JJ and his childlike curiosity. With Damien, though, he knows exactly why he's doing it. He genuinely wants to get into their pants. Some guys chat up fourteen-year-olds for the hell of it at parties, but Damien takes these things seriously, almost professionally. He'll size up which ones are cute enough to shag, but not so pretty that they can be cocky (this, in my view, means discerning). He'll work out the requisite amount of alcohol needed to get them off their faces but not incapable, and then ply them with it. He shared some tricks with me – and no, he's never tried anything on with me, not once. Like, there's the one where he'll drink vodka and orange with a girl and keep topping his own glass up with orange and hers with vodka. She rarely notices.

Damien's not exactly a liberal as regards women. He had this band at school, which he's currently trying to re-form. They recorded a song called 'She's a Bitch'. Some measure of its quality can be gleaned from the fact that the title rhymed first with 'never gonna get hitched' and later with the immortal 'All she needs is a hat and a cat / And she'd be a Hallowe'en witch'.

He sees me narrowing my eyes at him, and out comes another of the Great Sayings of Damien. 'If they're old enough to bleed,' he says, 'they're old enough to breed.' And he grins, his teeth crooked across his stubbly face.

JJ sighs theatrically, makes a mock-serious face at Damien and leans back with his hands behind his head.

'Do you want to hear my theory?' JJ begins lazily.

Damien waves his spoon. 'You never want to hear mine,' he points out, and dive-bombs his mint concoction again.

JJ continues, undeterred.

Let me summarize, right? Because I basically agree with him.

Industry has totally declined in the town. That is, industry in the traditional sense. Industry that makes solid objects for people to use. Cold steel. Hard plastic. But other little industries have slipped out from between the cracks, shifted from the shadows to take their place. And they have found a way to make money out of people's nothingness.

Even the poor can be customers if you know how to put your mind to it. Because if you're selling hope, you'll always find custom. Just look at the fucking lottery. OptiMystic Meg, a load of balls and the National Anthea for a doomed land. Perfect.

Of course, there are legitimate businesses that still survive in the town, because they do well no matter what the economic situation. Insurance firms, accountants, solicitors. They thrive off crime and deprivation. But there are others. No one can prove anything – JJ can only allege it from stuff we've heard in pubs, stuff we've picked up on our networks. Glaziers employing armies of kids to go round shops on the estates and do in the windows. Creating market need. Roofers with similar teams, armed with rocks and catapults to shatter slates and tiles. And there are, no doubt, those who can pay a monthly 'insurance' rate to these companies to ensure there are no occurrences of this kind. These are the new growth industries.

Some little cards started appearing in shop-windows round the Edge of the World a few months back. 'Earn £30 per 100, addressing envelopes from home. No typing required.' And an address. Easy money, it screamed. People all over town must have been sending off for details, getting their bin-liners ready for a deluge of junk mail to be addressed.

Ah, but it was better than that. You wrote to the address, and they asked for £10 to send you an information pack. You sent this off, and discovered that there was no junk mail to send: the task was to put *your* address on hundreds of these very cards, inviting people to write to you for information, then stick them up in newsagents. For another £10, they would send you your supply of cards and hints about where to put them up. And then *you* were a supplier. Brilliantly simple. I've always thought that if it spread unchecked, it could be a whole new subculture, and then more. There might, eventually, be more people earning from it than being used by it. My bizarre imaginings took me into a future society where no one worked, we all just exchanged cards and money.

This is the way the world is going. And JJ and I think it's quite funny, actually.

'This Saturday,' says Damien. 'Let's go for it.'

JJ and I exchange glances. I run my tongue over my coffee-roughened teeth. 'What do you mean, exactly?' I ask him, picking up my spoon and running it round the cup.

Damien leans back, his mischievous dark eyes surveying us both. 'Something new, beautiful. Destructive. Creative.'

JJ, his chin in his hands, looks from one of us to the other. 'I'm supposed to be going to this club with Imelda and Des. Sorry.'

I'm a bit annoyed, and I immediately try not to show it. Des is Desiree, by the way, Imelda's current shag, who's lasted a couple of months – that makes them practically married in Imelda's terms. I remember her talking about some dive where she wanted to take JJ. He'll probably be eaten alive.

'All right,' I say to JJ, 'if your aunt's more important than your friends, we understand.'

He opens his mouth, looking pained. 'She doesn't get out very much,' he protests.

Damien sniggers. 'Comes out, though.'

I, for some reason, grin and go along with him. 'The closet's bare, and she hasn't got a thing to wear. Are all the little girlies coming out to play?'

I feel bad about that. All right? I normally side with JJ against Damien. Course I do. It's just that I'm pissed off with JJ today. Sometimes, I feel like he's in tune with the oldies. Imelda's in her thirties, they get on really well, and by all accounts, he's *polite* to the various spiky-haired girls with pierced lips and ears who shamble out of his aunt's bedroom in the mornings.

I worry about JJ. He's mercurial, and I have not sized him up properly.

I'm worried that, one day, he might betray us.

'So what do you want to do?' I ask Damien carefully.

He leans back, hands behind his head, and grins at us. 'There's a ready-made playground, just out of town. Ashwell Heights.'

I can feel the smile creeping across my face, and I can feel my skin tingling in anticipation. Yeah, this feels right. If it had a colour, it'd be red.

Ashwell Heights, you see, is what my dad and Jeff are going to put out of business.

It's a shopping complex that seemed like a good idea back when it was built, in the heady post-recession days. Off the main road up to Maidstone, it stands like a castle of gold and silver and glass, a monument to stupidity. Someone had the idea that you could lure people into boutiques for dried flowers and expensive cafés selling teas from around the world – if you just bunged a few supermarkets and electrical shops in with it. Kind of like a cake-mix where you think you can get your victim to swallow the arsenic if you stir in enough eggs, brandy and nuts.

And it all went horribly wrong. What people want is everything at rock-bottom prices – which is what the Fallowdale Centre will be like, of course, only they don't know they'll be getting rock-bottom quality too. They want shops stacked high with cardboard shells full of cans and packets. Powdered mashed-potato mix that makes some slurpy white stuff not entirely unlike mashed potato. Sticky white bread which locks to the roof of your mouth. Beans for 10p a can, in runny orange sauce, oozing from their transparent shells as you look at them. Fizzy drinks of all colours, as bright and brash as you can make them. Frozen stuff for the kids, real food like the sort they get in burger bars, the only food they'll eat without throwing a tantrum.

God, you couldn't wish for better breeding grounds for anarchy and urban decay – houses where screaming kids, high on tartrazine, rule the roost. It was never like that at ours, and it won't be when I have kids. It may not be cool to say so, but I approve of the way my parents brought me up. If you didn't eat what was good for you, then you got it put in front of you again, cold, the next day. I remember my dad making me eat every last forkful of some cabbage and onion stuff. It tasted like my morning breath, but it pumped me full of vitamins. And there were tomatoes, loads of tomatoes with their slippy flesh and sharp little seeds – I hated them, mainly because Petra Renwick in my form once spat a huge gobbet at me that was full of chewed tomato. The smell didn't go away for days, but I must've got over it, 'cos I like tomatoes now.

You have to admire my dad, the way he sees a hole in the market and fills it. You can't beat capitalism these days. The alternative, to me, just means Communism, images from my childhood – tanks ploughing down Chinese students and Ceaușescu lying dead in the snow, and ancient Trabbies clunking their way round Berlin spewing out pollution. So your success in life depends on the extent to which you control capitalism. Anyone who tells you otherwise is stupid or poor. Or both.

So, yeah, he's going to give them what Ashwell Heights never did. A huge shopping centre full of what they want. He knows they don't want shops that sell real stuff. They want food where all you do is open a tin or add water. They want bright, flashy video shops selling Arnie, Sly and Jean-Claude blowing baddies away and Sharon, Demi and Winona getting their kit off. They want burger bars with orange plastic tables and Kiddies' Korners and chirpy Muzak. They want newsagents stacked high with life's priorities – cigs, sweets, the tabloids. And in the corner – brand new, gleaming, sparkling with the hope of the damned – the lottery machine. It's the only explanation for why there is so much of this shit. It's what people like. Think about that for a moment. Not just 'prefer', or 'put up with'. It's what they *like*. Jesus fucking Mary on a bike. This country.

Ashwell Heights is like a ghost town, fading from this world. The jewellers, flower shops and delis are popping out of existence one by one. Pop. Pop. Pop. Like bubbles on the wind. All that's left functioning are the shops like giant arenas. There's the huge, white aisles of the freezer centre, a remote space-station of a shop. The gigantic supermarket, with ghost bleeps from tills echoing up into the metal gantries night after night. The arcades, full of robotic terminals and pink space-age cars. The audio-video shops with their racks and racks of dummy boxes.

There used to be security teams out there at night, but I know from my dad that it just isn't viable any more. No one cares enough to spend the money now that it's condemned. So the half-human creatures gather there like rats after the nightly lock-up, clustering round fires and bags of glue.

'Yeah,' I say to Damien. 'We'll need to get a car.'

'We'll sort it.'

'But it's got to be disposable,' I point out. Thinking ahead, before JJ can get in. Besides, he's sitting there, arms folded, looking at us with slight contempt.

'No problem.' Damien's smile doesn't waver. 'We get it from one end of town, trash it at the other. Trash it properly, I mean.'

My heart's thudding hard as if with a rush of drugs, and I can feel my eyes beginning to tingle and moisten. My hands are clammy around my coffee-cup. This is going to be the best kick we've had in ages.

The point isn't to steal anything or trash anything, the point is just to go there and do whatever feels good. You don't know where the edge is until you ride out to it. This is where I find the problem with Damien – he thinks in mercenary terms. He'll be wanting to grab CDs and stuff. Still, I can cope with that.

JJ's got his detached face on again. So, what is it this time, I wonder?

Damien leans forward so that his nose is just a few centimetres from mine. 'I've got a condition,' he says quietly.

'Don't think I want to know. Does it involve lice?'

'A prerequisite, all right?' He leans back, drawing breath in from between his teeth. 'Marcie comes.'

'Oh, for-fucking-get it.' The adrenalin rush turns to cramp inside me. I turn away from him in disgust, shifting position in my chair. I reach for my coffee, but there's just a congealed brown sludge in the bottom of the cup by now.

JJ is chuckling quietly to himself.

'And you can shut up as well!' I snap at him. 'Look,' I say to

Damien, leaning forward and jabbing my finger in his direction. 'She fucked up last time. Marcie's all wrong, she's in the wrong time, wrong place. Wrong life. She thinks she's something she's not.'

Damien, arms folded, raises his eyebrows. 'For someone who professes not to like her very much, you seem to know her quite well.'

'Well enough.' I feel a sudden coldness and tightness, because neither of them knows about my little visit to Marcie and my arrangement with her. JJ's still chuckling. I dart a vicious look at him, but he just pretends not to notice.

'Marcie comes,' says Damien. 'And that's final.'

'Why?' I'm aware that my fists are clenched, resting on the table on either side of my coffee-cup.

Damien sighs. He shakes his head as if he is fed up with me and the rest of the world around me. Well, I'm not being put off by that. 'Because I promised her she could. She's feeling low. Needs to get out.'

Oh, brilliant. So now Damien, too, has taken on the role of decorator in Marcie's life, painting over the cracks in her existence. Matt or gloss, my love? Roller or brush?

JJ leans forward. 'I'm still going out with Imelda, by the way,' he says mischievously. 'Sorry. She's promised the girls they're going to meet me.'

I'm feeling let down, so I glare at him. 'Isn't that a bit like promising to take a vegan to a kebab bar?'

He grins. 'Maybe some of them are part-timers.'

'Don't forget your mirror,' I snap at him.

'Oh, I won't.' He doesn't look at all perturbed that I might be about to reveal his little secret in front of Damien.

'You still want to come?' Damien inquires, smiling.

'I'm coming all right. You can't stop me.' I lean forward again. 'But you keep your dog under control, or I might just be forced to shoot it.'

There is a long, cold silence, in which even I realize that I may have gone too far. Damien opens his mouth for a sharp riposte, then closes it again and hardens his jaw. My bowels go watery, pumped into action by the realization that he's definitely not happy now. He's not going to give me a verbal parry, with which I'd have been safe. He's really going to give me an answer, one based on the real world and not on our little construct.

Damien flares his nostrils.

Go on, then. Hit me. Hit a woman. I'm sure it's not the first time. I wonder if JJ will leap to my rescue?

He slaps his fist into his palm.

'Right, then,' he says. 'I'll see you Saturday. Down at the Star?'

'Yeah. Right.' I'm not shaken. No way. Not going to show it, anyhow. I'm going to save up my adrenalin for a good occasion.

'I knew you'd come,' says Marcie, her eyes like little oysters in their midnight-blue shells. She shifts position in her dress of mermaid green, extends a hand to me to sit down.

Let's go back a bit.

'*That you, Bel?*'

'Yeah, what? Who's this?'

Whoever it is has called me at 9.30 in the morning. Dad's left, Kate's out at a church bazaar or something, and, as is normal on a weekday, I'm under the duvet in the middle of listening to *Hits Hour*. I've just missed out on three points for not remembering 'Miss America' by the Big Dish, and now someone has to go and phone me, for Christ's sake.

'*It's Marcie. I just wanted to say thanks for the money.*'

'Uuuh. Yeah, all right.' My eyes feel stuck together. I poke around the edges and come out with some little granules of greenish-yellow stuff. It's interesting, actually. I sometimes wish I could collect it in a little pot and use it for seasoning. I pop it in my mouth and chew on it, enjoying the salty crunchiness.

Marcie is wittering. '*It's just that, well, maybe you didn't get me.*'

'What?' It's too early for this.

'*We said a hundred, Bel. Just so I can cover any potential costs. A hundred.*'

This doesn't sound like Marcie. It sounds like someone talking through Marcie's voice, using it for their own ends. I'm jolted awake, now, sitting up with the duvet round my sweaty body. Alert, like after the morning caffeine hit, and suddenly the radio doesn't seem so important any more.

'You said fifty. You said you'd take the blame for fifty!' I'm aware that I've raised my voice rather more than I'd like. Get a grip, Bel. You don't do this. You don't go over the top and let yourself get worked up on account of some stupid little bitch who doesn't know what a credit card is.

'*Fifty first of all, that's what I said. Just for the blame, like. I wanted somethin' to keep by in case of costs. Like I said.*'

'Has anyone been asking anything?'

'*No. Course not.*'

'Then what's your bloody problem, Marcie?' I hiss at her.

'*Money, right? Things you don't have to worry about, like council tax and the rent going up.*'

She sounds quite desperate. I'm hoping I've got her on the run. 'Look, Marcie, I don't have any money.'

'*Don't bullshit me. You're loaded, the fuckin' lot of yer. Comfy, anyway. Damien, JJ, you.*'

'That's the point.' I'm sounding agonized now. It's genuine, right? 'I don't have money of my own. I get an allowance in cash and I can't touch the rest till I'm twenty-one.'

There is a brief, disgusted silence.

'Yes, Marcie,' I tell her, answering the unasked question, 'I've got a trust fund. And if I want any cash up front, the bottom line is that I have to ask for it. Why can't you ask Damien?'

There is a strange, scrabbling noise at the other end of the line. For a moment I'm convinced that the connection has been lost.

'Hello? Marcie?'

'*Still here. Don't worry.*' She is breathing heavily. '*Damien won't lend me nothin'. I've got to have some more money, Bel. I've got to have it today. Please!*'

'Look – ' I'm floundering. It seems the truth wasn't enough to deflect her. Christ, how do I get her off my back? 'Look, Marcie, don't panic. I'll get it. I'll get you the money, all right?'

Why do I say that? Why the hell do I have to go and say that? Because it's the easiest thing, that's why.

There is some more breathing, and then, just for a second, I think I hear a man starting to say something. And then she hangs up.

I sit and hold the phone for half a minute, thinking, wondering.

I call her back, and get the engaged signal.

Fuckity fuckity fuck. Now what do I do?

Only thirty-six hours till our big night, and I've still got no more ideas. I'm just going to have to ask for some money, I suppose. I've done it often enough before.

With a little mental shrug, I stagger into the kitchen – the tiles are cold against my feet – and pour some cereal into one of Kate's ridiculous glass bowls. She has told me repeatedly that they're kept for special use, which is why I try and have my cereal out of them as much as possible. She's dead proud of her Le Creuset saucepans, too, so I try and scar them with ugly, black lumps of burnt porridge as much as I can. It's a futile exercise, because Kate never sullies her hands with soapy water – she snips a bit more of Jon's money to buy a Woman Who Does from the commune. She's called Liza Witherzedd (that's not her name, it's just how she always introduces herself). She has bangles all up her arm and the most amazing earrings. Apart from the fucking stupid New Age crap she believes, Liza's pretty much all right, so I feel a bit guilty about the porridge sometimes. I want to tell her not to bother with the saucepans, but she always does, without question.

I chew mechanically on my cereal.

I'm thinking.

Hi, I'm Bel.

I've got a knife in my pocket.

It's half-past ten on an autumn night, and I'm strolling down Canterbury High Street. Clothes, for the record – black wool jumper, leather biker's jacket, black jeans, black boots. Not kinky Honor

Blackman style – these are thick-soled boots, made for running. And to complete the ensemble, black shades.

No way was I going to try this where people knew me. I told JJ I was staying in, and I told my dad I was going out with JJ. I jogged to the main road and hitched. Looking like this, I knew it'd take me less than five minutes. It did. Three guys in a creaky Metro, on their way to a gig at the Penny Theatre, dropped me down by the Westgate. One of them pinched my arse as I slipped out of the car, so I screamed abuse at him and gave the door a hard kicking as they drove off. I was looking around for a brick, but they were halfway round the ring road already, and there were a few people around staring at me in disgust.

My foot still aches, but it was worth it.

So I'm strolling down the street. These shades look jet-black, but it's deceptive – you can see through them really well. They're designed to cut out the glare of the street lights but not their illumination.

I've just been sitting for two hours outside a pub called the Olive Branch, right by the cathedral gate. It's that time of year when they haven't quite dared take the tables and sunshades in yet because there's still the occasional warm night and it's good for custom. The cathedral, picked out in gold, glitters high above this small city, and the gate, in silver, stands in front of it like the entrance to an enchanted land.

Now, I'm strolling down the street. Groups of crusties are laughing and smoking in the square in front of Our Price. They turn and stare at me, so I stare back. I'm heading for the far end of the street, where it joins the ring road at the city wall. You can walk up on the wall, and there's an embankment that drops at quite an angle down to some gardens – I vaguely remember rolling down that when I was younger. This side, there's the bus station. I walk through the concourse – it's ghostly still, with just a couple of double-deckers chugging quietly to themselves. On the other side of the concourse, taxis are waiting, coffin-black and shroud-white.

The cashpoint is tucked round at the side entrance to one of the department stores, next to a bus shelter. I've picked my time right, so there's no one waiting yet. I sit on the wall, cross my legs and wait.

Before long, someone comes. It's two blonde girls, giggling and gossiping, their skimpy dresses stretched across lardy thighs. I wrinkle my nose in disgust. I watch them take out their money and stuff it into white-and-gold handbags, and head off in the direction of the taxis, cellulite in sharp relief under the street lights. Probably off to Luigi's in Herne Bay. A total dive, but it has a lot of attractions for the plebs – they let anyone in, stay open most of the night and serve cocktails at pub prices.

Now, here's a better candidate. Young, male, anaemic-looking. He's about eighteen, on his own and wearing a grubby denim jacket. He casts a few nervous looks from side to side – good, good, I like it – before getting his card out.

I wait until he's punched his number in before I slip from the shadows. My hand is tight against the handle of the knife. The night gathers around us. From somewhere deep in the old city, a siren sounds. Cheering echoes through the ancient streets.

I grin at him. 'Hello, my love.'

He smiles back, nervously. He's about to cup his hand over the keyboard. I like that. It's like the way a lot of men feel about their testicles.

'I wonder,' I ask him, leaning back without really looking at him, 'if you could do me a bit of a favour? It's just that I need fifty quid in a bit of a hurry.'

He's looking me up and down. I know what he's doing. He's looking at my designer shades and the smoothness of my jacket. I gesture with one hand, inviting him to look down.

My knife is resting gently on top of his belt.

'If you'd be so kind,' I add politely.

Now it's Saturday, at the Edge of the World. Eight-thirty. The houses and flats are vomiting their young, their disillusioned, their losers. Their faces are as white as Anthea Turner's grin. They will pour into the pubs and clubs, spend their easy-earned cash on sharp, fizzy lagers and complain that yet more of their precious lottery money – which, of course, they had to spend – is being put into a London opera house. I'm sure they'd all protest that they *ain't philistines, neither, went to see*

Pav in the park, but at the end of the day it's all sang in fuckin' foreign,
wop innit? or dago? no fuckin' difference, mate, but next week I'm gonna
winnit. Nuvver four pints over 'ere, darlin'.

I leave the house at quarter to ten. Marcie, her eyes black-rimmed
with five-hour nights, etched in midnight-blue mascara, is sipping a
gin and tonic at the window of the Bull. I have arranged to meet her
at ten, half an hour before the others arrive, and I told her explicitly
not to be late, so it looks as if she's listened, at least. She smiles when
she sees me, in a worryingly sophisticated way.

'I knew you'd come,' she says. 'Want a drink?'

I stand there with my hands on my hips, trying to muster as much
contempt as I can, thinking, I wouldn't piss on you if you were on fire,
and here I am doing your bidding. And she has stood up, would you
believe it? And smiled, and smoothed down the green silk dress she's
wearing. Normally, given something that colour, Marcie would have
gone all out for matching emerald lipstick and eye-shadow, with jade
earrings. But she's lightly, almost perfectly made-up in subtler, nutmeg
shades. I'm perturbed. I have to remind myself that this is the same
stupid little slut who, just last week, was curled up in a ball on the
beach, stinking of bile and lager, whimpering and fishy-pale.

So maybe she's not so green any more.

I sit down. 'I'm not staying.'

'I know. Meeting the others in the Arcade, aren't we?' She smiles.
She's confident and happy. Her voice is different, too, as if she's had
her peeling accent varnished.

Altogether, I feel quite at a disadvantage. I slam the envelope on
the table in front of her. 'Here. Take it.'

'Thanks,' says Marcie, quite unabashed. 'Mind if I count it?'

So how long does it take you to count ten five-pound notes? Let's
see if GCSE maths is up to it.

A glistening pint thumps down on the table between us, and Marcie
is quite adept in the way that she slips the money into her handbag.
My eyes follow up along a slim female hand, an arm in brown suede.
Earrings the size of table-mats glisten and spin in the dim pub light.
Above the stiff collar of a white dress-shirt, an ear-to-ear grin stretches

across a face which is smooth, Romany-brown. It's edged with crisp, black hair and floppy bangs which would have been in fashion in Manchester, circa 1990.

'Imelda,' I say languidly, trying not to show my surprise. 'Nice of you to join us.'

'I haven't, yet,' she points out, in a voice as spiky as her hair, and lights a long black cigarette as she sits down with us. She's wearing one of the supermarket aftershaves for men, and smells of musk.

'You . . . know Marcie, don't you?' Somehow I feel I have to say this, and I'm hoping desperately that she isn't going to make some predictable comment about biblical senses.

Luckily, she doesn't. 'By reputation,' she says, her big brown eyes flicking momentarily towards the girl. 'Imelda McCann,' she says, extending a hand. 'Pleased to meet you.'

'Yeah, right.' Marcie takes the hand awkwardly, and I'm pleased to see that she is unnerved by the firmness of Imelda's hand, by the way that her eyes try to grip like her handshake.

Their hands unstick with an audibly sweaty peeling sound. Marcie shifts uneasily in her seat and becomes preoccupied with smoothing down her dress again. I'm amused.

'So, what happened? I thought you were off out to Dykes-R-Us tonight.'

She chooses to ignore the put-down, and concentrates on waggling her cigarette up and down. It's got a strange aroma, like spices and ash. 'He persuaded me,' she says indistinctly, 'that a night out with you lot would be more of a fun option, darlings.'

'Hardly,' I mutter. 'We're all gender stereotypes here, you know.'

Imelda just flashes a mouthful of ivory. Maybe she's discovered that everlasting toothpaste that the market suppressed. She raises her eyebrows at us, and leans slightly forward so that her fringe blocks my view of Marcie. 'So, Marcia darling – '

'It's Marcie,' she retorts – rather sharply, with her arms folded into a barrier across her little bust. It almost makes me snigger out loud to see her looking so uncomfortable.

'Marcie. You're with dear Bel here, are you?'

I'm not quite sure what 'with' means. Luckily, neither is Marcie, and she just gives an indifferent grunt as an answer.

'I see,' Imelda says, her red lips closing softly over the black tube of her cigarette. She closes her eyes, so slowly that it's kind of mesmerizing, and then they snap open, big, wide, monochrome eyes out of a thirties film, and they're sparkling with life. 'You look very young, darling. Did you tell your mummy and daddy where you were going to be?'

Oh, dear. Not the right thing to say.

Marcie is cold, quite restrained in her answer. 'My mum went to live in Barnsley with a lorry driver. An' my dad's dead. He died a few years ago.'

'Aaah.' Imelda, not thrown at all, nods sagely, and shrugs. 'I'm really very sorry to hear that,' she offers.

'Yeah, well, so was I. I mean, fuckin' Barnsley. What a dump.'

Imelda smiles languidly and leans back in her seat, looking cool, poised, and of indeterminate age. I think she's thirty-two, but there's a five-year margin of error. JJ's granddad is dead now, but he was quite a randy old bugger, by all accounts – he sired Imelda quite some time after JJ's dad, so she can't be too old.

According to JJ, his aunt inherited quite a bit from her late father. She was the favoured one, and most of the fortune went to her, but she had no problem about sharing it with the rest of the family. These days, she lives largely off the interest – although she may have a job, too; I don't know.

Her father cut his losses just in time, and as a result of some shrewd selling, did very well for himself. What it came down to was that a rival effectively put him out of business. There's a rumour in their family, JJ tells me, that Imelda took revenge for this. With her financial security assured, she went to work for the rival firm about two years after. Over a period of months, she set about applying chaos theory to the company. A misplaced decimal point here and there. A couple of unfortunate computer viruses. Eventually, she did it once too often and was carpeted, then sacked. Imelda cleared her desk with a delighted laugh, and left behind her a company riddled with holes. She had to try not to break into giggles as she picked up her P45. All allegedly, of course.

'Where's the man himself?' I'm looking around the pub, but I can't see him.

'He's at the Arcade. He sent me out along the promenade to look for you.' Imelda, still cool and calm, raises her eyebrows and sips her pint.

So, JJ sent her to look for us. That means he's out earlier than planned, and he had some idea of where I was going to be.

That worries me.

It also makes me realize that we're going to be stuck with Imelda for the night if we don't watch out.

Trying to seem casual, I suck on an extra-strong peppermint as we head outside.

The wind screams across the sea, shaking and soaking the pier. Giant fountains of spray melt the sea wall as they have done for years. The old sea front quivers and groans, but stays up. Under shimmering orange light, couples scuttle through the spray. Groups of lads in leather jackets patrol the pavements, calling out to groups of girls shivering in skirts as they sail past, looking for somewhere to hang out. Fish-and-chip shops glow like beacons to summon ghost ships from the night mist.

In the long strand of pubs and arcades, a kind of skeletal life persists. It still has a throbbing heart. The Arcade.

Ten-thirty. Words can't quite describe the Arcade on a Saturday night. For one thing, it's not just a games arcade. It's warehouse-sized, has offshoots of dance floors and cocktail bars and shadowy corners where the dealers hover in their dreads and purple shell suits. Another strange success story in this failed place.

It's the only lively part of town. In fact, I often think that its cartoon-bright screens and its multi-dimensional worlds are reality, encased in a bubble around which there's a huge, fantastic simulation of a rotting seaside town where even the fish come to die.

Marcie has attached herself to some people at the bar. I find myself bobbed and butted through the seven circles of hell, looking for JJ.

The first thing to hit you is the wall of heat, and then it's the smell – beer, body odour, a hint of piss and sex. I grip the peppermint between my teeth and try to concentrate on the taste of that instead.

This primal scent, territorial pissing with sweat and lager, is today's equivalent of *lasciate ogni speranza voi ch'entrate* – I can imagine the slack-jawed looks I'd get if I said that here.

Grey smoke and dancing stubs of ash, like enraged fireflies, bombard me on all sides. Every one of the hot machines is surrounded by the eyes of young, male predators. They're all earringed, with hair either tucked behind their ears or short enough to reveal their shrivelled, rodenty heads. They leave slimy prints on warm beer glasses as they watch the world reflected in the screens.

This is a nightmare world of artificial noises, spewed from sound-houses all over the world, each trying to sound different and special, and each being just a variation on the clunks, bleeps and clatters of the rest. Dancing sprites on the screen pirouette with sharp-pixelled grace, dodge through mazes, hop the vast silence between asteroids as if they were stepping-stones, whirl themselves off branches on to bouncing platforms, crunch and grunt in brief bursts of white noise as they kick the living shit out of each other under desert sun. Worlds, worlds whizz past me as I'm carried deeper into the caverns of this place.

Wetness slops at my feet as two laughing boys push a friend over, with his beer in his hand. I shove him out of the way and barge on, angrily, my hair sticky with sweat against my forehead.

Girls, staggering in every respect (a point to share with Imelda), block my path. Lustrous blonde hair, silver mini-dresses. Bright, creamy cocktails. Tableau after tableau of tacky, garish life.

An arm grabs me, and I lash out. 'Fuck off! Get the fuck *off*!'

'It's me! For Christ's sake, Bel, it's me!'

Look at his big, grinning face, floating there in the blue-flickered darkness as if nothing mattered. I don't know whether to hit him or kiss him, so I do both. He tastes of apple and cinnamon. I feel him straining to pull away from me as I force him up against the nearest machine.

He pulls away from me, looking exhilarated but puzzled. 'Bel, are you all right?'

'Never better. I take it you're having fun in this hole?'

'Well, yeah.' He looks a bit shamefaced. 'Damien and I have discovered this new game.'

Beyond him, in the purple shadows of the alcove, Damien is hunched over the console, hypnotized.

'Anything I'd like?' I ask him wearily. Somehow, I know what kind of thing to expect.

JJ's face is bright with pseudo-teenage enthusiasm. 'It's called Repulse. You have to get this girl to undress, while picking off your rival voyeurs in the building opposite – '

'I get the idea.' I forestall him with an upheld palm. 'I'm out of this place. I'll see you outside.'

I turn and storm off, shoving two of the foil-wrapped girls out of the way as I go. They scream obscenities at me, so I gather a big, sugar-swollen gobbet of phlegm and shoot it in their direction. It hits like an exploding fruit.

Before I reach the bar, something heavy lands, hard and painful, on my right breast. The pain's indescribable, shooting up, down and across. Through a blur of salt water I see the floppy-haired boy I kicked out of the way before.

'You got in my fuckin' way,' he snarls, and I'm aware that there's his harsh, twisted mouth with its sickly-sweet beer smell on one side, and the metal wall on the other.

No – it gives way beneath my back.

It's not a wall, it's a door. I only realize which door as I stagger back against gloss-painted walls, realizing it smells stronger than ever of barely disinfected piss. The world wobbles and turns as I crash to the tiles, but standing above the door, legs apart, is that crow-black figure of a matchstick man, the universal gender sign obeyed by all. My peppermint's flown from my mouth and sits fizzing on the tiles.

I've never actually found myself in one of these before. The squat, teardrop-shaped urinals look far too high up the wall – Christ, what do they do, have competitions to lob it in from five metres? – but now is not the time to admire the scenery.

I try to get up – too suddenly. My shoulder burns in pain as something cracks against it. The washbasin. I can hear my own breath echoing in my ears.

Fuck shit fuck shit fuck. Get out of this one, Bel.

He's pushing me. Pushing and prodding my tits. The pretty-boy hair and suntan are misleading. He's got a really ugly face, close up, pocked like old stone under the tan; his eyes are dark slits and his nose a great hook. And the hair's pretty nasty, too. Blond strips hanging down. Yellowing lard. Like the Pardoner in the *Canterbury Tales*. Bizarre thought. He smells of recent lager and hours-old aftershave, a layer of sickly-sweet perfume which the sweat's already eating into.

'Bitch thinks she can push me around,' Pardoner says quietly, and I realize there's another boy in here, lounging against the wall of one of the cubicles. He looks a mean bastard too. Slicked-back hair, black, in a pony-tail. A squashed boxer's nose and two dragons tattooed on his arms.

Neither of them is particularly well-muscled, but they look full of hyper-energy, fizzing with edginess, ready to explode.

'Prick-tease, if you ask me,' says Pony-tail. He's got a voice from deep in his throat, a tar-clogged, phlegmy, smoker's voice. His little eyes narrow as his tattooed arms unfurl and he swaggers towards me, trousers bulging. 'All prick-teases, little girls like her. Only have to look at what she's wearing to see that.'

I fold my arms, put my head on one side and glare at him in contempt. But inside, I'm shaking.

Christ, what a stupid *stupid* situation to get into. My mind's going crazy trying to think of ways out. Collision, that's what it is. Car accident. If the cars hadn't been together in that place at that time, then no boom. I shouldn't have been here at ten-forty in this place. It's all a mistake.

Bravado isn't going to work. I smile, spread my hands. I open my mouth to explain.

Pardoner's right behind me, with his hand on my bare back. I whirl round, but he's grabbed my belt, pulling me back. It cuts into my waist, burning, and I scream. I can feel myself losing my balance.

'Get her in here,' says Pony-tail, jerking a thumb into the cubicle.

Reality smashes my mind. I look around wildly. My mouth's dry. I can smell and taste a nauseating mixture of piss and pepper-mint.

Pardoner grabs my hair with his other hand. He's got a grip on me as if I'm some tailor's dummy that he's hefting. My scalp burns with pain.

I hear my own screams echoing off the tiles. I'm pulling against him, now, slipping to the pungent floor, and I hear my stockings rip. There's nothing to dig my heels into. Pardoner shouts something decisive and throws me at Pony-tail. He's hard. I bounce off.

And something ram-raids my mind and kicks adrenalin into the synapses and screams at me to do something.

The cut the cut the *Cut* –

The knife is there, in my pocket –

I slip.

The toilet bowl smashes my skull. I feel my body weakening. Arms grab my wrists and bend them back. The arms are frizzed with disgusting hair – Pony-tail's. I scream. My mouth is smashed against the porcelain – *pain* – and I feel something smash in my mouth, chips of enamel splintering, and there's the warm gush of blood. My skirt is ripped down. I feel my flesh chilling. Right behind me, there's gasping, beery breath, the undoing of a zip.

Then I hear a crash, a thump and a squeal. My mouth spatters gore on the white lid, as I try to lift myself up and see what the hell is going on there behind me.

Through a haze, I see Pardoner go flying. He hits the tiles and a boot stamps on his head. The scream he lets out is animal, primal, a hideousness unheard before in this life.

Damien's on top of Pardoner, pinning his arms behind him, locking his head to the tiles.

JJ's there too. He's hit Pony-tail, whose greasy bulk smashes the mirror and the condom machine. JJ smacks him again, sending him crawling under the washbasins. Pony-tail's flies are undone, and his hands are clasped protectively over a wilting erection.

Shit, I'm gushing blood. It's wet and warm on my face. I can't move,

I can't stop it, salty tides across my face as if I'm crying the stuff. Like one of my Christ-shagging dreams when the nails go in.

JJ is there, pulling me to him. I'm dimly aware that I lose my skirt, and it lies in a wet pool in the cubicle.

There's no way I'm going to sob or scream. I wipe the blood away. Again. Again. Again. It streaks my shirt with huge, schlock-fest stripes. I'm coughing as it fills my mouth, warm and rusty. Jesus, this is happening and I have to deal with it.

Damien does something to his prisoner that makes him cry out with a deep, phlegmy rattle. Pardoner's suntanned face is contorted with pain, like a medieval woodcut of Agony.

Right, come on, I've got to take control. It's good. Now that the thumping in my bruised breasts is abating and I'm back on my feet, hands on my hips and taking stock of the situation, I think there's the distinct potential for some fun here.

I'm breathing heavily, sweating buckets. I wipe blood from my nose again.

'Who's outside?' I gasp to JJ.

He grins, keeping an eye on Pony-tail, who's on all fours with his tail between his legs, trying to shake his head clear. 'Aunt Imelda,' JJ says. 'If she can't hold them off, no-one can.'

An unbreachable dyke. Well, we might need her.

'Right.' I'm aware of my naked legs, my best and freshest cream knickers suddenly on display. Damien's trying to avert his eyes. 'Keep this place isolated.'

'Bel.' JJ's hand is on my arm. 'We came to make sure you were OK. Let's get out, leave these tossers.' He gives me his handkerchief, sloppy with water, and I press it gratefully against my gushing nose.

'When I'm ready,' I tell him indistinctly.

You must see this, JJ.

'Hold his face,' I instruct Damien. It's hard to sound assertive with a bloodstained handkerchief halfway up your nose, but I do my best.

Damien grins, and does as he is told.

I take a cautious look at the handkerchief. The blood seems to have stopped for the moment. I stalk over to the fallen condom machine, hefting it in my hands. It's a pretty heavy chunk of metal.

'Bel,' JJ says, again, holding out a hand. 'Let's go. Come on. Let's get out of here.' His little-boy eyes are bright with panic.

Luckily, Damien seems happy to hold his prisoner down for whatever punishment I want to administer. His face is red with exertion, and he gives me a crooked grin, his lips drawn back in a leer of pleasure.

I've stopped breathing hard and I'm not quaking with anger the way I was two minutes ago. My name is Belinda Archard and I'm perfectly calm, standing half naked in a Gents in the Arcade, my mouth salty with blood, hefting a cool, hard condom machine in my hands.

And bringing it down, hard, on Pardoner's knee. His scream's gratifying and the impact zings right up my arms, almost numbs my hands.

'Bel.' JJ's hand is on my arm.

'No.' I push him away. 'Hold him still,' I order Damien. I hurl the condom machine into the open cubicle. It lands in the toilet with a crash and a splash. There is a loud cracking noise, followed by a gurgle of water as the bowl starts to leak across the floor.

Ignoring it, I swing back my leg and smack my booted foot right into Pardoner's groin. It gives like a soft cushion. The noise he makes this time is rather less gratifying, more of a whimper than a scream. Damien laughs and slaps Pardoner about the face a couple of times.

JJ is going crazy, pushing his hands through his hair. 'Bel – we wanted – we had to come and help. This is mad – too mad, come on.'

I place my hands on his face, open my eyes wide and smile at him. I lean forward and gently kiss him. His mouth is warm and wet, but unresponsive. I've smeared blood on his lips.

'Shut up, JJ,' I tell him. I jerk my head towards Pony-tail, who's trying to lever himself up with the aid of the washbasin. 'That was quite a whack you gave him,' I say admiringly. 'Well done. Get him up.'

'You get him up!' JJ exclaims.

'All right.' I grab Pony-tail by his collar and slam him against the mirrors, facing me. His face twists in anger, but before he has a chance to lunge, my knee's in his groin and he's doubled up. I smash my fist into his forehead and he slumps.

Christ, it hurts. I'm wincing, sucking my knuckles. I never realized it hurt the punisher as much as the punished.

I can feel the urge for the Cut bubbling in my mind, trying to haze everything green and make me. It's hard and sharp, almost glowing in my pocket.

Pardoner tries to lift his head to see what's going on, but Damien bellows in anger and smashes him back down on to the wet floor.

Pony-tail's in front of me, still nursing his crotch. His forehead's bleeding. I grin at him.

'You wanted your oats tonight, didn't you, Pony-tail?' I say to him, prodding him with my shoe so that he knows who's being addressed. 'Well, we can't waste any of it. Don't want you to get prostate cancer.' I nudge JJ in the ribs. 'Watch this, my love. You could learn something.' I kick Pony-tail. 'Kneel up and face me.'

Incredibly, he obeys me. He seems to have become automated, or he would have if it weren't for the way he's shaking and sweating. He looks horrifically embarrassed, not daring to meet my eye. Blood trickles down his face and towards his mouth. He reaches up to wipe it away.

'No.' My voice is soft but commanding, and I slap his hand down. 'Leave it.' I put my hands on my hips. Despite the dried blood on my mouth, I allow myself a little smile. 'I thought you had a big stiffy just now, Pony-tail? What happened to it, hmm?' I raise my eyebrows.

'Bel, what are you doing?' JJ hisses.

'Humiliating him. Come on, Pony-tail, get some life into the old todger. You've got a job to do.'

Pony-tail, glowing with embarrassment, pulls his member out. Incredibly, it's still half engorged. The skin stretches as we watch, ironing out the wrinkles.

'Come on, pull it. Finish yourself off.'

'I ain't – ' He looks up at me, blood dripping into his eyes, blinks. He tries to protest.

I've moved like a huntress. I feel JJ tense behind me. For a moment, Damien looks as if he's about to release his hold on Pardoner out of sheer shock, but he soon recovers himself.

My knife snicks open, two centimetres from Pony-tail's sweaty cock.

'Come on,' I whisper to him. My voice mingles with the trickling water, like an enticing spirit from the underworld. 'You were all up for it before. Full of it, weren't you? Full of spunk. Where's it all gone?'

I nudge the edge of the blade against his foreskin. He's cowering, now, a great, humiliated lump.

Time seems to stand still in the Gents, and all I can hear is the heavy, anticipatory breathing of Damien and JJ, the gurgling of the water, and the occasional groan from Pardoner.

Pony-tail seems to have realized what he has to do. He takes his cock in his hand, squeezing the shaft with his four fingers and stroking his thumb along the head, as if he's working a computer joystick with a fire-button on the end. I start cackling with laughter. I didn't realize they did that.

He doesn't look at me. The knife gleams, still just a few centimetres from the organ, like a pure sliver of white light. My mouth is dry with anticipation, my eyes hurt because I don't dare blink.

'Keep going,' I tell Pony-tail. 'If you don't finish, I bobbit you.'

I remember hearing from Damien that the more you think about how difficult it is, the trickier it becomes.

Pony-tail is tugging hard, his hand a blur. I'd never realized quite how fast men could go on their own. I'm holding my breath, my hand tight and sweaty on the handle of my knife.

I can almost feel JJ's bright, wide eyes drilling into me, horrified with me. Damien, though, seems to be enjoying the spectacle, chuckling away to himself and occasionally twisting Pardoner's fingers back, just for the hell of it. Yeah, good stuff. I'm glad I left Damien in charge of Pardoner, because JJ wouldn't keep the prisoner in check. I can rely on JJ for swift, righteous anger like the kind that felled

Pony-tail, but he'd never stoop to gratuitous violence, and it's what's needed at the moment. A bit of stooping. A bit of careful, applied sadism, which Damien can do quite cheerfully.

Pony-tail gasps. He arches his back, slips, falls on to one hand as his cock erupts. *One! Two! Three!* The spurts of semen spatter his hand and wrist and dribble down to his trousers. He curls up, not daring to look at me, clutching his groin with one hand and his face with the other.

'There,' I say softly. 'Let that be a lesson to you.' The feeling of power is absolutely magical, coursing through me like sex. Like I've just turned the tables and raped him.

I stand up, snick the knife shut again and shove it back into the pocket of my blouse.

I push my hair back, wink at JJ, and signal to Damien to let Pardoner go.

'All right, leave them now. They're not worth shit.'

Behind me, Pardoner coughs and splutters as Damien releases him, and starts to crawl through the piss, looking for something to lever himself up. Pony-tail is breathing heavily, clutching with a sticky hand at the gash my ring's made on his forehead.

I suddenly realize I am desperate to go to the loo.

'Can you get them out?' I ask JJ.

As I emerge, drained, from the cubicle, a man staggers in, unzips and aims at the urinal just in time. He throws back his head, his eyes closed in ecstasy. He realizes that he's not alone, but he's too drunk to realize I don't share the same kind of genitals as him.

'My God, 's bedder. Farkin' bedder, innit mate?'

He emits a seemingly unending stream of dark golden piss, his back arching in pleasure, and for some reason he feels the need to share the joy of the micturition with me.

'Jeee-sus H. Like a farkin' tap.'

I frown, wrinkle my nose, and slip towards the door, trying not to look in his direction at all. But some fascination makes me linger at the door.

He finishes his piss with an orgasmic burst that sends the floating fag-ends spinning. He cheers with delight and staggers back out, seemingly blind to me, his cock still hanging limply from his unzipped fly.

I imagine he'll stick a beer-bottle on the end of the flapping organ as he and his comrades roll home along the shingle, calling out impossibilities to the girls. He might have some fish and chips, which to me smell uncomfortably like the dripping Gents.

Then, I suppose, he will vomit an acid, lumpy soup on to his doorstep, or another's, before passing into a fitful sleep on the sofa, and at noon he'll emerge from sleep with the sunlight spearing his eyes and his mouth ashy and reeking.

In the Ladies, I fill the basin again and again with red, then pink, then pinkish water. It stings my face with a snowy chill. The sharp pain in my mouth dulls and fades.

Girls come and go, laughing and gossiping, pissing and flushing, ignoring me. Maybe this is an everyday occurrence.

I peer into the mirror, having a close look at my chipped front tooth. It could be a lot worse. But I look like a street orphan with my bloodstained top and skimpy knickers. Time to do something about my clothes.

Imelda strolls in, dragging hard on her black roll-up. She collapses into laughter, while I stand there and coolly try to quell her with my gaze.

'I'm sorry,' she says eventually, her grin bright white in her brown face. 'It's just, well, terribly funny in a way.'

'So I'm the cabaret now, am I?'

Imelda pulls her jacket off and throws it at me. 'Haven't seen a fight that good in years. Jolly good stuff, girl. You gave it to them straight.'

'Yeah, well.' I shrug. 'They deserved it.' I rip off the bloody remains of my blouse and pull on her heavy suede jacket over my bra. It's going to be hot, but I'm grateful for it. I look up at her, see her pivoting on one heel and grinning like a schoolgirl. Yeah, right, enjoy it, 'cos it's all you're going to get. Somehow, I manage to mumble, 'Thanks,' to her.

'No problem.' She smiles, leans back against the washbasins. She's wearing a black cotton top, sleeveless. It shows that she's got very little up top, but smooth, brown arms, muscular but still feminine. 'So, can I always expect this level of entertainment when I come out with you and my darling nephew?'

'Only on days with a *y* in.'

Imelda grins, nods at me. 'Nice legs. Shall we go?'

I feel my face suddenly reddening, aware of my huge expanse of leg beneath the suede coat.

'Right, then.' I stalk over to the door, without looking at Imelda, but I can hear her chuckling behind me.

I'm glad JJ chose to be with us tonight. I couldn't really fathom why he would want to go to a gay club with Imelda, until he told me and Damien the other night, in our dining-room, about his interesting little fantasy.

He has a far-away look in his eyes as he contemplates the world in Kate's smoked-glass fruit bowl, running his finger round the edge.

'I've always wanted,' he says, 'to be able to borrow a woman's body for a few days. Just to know what it's like.'

'Yeah? What would you do? Apart from making sure it wasn't a period week. That goes without saying.'

JJ does that endearing little frown again, the one that's halfway between disapproval and incomprehension.

Damien sniggers. 'Know my mate Tom? He was in Russia for a year. They use slices of bread for sanitary towels there.' Damien never misses an opportunity to bring up bodily secretions as a topic of conversation. I think he feels that it's going to shock me or something, and he is always rather taken aback to find that I can talk about snot, earwax and thrush as happily as he can. 'I wondered what they did with the bread afterwards. Fry it up for breakfast, that's what I'd do. Nice with a bit of bacon and kidney. Like black pudding.'

'Only crunchier,' I agree.

I have a mental picture of this catching on as a delicacy, dark red slices of toast being consumed all round the world. I wonder if I should tell Damien that it's actually a thick soup of blood, mucus, uterus lining . . . But that's by the way.

JJ is studiously ignoring us. 'I'd wear the body round the house for a bit,' he says. 'Try on various clothes and things.'

'TV JJ. Always fucking suspected it!' Damien is crowing, leaning back in his chair and flicking a limp wrist at JJ in ignorant delight.

'What would you do, then, darling? And ignore him.' I lean forward, smiling expectantly, resting my chin in my hands.

'I'd wear something really tarty, you know, just to see what it was like. Tight skirt, fishnet stockings.'

'Tawdry!' I'm delighted. 'I love it. You're a cheap little whore at heart. Tell me what you'd do.'

'I'd go out to all sort of clubs. I wouldn't care what I did with the body 'cos it wouldn't be mine.' He smiles, shyly, but looks uncomfortably at the sniggering Damien. 'Does he have to be here?'

'Nature said the same thing, my love, but she let him live. Go on.'

'I'd . . . drink. Loads. Try new drugs. Get used to what the body could and couldn't take.' He leans forward, his face flushed now, his eyes bright. He's gazing into his own mind and seems to be forgetting the dining-room. That's good. 'I'd flirt. Lead men on for fun, see what happened.'

Damien whistles softly, shaking his head.

'Well?' I snarl, feeling supportive. 'He wants to know how we think. He wants to know how we operate!'

'And I'd go for girls. For variety. Get a reputation, maybe. When the owner got her body back she wouldn't have any idea . . .' He's grinning broadly.

'You'd have to clean it up,' Damien says with a smirk, lighting a cigarette.

'What?' JJ breaks out of his rapture, jerks his head towards Damien as if noticing him for the first time.

'Y'know, like giving a house back to a landlord. Hoover all the carpets, clean the bog out.' He does a big, deep laugh, which turns into a phlegm-sodden cough.

'Scrub behind the fridge,' I agree, leaning back. 'Hate to admit it, my love, but New Neanderthal here has a point. You don't give a rented car back with mud on the fenders and crumbs on the seat.'

I wonder if it was my body he was thinking of.

There is something in the air tonight, it shines so bright.

It feels good, having smashed those fuckers in their home ground. So I've got a broken lip and a chipped tooth, so what? I'm having fun.

Something in the air.

I need more.

I think –

– and, as the last-orders bell chimes in the caverns of my brain, the thought surfaces, frantically kicking and spluttering –

I think I need to kill.

12 *Definitely Possibly*

Eleven-twenty.

'Yes! Yes! Come on, one more!'

Claps and cheers resound along the sea front. Damien and Imelda are applauding JJ as he trots along the car roofs in Southgate Street, parallel to the beach. It's where all the pubbers and clubbers park, and it's lined with cars from one end to the other. All the cars look purple or white under the street lamps.

The game is simple. Damien's collected a bag of empty bottles and cans, and he runs on ahead and sets up the roofs – on each car roof an empty beer bottle with a can perched on it. (The cans are meant to be empty, but some of them aren't.) The player can't touch the ground, and he has to jump from one car to the next, kicking the can off and leaving the bottle. JJ's managed about one in six, so Marcie and I are following behind at a stagger, kicking our way through shards of brown glass.

He kicks with power. A can whizzes across the street in an arc of beer. It hits the window of an insurance company and kicks a wild alarm into action. JJ thumps the air, Damien claps and cheers, and now Imelda, her face showing concern for the first time, looks over her shoulder at me and Marcie.

'Look,' she says. 'I've got to go. Really. I'll get a taxi.'

'Are you sure?' I don't know if I want her to, any more.

'Yes, just–' She shudders slightly. 'Look after him. Get him home.'

'Do you want –?' I tug at the suede coat.

'Keep it, Bel. I've got dozens.' She backs down the street, heading for the sea front and the taxis, waving until she's out of sight.

'Yes! And – he – *scores*!' JJ kicks another can, and leaps on to the bonnet of a Vauxhall Astra. I can see him judging the gap between it and the boot of the car in front. It's a Rover coupé, one of the few cars I know straight away, because my dad used to have one. JJ's on the spoiler, wobbling. Somehow, he makes it, but he's not very graceful, and, forgetting that he's not on the roof yet, his foot goes right through the Rover's back window. The glass erupts into small squares, tinkling, hitting the ground like a frozen waterfall.

I'm gratified that Damien chokes back his cheer and gives a sort of stifled giggle. I always enjoy seeing Damien taken aback.

So I'm showing him, running forward to catch JJ by the shoulders as he tumbles and falls among the cubes of glass. I give a great whoop of delight. There's something I really like about breaking a window; it's like trampling fresh snow. 'Yeah! Way to go, my love.'

JJ's looking up and down the street, wild-eyed, as I help him up. Marcie, not quite sure what's going on, swigs from her can and slumps into Damien.

'Let's take this one,' I hear myself saying, suddenly.

They're all silent, looking at each other. The alarm is still whooping in the insurance office down the road.

'Well, come on! No one's going to want it now. Are we going up to Ashwell or what?'

'We were,' JJ says uncertainly, with a hand on my shoulder. 'It seemed like a good idea after . . . two drinks.' He giggles nervously, and I hear it frothing up his nose.

'Jesus. You're all so fucking boring. Come on.' With one swift move, and not caring much for injury any more, I'm in the back window and flopping on to the warm leather seat. I swivel my legs, keeping my dignity, and unlock the doors for them.

Midnight – not at the oasis, but on the road. We've got the best ever car ventilation system on this warm night, otherwise known as a missing back window.

I'm taking it really slow for the moment, and I've driven us on the back route up to Ashwell Heights, avoiding the main road. There's no point getting pulled over now, ending our fun. And I don't especially want to smash into pedestrians – it would cause a hell of a lot of hassle.

There it is, up ahead, the pyramid-shaped roofs silhouetted against the night sky.

Damien's in the front with me, smoking constantly, a broad, stupid grin fixed on his face. JJ's behind me, biting his nails, tousling his hair. I wish he'd stop doing that. He looks rodentish.

Marcie lolls from side to side, her mouth and eyes propped open by invisible beams. That grown-up woman's dress and superficial demeanour didn't really count for much in the end, because she always reverts to type after three Martinis and whatever she had in the Ladies. Imelda, I know, was coked up to the eyeballs – not unusual, according to JJ – but in her case it seemed to have brought on a crashing reality-attack, also known as sudden departure of bottle. Good, in a way.

A couple of fires are flickering in the scrubland beyond the car park. Otherwise, it's all dark. I've taken the car down to a crawl, just twenty miles an hour. I feel bright, alert, in control, adrenalin coursing through me. The night helps – it's as if the landscape has been sectioned off so that there are only primal elements. Darkness. Fire. Earth.

I bring the car into the deserted car park. We drive right up to the doors, passing the shuttered kiosks, the neon-lit petrol station. My heart thumps for a moment, but the shop and counter are dark and uninhabited. I grin across my face, so hard that it aches.

'Hold on, children,' I tell them.

I slam the car into reverse and take us back – five, ten, fifteen metres across the car park.

'Take it steady, Bel,' JJ says. I think he's just realized what I'm about to do, and I'm galvanized into action by the terrified thought that he might be about to get out of the car.

I can feel the power building up under the pedals. I'm torturing this Rover, making it do what I want. You always forget how much power there is in a car. You always forget the way it takes over and sends throb throb throb through your body and sends your feet quiver-shivering on the pedals. I can feel it straining at the leash. Up ahead, the lights glow bright in the glass surface of the precinct wall.

Marcie lifts her head, whimpers.

JJ has his hand on my shoulder. I'm angry. He's trying to stop me. Trying to make me do it his way.

'Bel,' JJ ventures. 'I think you should let someone else drive.'

Well, he seems to have sobered up quickly.

I give him a grin in the rear-view mirror, then I release the clutch. 'No way, darling.'

We hurtle across the car park. The orbs of my own lights zoom towards me. I grit my teeth and take the car right through.

The crash, the fragmentation of the boundary, lasts a mere millisecond – and then it's a gateway. Smooth.

Almost like passing through water. You'd think the glass would be strengthened, but it billows around the car as if it was intended to let us through. I feel the impact, and it slews the car off track, but I rectify that.

We're turning, fast, on a slippery surface now, fake marble. Purple night-lights bathe us – I glimpse Marcie's face, hollow-eyed with terror, in the rear-view mirror – as we scrape up against a giant bowl brimming with foliage. I slam into reverse and pull the car clear with a grind and a choking burst of fumes.

Glass walls and balconies rise on either side of us, like the tombs of consumerism. There is a chilly silence.

'Good car,' says Damien.

He's right, of course, and I know what he's thinking of. His mind's on looting, and he means it's got a good solid bumper and some power behind it.

'It's just for getting around.' I turn to him, keeping my face hard and expressionless.

Damien just snorts with laughter and lights a new cigarette.

'I mean it, Damien!'

I'm not quite sure if JJ, in his innocence, is aware that Damien's serious about coming here, if he knows, or has worked out, about his taste for raiding expensive items. No, I wouldn't put it past JJ not to have noticed it at all. He's more concerned with building Meccano sculptures to look right up the cunts of the girls who walk above his grating.

'Look,' I say to Damien, keeping my voice level. 'We start nicking stuff, we draw attention to ourselves.'

'Oh, yeah,' he sneers. 'And a fucking great hole in the side of the building's pretty inconspicuous.'

'It gets trashed night after night. Kids come up with bricks just to have throwing contests, Damien. Don't you listen to the buzz in the town?'

He's silent for a moment, blowing smoke at the Rover's windscreen. Then he says, 'I want it to be worthwhile, our coming here.'

'What you want doesn't count for shit.' I don't know why I say it, but I have. It's out.

'Shut the fuck up,' Marcie offers from the back seat. 'And find me another drink.' She belches loudly, and follows through with a suspiciously wet gurgle which she almost manages to suppress.

'Look, whose idea was it to come here?' Damien snarls. 'If it hadn't been for me you'd be sitting at home watching vids and drinking coffee.'

So he thinks of himself as our liberator. Give me a break.

'I need some air,' says JJ, and he swings himself out of the car. His feet crunch glass as he surveys the car-sized hole in the glass wall.

Sighing, I get out to look at him. He's running his hands through his hair, and when he turns to look at me, his eyes are wild, red-rimmed.

'I – don't think we should have done this,' he says worriedly.

'Bit late now.' I slam the driver's door behind me, and come round to put a hand on his shoulder. 'Look, we won't be long. No one will ever know we were here. The crusties and glue-heads hang around outside with their fires. No one comes in. And no one cares about this place. It's practically condemned. It isn't even alarmed.'

He thrusts his hands deep into his pockets, breathes the chilly night air through the gash. 'Why did we come here?' he asks.

I shrug. I haven't really thought it through, not the way he wants me to. It's something to do, isn't it? The way I see it, people of our age get blamed for everything, so we might as well start doing some of it.

That's as close as I've ever got to a proper reason, and it hits me there, in the purplish, echoing halls of the dead shopping centre. The idea that I've always suffered through the antics of the stupid, and I always will, so I might as well enjoy myself.

Things like – all through school, when we'd be plagued by the antics of those few Fallies who'd slipped through the net. They, losers with no hope of a GCSE, torched the three chemistry labs with bunsen burners and acid, which meant we had to bus it out to Canterbury for practicals. No wonder most of the top people only got Cs. And there was the time the motor bikes were burnt, out on the cricket pitch. The groundsmen couldn't repair the razed turf in time, so the season was cancelled – and, since they never admitted to it, the whole school got a letter home explaining the situation and begging for more School Funds. I'd just got a girls' cricket team together for the very first time, which turned out to be worth nothing.

All blamed, all punished. There's no point being young if there isn't someone out there, somewhere, who thinks you're appalling – and if they're going to think that anyway, then you might as well take advantage of the headstart.

The engine suddenly changes note – I hear a shriek from Marcie, and a brief, heartfelt, '*Oh, shit,*' from JJ.

I run forward. I slam my fist on a ton of metal that's disappearing fast from us.

The driver's door swings open as Damien careers down the main precinct. He clips the corner of the inert escalator and the door shears away with a scream of metal. By some miracle, it hangs on at one hinge, clattering behind the car like a broken wing, and the drag temporarily slows him down.

JJ and I are in pursuit, but the Rover is accelerating again. All I can hear is the tortured roar of the engine as the gears are crunched up and down and back up again. Marcie screams and screams. Choking exhaust fumes billow in the mall.

Damien, with an audible whoop of delight, swings the Rover round the corner by Boots, and we run after him, our feet slipping and sliding on the marbly surface. My shoes weren't made for this, and I'm slowed down by pulling the too-small suede coat around me where it won't quite hold together.

The car slams into the façade of Woolworths. The doors vibrate as if bombed. Incredibly, there is little damage – those glass doors are tough.

JJ and I are pounding along the precinct, and we get ten metres behind him just in time to see the reverse lights come on. JJ pulls me out of the way – so hard that the coat rips – just as the Rover screeches into reverse and then pounds forward again, a huge metal battering-ram, smashing open the entrance to the store like an eggshell. It ploughs on, hitting a display stand of CDs with a crash that echoes up through every hall and balcony of the place.

JJ and I crunch our way into the store. There's a light flashing above the entrance, strobing red. Something tells me that it's not an intentionally silent alarm. Someone has been here before us.

Damien, not looking at all shaken, gets out of the car and manages to push the door back into its hole. He spreads his hands. 'Load up, kids.'

JJ lunges forward, but I hold him back. I kick aside a fallen video-stand and look in at the car window. I don't know quite why, but I lean down to Marcie, still slumped in the back seat.

'Are you all right?'

She looks up at me from somewhere deep within her own world. 'Yeah. Fine,' says a small voice.

'Come on.' I offer her my hand. I'm aware that JJ is looking at me uncertainly, and Damien just with contempt. I grab Marcie's slippery hand, and pull her up.

Damien, casually, is stuffing CDs into various pockets. Most of the time he doesn't even bother to look what they are.

'Damien – '

'Fuck off, Bel.' He grabs a disc from its box, frisbees it towards me. It whizzes past my ear.

'Listen to me!' I'm angry now, and I can feel the heat rising to my aching head. 'I chose the car, I'm driving the car. We do what I say tonight.'

Another low-flying CD buzzes my head.

'Try and assert your authority, Bel,' he says. 'It's amusing.' He storms over to me, slams me up against the record counter and grabs me by the collar of Imelda's jacket.

His eyes are brown, deep, quite abstracted, and his sleek face glistens with an unnatural wildness. 'You listen to me. I saved your life tonight. D'you realize that? I sorted things out for you.'

'Yeah, and you took your time.' I'm aware that my voice isn't quite steady any more. 'A couple of seconds later – '

'And you'd have been fucked. In every sense. I know.' Damien grins. His crooked teeth look huge, hideous under the strobing light. 'You owe me, Bel. You owe me your life.'

Now JJ moves, and there's nothing I can do to stop him. 'Just leave her,' he says quietly. He says it like a request, not an order. I've taught him nothing, it would seem.

He taps Damien lightly on the chest, as if he wants to push him but hasn't got the bottle. Hell, that's worse than a full-scale push.

'And what's it to you?' Damien snarls. He catches his breath, seems about to say something, then says it anyway. 'We know why *you*'re so moody tonight.'

JJ steps towards him.

I frown for a moment. There's something about what Damien's said which disturbs something deep in one of the dusty cabinets of my mind. It was almost as if he wasn't sure if he dared say it or not. For the moment, though, I've got other concerns.

Their threats, the potential violence, seem to sublimate into a dark, black-purple cloud and hang in the air between the racks and the Pay Here signs. Marcie's tugging at my sleeve, but I'm sure I can hear a distant commotion, like sounds outside a pub at night.

'Come on,' says Marcie. 'I wanna drink. Let's have a drink.'

I'm definitely right. Clattering feet and raucous shouts are echoing through the hall outside. I'm sure that I can hear someone coughing, painfully, again and again. There's a distinct sound of breaking glass.

And now our faces, in unspoken unity, have turned towards the shattered entrance of the shop.

It sounds like an army of darkness arising from the shadows. Only it's coming from above us.

Even Damien is looking now, his hands frozen above his spoils. His mouth opens wide.

We've moved to the glowing, red shell of the doorway. I can see shadows up in the balconies of the next level, half hidden behind the spidery plants and other trails of foliage. The clanging and shouting grow louder and louder, and so does the coughing.

At the top of the frozen escalators, the shadows start to resolve themselves into figures. Under the purple lights, I can see a flicker of combat jacket, white dreadlocks, swirly tie-dye. Behind, a couple of leather jackets.

I've realized that the coughing is not coughing at all. It's the sound of two hungry-looking dogs barking again and again.

There are, as far as I can see, about five or six pairs of feet descending the escalators with the security neons glinting in their eyes like alien, robotic light.

Damien draws breath quietly behind me.

'What are they?' JJ murmurs.

I hear the soft click of Damien chewing on nothing, as he gets his mouth round the answer.

'Fallies,' he says grimly.

13 *Force Majeure*

It is three o'clock on Sunday morning and I am sitting in a very small room with a white light shining in my face and a tape-recorder going beside me.

I'm not saying anything. I'm listening to the rain.

It was just three hours ago at Ashwell Heights.

'What's this, then? Looking for Santa's Grotto?'

The leader is a tall, blond guy with stubble in an army jacket. His hair's twisted into stumpy dreadlocks whose shape reminds me of root ginger. He speaks in a rough-edged town drawl, the Fally voice.

'No way,' I say to him, folding my arms, opening my eyes wide in my usual challenge posture. 'Saw him last year, asked him for a life. Did I get one? Did I hell.' I keep my voice light, keep a grin that's friendly and not knowing. You never know, humour might defuse this one.

They've met us at a point halfway between Woolworths and the escalator. Well, they've exchanged a smile or two among themselves. They carry various odours: a pungency, maybe petrol or meths; scented smoke; the meaty dampness of dog.

There's Dreads, with his twitchy hands and his army fatigues. Behind him, two leather-jacketed skinheads, one chewing, the other grinning. Grinner's holding a well-fed looking Alsatian on a leather lead.

Behind Chewer and Grinner, there's a boy in denim and a purple tie-dye shirt. He's got a trowel-thin face, dripping with oily black hair.

He's holding the other dog – it's a skeletal creature with white, rune-like scars etched into its fur, and it's straining at the string.

Then, behind him, higher up on the escalator, there's the only girl of the crowd. One side of her head's shaved to little more than stubble, with spots poking through, and the other's a cascade of well-nourished hair, the colour of blackcurrant. Her arms are folded over a clashing patchwork coat. Her face is striking for three reasons. First, she's staring at our group, her bright eyes filled with amazement. Second, she's got royal blue lipstick. And third, the whole right side of her face is scorched with a bright, crimson birthmark.

No obvious sign of any weapons, at least. I've got my hands in the pockets of Imelda's jacket, and my hand clasped round the knife. Just in case.

Dreads sees the Rover sitting among the chaos in the smashed shop. He sees the flashing light of the dead alarm and grins. 'Been busy. What a way for nice little kids to spend their time.'

I shrug, aware that I seem to have appointed myself spokesperson. Why's Damien so quiet now?

'Well,' I say quietly, 'nothing on telly, the theatres are closing, the British novel's dead. What's your excuse?'

Dreads doesn't grin this time. He comes right up close to us, looking me up and down. He's trying to work us out, I can see that. It must be obvious that the coat I'm wearing is expensive, but he must be wondering why it's ripped and why there's nothing on my legs. His eyes sweep over the rest of us. I imagine him looking intently at us all. JJ, cool in his checked shirt (also borrowed from Imelda). Marcie, quivering and hollow-eyed, mermaid-like. Damien, sleek and arrogant, a dark shadow in his private-eye coat.

'We've had this planned for weeks,' Dreads says quietly. 'Weeks.' He's shaking with suppressed anger.

'Look,' I say to him, 'you keep out of our way, and we'll keep out of yours. Deal?'

Birthmark steps forward, places a hand on Dreads' shoulder. Her nails are long and black, and her left index finger is inlaid with a bright jewel. She seems to carry some authority.

'Why don't you get off home?' she says. She's got a deep, rounded voice with a few edges knocked off. 'Back to Mummy and Daddy and your nice houses.'

Damien starts forward, but my arm's in his way.

'Hey, we don't want any trouble,' I say quietly, but I'm aware that Birthmark's crisp, blue eyes – might be contacts – have fixed on Marcie. She stares at her for what seems like a long, long time.

Behind us, the red light flashes again and again and again, like blood, giving us all birthmark hues on our flesh.

The dogs growl quietly.

Birthmark nods to Dreads and the two of them retreat for a conference in the shadows behind the escalators.

Grinner and Tie-dye each pay out more of the dogs' leads, and the ugly mutts skitter forward, straining at the leash. I feel my heart pounding. I don't want to get too close to that meaty-mouthed Alsatian with its yellow fangs.

Chewer spits out his gum. It hits the floor, sticking there in a pool of saliva, like some mutant limpet.

'I think,' says JJ softly in my ear, 'that they'll want the car.'

I give him a brief, admiring glance. It's an idea that had occurred to me, as well. 'Is that a problem?'

'I can't see Damien agreeing,' he suggests quietly.

'Too true.'

They're strolling back towards us, the girl looking strangely noble with her emblazoned tribal mark, and Dreads just edgy.

Birthmark narrows her eyes. 'Don't I know you?' she says to Marcie.

Marcie shakes her head so hard I think it might fall off.

Well, that's really going to convince her, I think grimly. My mouth is dry with beer, just starting to get that clogged and cabbagey taste. I want to swallow but I don't dare.

'No,' says Birthmark quietly. 'Perhaps not.' She turns her eyes away from Marcie, and Dreads follows her gaze, uncertainly. Birthmark's hand droops over Dreads' shoulder.

She stares at me. I swallow hard. It hurts.

'I don't know you, either,' says Birthmark. She glares right through JJ. 'Nor you,' she adds thoughtfully. She slowly lifts her hand from Dreads' shoulder, and her jewelled finger glints red as she extends it towards Damien.

Oh, no.

'But I do know you,' she breathes softly.

And then she said to Damien that she knew him.

The light is even brighter now in my eyes, making my eyes sting and my face glisten with sweat.

It all seems like another world. Out there in the darkness, in the chemical-coloured light.

I can just hear the sea swishing quietly at the edge of existence. I wonder if the future-ghost in her silver cape is out there, somewhere, picking up my thoughts on her mental plane.

Damien backs off.

This is ridiculous. 'Don't be stupid,' I say to her. 'So what if you do know him?'

'I know him.' She's looking at me, now. Her voice is glass-hard, her blue-painted lips spitting out the words. 'I've seen him on the estate. With his *father*.'

It hits me then that the Fallies know more about their enemy than we could possibly realize. They must have been watching Jeff Ash for weeks. They must know that he – and Jon Archard, *hell* – are ready to evict everyone from Ferris Court flats and blow the whole lot sky-high.

From behind us, there is a loud crash and a screech of wheels. The Rover has turned, and Damien's at the wheel.

Marcie's shaking in terror and JJ looks uncertain. Someone's got to move.

In front of us, Tie-dye and Grinner are looking round, uncertain as to what they should do.

I grab Marcie and yell to JJ, just as an angry Birthmark and Dreads start running towards us. Somehow, we've piled into the car.

'Go, Damien, go!' I scream at him.

He revs the engine to give us a good impetus. Fumes billow in through the smashed window, and there's an acrid smell as the clutch starts to burn.

Some reflex makes me pull my seat-belt on. Conditioning, no doubt, from years of being a good little girl in public. Or do I just think it's safer?

The Rover hurtles right towards the escalator, and the Fallies scatter. For a split second, the Alsatian, growling and slavering, is scratching at my window, and then the car swings and it's gone. We're screaming along the precinct and we scrape the edge of the escalator, before hitting an open plaza filled with tables.

Somewhere, now, an alarm is going off. Behind us, I can hear shouting, barking. The Fallies are in pursuit.

Shops whizz past in the purple light. JJ, remarkably calm, directs a sweating Damien from the back seat. 'Not down there, it's the stairs. Keep going straight. Round the edge. Don't hit the tables.'

I have to suppress a giggling urge to yell, *Where's the crystal?*

Damien's slowed down, because we can't find a way out of the plaza. We have to drive round the edges because white tables are clustered like giant mushrooms in the middle, and there's no room between them.

There is (a) the stairs. No go.

Or there is (b) back the way we came. Blocked by Fallies.

Jesus(') shit.

I stare into the light, and the tape churns on beside me.

It is vital that I recall exactly how it happened.

Damien takes slightly too long to turn the car around.

They're coming through the plaza, leaping over the tables. Grinner, Chewer and Tie-dye smash some over, blocking our way in front. The barking echoes off every wall as they unleash the dogs.

Damien's out, making a run, leaving the engine going with no one at the wheel. Bastard. He vaults over one of the tables with a great swish of coat, like that *Interceptor* guy.

'He's gone!' JJ is furious. 'Bel, get the wheel!'

'I can't take this,' Marcie whimpers. 'I want to go back.'

'Marcie, no!' JJ lunges at her, but too late – she's off in her tight green dress, dodging the Fallies, and is swallowed up by the shadows of the stairs.

I can't get out of my seat-belt. '*Shit shit shit*!' The car, still trundling at about ten miles an hour, clips a bin, and Grinner and Chewer leap for cover. I'm straining at the belt. My thumb stabs again and again on the red release button, with no effect.

Something wild and angry lands on the bonnet. It's the scabby dog, scratching the paint up into fountains, barking like a hellhound. Its eyes are skewed, looking in opposite directions. I've never been so frightened of such a scrawny creature before. It looks mad and hungry.

It slides, trying to get a grip on the windscreen. The car slams, still quite hard, into the side of a burger bar. This time I hear the headlights smash. The dog slithers but regains its balance.

JJ yelps – the creature's filthy jaws are right up against our windscreen, trying to bite the glass, clouding it with foul breath and spittle.

The creature won't take long to find the back window's gone.

Behind us, the Fallies are approaching at a run. Except Birthmark, the arrogant bitch – she's standing on a table with her arms folded, smiling.

The Alsatian's in the far corner. It's watching Damien, who can't see which way to run. Dreads and Tie-dye are right behind the dog. Dreads has a broken bottle.

Another smash with those paws and the dog's going to be right inside here.

I finally break free of my seat-belt. It whips across my neck and I slam, decisively, on the button for the windscreen wipers.

The first high-speed wipe smashes the mutt on the side of the head. It gives a terrifying yelp, almost like a human scream. Its teeth are flashing as it tries to bite into the wiper, and in the process the wiper goes right up inside its collar. The blade flips across the bonnet, dragging the yelping dog with it.

JJ and I watch in horrified fascination as the mutt slides to and fro, trying to get a grip with its legs on the bonnet. It's obvious that the twisted collar's getting tighter and tighter, and the dog thrashes impotently. Foam and blood are welling out from between its jaws.

The Fallies seem to have forgotten JJ and me. They've formed a crescent in the corner around Damien. They maybe haven't realized about the dog.

'Get us out of here, Bel,' JJ snaps. 'Now!'

Tie-dye's smashed his fist into Damien's stomach. Damien, bent double, hits the wall, his face red and screaming.

I'm in the driver's seat, jiggling the wires again and again.

'I can't do it!'

'Move out,' says JJ, coming round the front. I try to ignore the kilos of thrashing dog being slammed again and again across the bonnet. I move back across and he gets into the driver's seat.

Dreads pulls Damien up by the hair. He does it with surprisingly little effort. It's like watching a skeleton lifting an undertaker. Dreads spits at Damien and slices with the bottle, close to his face.

The engine coughs, splutters.

I can feel my nerve going. 'JJ, come on!'

'All right, I'm trying my best!'

I risk another look over my shoulder. Damien's face is bleeding from a broad red stripe across his cheek. Tie-dye slams him against the wall again and does a high kick right into his stomach. Damien's on the floor, now, and Dreads is standing over him with the bottle.

The engine catches. JJ slams the car into reverse. The broken windscreen wiper skews off, taking the throttled dog with it. I hear a sickening thump.

My body shakes again as we hit a table behind us. Other tables fall like dominoes, sending Birthmark off-balance and crashing to the floor. I can't resist a scream of delight as adrenalin pumps into me, and I thump the roof. 'Come on! Come on!'

JJ obviously doesn't like this. He's sweating and gritting his teeth as he swings the car around.

We're ready. JJ has his hands steady on the wheel.

'We can get out,' he says. He doesn't look at me. All we can see is

Dreads screaming, brandishing the bottle, and Chewer and Grinner hauling Damien to his feet by his collar.

Tie-dye is looking in our direction. His eyes open wide and I can see his finger lifting to point at us.

'No.' I'm firmly gripping JJ's arm. 'We don't leave him.'

'Then we're dead!'

'Get him, JJ. Or we're finished.'

His eyes meet mine. For a second, no more. He looks cold, resolved, so unlike my JJ that I almost flinch. I realize he is actually prepared to leave Damien. And I have to ask myself whether I am too.

Then JJ hits the accelerator and heads straight for the Fallies.

I sigh, lean back in my chair, because that's the hardest bit to remember.

The tape isn't going to stop. I close my eyes against the harshness of the spotlight. I can see an angry, greenish after-image. I can see foam gushing from the mouth of a dead dog. Foam and blood.

I can smell the roasting flesh of the dog, mixed with the scent of bergamot and orange.

No, that's not right, surely?

JJ slams the brakes on, jolting me back and forth. The Fallies scatter, dropping Damien. JJ then edges forward in jerks, keeping them on their toes, as he finds the switch to get the side windows open.

Behind us, I see Birthmark scuttle for the cover of the stairs.

Momentarily, I think of Marcie.

Damien, his head bleeding, is heaving himself up on my door handle.

'Come on, then, if you're coming!' I scream at him, and pull him in the open side-window. He lands in the back with a thud and a gurgle, and before his legs are even inside the car, JJ is moving us. With one intact wiper still swishing uselessly across the bonnet – across the dog-blood – the Rover smashes a path through the scattered tables.

We make it to the mall in just a few seconds. On the back seat, Damien, head in hands, yowls like a wounded animal.

JJ's handling the car like a pro. As horses go, my little JJ is pretty dark.

'We haven't got Marcie,' I say to him.

'I know. She'll have got out. We'll pick her up.'

We're back at the escalator and the shattered Woolworths entrance.

About forty metres to go.

The red light is still flashing on and off. Police from hell, I think with a sudden chill. I glance on to the back seat. There's a pungent smell of bile. Damien, bleeding profusely, has been sick. He's got his head between his knees, but he's still breathing.

Thirty metres.

The car picks up speed. I close my eyes tightly and all I can see is a pair of opaque lenses above a plaice-white face, with –

Twenty metres.

With a jagged, Zig-zaggy-Stardust-stripe of a birthmark –

My God – no! –

She is there in front of us, white legs straddling the glassy gash of our exit.

Birthmark. Her face contorted in rage.

Fifteen.

Something in her hands is gushing out white clouds, spewing globules on the walls and floor around her.

Ten metres.

Birthmark, screaming profanities, shoots the fire extinguisher like a gun, splattering our windscreen and wheels.

'JJ, slow down!' I scream.

He hits the brakes. The car's gripped by the foam as if on a moving pavement. There's nothing JJ or I can do. The windscreen is almost totally covered. There's a soft thud of flesh.

'Jesus.'

It's a white-out, everything's white and bright, we've stopped dead, white like that toilet seat (so long ago) and I don't want to look in case I see red, the splash of blood on snow, the red of a crimson harlequin-faced demon. 'Jesus Jesus Jesus.' As I say the name, it becomes more than a name, I realize what I am saying and I see his face, I see the whiteness of the Turin shroud in my mind's eye and I see his kind face reaching down to kiss me, I feel the nails driven into my body, I feel the knife in my hand cutting skin, opening his wrists and I'm watching the white clouds of his spirit pour out and over me –

'Bel – '

Focus on something. Focus on clarity, like white and red. I'm back in primary school saying, *Our father which art in heaven, Harold be thy name, the king don' come, Di will be done.* That's what we said. I really thought the Lord's prayer was some sort of allegiance to the Princess of Wales –

'Bel, for God's sake!'

There is a boy shaking me by the arm. He's got big, endearing eyes and a floppy fringe, and his face is filled with panic. His name is Joshua James McCann.

His name is JJ.

'Bel! Come on, we've got to get her in!' He's opened the car door.

'What?' I am confused.

'The girl! Come on!'

In front of me, through a haze of drying white foam, a single windscreen wiper judders across the bonnet of the car. There is something caught up in the blade. It looks like a clump of bloodstained hair.

I twist round in my seat. Damien still has his head down, breathing hard, sounding like he's about to retch again.

The first rule of disaster, someone said once, is to panic about one thing at a time.

So what happened then?

I sigh, closing my eyes against the light.

We – JJ and I – got out. She was crouched on the floor next to the fire extinguisher.

And was she badly hurt?

Yeah. Well, no. Well – she didn't seem to be. No blood or anything, and she was breathing and that. Kept sobbing something about her leg.

And it was JJ who suggested . . . ?

Putting her in the car, yeah. (Shrug.) Well, we had to do it. There was nothing else we could do. We threw her in next to Damien and hoped for the best.

And then?

And then we went out the same way we came in. We found Marcie sitting in the car park, dribbling into her dress. She had foil crumpled in her lap and a straw up her nose. We didn't say anything. We just picked her up and shoved her in the back as well.

And . . . that's when it all started to get rather worrying. Right? Right.

We've managed to clean the windscreen up and to fix the wiper vaguely back into place. No one's in control except for JJ and me.

The road swishes past. Night air, more chilly now, floods in through the back window. Lights of tartrazine-orange against dark blue skies. Even in September, the sky's not totally dark at this time. There are clouds, moving like great, monolithic spaceships.

JJ and I are not looking at each other. We are quiet, the car is quiet. It smells of rust, engine fumes and vinegary bile.

Marcie, fish-eyed, smiles to herself as if she has discovered a secret in her little world. I doubt she's noticed the extra passenger.

Damien clutches a handkerchief to his cut. It was messy, but not that deep – he's suffering more from the punch and the kicking. He's a big lad – he was prop-forward in the First XV – and it takes a lot to knock him down.

'How are you doing back there?' I ask, without looking round and without sounding like I care too much.

'Not . . . too bad.' Damien coughs and splutters, producing something that I don't especially want to see. 'What happened? What's she doing here?'

He nudges the semi-conscious Birthmark, who's lolling against him. I glance in the mirror. She's a greyish-white, mushroomy. Her mark's like a giant bloodstain, and her mouth's slack and glistening.

'Don't ask me.' I nod to JJ, who's concentrating on the road. 'He picked her up. I haven't yet found out quite how far off his rocker he is, but I'm sure he'll enlighten me.'

A boundary sign looms, an angular ghost in the night: Teysham.

'You're going home, Damien,' I tell him. 'And you're taking Miss Mermaid there with you.'

He groans, clutching at his head. 'But – wait – I've . . . got to get cleaned up first – '

'Got a bathroom, haven't you?'

We've arrived at a village square with a war memorial and a telephone box as its two silent guardians. Not far away, a vixen yelps, sounding worryingly human.

'Right, get out. You too, Marcie.'

'Me too, Marcie,' she says in a far-away voice. 'Meatoo Marcie. Meat two veg.' She chuckles, opens the door and waves vaguely at me. 'Bye, then.' She falls out of the car and lands on the verge by the telephone box.

Damien, staggering a little, helps her up. They're like a couple of lost souls in the moonlight. I grin at them.

'Come on,' I say to JJ. 'We've got to lose this car.'

I just hope that neither Damien nor Marcie is going to have too clear a recollection of tonight.

We accelerate away in the dark. Through the shattered windscreen I see them hugging each other in the village square, like the last people on earth.

We slow down at Marsh Avenue, a big modern development. Tasteful five-bedroom houses, with twisty porch pillars like barley-sugar sticks. Garages, big enough to be little houses themselves. Gravel and neat lawns. Not unlike where I live.

We stop for a second.

'Listen,' says JJ.

There's a whine, like a motor, echoing down in the valley, and a faint clanking of glass. I peer out, down the hill, try to see. A square of light is disappearing down towards the coastal road.

The milkman's been. I need to clear the dry, beer-cask taste from my mouth. First of all I take great gulps of the fresh night air. Then

JJ stays and watches Birthmark while I hop over a couple of gates and grab some sleek white pints from Marsh Avenue doorsteps (dodging a cat in one of the drives). They're so smooth, like little bombs of milk. We gulp them as we judder along, down into the valley. Out through the country lanes, towards the downs and quarries.

Birthmark is lolling quietly in the back seat, sometimes making a low moaning sound. I'm not quite sure what we're going to do with her. I lean back, try and give her some milk, but she won't lift her lips to the bottle.

At one point we have to cross a B road, and a bright coach thunders past, followed by a petrol tanker and three cars. Hearts thumping, we get across, back on to the lanes and a world of darkness and over-hanging trees, where no one will see us pass.

The night washes in through the car, smelling of pine needles and dung and the burning of petrol.

We drive on, in deathly silence.

Getting rid of Damien and Marcie was a smart move. They're dead wood in lots of ways. One too brash for his own good, too anxious to prove himself, and the other just a stupid whining bitch.

We could have found out where Birthmark came from, taken her home, lost the car and forgotten it all. I kept looking at her in the mirror, that strange, segmented harlequin-face, and shuddering as I thought of the Fallies descending the escalator, and the frenzied dog clawing at the Rover's windscreen.

She didn't look or smell like a Fally. More like a Trav. So did Dreads, too, actually. Like one of that band who hang around Canterbury in their combat jackets, smoking draw and barking at passers-by for money. Keeping a scrawny dog so they can claim an allowance, which they spend on drink while feeding the dog on scraps.

We drove on. This is how it was.

I notice that her eyes are closed now.

I tell JJ to stop the car, but he doesn't.

I scream at him to stop the car. There must be something frightening in my face, because he takes one look at me and swerves into the verge.

It's silent and still in the valley.

I look down at Birthmark.

Her face tips towards me, sending my heart pounding. Her mouth drowns in a sudden gush of clear fluid, frothed with a white foam. It's welling up, drenching her face, glistening the birthmark. It leaves the flesh tight, glossy; it's like frozen meat shrink-wrapped in plastic. The sound of the fluid dripping on to the floor of the car is gunshot-loud in the night. Still her eyes have remained closed.

'Come on,' I say to JJ. 'Help me get her out.'

You got her out of the car?

Yeah, that's what we did. It was totally dark and still and we couldn't even see any lights of houses for miles around. On one side of the road there was woodland, sloping down.

And the jacket? What happened about the jacket?

We – I – well, I don't know. It must have come off as we were . . .

Yes?

Dragging her along.

Dragging her along. Right. You didn't know if she was dead or alive, and you didn't stop to ascertain. And what did you do then?

We rolled her down the slope.

And then we drove away.

The car judders and protests as it is put through one of its final punishments – the dirt track down into the old quarry.

I need some air, so I'm out, round the front of the car, leaning back against the bonnet with my hands deep in Imelda's jacket. I gulp down the last of the milk, wipe my mouth and sling the streaked bottle away into the bushes.

The moon's crept out from behind the clouds, picking out some details of the old hollow. There's a few old stumps of tree, deformed and knobbly, like trolls. Mangled metal, almost natural sculptures of rust reaching up into the night, with twisting green leaves trying to reclaim them for the earth. On the crest of a rise just in front of us, there is the crumbling brown skeleton of a car – looks like it was a small hatchback.

There's a gentle rustling sound, and some scurrying and scrabbling in the bushes. Otherwise, it's still.

What a night. Exhaustion is beginning to wash over me now, and pain's coming back from that cut on my head. I feel slightly dizzy, and put a hand to my forehead, but the Rover steadies me.

Belinda Archard and JJ look at each other across the scratched and battered car.

Belinda Archard says, *We have to get rid of the car.*

Belinda Archard tells JJ to step right back.

Belinda Archard gets the knife from the pocket of Imelda's jacket.

'Just keep back, JJ. I know what I'm doing.'

The moonlight is bright and cold on my knife. It's a slice of light, white as a mother's pride. Sliced from ice, pure and cold, the moonday light that shone on the golden helmets of Armstrong and Aldrin. The brightness that fell on Iphigenia and Clytemnestra from the flames of the towers –

And JJ is frozen, watching, which is what he does best. He's sitting on a flat rock with his knees drawn up and his face blank. He never really wanted to be a part of this, never wanted to come along.

I've sliced down through Birthmark's patchwork jacket. It comes apart with a fraying of threads, a rainbow tatter, and I pull it clear of the car.

JJ is sitting on his rock and staring across the wasteland. I hack the jacket apart, making incisions from one side, then the other, then the first again, so that it unfolds into a long strip of wool. JJ is shaking quietly.

I tie a smooth, heavy stone to the tattered rope of wool. I open the petrol cap and lower the material in until it hits something. I'm breathing hard, sharp as acid, and my heart's hammering away in my chest.

Then I unfurl the ragged thread, giving myself a good length, with odd bits of armhole sticking out here and there.

I call JJ over. In a daze, he comes and squats down next to me.

'Someone will find it,' he says. 'Someone's bound to find it.'

'Here?' I shake my head. 'Wrecks end up here all the time.'

I click my lighter into action. Our faces flare orange in the dark for a second.

'No one ever comes here,' I say to him, widening my eyes.

'We did,' he says.

His words hang in the air as I touch my lighter to the long thread of wool.

And then the light erupts, finds a path, blazes a trail into hell. Down and down it burns, hot orange light pointing to the car. I pull JJ with me to the ground.

It's nothing like as spectacular as I'd imagined. When it gets to the car, there's a brief *whoomph* and a flash of orange as the rest of the petrol ignites.

I hear the windows go, with sharp cracks, and then there's a larger burst of flame which possesses the car from the inside and eats it up. The flames, roaring like a crowd, reach up against the night sky – two, three, six metres into the air. Black smoke blots out the stars and the clouds.

I lift my head, trying not to look right at the flames. There's a strong smell of hot, burning petrol, mixed with rubber and metal. I start to cough. JJ, next to me, is staring, transfixed, into the heart of the inferno.

I touch his arm, gently. 'Come on, let's go. It's over.'

Something cold and wet splashes my head. I look up. Two more raindrops hit my face.

'Oh, shit.'

JJ appears to have recovered. He's standing up, and helps me to my feet. The rain lands on Imelda's coat, spattering it with big spots of darkness. We hold hands and run down to the edge of the quarry, the rain getting heavier and turning the dust under our feet to mud. I look behind us once, but I can't see any smoke or flames.

By the time we get to the embankment and the main road, it's established a rhythm, and it's hammering on the tarmac, making it glisten like pitch under the soft street lights.

I realize that I haven't given any thought as to how we're going to get home. I look at JJ now, in the rain, our faces shiny with sodium-light and rainwater, and it seems that we've both suddenly thought of the same thing. We can hardly attract attention by getting a lift, certainly not the way I look.

So we hit the verge and walk as best we can along the slippery grass, ducking into the shadows every time a car swishes past. Luckily, the approaching headlights give us adequate warning.

After about fifteen minutes of miserable, snuffly trudging, we get to the roundabout, with its sign announcing that it's a mile to the town centre.

We know the way across the fields from there, and it's another ten minutes before I've found the way to our street.

We stand in the rain at the end of my road, both of us drenched, and suddenly everything hits me like a giant juggernaut and everything inside my body seems to shatter and release floods of weakness, horror, self-hatred.

JJ holds me close, kisses my soaking hair.

'Come in,' I eventually manage to say to him. I sniff back the mucus into my nose, try and wipe some of the rainwater and salt water from my face. 'Sleep on the sofa. Dad won't mind, and Kate can go to hell.'

'I'm not sure . . .'

'It's miles to yours. We can ring Imelda in the morning.'

'All right,' he says.

I let us both in, and I give JJ the bathroom first, supplying him with a fluffy towel from the airing cupboard and a sweatshirt and a pair of jeans of mine. I trot along the corridor, dripping in wet suede, and listen at Dad and Kate's bedroom door. I can hear deep, undisturbed breathing.

When JJ comes out of the bathroom, I'm down in the lounge, but he doesn't say anything to me. He just curls up on the sofa. I cover him up with one of Dad's coats, then I finally get out of the soaking suede jacket, which I throw in the airing cupboard. I go and get under the shower, which pummels me like liquid mud, warm and invigorating. Then I wrap myself in a towel, go to my bedroom and switch the Anglepoise lamp on.

I'm warmer, but still shaking, and my breathing sounds unbelievably loud. I get myself a couple of aspirins and gulp them back with some water.

I put my tape-recorder on quietly, playing Albinoni in the background. My curtains are still open so I leave them, watching the rain twisting the patterns of the glass, hazing the distant lights beyond.

I sit and I sit, listening to the rain, for what seems like hours. The light shines in my face and I try and force myself to remember everything.

The tape clicks to an end. I don't turn it over.

I blink, realizing only now that the light is unbearably bright.

So I switch it off and lean back with a sigh, as the rain thrums and clatters all around me, around the house and the garden and down in the Town at the Edge of the World.

I think of the rain pummelling the deserted promenade, with no one to hear it but the sea-wraiths and ghosts from under the pier. I think of the sea, grey and foaming, eating up the land, dashing the pier and the sea wall.

And I think of the rain screaming into the hole in the side of the Ashwell Heights complex, where the red light must still be flashing, sending out its silent signal all across the valley.

And I think of the rain hammering down on the charred wreck of a car in an abandoned quarry up beyond the town. I imagine the metal hissing and steaming as it cools.

And I think of the rain on –

The rain on cold, still flesh –

– as I fall asleep in the chair.

14 *Dreams are not Enough*

I am walking up the long, cold nave to a stained-glass window of the Crucifixion. Christ detaches himself from his cross and from the bright fragments of colour, and flies down on wings of gold to embrace me.

As our mouths are about to meet, he throws back his head and laughs, and I see the great red blotch of birthmark, scarring and blistering his face as it erupts in smoke. Flames gush from his face. His flesh drips like candle wax on to the floor of the church and I'm covering my own face, trying to scream, trying to drag my leaden feet away.

I turn away, sobbing, dodging the pillars of rain that hold up the roof. Standing behind me in the nave, there's Dreads in his combat jacket, eyes white and sightless. He's thumping a mallet into his hand again and again. Behind him, with their sunglasses reflecting my terrified face, are Chewer and Grinner and Tie-dye, with their dogs straining on clanking chains, barking great clouds of blood. The rain thunders on the roof.

Chewer, Grinner and Tie-dye open their mouths, revealing flint-sharp teeth. They exhale in unison. It sounds like a storm, like the howling of the wind.

There's a shadow at my shoulder.

It's JJ.

There is something not quite right about him – something off-key. He turns to look at me, his eyes bright and feverish – but he looks through me, and I follow his gaze over to the door of the church, where a bright light is flashing. Orange, like a car indicator. On-off. On-off. An insistent bleeping fills the vaults of the church. Beepity-beep. Beepity-beep.

Slicing through the scene, my alarm clock is screamingly loud. I thump the switch and roll over.

I am shivering.

15 *Everybody Hurts*

And when Belinda Archard was sixteen, her mother died.

Sod the false bio-data. Ghost-written in a spectral light. This is me we're talking about. It's me. It's always been me.

I hated her for it, afterwards. I hated her for leaving us and making us move away from the country.

It wasn't her, directly, of course, I can see that now. But my father just threw himself into his work, made all these great moves which led to his own business. Just right. Sorted. Quids in.

It seems that all that remains of us is money. We weren't exactly doing badly before, but now? Now we were coursing the white waters of solvency. And in the middle of the country's biggest recession, too.

Jon kept telling me how lucky I was to be born under a government that allowed this sort of thing. Not sure I quite believed him. I've got a healthy cynicism for any party that preaches basic morality on the one hand and shags its secretaries on the other. He took it seriously, though. Told me all about the strikes, showed me all the videos of the bin-liners in Leicester Square. Yeah, yeah, OK. So it happened and it was loud and it was shit and it was just before I was born. So was punk. Point being?

We had all this money and he was getting somewhere, and he said we would never want for anything from now on. And that he'd never deny me anything.

I don't know if he ever wanted to meet anyone else. I've never asked him.

Another golden afternoon in 1992. The summer was one long, treacly string of them. They merged together into one, as if the battle in the garden had gone on for ever.

Belinda, in her armour of dock-leaves, was sliding on her stomach and gripping a slim gun of hazel wood. The demons of the garden cowered from her – the dragon-headed rhododendrons with their spiky eyes and snapping mouths, the serrated nettle-monsters. On her way to the targets, there was always a bush sprouting papery white tokens full of seeds. She gathered them, because she knew the land where they were the currency. She kept an eye out for the advance troops, the little patrols in their armour of black-spotted red or yellow-and-black stripes. She navigated the land by smell and touch.

The grass had turned yellow and brown. Before, Belinda had only ever seen grass that colour on camping holidays, a neat oblong of civilization/destruction left where a tent had been standing for a few days.

Overhead, a plane gave out a near-animal groan and then its sound cut. Belinda knew that meant parachutes, and normally she'd have been scanning the skies, ready to aim at the little coloured mushrooms with her sharpened stick. Not today. Today she sat and listened to her breathing and smelt the earth and the herbs.

When I get older, she thought, I want to get a knife. Some of the girls in school have got them. Some of the prefects, even. They have to have them, 'cos the troublemakers have them. They go round to the bins in lunch-hours and tell the Year Ten girls to stop smoking, and if one of them pulls a blade on a prefect, then they have to match it. No respect otherwise. It'd all fall apart. See what I mean?

Dying's easy. Anyone can do it. You don't need any special gear like guns or knives or poison. You just need a quiet place to sit and get on with it. And a weak heart helps.

It was another summer. August, 1997. Hottest day for years. I found her sitting out in the garden – right out in the long grass – next to her easel.

The picture wasn't of anything in view. I remember noticing that at the time. She must have been painting from memory. It was a bridge, a big arc of metal over a river. Thinking about it since, I realize it must have been Newcastle, where she lived for a year before going to York University. There was something brick-red in the distance on the picture – maybe the roof of a house or something – and it had turned into a shapeless blot. Her brush was lying on the grass and her head was on one side. She wore a hat, usually, when she was painting out in the sun. It was lying upturned at her feet as if ready to collect money.

Her eyes were shut, I remember. I went weak as I touched her, and I felt my legs giving way. Not just because I knew she was dead. Not just that. It was because I had looked out of an upstairs window two hours before and I had seen her reclining in exactly this pose. She had not moved.

And the right side of her face – her normally pale, fragile face – was burnt lobster-red.

I touched her head. It felt heavy. The sun hammered my skull. It was the kind of weather where you might be blinded in the light and shoot someone just because you couldn't cry at your mother's death.

I held her face, on the pale, cold side. She looked like a red-and-white harlequin. Her right eyelid was puffed like a soaked prune.

And then I had to let go, and a mist blurred everything, and I was running, running back towards the house with every step thud-thudding through the earth and my head and my life.

Black suited me. Mourning became Belinda. It was the smartest gear I'd ever worn in my life, to be honest.

Jon looked amazing, really cool and calm, and not in one of these cheap rented suits either. His was Savile Row, double-breasted. A suit to keep for next time round.

He asked me to read the lesson. I said I'd rather not. He said that was all right. I asked him if he wanted to know why, but he didn't. In the end, my Uncle Graham did it – my mum's brother – and Jon never did ask why I refused.

But I know what he thought, and I let him think it. Adolescent rebellion. Going through her God Can't Exist, Or If He Does, He

Must Be A Total Shit phase. Way off the truth, sorry. *Nul points*. What would that make me? Hey, I kept believing in the Bible all through the news from Ethiopia and Tiananmen Square and the Gulf, I remained faithful during Bosnia, I was unshakeable despite the existence of Mr Blobby. So does one quiet death in a garden get me railing against the heavens and saying, see you, God, you're a shit, you are? Really, I have more perspective than that.

As a matter of fact, I've always been deeply spiritual. Even down to the screen saver on my computer – an enhancement of the Turin Shroud image, pulled off the Web. Touched up and made less ghostly, of course. And I did it before they proved it was a fake. But what does it matter that it was? Most of the trappings of Christianity – certainly in the English branch office – are fake. The most important matters seem to be stuff like who does the flower rota. But none of that matters, because no matter what transient stuff you build around them, the truths remain.

People never believed me when I used to tell them I saw Jesus in crowds, so I stopped telling them after a while. I had this horrific paradox. I hated Christians but I loved Christ. None of the Christians I've ever known has been true or real – they all let their relationship with God get in the way of their day-to-day stuff, you know, people, and yet they all think they're going to heaven at the end of it. Me, I've no idea where I'm going, or even if I just atomize into a void at the end of it all, and for your average Born-Again, that makes me some kind of heretic or freak. And yet I know that, if I could ever actually stop Jesus and find a moment of his time and tell him all about it, he'd be more understanding than any of his so-called supporters. He'd probably say, 'Yeah, well, that's pretty normal, actually.'

If the Jehovah's Witnesses came round and said, 'Will you let Jesus into your home?' I used to say, 'Him, sure, but you stay outside.'

As for the actual ceremony, it's become a series of stills in my mind, rather than a continuous videotape. Just the bits I most remember.

The heat. The blasting furnace-heat of the sun, making everything yellow and white and coating my body with a sticky film directly under all the black stuff. The earth at the edge of the grave, crumbly and dry like that powder you use for milk shakes.

The colour of the coffin wood. It was beautiful. Dark, dark oak, polished and cool-looking, as if it would not allow the sun anywhere near. I was impressed. I wanted to stroke it.

Jon slipping on his shades when we got back to the car, and touching my elbow briefly, and looking away when I looked at him. My sweat doubling as I felt his hand on my arm. We've never really *done* physical contact. Don't feel happy with it. No need for it. Seemed to be more for the benefit of everyone else.

The taste of the extra-strong peppermints we sucked on the way back to the house, to disguise the quick mouthful of whisky we each had from his flask. Not even death could break our complicity.

And later, much later, after he'd gone to bed, there was me alone in the lounge with the debris of departed guests around me, a plate of sausage rolls beside me and a jug of lemon squash, and MTV on loud loud loud, smashing the house down, ghost lights strobing in the darkness as they destroyed the physical world. Bel blitzed, tuned-out, must have slept at some point but doesn't know when. Kept being pulled back, grabbed by the remorseless pace of the TV. Didn't, couldn't switch it off, and eventually smoked the last of a dwindling batch of spliffs just to get unconscious for an hour or two.

I went away for a while. A couple of days, no more. I took all the money I had from my account and left Jon a note, telling him exactly where I was going and when I'd be back, because to have known he was worrying would just have acidified my stomach, made it all hell.

I phoned him from Calais when I got there. I couldn't be on for long, because I wanted to save my money – the exchange rate hadn't been favourable to me. He sounded puzzled at first, but he was OK about it when I assured him I'd be back in a couple of days.

And I was. I never let him down. I went to Lille on the train, which used up most of my money. I got round paying for accommodation by picking up a bloke in a bar – but only after three hours leaning against the radiator and swigging Kronenbourg from the bottle, watching them all, deciding who was the safest to go for. Anyone who came up to me and tried it on was a non-starter to begin with, and, of course, there were plenty of those.

Eventually I went to a club with a bunch of students. It was a mixed crowd, so I never felt uncomfortable. Memories are hazy, but I do recall telling Luc at one point – loudly, in his ear, in dodgy French and over the beats of some Euro-pop or other – that my mother had just died. It was easy from there.

I left Luc at dawn – he was still asleep and I didn't wake him. He was nice, and a great lay, but he snored.

Before I left Lille, I chose a backstreet shop where I was to prepare myself for the rest of my life.

I was vulnerable now. I felt alone, unprotected in the world. I had seen just how easy it was to leave this little place, and in the two days since my mother's death I had suddenly found myself suffering from a heightened awareness of the harsh, spiky, poisoned nature of the world. Every step could be the one to lead you into chaos or destruction. And a growing conviction had burned itself on my mind. The knowledge that there was something I could do about it. Something which had been at the back of my mind for literally years.

Throughout the eighties, the years in which I had lived the first years of my life, the governments of the world had been poised, ready to obliterate each other. Through simple fear – and, I'm sure, mutual ignorance about what the other side could actually do – they had not. They had survived. We had survived.

Dying's easy. Anyone can do it. Well, it wasn't going to be easy for me. It was time to acquire myself a deterrent.

Inside the shop, which smelt of polished metal, leather and wood, I found an indifferent old man looking at me over half-moon spectacles and a copy of *Le Figaro*. And a counter full of flick- knives.

I pointed to one at random.

'*C'est combien?*' I asked.

16 Cat's-paw

The town is full of sky today. This is a thin town, a fragment floating on the surface of the world. Above it, so much sky. Even before you get to the clouds, there's a big open space, with a pale hole where the sun should be.

An irritated wind scuttles across the pier, pushing a polystyrene tray, chip paper, a drink carton. Pungent vinegar and grease smear the air, daub their smell on your nose and mouth.

I watch the empty sea churning, grey and white. My hair tangles up like sea kelp. When I get it home, it'll be stuck together with salt, sculpted into a mess as if it's made of clumps of dead mermaids' hair.

I suck on a cigarette, and its hot, savoury harshness blocks out the rank smell of the End of the World. Sometimes it smells like death up here on the end of the pier, especially now in the grey zone between summer and autumn. It's like there are bodies under the sand, decaying into a spinachy mulch of seaweed.

A long way out, beyond the headland, spray's being kicked up by a hovercraft. Going to Dover or Folkestone. Those towns might be dilapidated in places, but they still have a haunted nobility, and they still do business.

But nothing comes near here; this town's no businessman. More like a decrepit whore, built for pleasure, but unable to give it any more. The juice has been squeezed from the flesh, the skin's gone putrid, and her lush sweetness – once a honey-trap for sailors, students, drunkards and artists – has turned fishy-stale.

I'm leaning on the rail, smoking, trying not to singe my hair. I wonder how much longer I can stay here in this chaos of salt and chill.

I glance down at the end of the pier, past the stilled arcades and the faded booths. There's a small blonde figure in a black coat, scurrying against the wind.

I know that she can see me, so I don't try to hide, but I pretend to be looking through a ten-pence telescope when she approaches me.

'Hi,' says her croaky voice.

I look up. 'Hello.' I can't help wrinkling my nose as I notice that she is wearing cheap plastic earrings, moulded into flowers of disgusting pink and purple. They're the kind that you'd win on a shoddy hoop-la stall and wear as an ironic joke.

'Kate said you were here.'

'Yeah, well, good for Mystic Kate.' I spit a stream of smoke into the wind, and it comes back at me, a spiky cloud.

Marcie leans on the rail beside me. I look at her again, and for a moment I'm shocked to see how rough she looks. Her face is ghost-white, with fever-red splodges on her cheeks and nose, and her eyes are scribbled round with fatigue and mascara, etched with outlines so deep that they look hammered into the skin. Her blonde bob's scraggy, fraying above those horrible earrings, hacked and slashed at the back in a vain attempt at home hairdressing. A pig's ear of a duck's arse. There's a haze of cheap soap around her.

She twitches her lips in a sideways smile at me, and a scabby cold sore lifts its head out of the white make-up to say hello.

'How have you been?' I ask her. I realize I have not seen her for several weeks.

She shrugs. 'Could be worse.' She looks at me, and I can't meet her gaze – I feel it almost blinding me with its bone-whiteness. 'I'm gonna lose the flat. Can't pay the rent.'

I feel the chilling burden of other people's problems, and a strange guilt. 'What happened?'

'You know that green dress what I wore out?'

Mentally, I translate Marcie's vernacular. I assume she doesn't mean she used it to the end of its natural life.

'That night?' I ask.

There's a pause in the conversation, as if we are acknowledging something unspoken.

'Yeah. Cost me a hundred and fifty.' She looks up, a brief, shy, tangential glance. 'I wanted to wear it 'cos it was good. Made me feel good.'

My cigarette burns down further. Sparks cascade into the sea. I nod quietly to myself. 'And the coke?'

'Your money,' she says in a small voice.

'Ah. Right.'

'I think . . . I mean, I . . .' She flips her fingers, slumps into her arms on the rail. 'Dunno, I can't . . . I'll have to leave this town.'

'And go where?' I look at her properly for the first time. 'Why do you want to go away? Tell me something you've considered, Marcie, tell me something you've thought through for once. Talk to me, not off at a tangent. Take some fucking *control*, for God's sake!'

She seems totally numb to my outburst, and I turn away from her, tutting, feeling my face roar with colour. I wonder why I care.

'Damien's not been out since. He's sold them CDs. Planning another raid, he is. Thinks it's easy money.'

'Ah. Right.'

'What did you do?' she asks suddenly.

'When?'

'That night. I don't . . .' She sounds embarrassed. 'I don't remember it. I mean . . . I remember all them Fallies, and I was in the car park at one point, yeah?'

'You were in the car park. In body. We got you home.'

'Wet. I got wet. I woke up in the spare room at Damien's.' She shudders. 'His mum was so good to me. It was terrible. I'd, like, gone further than when you ask what someone's done, you know? It was like she'd took me in off the streets to give me breakfast.'

So Marcie wants to know what we did.

And I am confronted with a question about my own actions, when I have hauled myself through these last few weeks just by not questioning what we did, by telling myself that we had to do it. There was no other alternative.

*

JJ scratches at a night's stubble and then wraps his hands around a cup of coffee.

Opposite him, on the sofa, I sip some orange juice. The clock clunks to itself, the land dries out under a morning sun.

'It was an accident,' he says. He almost offers it as a suggestion, as a starter in a game of Chinese Whispers.

'It was an accident,' I agree. 'She didn't get out of the way, and there was no way you could stop.'

It's as if we have to find this common ground. It has to be said. We don't say what really needs to be said. We talk about the car.

'We . . . couldn't have left it,' he murmurs. He's looking at the floor, his fringe falling down and hiding his eyes. 'If we'd left it someone would have seen it.'

'But no one thinks anything of another burnt-out wreck.'

'Nothing at all. Joyriders.'

'Fallies,' I offer. Our eyes meet. 'Fallies,' I say again.

And since then, we have drowned in silence.

I thought there might have been something. An item on the news about the girl. But no, it seems I must have been right about her being a Trav. Could it be that no one's going to miss her? My God.

I've relived it again and again and so has JJ, I'm sure. I don't know if he still has the same conclusions, but I have convinced myself that the actions had to be taken, swiftly, decisively.

Evidence was purged in flames. Not all the evidence, though.

I have to tell Marcie something.

So, the truth. But not the whole truth.

'We drove the car out to the quarry,' I say to Marcie. 'It was quiet, still. We set fire to it and let it burn.'

I can feel the fire-bright face searing me again. Is she going to burn through the spaces between the truths?

'And then what?'

'Nothing. It started to rain, so we ran. Got soaked. Went back to mine.'

'Oh. Right.'

It's essentially the truth. A component may be missing, but it's not a vital component as far as Marcie is concerned. And it actually seems that she's prepared to accept that. Marcie missed the whole bloody lot, and all she knows is that we had to get rid of the car.

'Bel,' she says in a small voice, 'I need some more money.'

So that's it. She didn't come out here to the furthest point of the Town at the End of the World for the pleasure of my scintillating company. Even on the pier, I can't be an amusement.

I give her a brief, empty laugh and a shrug. 'I don't think you've come to the right place. Why not try the bank?'

'Bel, I ain't joking.'

OK, so Marcie is obviously not in the mood for banter. Nevertheless, what does that change? She has already taken quite enough from me, in return for some blame that never materialized, some security I didn't need.

'I was thinkin' about an idea,' she said. Her fatigue-bruised eyes carry desperation in their hollows. 'I was thinkin' that maybe I was drivin' that night.'

I push my hair out of my eyes, angrily. 'But Marcie,' I hear myself saying, at the risk of stating the obvious, 'you weren't driving. I know you weren't. And the problem is, no one knows who was. We were in town, as far as everyone's concerned, and I want it to stay that way.' I stare at her, wanting to pierce that pale, limp body. To harpoon it with truth, bright and ineluctable.

'But they might come and ask us about that night. About the Fallies.'

'Yes, they might. In which case, we know nothing.' JJ and I have thought this over, and decided that this is our policy.

'But if they do,' Marcie ventures, 'wouldn't you like the security of knowin' someone would take the rap for the wrecked car?' We are both looking out at the choppy sea now but I can sense her as strongly as if her eyes were on me. 'I've got a record already, it wouldn't bother me. I'd take the blame for it, if they came askin'. If we'd made an arrangement.'

I'm not stupid, and I can see where this is leading.

I can see the flames riding high in the night sky, vortices of orange stars. A husk of a car, crumbly to the touch like an old fire.

And I can see white globules of fat, fused to the earth at the bottom of a wooded slope.

'All right,' I hear myself saying to her, and my voice is roughened by smoke and salt. 'I'll find you the money. What is it, another fifty?'

'Fifty'll do,' says Marcie with quiet satisfaction.

Why? I don't know. I feel, maybe, that I am paying something beyond mere Marcie.

A ghost that hovers one fragment of space and time beyond her. Its face bright red on one side and virginal white on the other. A scythe swung up to its shoulder perhaps.

I am trying to pay my dues.

And Marcie doesn't know exactly what she's taken on.

I go round to JJ's flat but he's not answering the door. The only sounds are the echo of the bell, and the swishing of cars on the spray-dashed promenade. I even try standing above his voyeur-skylight and peering in. The place looks much as normal – mouldering dishes on the draining-board, caseless videos scattered around the blue carpet and over The Rapy Couch.

I have to see him. This whole business is just eating me up. I can get a tram out to the suburbs, see if he's at Imelda's house. I hurry along the promenade, past the dead and dying shops, my boots smacking the puddles.

I see myself pictured in each window, sometimes clearly, sometimes just like a ghost. There are other objects in these half-abandoned shops, and they all seem to be watching me. One, which looks like a dark crustacean ready to pounce, is just a wide-screen television on a stand.

The most sinister shop-window is just opposite the tram-stop. There's something in it like a metal skeleton, a two-foot-high match-stick-man made from rusty steel. I realize, as I hurry past and reach the tram-stop, what it must have been. That shop used to be an optician's, and it had a little bespectacled dwarf in the window who used to bob back and forth, pointing at a board of letters. Now he's gone, and, as with the town, only the bare bones are left. I shiver as I wonder whether the little skeleton still dances there on a dark night. I picture him nodding sagely at the strolling couples, the shivering drunks and the snivelling druggies. I see him bowing to the gaggles of cackling, Lycra-sheathed creatures as they surge from night-club caverns.

It's grey now, the off-tuned autumn grey which this place attracts. There is only one other person at the stop – a girl with scraggy black hair and a beaky crow-face, slumped in contemplation, a sloppy Asda carrier bag hanging from one hand.

A tram approaches from the other direction, from East Bay. It moves with the sleekness of a barge. For some reason, my eyes become fixed on it, even though it's not the one that I want. There are quite a few passengers on it.

The tram approaches, whining and clanking. I am watching the windows. There are three people sitting on the back seats. Momentarily, a fragment of sunlight breaks out and brushes across the windows, and I see a white face outlined in blackcurrant-coloured curls, and glowing with a garish red birthmark.

I actually take a step backwards, almost crashing into the Scrag, who mutters a lacklustre obscenity.

The tram is slowing down. The face has receded into the shadows, but I can still see the candyfloss outline of that hair.

I can feel my eyes pulled open wide with horror, and my heart hammer-hammer-hammering away.

I hop across the tracks and on to the other platform, but the tram has already started.

I'm running alongside it, back the way I came. I'm trying to keep pace with the tram, reality bouncing up and down like I'm running with a hand-held camera. The tram's getting faster and faster, its whine building up.

The figure's turning now, turning – the whiteness of her skin, the aurora of the hair –

And an unblemished face, staring back at me in puzzlement.

The tram trundles off along the sea front, and I stand and shiver and watch it until it's just a toy in the distance. It rounds the coast by the abandoned fairground. It slips into suburbia. It disappears into perspective-oblivion.

I go to the cashpoint, and take out fifty pounds.

17 *Slack*

Up here, we can see houses, sky and some patches of green. That is, they would be green if they weren't clogged by experience, adorned with the envious meals consumed and vomited upon them. Up here, no greenery is silent – it is alive with colour and texture. It *twitters* with skittery chip cartons and *scrunches* with yellow plastic Quaver packets and *pssshutts* with red-and-white Coke cans and *squelches* with pitchy dog sludge. Living history. Beyond the green, there's a row of blinded windows, and one still-active video shop, plastered with larger-than-life posters.

'I wonder,' JJ murmurs, 'if this is the kind of place people mean when they say they've come to the University of Life.'

I'm at Imelda's house within half an hour. She finally comes to the door with her hair arrayed in tar-black needles, and a lime-green towel pulled taut around her shoulders. She frowns first of all, and I smile nervously, taking in what she's wearing – an apple-coloured dress, little more than a long T-shirt, rumpled and stretched in places as if she's pulled it on while coming down the stairs.

'Oh. Hi,' she says at last. She looks vaguely surprised to see me, and folds her arms across her breasts, as if she's trying to hide something.

'Sorry to wake you,' I find myself saying glibly. 'It is only four in the afternoon, so I could come back later.'

Imelda grins. 'You've caught me conscious. Kettle's just boiled.'

I settle myself in the kitchen, and she flicks the kettle on with one hand while towelling her cropped hair with the other.

'Is he here?' I ask her casually. I hold my breath, because I haven't contacted him for nearly a week, and for all I know he might not even want to see me again.

'Yeah, he's here.' She clicks the TV on, restlessly, as if her hand needs something to do, while still drying her hair with the other hand.

'JJ!' she calls upstairs, and then, when there is no answer, with a mother's commanding tones, 'JJ! Get off your bed and come and see Bel!'

'You keep him in order,' I say, amused.

'Someone has to, darling.' She pours boiling water into the teapot. 'So, I hear you lot had quite a time the other night.'

I'm instantly alert, but I have to try not to show it. 'Yeah, well, you know. We're young, stupid and white.'

'What?' She glances up with a brief frown, as if I've said something strange that she can't quite place.

'Never mind. It's a song.' (By XC-NN. Damien played me it.)

JJ shambles down, in a loosely-tucked-in check shirt, his hair frightened into a quiff, his eyes crumpled. He waves absently at me and collapses with a yawn into the armchair.

'You just can't get the staff, can you?' I sigh to Imelda, grateful for the chance to slip out of this conversation about our activities the other night.

She looks up from stirring the tea, and raises her eyebrows in a brief, arch way. It's Imelda's way of saying *fnarr-fnarr*, I think.

So we're here up on Fallowdale. Drawn by something unknown. No, this isn't the University of Life. It's the down-market version. The University of Central Lifeshire, formerly Life Polytechnic.

Well, you can stuff it, I think to myself. At this particular establishment, my year group is full of tossers. I can't do my preferred course modules. And the catering, cleaning and accommodation all 'suck dead bunnies', as the Americans say.

It's inevitable, really – been happening for years, ever since Mrs T and her option-to-buy innovation. Less and less money coming into councils, no one really being bothered about keeping up repairs on no-go estates.

And you know what else this brickwork world is full of? The bus-stops. The buck stops here at the bus-stops. Where the bus stops, life stops. Life banks up, like scummy algae. The specimens gather, gossip, shove, smoke and drink there. It's as if the bus shelters, in their urine-pungency and their blood-and-bile technicolor graffiti, are nexus points where intensity of life burns through, searing them all and anyone nearby. You only have to watch to know this.

You see, there's a bus-stop just here, on the other side of the green, and there's a collection of specimens there right now that proves my point.

There's Sad Old Bugger, tottering in ill-fitting clothes the colour of dung, with a face like a corpse under a flat cap that's probably crusted on to his head.

There's Mrs Blobby, wire-haired and double-chinned, wobbling in a knobbled pink jumper and barrel-slacks. Say that word again and again, say it with venom – *slacks* – and spittle – *slacks* – and phlegm – *slacks*! It sticks in your throat after the third time, doesn't it? A word that describes ruched old cloth round a putrid white belly. Describes a world slipping away. Describes a stumpy-toothed mouth dribbling over a jawbone.

Slouched against the glass is Ms Grunge, hair knotted with coloured threads, big crunchy skirt over scuffed boots, Walkman welded to her ears.

Standing behind is Miss Confection, a dolly-stick with yellow, scraped-back hair, striped tights, blue plastic belt clasped with a flower around a navy pencil-skirt. A small black vinyl rucksack is slung across her back, just big enough to hold a lipstick and a mirror, like some glossy insect slithering up towards her neck.

'Half their life must be spent waiting for buses,' I mutter.

'Always waiting for the one that's going to take them away from it all,' suggests JJ. He doesn't really say it to me, though; he's absent, staring into the fluffy, open sky that you find this far above town. 'You can understand why the place looks so beaten-up.'

I can see the beginning of a familiar argument. I've never held with this stuff about poverty breeding crime, actually, and I don't have any sympathy with people who are so frustrated that they trash their own neighbourhood. Pissing in your own back yard – that sort of thing just transcends mere stupidity.

'If their lives are so shit,' I mutter, 'why don't they do something about it, then?'

JJ shrugs. 'Maybe they can't.'

'Bollocks. Everyone can do something.'

Across the way, Ms Grunge opens her mouth wide as if to yawn, leans forward slightly and projects a glistening arc of spittle through the air. It lands on the pavement. She licks her lips, closes her eyes and retreats back into her Walkman-world. Sad Old Bugger stares at her, his jaw working silently, while Mrs Blobby turns away in disgust. Miss Confection brings her watch up to her eye with a smart, robotic movement, drops her arm and resumes waiting.

'Well, I'd never have had you down for an optimist. What's this, a sudden new faith in humanity's potential?'

'You know what I mean,' I snap at him, pushing my hair back angrily. I glance at JJ and he's smiling in a quiet, superior way. 'Nobody needs to smash windows and nick things.'

'Which we've never done, of course.'

'That's different. I don't try and justify it.' I feel smugly content with my answer, because it's the best one I can think of, and I've been wanting to use it for a while.

'No one tries to justify. Only to understand.'

What is this? It sounds like he got that straight out of a book. Or else the Fally air must be addling his brain, turning him against me. What the hell does he mean, *understand*?

'You can understand,' JJ offers, 'why people feel aggrieved at not having things, especially when it gets near Christmas and the shop-windows are full of stuff. All these glitzy stereos and TVs and things. Putting them in the windows just rubs it in the face of the people who can't afford it.'

I don't believe I'm hearing any of this. 'Oh, yeah, so it's society's fault for daring to advertise consumer goods. Brilliant, JJ. So we should all pretend to be fucking poor, so as not to piss off the underclass.'

JJ's argument is dangerous. You put the goods in the shop-window, so it's your fault? Worryingly close to all that crap about rape and short skirts, in my opinion.

If I don't watch out, he'll turn into one of these nannying types who spout neo-Marxist justification for crime. Why should I make allowances for someone who thinks he can walk off with electrical goods out of a shop-window, when I have to pay for mine? I mean, if I ever got caught, I'd be punished more heavily than him, on the grounds that he's more 'needy'. Yeah, like everyone needs a video-recorder to survive. One of life's essentials.

The bus scoops up the little crowd of losers. Ms Grunge slouches on. Miss Confection totters, picking her change from a prissy little purse. Mrs Blobby hoists herself up like a whale on a crane. Sad Old Bugger totters on last, and I see the bus move off as soon as he's got his ticket. I snigger as he staggers.

So here I am trying to articulate my anger to JJ. 'If you're poor enough to need to nick stuff, surely nicking food and clothes makes more sense? You've been doing the wrong sort of thinking.'

He looks amused for a moment, but when he glances towards me, he seems more disgusted. He sighs and slips off the wall. 'I've had enough of you, Bel. Let me know when you're feeling less confrontational.'

I can't believe this. I hop off the wall and pursue him down the hill, but he's walking on ahead, glancing just once over his shoulder.

'What's the matter with you?' I'm scurrying along to keep up with him. Fally houses scroll past, dirt-coloured, their different-coloured doors flicking up one after another like cursors on a screen. 'What do you mean, I'm being confrontational?'

'I don't want – '

'Look, I need to know!'

'That old one again. Need to know. Yeah, yeah. Leave it, Bel.'

We hurry round the corner. No sign of anyone else on the round-about, or in the street stretching out in front of us. Just gardens full of washing. People cower in their houses in Fallowdale. People hide.

'I thought we had an understanding!' I yell at him.

'Did we? I thought we had a shag.'

'But we've been having a laugh together!' I've finally got in front of him, finally caught his eye, and I fling my arms out like some stupid scarecrow and he tries to dodge past me but he can't. 'So what's the matter?'

He sighs. He starts to say something, looks away, then opens his mouth again. He blinks quickly, eyelashes fluttering in that girlish way of his.

'Go on!' I can feel that we're teetering on the edge here. It could go either way. I've got to pull it out of him.

He folds his arms, kicks at the ground, meets my eye for a second then looks away. 'I don't care much for – '

'Yes? Yes?'

'For your contempt.'

'My contempt?' I frown, draw back from him. 'You mean my natural wit and intellectual cynicism?'

'No. No, I certainly don't.' He sighs, shakes his head. 'Look . . . You've – we've – never lived like these people. Why do we talk about them in such a cavalier way? How can we know what it's like to live like they do? How can we possibly know?'

I shrug. 'Do we want to?'

He says, 'It's like with your dad.'

I feel hot anger prickling my forehead. 'What about him? Why do you need to bring him into this?'

'Well, he doesn't care, does he? Knocking down those flats.'

Shit, have I been telling him about that? I suddenly realize quite how much you open yourself up to someone when you're seeing them. How much ammunition you give. Like handing them a knife, and telling them to cut you. I'm going to have to be careful.

'It's for the best,' I say guardedly. 'The complex'll bring employment to the area. Worth losing a few dodgy sixties high-rises for.'

JJ, arms still folded defensively across his chest, shakes his head. 'Did you hear him say that? I mean, do you know when the sixties were? We were born in the *eighties*, Bel. Get your head round that.'

'Yeah, I know. Thatcher's bottled sperm. Do you have a problem with that?'

'I don't like your attitude, Bel. I don't like your mindset, your assumptions. All the things you get up to.'

'On my own?'

'All right. We. The things we get up to. It's pointless. And it isn't fair. It isn't helpful, the way you talk about all these people.'

'Helpful? JJ, what the hell have you been reading?'

He doesn't answer. He ducks round me and starts walking again. He leaves me standing there, uncertain as to whether to follow him.

Those long, slim legs are striding back down the hill towards town and he isn't looking back any more.

I stand there, hands on hips, and watch him until he's just a speck in the distance.

18 *Insurance*

JJ has not called. I wonder if I'll ever see him again.

It's a place for endings, this town at the end of the world. People think they come here for new beginnings, but no, they find closure, completion, even death sometimes. It's that whole thing about there being nowhere to go. When you get to the edge of a cliff, the only way is down.

I don't know how I ever imagined anything could start here, in this desolate place.

Funny how people get together by mutual assent, but when they split up it's almost always at the wishes of one or other of them. Not both. It's like losing your job. I'm going to go to the library one day and see if there have been any sociological studies done on the similarities. They have a similar crashing, disruptive effect on your life.

The only difference is that with a job, you normally get some notice. That would be good, actually. Notice. Pack your bags, I'm dumping you in two months. I'm giving you that time to get your life together and find someone new, all right?

But no. You're out on your ear that very day. And there's no such thing as Emotional Income Support.

Part of me says: wise up, get real, the world is never going to end unless you really want the world to end.

Part of me says: but I just want to know where he is, and where things began to go wrong.

When you're at school – doing, say, English A level, like I was –

you're in the incredible position of having some older woman or guy take you aside every few weeks and say: yeah, this is good, a B-plus, I'd say, but it could be an A-minus if you'd tighten up your argument just here, look, where there's all that waffle, and use a few more pertinent examples just here. In other words, someone tells you exactly how you could do better.

Life needs grades. Life needs a pigeon-hole where you hand in your essay every two weeks and get told just exactly how much of a waste of space you are. Because then, at least, you know, don't you? Reports on life, to take home. 'Bel has done quite well in the past year, although a neo-religious mutilation fixation and the haunting guilt of violent crime are combining to produce adverse effects in other areas of her life. She would do well to maximize her interpersonal relationship strategies, and to GET A CLUE. C-plus.'

So now it's dusk, and I'm on the cliffs.

I had to get out of the house, because it was just starting to get to me far too much.

I told that bitch Kate, though. I told her. Shit, I wish my dad would divorce her and find someone vaguely human, someone who'd let him be himself, and not try to have any say over me, none whatsoever.

It was just an hour ago, like this.

'Bloody hell,' says my dad, shaking his head as he examines his tax return at the dining-room table. 'I've just about written off as much as I can. What else can I put on there?' He taps his teeth with a Biro, the end tapering and chewed – like the mountain-shapes those people in *Close Encounters* are all making, or a recently sucked stick of Brighton rock.

Ever since the law was changed on tax self-assessment, Jon's been slightly dislocated. A bit like when you never quite catch up from that lost hour after putting the clocks on. He had it sussed for April – all the cashflow neatly trimmed to his best advantage, and just the right number of trips to conferences that he could get away with.

He took me to one last year, an Independent Redevelopers'

convention in a hotel in Bath, just so that he could count me as an observer and claim for my train fare and expenses too. In the car, he told me gleefully to drink as much as I wanted, because it was all going on the account. After that, it all seemed pretty bloody pointless. I don't like it when Jon sanctions things, tries to be liberal and cool. Sometimes I wish he was a reactionary old fart like other people's dads.

Anyway, it was a neat town – better than this dump, I thought. I spent a morning strolling around, looking at Georgian crescents, furrowing through musty bookshops. At lunchtime, back at the hotel, most of the delegates were ploughing into the bar, carrying off gleaming pint trophies as they yapped and pointed at one another like schoolchildren. I escaped to McDonald's at tea-time, and just as it was starting to get dark, I hung around a pub off the main street and leant against the bar, sizing up the guys who approached me, telling each and every one to get lost, until the right one came along. Suede coat, loose checked shirt, earring – in other words, he looked the part for getting me some gear. And I was right. I spent quite a good night in Bath after that, in a sea of light and darkness, wrapped in techno, jostled by bodies of varying ages and genders. I learnt nothing about Independent Redevelopment. However, I found out at breakfast that my dad didn't, either. Also, he was so gloriously hung-over – while I was fresh-scrubbed, gleaming and straight – that we had to leave the car and take the train home. So much for the great alcohol-versus-drugs debate.

'Can you think of anything else tax-deductible, Bel?' He dangles his glasses from his hand and sucks thoughtfully on the earpiece.

I'm slumped on the sofa, hopping through the satellite channels. 'Stationery. You always forget to put down stationery for invoices.'

He shakes his head in despair. 'No, no, I've written all that off. Think of something else. Remember, Bel.' He points his glasses at me, and I know what's coming. 'First food . . .'

'Then morality!' I cap the quote with a brief, affectionate grin at him.

I like doing this – one of the rare events in the year which unites us. It's better than Christmas, in a way, because rather than both having paid ridiculous amounts for things that neither of you wants, you're conspiring to get more money out of the system. And this year, it serves an extra purpose – it helps me to forget my screwed-up life.

Every year since they started the business together in 1988, my dad, who studied economics, has done the accounts himself. All the little bits and bobs add up. More yummy money for us. What I like about my dad is that he's never pretended. That quote – he uses it a lot. 'First food, then morality.' It gives me a little twinge to hear it every time, because it's something Mum used to say as a joke. She did German at university, and it's from a German playwright called Brecht. It tells you that it's all very well having principles, but you need to be alive to put them into practice – so if you don't get yourself and your family looked after first, you're stuffed.

Jon's always been scathing as fuck about the people who pretended to have a social conscience at university. They'd hang round outside the Union with placards and copies of *Marxism Today*. He tells me to watch out for them when I get there, because although the names will have changed, the attitudes will remain. They'll have spiky hair, earrings and ripped jeans. Always ripped jeans, as if being left wing means you have to brag about how poor you are. They go home to Mummy and Daddy in the holidays and eat all the nice food that Mummy cooks, without having the smallest of urges to take it all down to the local Salvation Army hostel. Funny, that. And in two years they all have nice suits, nice cars and mobile phones. They'll blush as red as Tony Blair's tie whenever they think of their fingers being blackened by the *Socialist Worker*. There was a song out when I was in the lower school: something about a rich student girl who wanted to go and live with commoners, and didn't realize they were all laughing at her, because she thought that it was cool to be poor. Says it all, really.

They were capitalists when it wasn't fashionable, my dad and Jeff Ash. And then, after the alternative conveniently exploded in the Romanian snow and the Berlin night and the empty shells of Sarajevo's tower blocks, people sat up and said: Oh! Right, maybe it is a good idea to have a decently regulated economy after all, and where did I put that lap-top? And Dad and Jeff were laughing. Yeah, OK, we've got a new government – which may as well be the same old shit for all the difference it's made – but business is sorted. I have a vested interest in helping them stay beautifully solvent, because I've got no intention of ending up like a Fally.

'I know,' says Jon, and starts scribbling away. 'The window cleaners. I forget them every year, because they hardly ever come.'

'Do you know them well?'

'Yeah, everyone does. One of 'em does the car windscreens too, at a fair price, if you get to know him.'

'Get receipts from them,' I tell him, skipping to UK Gold. 'With a few quid added on.'

He looks up, his glasses filled with light for a second. 'Very good idea,' he says, and taps a note into his electronic organizer.

I grin to myself. Hey, I'm wasted in slackerdom. I should be a tax consultant.

Kate swishes across the living-room, blocking my view as usual, as she pretends to dust the top of the television. Kate doesn't need to dust, that's the stupid thing, as she could easily afford to have Liza Witherzedd in every day – but she has this urge. There are stranger perversions, I suppose. The thought of my father actually shagging her is pretty gross, so Kate's affinity with bits of dead human skin and ugly little microbes is mild by comparison.

'I hope you're helping your father, Berlinda,' she says – without turning round, so I have to endure the view of the swirly leggings stretched to breaking-point across her fat arse.

I grin, and try to exchange a complicit glance with Jon – but now he's got his head down, and barely acknowledges me. So Cowbitch is manipulating our relationship without even looking at us. Christ, I hope this woman gets a steering-wheel right through her chest one day.

She folds the duster, sighs – as she always does – turns down the volume of the TV ('Your father is trying to work,' she snaps), rearranges a couple of ornaments (in the vain hope that they will make the lounge look more *Country Life*), and comes and sits down beside me.

'Berlinda, I'm worried about the late nights you've been having and the times you've been out late drinking,' she begins.

I smile sweetly at Kate. It's really just too much effort to bother to keep up the pretence any more. I yawn and stretch my arms high above my head.

'Kate,' I say with a sigh, 'if you knew the half of what I did, it would blow your fucking cosy little world inside out. So why don't you piss off back to your stupid coffee-mornings and keep out of my life?'

I'm halfway to the door before her jaw has even had a chance to drop. Outside in the hall, I punch the air and allow myself an enormous, clenched-teeth 'Yeeesss!'

A small victory.

A battle, not the war.

So now it's dusk. The sea swishes calmly to itself far below. The town's lights are spread like stardust to my left and behind me, as the promontory and the skies start to merge into a dark unity. Far over to my left, the coast rounds out a little, and I can see along the miles to the next town, which isn't quite so screwed-up as this one, and where there's an all-night funfair – I can see whirling cones of light, glittering trees and arenas of colour from the distant shore. Occasionally, a burst of music will detach itself and slip through the air to me, half-dissolved.

Dusk is a gateway. It's when the borders of the world start to fuzz away, and shadows steal across everything, leeching off the light. The air goes different too, tasting cooler as if it's jostled by ghosts all ready for a night on the town, piling into phantom coaches and going down the bay to skim the water, froth the waves.

The sun bloods the sea, light spreading like a birthmark.

When I look beyond the light, I'm sure I can see her face smiling at me, beckoning me.

I am permanently taut now, shivering every day, afraid that I will see a sliver of her in the surface of a knife, a ghost of her in the face of the long-case clock or in the screen of my computer.

I dreamt her again last night. She was looking at me in church, cut into chunks as if in a stained-glass window, but standing on the altar, her neck outlined in a white dog collar of bubbling milk. Her face grew bigger and suspended itself above me. Her birthmark was of molten stained-glass, encasing her face in a waxy mask, shrinking into the gloss-coat of a toffee-apple. And then it cracked, bursting as if under enormous pressure. The sea cascaded out, glutinous like pea soup or gallons of pus, and it roared towards me, coming to engulf me.

I awoke drenched in sweat. For a few seconds I was chewing the chill air with a sandpaper mouth, and then I sank back on to the cold pillows.

So now I'm sitting up here on the cliffs. I'm sure there is one single moment when the sea loses its sheen, but I can never pinpoint it exactly. It gets darker and darker until it's just a cloth, shot through with the odd flash of silver, rustling quietly under the chilly darkness.

An electronic chirrup shatters the stillness. I realize it's not a creature of the night – the warble is coming from deep inside my coat.

I sigh, and take out the mobile phone. It was a birthday present, but I've hardly ever needed to use it. The whole idea – being contactable when you're on the move – is anathema to me, and I've given hardly anyone the number. So I'm irritated as I answer the call.

'Yes?'

'*Bel? We have to talk.*'

It's a girl's voice, small and hard-edged like a little dagger. Sounds like it's embedded in someone, too.

I gulp deeply, tasting the night air. 'Hello, Marcie. What can I do for you?' I need a cigarette. I start to rummage in my pockets, sending a fountain of sweet wrappers, ash and other oddments over the glistening grass.

'*I think you can do something for me, Bel.*'

Either it is a very bad line, or there is someone doing a heavy-breather act on an extension. Which of Marcie's shags is it this time, I wonder?

'What is it now, Marcie?' Perhaps I sound more irritated than I intend, but she is really the last person on my mind right now.

'*Things are bad. Really bad. I'm gonna get my electric cut off soon.*'

'Marcie, babe, my heart menstruates for you. Light some candles and sit it out, darling.' What does she think I am, some sort of fairy godmother?

'*I'm not jokin'*, *Bel. I need some more cash.*'

A chill pervades me, as if one of those frolicsome spectres on the cliff top has touched me with its liquefying bones. This is just too bloody much for words. She can't do this. Especially not now. Doesn't she realize I have problems too?

'Marcie, listen to me – '

' *– else the gas an' all –* '

' – agreement, didn't we?'

' *– landlord came round yesterday and –* '

' – just haven't got that kind of money – '

' *– got to, Bel, please!* '

I close my eyes and count to three. The stupid bitch probably blew the last lot I gave her. I expect she doesn't know how to put it in a bank.

'Marcie, have you got a job yet?' The night gathers around me, and on the blackening horizon, the lights of a hovercraft skim towards the ports. Its muted thunder reverberates across the bay.

'*Tryin', ain't I?*'

I am tempted to reply, *Yes, very,* but I restrain myself. 'So you just have to live with it. I'm not made of money, and I can't keep giving it to you. As far as I'm concerned you said you'd take the blame for something, well, two things. And believe me, I'm grateful, Marcie. I really am.'

'*Yeah, so you can show it –* '

'Marcie, the fact is that there's nothing to connect us with anything. We're clean. They'll probably have arrested the usual Fally suspects by now for the Goodmans' window and the . . . the other thing. Ashwell Heights and the car. Think of yourself as having offered an insurance service. You can't come and demand more down-payment just because the fire, flood or act of God hasn't happened. Can you?'

I hope my voice doesn't sound as squawky with desperation to her as it does to me.

She says: '*Come round. Now.*'

I say: 'Marcie, get a life.'

She says: '*Come round, or I'll tell. I'll say it was you all along. Driving that night on the beach.*' She says: '*And at Ashwell Heights. I'll say it was you, all of it.*' She says: '*They'll put you away. You'll go down.*'

You fucking evil little bitch. You nasty, screwed-up, loose-pussied little whore-bitch, telling me, telling me what to do.

I'll kill you.

Stupid thoughts course like lightning through my head.

We did post-modernism in General Studies. Umberto Eco said that post-modernism means always having to say the words 'I love you' in inverted commas.

Just like 'I'll kill you'. Something a parent says to a wayward daughter. Something a houseproud wife might even say to her husband. 'Don't drop wine on that carpet or I'll kill you.'

Some stupid road-safety advert from a few years back. A kid saying, 'You're going to kill me.' (Yeah, because you ran out in front of my car, wank-brain.)

Always in inverted commas, until you start to think about it. I might well have said it to Birthmark or Dreads or any of those other Fally bastards. And not meant it. Now one of them might be dead.

And Marcie, the stupid cow, just for the sake of a few quid, is going to drop me right in it without even realizing what she's doing. Because she was off her face, incoherent, when we picked her up outside Ashwell Heights, and sound asleep – I assume – when JJ and I took the matter to its next stage, its logical and inevitable conclusion.

'Give me half an hour,' I say, and cut off the call.

On the way to Marcie's, I have to go through the subway to get to the main part of town. It's fetid, rubbish-littered. Right at the end, there's a huddled figure. I quicken my pace, trying to avoid looking at him. But as I approach, I glance in his direction. My body goes cold as I see a grubby combat jacket, but the eyes meet mine for a second and I see it's not a face I recognize.

'Spare some change, love?'

I'm ready to do my usual thing, which is to hurry past without giving them a second thought.

When I get to the end of the subway, I slow down. I don't know why, but I can feel myself turning. I sigh, take a deep breath inside my thick coat. I'm thinking about where I'm heading now, and the mess I'm in. I'm aware that I have turned, now. I'm wandering back towards him.

Why not? Just for once, why not? It might make a difference.

His eyes are open wide, big whites glittering in the dark. 'Spare any change, please, love?' he asks again.

'I'm not going to give you money,' I tell him, and my voice sounds strained and unnatural in the dark subway. 'For all I know, it might go straight to your dealer. But when did you last eat?'

His stubbly face looks more hopeful. 'Yesterday,' he admits. His hands are pulled up inside the sleeves of his old army jacket.

'All right. Hang on.'

Quickly, so that I can do it before I change my mind, I hurry up on to the pavement and along to the Burger King. I wait impatiently in the queue, jingling my change. I buy one of the largest I can find, and a big portion of fries, and reflect that it doesn't actually cost me a vast amount.

Clutching the stuff in a brown bag, I head back down to the filthy subway. He's still sitting there, shivering and looking hopeful. I hold out the bag to him. I just want to give it to him and get away. Maybe it'll make me feel better.

'Here. Have this.'

He grabs it like a child, practically rips open the bag. The burger in its wrapper falls out into his lap. He picks it up, and I watch his face freeze with disappointment.

'Sorry,' he says. He looks up at me, not quite daring to meet my eye directly. 'I'm a vegetarian.'

I can't quite believe this. This is actually what he has said. I give him my most contemptuous stare for about two seconds, then I snatch back the paper bag – which still has the fries in it – and clutch it like a baby or something. I'm not going to touch the burger, which has been in his scabby, snotty hands.

'Fuck you, then,' I mutter to him, and hurry back into the sodium-orange overground.

I no longer have JJ to buoy me up. I am alone, adrift in this town of rain and ghosts and danger.

The rain has wrapped me in a cocoon of wetness by the time I get down to the town.

I stand outside the four-storey building on Westcliff Promenade where Marcie lives. I watch the raindrops dancing like little sparklers on the tarmac sea-front road, and I listen to the sea growing stronger and angrier behind me, crashing into the sea wall. The coldest, angriest air howls around me, bounces off the cliff of seaside houses in front of me.

Far along the promenade, there's a couple having a vociferous argument. Their voices echo off all the houses.

That rank smell hangs in the air as usual. Fish and chips and seaweed, all merging into a general odour of decay. The edge of the world, slipping away in fleshy, gangrenous chunks. Sliding into crumbly nothingness, like boil-in-the-bag cod poked with a fork.

This is – has always been – a place where people come to die.

My name is Bel.

I'm standing in the rain.

I've got a knife in my pocket.

19 *Kicking into Touch*

'*Bel?*'

It's noon. I'm sitting in Canterbury Cathedral, and I've just stuck two fingers up at the pair of obviously American tourists (him with baseball cap, Chicago Bears sweatshirt and camera, her with elegant white hair and a designer blouse) who glowered at me when the phone went off in the echoing vault.

'Yeah?' I put my feet up on the pew in front of me, prop a hassock up behind my back for comfort, and settle the receiver against my ear.

'*It's Imelda, darling. Are you all right?*'

Imelda? Did I give her the fucking mobile number as well? God, I might as well have it on a T-shirt. I'm instantly on the defensive.

'Yeah, I'm fine. Why shouldn't I be?'

She breathes a sigh of relief, which sounds just understated enough to be genuine. '*Shit, I thought you were in some kind of trouble. Your stepmother rang yesterday. Katy, or whatever.*'

'Kate. Yeah. Commonly known as Cowbitch. She's got fat thighs and wears inch-thick make-up. You wouldn't like her.'

'*She sounded like a prissy know-all to me. Kept calling me "young woman". Is she the kind of person who has to match her serviettes with the tablecloth?*'

I smile to myself. Whatever's happened, I like Imelda. She's cool, and she lent me her coat, after all, and kept guard while I beat the shit out of a couple of social misfits. 'Yeah, that's Kate. Look, what did you tell her?'

'*What did I know, precious? Sweet Fanny Adams, of course. Where the hell are you, anyway?*'

I tell her.

'*I see. So I was wrong, you're quite far from hell, as it happens . . . Are you trying to save yourself? If you are, don't bother. I tried it once, but it needs a kind of long-term refrigeration I didn't feel capable of.*'

'Christ, Imelda, keep talking.' I'm feeling better already, and I lever myself up into a sitting position. 'You don't fancy giving up the girls and the one-night stands to marry my dad, do you?'

'*'Fraid not, but if you're still single in ten years, remember me. Look, your stepmother . . . she said you left the house last night, at sunset. You didn't say where you were going but you seemed pretty cut up about something.*'

'Uh-huh.' I've got to keep my voice neutral. Even Imelda can't be allowed to know everything. 'Look, is JJ . . .?'

'*He's out. Forget him, Bel. We can still be friends, whatever's happened between you two, can't we? Right, then. Let me come and get you.*'

'I'm not sure . . .'

'*Aren't you? Bel, do you ever trust anyone?*'

That's a shock, but at least she forces me to confront the question. Last night, I would have thought that I still had somewhere in my heart for trust. I stroll down the nave, my footsteps like gunshots, and leaf idly through the pamphlets and the books.

'*Are you still there?*'

'Yeah, I'm here. I'm thinking. All right, Imelda. You know the Flying Horse?'

'*On the ring road, near the cinema?*'

'Yeah. I'll see you there. Soon as you can.'

I switch the phone off.

Before I go, I decide to do something. When I leave the cathedral, one more candle is burning inside that vast and cool space.

And then I'm walking out into a cold but surprisingly bright day.

I turn left at the door, heading through the precincts towards the city wall. I walk in the shadow of the cathedral, and I remember myself thumping on Marcie's door last night.

'All right, I'm comin'. Calm down.'

I step back from the door, hearing my own breath echo through the stairwell. The rain brushes the windows like ghosts trying to peer in through the cracks, and my heart is marking the time of a hellish dance.

She opens the door. She's shrink-wrapped in a denim skirt and a red Lycra top. With her hacked-about baby-doll hair and hard-ringed eyes, she looks about fifteen.

She shrugs. 'Come in, then.'

As I hurry through the gardens in the shadow of Canterbury Cathedral, I recall that she didn't seem especially pleased or displeased to see me. Just indifferent.

I scurry down the steps from the city wall, into the car park. I'm facing the Christ Church side of the ring road now, with Lady Wootton Green and the looming, prison-like gate to King's School facing me on the other side of the busy road.

I hurry along, through the car park and then on the pavement, passing Burgate on my right, and I cross just opposite Parrot Records and Tandy. The crossing's got one of those whooping, triumphant signals like some sort of electronic bird-call, and it thumps my eardrums.

A scruffy figure brandishes a pile of magazines under my nose, and says, '*Big Issue*?'

'*Gesundheit*,' I reply over my shoulder, without stopping.

I wonder where JJ is, and who with.

Marcie's flat stinks of cheap perfume, mixed with recently cooked meat (that old, dead smell) and the lingering hint of her new paint. I sit myself at Marcie's kitchen table, and she slumps in the scabby armchair she keeps just by the door.

'How have you been keeping, Marcie?' I ask her quietly, flicking through the pile of *Best* and *Bella* and *Chat* on the kitchen table.

'All right.'

'Hmm.' I glance up at Marcie, who's picking at the arm of her chair. 'Don't you get worried,' I ask her, 'living on your own, and picking up all these men?'

She looks nervously from side to side, as if she can see creatures lurking in the shadows. 'No. Why should I? Can look after myself. I might go to evenin' car-eight sometime.'

I look up, I put my head on one side. I digest what she's said. Yes, that is what I *thought* she said. 'To what?' I ask. 'Some sort of motor maintenance class, is that?'

Marcie looks at me like I'm stupid. 'You know, like judo, only with . . .' She makes chopping motions with her palms. 'When you hit people. Bruce fuckin' Lee an' all that.'

I shake my head in despair. She is still peering at me across the kitchen, her face slightly spaced and terribly earnest.

'Business, Marcie,' I tell her, with a stern gaze. I glance at page sixteen, which is 'Be Big and Happy: Twenty Great Fashions for the Larger Lady'. I look up at the scrawny girl in her armchair again, and raise my eyebrows to indicate that I want to get on with it.

'I want a hundred,' she says in a small voice, without looking at me.

I don't look up. I'm staring right through page fifty-five, 'Ten Great Diets: Get the Perfect Figure This Autumn'. 'Go to hell,' I reply.

'Fine. If that's what you want.' She reaches for the phone.

I'm there first. Christ, I've jumped so hard I must have strained something, because there's a spasm in my leg. Ignoring it, I pull the connection out and hurl the telephone at the wall, where it hits with a satisfying crack.

Marcie and I stand there, looking at each other and breathing hard, for two seconds. Sizing each other up.

I stroll into the Flying Horse and check my watch. Imelda's not here yet.

I order a pint of the local bitter. For some reason my heart is hammering, like it used to when I was under age. Stupid, really. Like I think the barman knows something about me.

'You can't silence me,' she says quietly.

'I can.'

'Yeah, and you'll get into even deeper shit.' But her voice is not steady now, her words carry no resonance.

My fingers close over the handle of my knife. I've got a bladder like a ripe melon, but I ignore the ache.

Here and now.

Is this the Cut?

I take my pint to a quiet corner of the Flying Horse, and sip it gently. From my seat I can see out into the road, and I can see the grey city wall with the honey-gold cathedral, jagged and powerful, reaching up beyond.

I drink, and I wait for Imelda, and remember Marcie's frightened, drugged-up eyes.

'I just want money,' Marcie says. 'That's what it's all about, innit? This thing. Movin' up, gettin' out of the fuckin' class that society's spewed you into.'

I narrow my eyes. I move closer to her. She shrugs, folds her arms across her tight little chest and puts one leg out in front of the other, swivelling on one heel as she must have done in the days when she was touting for trade.

I could argue, I suppose. There's a good case for education, not dosh, being by far the best elevator to the middle class.

But Marcie's mind doesn't work like that. She thinks like a Fally. She thinks that all you have to do is win a hundred thousand on the lottery and you're one of the world's movers and shakers.

I suddenly realize that I pity her. My hand has been tight on the handle of the knife for the past minute and I just cannot take it any further.

Oh, shit, the rationality circuits have kicked in already. That means I'm going to have to try and talk her out of it.

'Marcie,' I say hoarsely. 'What do you *want*?'

'Told you. A hundred.'

'No. I mean really. I mean at the end of it all, what do you really want? Don't you ever feel that you need to get out?'

Her lip's trembling. She doesn't know where to look.

'To do things that aren't seen as right, aren't sanctioned?' I'm practically shouting at her. I fling open her fridge, and a six-pack of Stella and a packet of cheese spread fall out on to the grubby lino. 'Is all you want to get a stable job in this end-of-the-world shit-hole, to have two kids and a nice semi? Is *that* your life, Marcie?'

Marcie sinks back into the chair, shivering and sobbing. Well, I think to myself with some satisfaction, she's certainly been on something tonight, which gives me an advantage.

I glance into the fridge, and I see them again, those weird little bottles, all neatly stoppered and labelled.

This time, there's no rules to get in the way, and I just have to look. I pick one out and lift it up to the light.

'Leave those,' Marcie whines. 'They're mine!'

The bottle I have in my hand is labelled, like the others, in Marcie's childish handwriting, with a name and a date. This one says 'Steve, 21.09.98'. I pull out the stopper and sniff. I recoil almost immediately from an all-too-familiar, fishy pungency. There's not much of the stuff in there – just enough to cover the bottom of the bottle, really. But it's white and it's sticky and yes, I know what it is, thank you very much. I put it down, gingerly.

Marcie shrugs. 'Souvenirs,' she says.

There must be thirty bottles in there. 'Don't tell me. This is just this year's batch.'

She doesn't dare meet my eye as she nods.

'Jesus, Marcie. Have you ever thought of taking up stamp-collecting?' I grin at her. 'Philately gets you everywhere, you know.'

'You what?'

'Never mind.' The ache in my bladder has grown unbearable. 'I need your bog. I'll be back in a moment.'

Imelda waves at me and gets herself a spritzer, which she carries elegantly across to my table. Her bangles and earrings clatter as she sits herself down.

'So,' she murmurs, 'what happened?'

'When?' I take a cautious sip of my beer.

'Last night, Bel darling. Don't tell me, you went for a *Sturm und Drang* rail at the heavens up on Westcliff?'

I shrug. 'No.' Then I sigh, leaning back in my chair. 'If you must know, I went to see Marcie. I went to see her wanting to smash her stupid little face in and kill her, for reasons that are just too fucking complex to go into right now. And for various other reasons, I didn't do it. Right?'

Imelda grins. 'Right.' She raises her glass. 'Well, here's to life in all its fucking complexity.'

I feel a sudden chill, and then my face flushes red. 'You don't believe me. Imelda, how could you?' I pull the mobile out and thump it on the table, sloshing some of her spritzer over the edge of the glass. 'Ring her. Go on, ring the stupid slut! You'll find her probably in the more shivery stages of comedown, but basically alive and well, OK?' I fold my arms and glower at her.

Imelda laughs in delight and claps her hands together. 'Darling,' she says. 'You're wonderful.' She sips her spritzer. 'I won't take you up on that offer. But I love being with you. Do come round one night, won't you? Before the party.'

'You're having a party?'

'No, you are. I've decided it's what you need, to mark the transition to the next stage of your life.'

I can't help being amused. 'Next stage of my life?'

She shrugs. There's that impish, bone-white grin, flashing across her Romany cheekbones again. 'Let him go, Bel. You have to do it even- tually.'

In normal circumstances, yes. Imelda does not know what we share, though. The secret that still ties me to him.

This is what I did to Marcie.

'Marcie.'

She doesn't look up. She seems spellbound by her portable telly, which is showing some soap or other. People standing in a room and arguing. Their light and shadow play on her face.

'Marcie!' I grab her top, twisting its stretchiness in my hand, shaking her by it.

Slowly, her head turns round to look in my general direction, but her eyes can't focus on me. She turns back to the TV.

'Listen, Marcie.' I squat down, physically placing myself in the way of the screen so that she has to look at me. 'Don't go saying anything stupid to anyone. To *anyone*, understand? It'll get us all in a lot more trouble than you realize.'

She stares at me with her eyes laser-sharp now. Honed by her chemicals. She looks angry and dangerous.

'I don't care,' she breathes. 'I just need the money.'

I look at her, long and hard.

Part of me's thinking: hell, it's only money, and this'll be the last time. There's always a way – Damien, maybe, or my dad. Or Kate, without her knowing. But I don't think they keep that kind of cash in the house.

I pat Marcie on the cheek. 'Give me a day or two, kid. I'll get it to you.'

At the door, she calls my name. 'Bel.'

I turn, for one last look at the scrawny, pathetic figure with her big fish-eyes. 'What?'

'Three days. Then I tell.'

I slam the door behind me, stamp down the stairs, back out into the rain and the night again. It's got colder. I zip my jacket right up to my neck, and hurry for my tram.

We leave the Flying Horse as the cathedral clock is striking three. I feel fuzzy, warm, and rather happier with life thanks to four pints of bitter. Imelda kisses me warmly on the cheek and I wave her goodbye. I wave and wave her goodbye. I take up great scoops of the air and hurl them across towards Ricemans, towards her receding figure. I wave and wave, hopping up and down, and she's gone.

I realize that I still don't know what Imelda does for a job, although I know about her money. I never did ask JJ, did I? But there's no way I could get the money for Marcie from her. No way at all.

Just one day left.

Suddenly, something in front of McDonald's catches my eye. I squint across the road, hanging on to the rail.

A combat jacket, in the shadows of that doorway. The pedestrians bustle past him, oblivious. But his eyes are staring at me. From underneath a head of short, stumpy dreadlocks.

I want to run after Imelda and get her back. I'm on my own.

Those eyes are cutting across the street. The whole of Canterbury seems to be humming, the air like treacle. I want to turn and run, but my legs have gone flu-wobbly, and my brain just cannot send the right commands.

He is just looking at me.

And then three gossiping mothers bustle past the front of McDonald's, with their entourage of tottering toddlers and trundling pushchairs, one of which has a heart-shaped, silver balloon tied to it.

And in one blink, he's gone again.

I push my hair back from my sweating face. The sun is so bright for an October day, slicing the town into yellow light and black shadow.

I am shaking.

For the first time, I'm aware that I'm being watched.

What the hell is going on?

On the bus home from Canterbury, I call Damien.

'I've got a funny feeling,' I tell him. 'Those Fallies. Is there any way they could have traced me through you?'

It takes him a moment or two to work out what I'm on about. 'Well, my dad papers his wall with hate-mail. They know who *he* is.'

'But what about me? Or JJ?'

There's a telling pause at the other end of the line. 'Why you and JJ in particular?'

'Never mind,' I say quickly. 'Damien, my life's in need of some serious stim. What can you offer?'

Another bewildered pause. 'You're asking me?'

'Yeah. I am.'

'What happened to golden-boy JJ?'

'I bit him, and he was chocolate. All right?'

Damien gives a snorty, phlegmy laugh. 'Yeah. Right. Come round and I'll take you somewhere.'

20   *A Fragile Thing Called Trust*

The picnic table is like a great monolith being uprooted, a standing stone being stood up. Tearing up time. Slowly, it falls, and in its creaks I hear the sound of societies toppling.

Damien gives a great whoop of delight. I scream as if I'm in the front row at a gig, and I kick the table's underside. It flips over, hits the mud and splashes into the river, cutting a clean rectangle which gushes white froth.

I still have my heart thumping madly at every crossroads, every traffic-light. I'm waiting for the sight of a combat jacket and dreadlocks, with revenge in his eyes.

Damien's the only thing I've got to cling to in the wreckage. The only way I can actually feel better about all of this. I don't know what it is about him. He's sometimes almost painful to be with, but he's more alive than JJ, more vibrant. Not exactly Reconstructed Nineties Man, though. I mean, we had an exchange just now, in the pub, about his motto for living.

'Yeah, I've got one. *A woman's place is in the wrong*,' Damien says, quite earnestly, and lets loose that barking laugh of his, as he leans forward, shooting a fountain of ash all over the floor of the pub.

I fold my arms and glare contemptuously at him. 'I'm supposed to think that's funny?'

'Oh, yeah, 'cos that was the old one.' He grins, teeth hooking over his lip as usual, about to form a fricative. That, for the uninitiated, is the first F of Fuck You.

'Don't tell me. You've reinvented your motto. Re-established your credentials. Turned yourself into New Damien, same old shit in a nice new bowl?'

'Yeah,' he says, and takes a gulp of beer with an audible slurp.

I grin, lean back in my chair and press my fingers together, ready for the great philosophical contribution he's about to make. 'So. I can't wait to hear. Hit me with it.'

He lifts his finger, looks at it for a second as if trying to remember what it's doing there, then opens his eyes bright and wide as if it's all suddenly come back to him.

'This is it then,' he says, softly and earnestly. '*Hell hath no fury like a bitch with PMT.*'

You wouldn't believe it, would you? Ten million sperm to choose from, and that was the winner.

I tell you, if Damien ever gets some girl pregnant, I'm going to advise the poor cow to put the creature out of its misery. I'll find a clinic myself. I'll say they're so good I'd trust them with my own mother.

Earlier still, Damien comes to the house. Kate lets him in, with her face showing exactly what she thinks of him. He grins at her, teeth Stonehenge-askew; for a moment, I watch them, there in the hall, Damien grinning and Kate, arms folded, face hidden behind her tragi-comic mask of make-up.

I see Damien as some predatory lion and Kate as a performer, a pretender about to fail, as others have failed, in taming him.

'Don't mind her,' I say to Damien. He flops into a chair as I make some coffee, and just about restrains himself from putting his feet up on the table. 'She's just a social climber. With a social axe and social crampons, probably.'

'So, where's boy wonder?' Damien asks, pulling out a cigarette as usual.

I pluck it from his mouth, millimetres from ignition. This is the kitchen, where I ostensibly play along with them. Subversion has to be subtle, and invisible. 'He seems to have become indifferent,' I say with a shrug. Trying to sound it myself.

He grins. 'You'll have to watch yourself. Don't you think he might have found himself another bimby-fuck? Are you going to do anything about it?'

I don't meet his eye. 'What am I meant to do?'

Damien shrugs. 'Never thought you'd let anyone get one over on you.'

'No,' I tell him quietly. 'I don't believe I would.' A sudden thought occurs to me. 'You haven't got a hundred quid you could lend me, have you?'

He laughs hollowly. 'Lend you? Are you serious?'

I already regret having asked. It might lead to other questions. 'Never mind,' I mumble. Luckily, he doesn't pursue the point.

The wind's fighting us, and we love it. I turn to Damien and grin. He raises his eyebrows back at me.

'You like getting pissed, don't you?' I ask him.

'Yeah, well. You have more fun.'

'Yeah, and you can't have totally inane conversations when you're sober.' I give myself a little sniff of a laugh. 'Well, even though you try your best.'

'You think you've experienced drinking? You ain't even had my homebrew.'

'Homebrew? The last resort of the alcoholic with no taste? Please, do me a favour.'

He hits the stereo, and the car shakes to the sound of something tuneless and explosive.

'Who's this?' I ask him.

'Sic Transit,' he tells me.

They sound like four blokes hitting each other over the head with their instruments, but I'll take his word for it. 'Are they on Broken Records?' I ask, hopefully plucking out a name that he's told me before.

'Nah. They're on Accurate. They used to be on Squid, but that was only for the first E P.'

Damien's got a job now, incredibly, working in a record shop, and he's become something of a catalogue trainspotter. Broken, Extensive and Accurate are his fave labels.

The band he used to be in couldn't actually play any instruments, but that didn't seem to stop them. The problem was that whoever was in charge of choosing their name had this idea that they'd got a sense of humour, so their first name was Plus Support. That didn't work, because people were turning up at all kinds of gigs expecting to see them, and being disappointed. Then they were called Gather No Moss for about a week, until someone got the joke and realized how crap it was. Finally, they called themselves Cancelled (oh, please, someone, fix my sides up with insulation tape) and played a gig in Canterbury to precisely five people, probably due to the big sign outside the pub that said 'Live Music Tonight: CANCELLED'.

Eventually, they settled on calling themselves Boxx, which had rather less stupidity – but at the same time, less style – and recorded a demo CD called 'Life's a Beach (And I Forgot the Sunblock Cream)'.

The music pounds my skull. The light and the wind rush past me as we drive along the big coastal road. I think back to what we were saying in the kitchen.

'Tell me what to do, Damien.'

'No idea.' He sounds as if he doesn't care.

'Can I try and catch him in the act?'

Damien makes a grunting noise, and picks at the grain in the table. It's obviously not a good topic of conversation. He wanted to make a casual remark and not want me to elaborate on it. How can I help that? How can I help voicing the thoughts that are consuming me day and night?

And Damien can't know what I'm really panicking about – the thought that JJ might be whispering pillow talk, telling someone about Ashwell Heights and Birthmark.

It occurs to me that I share a secret with Marcie, and I share a bigger secret with JJ, and I don't yet share one with Damien. He's just this guy I drink with, a bit of a lad – a bit of a tosser, frankly – who's always been there.

'Imelda's having a party,' he says, tapping his unlit cigarette against his teeth. 'Maybe you'll find out more there.'

'Nah, get it right. Imelda is organizing a party – for me.'

'Yeah?' He sounds only slightly surprised. 'Might be good.' He grins. 'That Imelda. Shame, innit? She is one fit, babetastic babe. What a waste.'

'Not bad legs, either. Do you have anything to contribute today, or are you just here to drool on the table?'

'All right. I can tell you what to do. About JJ. If you wanna hear. It's pretty disgusting, though. You know how you get back at an ex's new lover?'

I get the feeling he's going to tell me. 'Go on,' I say with weary resignation.

'Hire a rapist.'

'You *what*?'

'Honestly, it was in this revenge manual I got from the library. Loads of fucking brilliant stuff in there. Translated from Japanese. It's quite common over there, apparently.'

'You – are – *kidding*.'

'Nah. Even better.' He leans forward, teeth looking suddenly even sharper. 'What you do is to get her buggered with a vibrator. Or – this is the worst one, are you ready for it?'

I open my mouth, crunching on nothing, still reeling from his suggestion. No words come out. It takes a hell of a lot to shock me, I can tell you. 'All right. Go on.'

'Get a bloody massive, randy dog to do it – '

' – I do *not* want to hear – '

'Some crazed creature on heat that'll shag anything – '

' – fuck yourself, Damien Ash, I do not – '

' – and she'll be so embarrassed, she'll never go to the police!'

There is a breathless silence. Our faces, reddened by shouting, are inches apart. Hot breath and pungent sweat. I've been repelled. Congrats. Someone's finally done it.

'I would *never* do that, Damien. Never fucking ever. It is just the most fucking gross thing I've ever heard.'

'You should get out more,' he says, leaning back with a lecherous grin.

'It's not a laughing matter, Damien.'

He raises his eyebrows. His sleek face is full of an expression I haven't seen before – something like the passion of knowledge. 'You don't like it,' he says quietly. 'You wouldn't ever do it.'

'No.'

Damien breathes deeply, and his brash, laddish voice seems to wash away like the tide, revealing something softer. 'Then whoever she is,' says Damien with quiet smugness, 'you don't hate her as much as you think you do.'

I open my mouth. Nothing comes out.

I blink, realizing what he has said. And I slump back in the chair, because it's so close to a sensible remark that it's totally thrown me.

Damien drops me off in town, my head ringing from Sic Transit.

'Later, then,' he says, raising his eyebrows at me.

I lean on the car door, gazing at that sleek, reddish face. It's got a wicked allure about it which I never noticed before, actually. Brick-red like a wall that you want to scrawl graffiti over.

'JJ,' he says, 'thinks he's a rebel. People like him aren't rebels, Bel. He holds you back, yeah? Keeps you in the middle. Just scratching the social veneer.'

Yeah, right. My stomach's tight and I'm longing to tell him. But I can't. I can never tell him.

JJ and I are bound together by a night, a face, a truth darker and stronger than anything else we will ever experience. This is why I know it is not over yet.

But I need Damien's company. I need the sleek, angry entertainment he offers me.

I go to the road outside JJ's house. Well, Imelda's house, I mean. Under the leafy suburban trees, there's a new, gleaming bus shelter. No graffiti here. It's even got an intact timetable, neatly fixed on to the wall of the shelter in a perspex square.

I sit in the shelter, slip my shades on and watch the house.

History has forced me into the role of private detective.

'Fancy a fuck, darling?'

I turn to glower at the scum with the fullest and best contempt I can muster. It's leather-jacketed, grinning broadly, under a reddish crew cut.

I look him up and down. His skin seems to be the same rubbed and cracked texture as the old leather of his jacket. His hands are plunged deep into the stretched pockets and they're rubbing against his grubby, denimed groin. Oh, please. Is it possible to be this much of a sad loser?

I lean against the bus shelter. 'You wouldn't know what to do if I said yes, would you?'

He opens his eyes wide, and his mouth slightly, looking exactly like someone who doesn't know what to do.

'A hundred quid.' I throw that in his direction, just to see how he copes.

He's rubbing harder. With a sudden flurry of activity, and a triumphant yelp, he unzips his fly and pokes out a semi-tumescent cock.

So I look down at it with my full disgust – and with a brief click and a smooth shine, the knife is out, gleaming in the afternoon light.

I watch him running, as fast as his legs can carry him. I notice he didn't have time to do his flies up first, so I rather hope he does himself a nasty injury.

I snap the knife closed.

After that little bit of excitement, I wait.

Shadows grow longer, and the light starts to thicken around me. It's only three-thirty in the afternoon, but I've got that feeling again, like the days are constricting me, like we're heading towards something big just around the corner of the next year. Hell, that's nothing new. Just perfectly normal autumnal paranoia. Season of mystery and mellow fruit fools. Conditioned by the academic calendar, I always see it as the beginning of something when all the leaves start to go crunchy and fill the pavements. So that's all it is. Nostalgia, mixed with regret.

Yeah, that's all it is. It's not as if I've got anything to be upset about, or anything like that, after all.

There he is.

The loose jacket, the floppy hair. I must admit, I feel a pang as he strolls down the gravel drive. Crunch, crunch, crunch, like he's treading the carefree dreams we once had, not giving a damn.

Still on the other side of the road, he turns and walks towards town. He checks his wallet. Puts it away again. He's off to the shops, heading into a great untrodden tinsel-decked Christmas full of new life.

We keep heading down, down towards the sea. The sky empties of detail, bit by bit, as the streets level out. The air becomes crisper, saltier, and seagulls shriek overhead.

We're joined by an invisible, taut string exactly a hundred paces long. I keep that far behind him, and he's not all that difficult to follow. Once or twice I almost slip on the leaf-slicked avenues – but he doesn't look round. I nearly get run over on the roundabout on the edge of town – but he doesn't look round. A huge, muzzled mastiff pounds against a gate as I go past, scrabbling at the lacquered wood, tearing it, demanding to come and get me, growling like Cerberus on acid. (I shiver, recalling those dogs in Ashwell Heights.) But he still doesn't look round.

In the streets of the town, dodging the sad losers with their carrier bags and their chocolate-mouthed kids – faces stained in a permanent, slack-jawed O – I find it easier to keep myself hidden. I duck and weave, keeping him no more than fifty paces in front.

He goes down Fisher Avenue – past the rank back sides of all the chip shops on the sea front – taking the short-cut to the shopping precinct.

I follow him into the large chemist-cum-department-store, and hover by the rows of multi-coloured shampoos as I watch him select some toothpaste. And then he moves over to the pharmacy counter to pay.

This is stupid. I sigh, toying with the bottle of penny-royal shampoo I'm pretending to be interested in. The lights are bright and angry. The place is full of disgusting, fish-coloured people with scabies, who seem to have brought their kids here for the afternoon in order to smack them. And he's bound to turn round and see me in a moment.

He scoops up a packet of condoms from the counter beside him and slips them into his pocket.

I'm standing there open-mouthed for a good few seconds, so I must look like one of those fucking stupid kids. I suddenly feel ridiculous, as if morality has seized me. He's paid for his toothpaste and now he's walking out of the shop. No one's making a move to stop him.

He's out of the door and absorbed by the shifting crowds on the street. I don't get to the door in time even to see which way he goes, because of a barrier of hard-edged pushchairs and baskets that suddenly seems to move my way. I push past them, aware of a screech and a sudden flurry of movement on my right. There's a cascade of crunchy cereal bars and low-fat crisps, crushed beneath a fat mother with obscene orange lipstick – this I see, flash-framed, in the briefest of glances backwards.

I'm out on the street, looking up and down, whirling round, buffeted by sweaty, stinking shoppers on all sides. A light drizzle is starting to fall, tickling my hair and neck. Everything's going grey and the seagulls are laughing overhead.

Sudden fear grips me, and I want to run back into the shop. I look up and down the street, watching for movement in every shop doorway. But there's no Dreads, no Birthmark.

Christ. I'm losing it.

21   *Down Payment*

Still nothing on the TV about Birthmark.

It's the day after, and today I have to pay Marcie her hundred.

Luckily, I can. I'm on my way.

I think back to last night.

My father sighs, as if he's drunk too deeply of the air, and leans back.

'Bel,' he says, spreading his hands, 'you're almost of an age where I can't really tell you what to do any more.'

I've got my arms folded, doing that not-quite-looking-at-him trick by playing with my hair, twisting it in front of my eyes so that he's sometimes in vision, sometimes not.

'Almost?' I mutter.

Jon sighs, takes his glasses off and spins them around in that tutorish way of his. 'I managed to save us all a great deal of embarrassment,' he says. 'I don't suppose you know Jeff Ash plays golf with Derek from the Spindle?'

'Who? The what?'

'The Spindle. The public house where you and friend Damien, in your youthful exuberance, tipped a table into the water in front of several witnesses.' He shrugs. 'Derek's the landlord there, and luckily he's known Jeff for a few years, so we were able to come to an arrangement. But I hate to think what might have come of it if you'd picked somewhere else.'

I shake my head. 'Dad, you make me sick.'

'Really?' He sounds no more than faintly surprised.

I'd expected him to shout at me, at the very least berate me for being a teenage hooligan and lock me in my room or something. I try to articulate this. 'I mean, for f– for God's sake, would you buy me out of *anything*?'

'You're my little girl,' he says calmly. 'I couldn't do the tax without you, don't forget.'

'Oh, yeah, right. I knew I was important.'

'It's my job to get you out of trouble. When you were younger, well, that was different. I had to stop you getting into it in the first place. But now, it's your problem. You're eighteen. What can I say? If you want to run away to a commune with the local drug dealer, all I can do is spell out the pros and cons to you and let you choose. And if you cause trouble, well, Jeff and I both agree that the best policy is damage limitation.'

I'm quite disgusted with him, actually. Is this the way it's done nowadays? Buying people off? 'And that's it? No fine, no grounding?'

He sighs again. 'We have a great life, Bel. We're well-off, we're warm and comfortable and I don't want anything spoiling that.'

My gaze is fixed on the way the velvet of the chair is like sand, a surface you can stroke and indent with patterns. Stupid, the way you fix on these little things when you're trying not to look at someone.

'How . . . far would you go?' I ask him, and I realize my voice has come out smaller than I intend.

'What do you mean?'

I hear the creak of his chair as he leans forward. The afternoon is still, suspended in greyness between day and night. A pre-winter afternoon, on the boundary. Rooks are cawing outside, and I shiver slightly.

'Well, suppose – I'm not, right, definitely not, but – what if I was pregnant, say?'

He shrugs. 'I'd support you, whatever you wanted to do. Anyway, I know you too well. You wouldn't get tied to a mewling and puking infant, not yet.'

All right. What if I'd stolen a car, smashed up some Travvy girl and left her for dead, then destroyed the car . . . ?

Go on, Bel, you fucking coward. Say it.

184

'What if I'd – '

Time hangs like dust in the grey room. My father lifts a hand, inviting me to continue.

'What if I'd – '

I look at him for the first time, and see his pale, grey eyes, expectant, loving. I suddenly realize I am having unconditional love fired at me in hot, radioactive streams and I'm not protected. I can only absorb and not reflect. It cancers my cells and crisps my blood to black ash. I cannot live with this love. I cannot.

I break my gaze. 'No. Nothing. Nothing. Can I go now?'

'If you want.'

'If I want? Is that it?'

'Yes,' he replies.

'I'm going to the beach. I have to think.'

He nods, picks up his newspaper. 'Take care. See you later.'

As I get to the door, I have a thought. 'Jon?'

'Mmm?'

'Can I have a party here?'

'Choose your date,' he says, and turns the page.

'What about Kate?'

'I'll sort it with Kate. All I ask from you is a guest list.'

The beach is almost deserted. My hair's being whipped up into a sticky, salty tangle, as messy as the black ganglia of seaweed under my feet.

I was right about JJ. As far as I can tell. I certainly don't intend to go and peer through his grating to see exactly how he's used his little purchase.

I sit at the edge of the water and skim stones.

There must be ghosts around me, whispering about the people I know – the people I can no longer trust?

They all had their own reasons for being there, that night at Ashwell Heights. I went because it was fun, and moral considerations didn't come into it. Damien, I think, veers more towards the immoral – he takes a sordid delight in smashing up the trappings of society. Marcie's

185

just too stupid to know whether what she's doing is right or wrong. And JJ? He just came along for the ride, an innocent abroad. Because I was there. Or that's what I thought at the time.

And now, JJ and I are trapped together in the memory of a haunted night, a wasteland of rain and fire. Whether we like it or not, we are still joined by a secret which neither of us wants. I no longer see him every day. I no longer know how his mind is working from minute to minute, what he is likely to do. I wonder what he murmurs to her, whoever she is, in soft and warm moments.

Damien and I are linked by mutual hedonism. We both take pleasure in the turning of tables, and such things. But I feel uneasy about the way I'm caught up with him. He's like a drug, or the dark side of me. He's like a beautifully detailed painting of a blood-soaked battlefield.

And Marcie, too, is trapped with me. Caught in the mesh of the blame game, started as such a small thing all those weeks ago. It could go on, I realize in horror. If I give her this hundred, it has to end here. One way or another, it has to end.

My life is being over-complicated by the people who were my friends. Each one of them has me snared as firmly as if my feet were in a rusty man-trap. I'm being controlled.

Two hours later, I'm watching Kate and Jon, canoodling disgustingly down the end of the garden, down by the bonfire. I know what the conversation is about. He's trying to soothe her. He's winning her round about my impending party.

Yeah, so they're swathed in smoke and in each other. I snarl quietly to myself, but I've got a satisfied grin on my face as I stroll along the upper landing, past Kate's blue porcelain vases and lacquered tables and hanging baskets bursting with dried flowers.

In the room she shares – for now – with my dad, I find her handbag, which contains just twenty pounds. Hell. Not worth taking.

Five minutes later, I'm in front of my mirror. I've crossed my legs, my legs are criss-crossed, with a mesh of black diamonds from my most tawdry pair of tights. My movements are constricted by the most uncomfortable of little black dresses, and glossy black high-heels pinch my feet. I have put up with discomfort before, and I shall do so again. I grin into the mirror. My silver earrings spin like little mirror-balls.

I'm putting my lipstick on. The radio is jabbering away in the background. To my annoyance, it's one of those stupid public-guilt ads again, trying to persuade the middle classes to sponsor the Third World. Some tosser's talking about his journey to the office, and saying how hectic it all is, bumper-to-bumper, all these people behaving as if getting to work is the most important thing in their lives. And then, as if in a sudden epiphany of conscience, he remembers little Kwame, the African child he's been blackmailed into sponsoring, who doesn't even have fresh water every day. We're supposed to experience a vicarious 'Aaaah' moment as he comes over all caring and perspective-hit. We're informed that the organization still has 400 children 'available' for sponsoring – like a sale, Last 400 Must Go! – and we're expected to give them a call and grab one off the shelves. Well, they can fuck off. There's too many people in the world as it is.

I scowl into the mirror. I finish applying my lipstick, grab my bag and wink at myself. 'See you later.'

Not Domingo, tonight. Too many memories.

No, instead I get a taxi right down the sea front, along through the next town and to Paradise City, major haunt of the techno-crazed, Lycra-sheathed and generally over-excited of the South Coast. Half the clubbers of the region don't know it exists, and that's the way the other half want it to stay. I only found it because Damien gave me some covert flyers from the record shop. (I don't know what he imagined I'd do with them. Maybe he thinks I'm still in the schooldazed habit of sticking them on folders next to Ryan Giggs and the well-eyebrowed Gallagher brothers.)

They're a whole subculture, these coastal clubs. Tackiness sheened with surface gloss. Drinks at London prices without London style. Posh and pretty Sussex girls called Hannah and Pippa and Emma, shimmying and shimmering in silver mini-dresses. Or 'Babe' T-shirts tight across their nipples. Tripping in the fantastic light, stretching under the strobes. And later, puking bad-E bile into cracked Armitage Shanks, before rinsing their mouths and going home to Daddy.

I'm reasonably confident of not being turned down by the bouncers – although their system is a law unto itself. I don't intend to pay for the ten-quid ticket myself, though. No way.

I lean against the cold brick wall along from the pounding entrance, raising my eyebrows at any groups of men who pass. Some of the young posers pause. They suck thoughtfully on their cigarettes, making little flares of hesitation in the darkness, before lumbering on after their mates, deciding a pint of Stella is a better option than me. One or two laugh raucously after making secret little comments in each other's ears, so I just look down at their groins with disgust and contempt, then back up to their eyes, holding that expression.

Soon, as I knew there would, there comes a boy who approaches me. He's not bad-looking, but he's got gingerish blond hair with a centre parting. He asks me in a slight Scottish lilt if I am going in, and I shrug, telling him I might be, if I could afford it. Within seconds, he is snared, and he's paid for us both. I smile, and I'm all over him, stroking his leather jacket as the crowds thunder down the stairs into this outer vestibule of the Inferno. I'm telling him my name's Jane, saying I've just got enough to buy him a drink when we get in.

When the wall of smoke and sweat hits us and the harsh, industrial noise swallows everyone up, I cut myself adrift from his arm, slipping into the reddish darkness, ignoring his plaintive wails.

Now we enter the second stage. I need to pick a target more carefully.

First, I shoulder my way to the bar. My dress is still tight and uncomfortable and I have to keep hoisting the shoulder back up. I manage to get served fairly swiftly by putting on my best smile. After paying the price of a decent meal for a vodka and tonic, I mix with the shadows, holding my glass like a lantern, and move up to the gantry between the two dance-floors.

I slink discreetly between the slobbering couples to observe the Bacchanalian frenzy below me. I've got a very precise idea of what I am looking for, and I'm not sure that I'm going to find it.

I can feel clouds of boiling moisture gushing from the maelstrom of clubbers like some primal energy, a creature raised from another dimension by the whirling of their arms. And then there is the noise, the bedlam so intense that it seems to transcend normal hearing and instead go straight for the nerve-centres. The allure of Paradise City, so I'm told, is its wildly eclectic mixture of styles, but at the moment, we're in jungle phase. One record merges seamlessly with another, cranked up into Uzi-fast drum rolls. I can see, in flashes of light, the tiny figure of the DJ – like some celestial techno-mage behind the great ebony curves of his decks – bobbing frantically, mixing, matching and scratching. Piercing whistles sometimes cut through the throbs, or are they screams? It's so hard to tell. And through it all, the heat gets thicker and every movement drenches me in a tropical sweat.

I lean on the slippery rail, blinking the smoke out of my eyes. I sip my rapidly warming drink and move half-heartedly from side to side as something I vaguely recognize comes on. Goldie, is it? Hmmm. I start to wonder whether this was such a good idea. I'm not going to find what I need here.

The DJ lifts the mike, almost eating it with his big black mouth, and the words boom out, stentorian but crunched-up like it's the voice of God(zilla). 'All right, massive, massive.' I've never been a particular fan of this pretentious, surface culture, so I don't know what's so fucking massive. His ego, probably. He's giving out 'respect' to some posse or other. Again, I've never understood why gangs of clubbers qualify as posses, nor the criteria for getting respect. I imagine it's something to do with having the right designer clothes and 'attitude'.

I sip my vodka and sigh.

'Sheep, aren't they?'

The speaker is a young man, twenty-ish, with blond hair and wire-framed specs. He raises his eyebrows at me and I smile uncertainly back.

I grin at him, sipping my drink. 'They all need a sheepdog. Or a dip.'

He sighs, nodding as if under a great melancholy. 'It doesn't need much for the pack instinct to take over.'

All right, so I'm sizing him up. His voice is calm, educated. His shirt and paisley waistcoat look pretty expensive, and I'm fairly sure those are designer lenses. A graduate professional, I reckon. A man at home with sleek cars and pints of real ale – someone who, given the choice, would rather be at home listening to CDs of Paul Weller or the Beautiful South.

OK, so this is as good a place as any to start. And you can just about hear yourself think, up here.

I open my mouth. I close it again, then decide to say it anyway. 'So why did you come, if you hate it so much?'

He sips his drink coolly and raises elegant eyebrows at me. 'I might ask you the same question.'

Might you, indeed? Great. Sounds like you got that one straight out of a book. So, now what? Ask him what music he likes? Never a good move, as he might mention someone totally unknown, and go on about their difficult third EP for half an hour. Or we could opt for the *Pulp Fiction* school of conversation and babble about names of hamburgers and the best way to shine your shoes. Bollocks to that – I believe in getting to the point, don't I?

I lean forward so that I'm closer than would normally be comfortable. There's a scent of some rather nice aftershave around him. I quite fancy him, actually.

'Would you pay a hundred pounds,' I ask him, opening my eyes wide in what I hope is a seductive gaze, 'to have sex with me?'

He laughs first, looks down at the throbbing throng below, blushing slightly. Then he looks back at me again, sees my perfectly serious, enticing face and holds my gaze. For that all-important moment.

Beneath us, the music suddenly cleans its sound, is sheened with synths. The club slides (via Baby D) into its classic Euro-pop hour. And still he doesn't break eye contact. I feel hot.

'Well, I – I mean.' He takes a gulp of his cocktail – more than he intended, judging by the way he has to blink back the impact. 'It's not the sort of thing I was expecting to be asked,' he admits eventually, and pushes his glasses back up into the little white dent at the top of his nose.

I rather like him, actually. I grin, and swivel from side to side ever so slightly, drinking deeply and slowly from my glass and letting my cheeks flush with the scarlet of promise.

The beats hammer beneath us, shifting into Ace of Base. Incongruous Nordic reggae, icy and blond.

'Don't tell me,' I say to him, with a quick, full smile. 'You'd thought that if you kept me talking for long enough, bought me a few more drinks, had a dance and then another little drink or two . . .' I move even closer so that I'm almost nestling into his body. 'You thought you'd eventually have got it for free?'

His mouth makes incoherent sounds of protest, but his smile is as broad as my own.

I laugh. I'm surprised, actually. It sounds genuine, unembittered. Must be the drink. 'Good try,' I tell him.

He shrugs. He turns away briefly, carrying the strobes in his lenses, then turns back to me as the light whirls and fragments over our bodies. 'You seemed to be rather nice,' he says with another shrug.

'I am, when you get to know me. I just think it's a bit pointless standing here for six hours, shouting into each other's faces over music that neither of us really likes all that much, drinking over-priced cocktails – and probably dancing to Whigfield, or something equally horrendous, yeah? – just so that we reach the stage where you ask me for a drunken fumble up my Channel Tunnel. I mean, it's all a bit fucking pointless, isn't it?'

He looks deep in thought for a minute, then laughs again and runs a hand through his short blond hair. He shrugs. 'I don't know. I suppose I'd never really thought of it like that before.'

'No, well, there you are. And the truth is, that I need a hundred quid, and you could probably rather do with a shag. Girlfriend just left you?'

I throw the last bit in as a hopeful spice, like that stuff labelled 'Mixed Herbs' that you put in each and every pasta dish because you know it won't do any harm.

He pulls a face. 'For the moment,' he says in a hollow voice, and drains his glass.

I finish mine off too. 'Right, then. That settles it. Shall we go?'

'Look, I think – don't get me wrong, you're very pretty and all that, but I just – '

'Just what? Don't think I'm worth paying for? Look, think of it as a consultancy. A small business enterprise.' Hands on hips, I gaze up at him, seeing myself twice in his glasses. 'I mean, just look at the market competition. You can spend thirty quid and get some slapper riddled with diseases, smelling of rubber and cheap soap. Or you can have me. A nice girl. The sort of girl your mummy would be glad to meet. Mmm?' I tap him on the cheek. He's quite stubbly, but soft at the same time. 'Come on. Let's go.'

I grab his hand and lead him from the balcony. He doesn't resist. As we get to the cloakroom, it starts up – the familiar da-da-da-da of 'Saturday Night' by Whigfield.

I just love being right.

It was that git at the bus-stop who first put the idea into my head – when I, just as a joke, told him it would be a hundred quid for me. And it came to me, after I saw JJ so casually preparing himself for a night without me, showing how little he really valued me. I realized that I could very easily know my own value, and know it in cold hard cash, thus solving a major problem.

If Marcie ever knew, I doubt she would appreciate the irony. But it's different from any time she ever did it. I was careful, I was discreet, I was choosy. And I had a particular purpose in mind.

He saw, he came, he paid. I have to say that it wasn't exactly an unpleasant experience. He had expert fingers, and managed to find places that I thought men were oblivious to.

I've read about it, how these women detach themselves from the act. How it becomes just a transaction. Jesus, I couldn't. That was the problem.

Anyway, Chris – that was the guy's name – was really decent about it, actually. Decent, fucking hell, what a word. Didn't think I'd ever use it, certainly not about a bloke. I made him go to the cashpoint before we went back to his, just so that I could be sure. He put fifty in my purse before we started and got the other fifty out almost straight away afterwards.

My general impression of him turned out to have been more or less right. He had a little flat not far from the harbour, quite tidy and tasteful. A couple of large plants – he said one was called Robert, and I laughed politely. (Robert Plant, get it?) Athena prints on the white plaster walls. Nice hi-fi system, wooden coffee-table with wicker mats. Books abandoned on the sofa – William Boyd and some sci-fi thing.

And yes, he was really gentle, almost too much so. He kissed me at the end, and stroked me, and said in a small-boy voice that it was a shame he wouldn't be seeing me again.

I shrugged and said something about how things might have been different. He blinked – he'd not put his glasses back on – and I looked again at that little white indentation at the top of his nose, and the slight, untrimmed bits of stubble on his face. It occurred to me that maybe these might be the kind of things you learn to know and love about a spouse, a lifelong partner. You realize that they're not perfect, but because they're nice and they put up with you, then you come to love their little defects.

Maybe my dad loves Katebitch for her fat thighs and her red lips.

My mother was a sword-thin woman, with albino-blonde hair. She was elvishly beautiful, but horrifyingly pale, as if someone had turned the colour down on her picture. She was painted in pastels. And she faded from this world.

I can't see Kate fading. She's ominously, colourfully present. Splashing herself on the world in bright oils – that emerald garden, those chocolate flowerbeds, those strawberry tablecloths. Maybe that's it – my father is so frightened of losing a partner again that he's found himself someone so hideously larger-than-life that she can't possibly disappear.

And I stared into the darkness, and lay awake in the stranger's flat, with his money in my bag and his body slumbering beside me under a soft duvet.

I breathed strange-smelling air – pot-pourri of some sort – and listened to the alien sounds. Cars on the sea front. The distant hiss of the sea. The occasional shriek, a crunch of pebbles from the beach.

I lay awake, wondering what kind of person I was, thinking – as I had so many times in these past few weeks – that I ought to hate and despise myself, but feeling nothing inside. A hollow. I would say it was like hunger, only hunger needs to be satisfied and is only temporary.

I looked at him, the stranger who had given me my one and only taste of prostitution, and wondered how familiar that close-cropped head might have become if I had met him on an ordinary night out. If I had met him instead of JJ. I would have got to know the name of that aftershave, rather than just its scent, and I might have got him some for Christmas in a little cardboard gift-box. I might have got talking about William Boyd, or that sci-fi author, and started to read their novels just because Chris liked them. I might have found out what his favourite children's TV programme was, and bought it for him on video. (I've always wanted someone to do the same for me. Mine was *Willo the Wisp* – it was just so bloody surreal and psychedelic, I could watch it for hours.) These night noises could have become as softly familiar as his dressing-gown and his sheets. They might have moulded themselves around my life and comforted me. But no, it was never to be; I was fated to be his fuck, and that alone.

I lay awake, swaddled in thick sadness, for hours and hours, watching the orangeade-light from the street and feeling that old numbness deep within my soul.

Twice, I almost slept. Once, I nearly touched his shoulder to turn him round, wake him, tell him everything.

Everything.

But I left, in silence, before the break of dawn.

22   *Shadows*

We meet in a cold, grey no-man's-land, on the footbridge above the roaring motorway.

It isn't quite raining, but drizzle hazes the world, makes the air taste cold and damp above the petrol. Underneath the bridge, the traffic thunders on: great slabs of freight trucks heading for Dover, cars of all colours, buses with sleek black windows.

I mount the last steps and I'm up here on this giant span of concrete. She's there at the other end: scraggy blonde hair blowing in the wind, stripy stockings, hands in the pockets of her black PVC coat.

I smile wryly and walk towards her. She approaches me, and we meet in the middle of the bridge.

We are here at Marcie's own request. It was quite strange. I called her, told her I had the money. She told me to bring it round, and I was halfway to the tram-stop when my mobile went again. It was Marcie again, telling me this location. She said exactly which junctions it was between – I didn't think her capable of that much precision. So I had to get a cab out to the edge of town, worryingly close to the wasteland where we left Birthmark. I got out on the nearest road bridge, in the grey land of open skies and swirls of tarmac threading round each other and, in the distance, a half-finished hotel site dotted with yellow JCBs.

I'm opposite those hollowed eyes again. I can see that she still looks terrible. Scrawny, waif-thin. Her eyes and mouth seem too big for her face, as if they're stretching the skin to tearing point.

'Marcie,' I say to her, 'you don't look too good.'

'I'm fine.' Her gaze, I notice, doesn't quite meet mine. She's always looking at a point just beyond me, or just to one side above the thunderous motorway. 'Have you got it?' she asks.

'Yes. I've got it.'

She holds out a hand. Her nails are painted a thick black.

I put the envelope into her hand. 'Quits now. Right?'

She opens the envelope and peers in, thumbing each one of the ten-pound notes.

When she doesn't answer me, I feel myself growing angrier. 'Marcie, you stupid little bitch – '

'How'd you get it?' she asks casually.

'What?' I'm irritated. She's caught me off-guard.

'The money. You said all yours was tied up in them trust funds and things. How'd you get it?'

'A commercial transaction. All right? In other words, it's none of your fucking business, Marcie!'

She shrugs, reseals the envelope. 'All right,' she says, and stuffs the envelope inside her coat. 'I'll go now.'

I don't know what makes me stay. I could have just shrugged, said, Fine, right then, and turned and walked back along the bridge and left her.

'Look, Marcie,' I say awkwardly. 'Is everything all right?'

She's turning to go, and now she turns back, her face hostile and suspicious. 'Yeah,' she says, scowling. 'Why shouldn't it be?'

I shrug. 'Fine, I . . . just wondered. I only ever seem to see you these days when you want something, that's all.'

She shoots a contemptuous glare at me, and turns to leave.

'Look, are you . . . doing anything on Saturday?' I don't know why I've asked. Maybe I've just got this strange desire to have as many people of all kinds there as possible.

'Workin', maybe,' she mutters reluctantly.

This is a surprise. 'You've got something?' I say, trying not to sound too shocked. Hurriedly, I move on. 'Look, Imelda's throwing a party for me. Why don't you come?'

'I'll think about it.'

'Yes, you do that.' The wind blows cold around the discomfort of our silence. 'It'll . . . have got going by about ten o'clock,' I add, hoping for a response.

'What will?'

'The party.'

'Oh. Yeah.'

Eventually, I clear my throat and turn to go. 'Right, then. Be seeing you, Marcie.'

She nods silently, hands thrust into her black coat. She is watching me, now, intently and perhaps with a small amount of puzzlement. I find her gaze quite unnerving, and I keep looking over my shoulder until I reach the steps at the end of the bridge. I look back one last time, and she is still there, motionless.

She's got the look of someone who knows too much about me.

I don't like that.

I have to see Damien again, before Saturday. Obviously, there's a lot I'm not going to tell him, but I want him to know he was right about one thing.

I slip into Damien's car and I feel it accelerate before my bum's even on the seat. In fact, before I even realize it's a different car.

'What is this?' I ask him in astonishment, marvelling at the leg-room, the tinted windows.

'Like it?' He looks smug.

'Well, yeah.'

'Mm-hmm.' We're driving out of town, along the high, old coastal road, with the sea shimmering off to our right. 'We'll have to lose it. They might miss it before long.'

'Ah. Right. You stupid fuck, Damien.' It's a half-hearted curse, though, sour and drippy like an ice-cream that's been left in the sun too long. 'Where did it come from?'

'Olympus Hotel car park. It's the Conservative Club AGM today, didn't you know?' He flashes me one of his wobbly, toothy grins. 'They'll all be in there all day.' He sighs with contentment and moves up a gear.

I decide to forget my misgivings and just enjoy the ride. I

have to tell him something else, though. 'About JJ. You were right.'

'Yeah?' He sounds surprised. I realize it isn't because he's right – Damien just naturally assumes that all the time – but rather because I have been satisfied of the truth. He's obviously dying to know if I found JJ in a mass of thrashing limbs and sweaty sheets in his basement flat.

'I saw him buying some rubbers. Didn't use them with me. Said he hated the way they feel, and I thought he was telling the truth.' I know Damien cannot see my eyes behind my shades, so I still haven't weakened myself with any confession of emotion or anything stupid like that. Wouldn't be good.

'Uh-huh,' says Damien.

I lean back in the seat, letting the throbbing of the engine massage my thighs. 'Come on, go a bit faster.'

Later. The sun's getting low in the sky. We've bought a bottle of vodka and it's swinging from Damien's fingers.

First of all, he wants to know why we've stopped here, and he's angry. I just say I wanted to, though. We leave the car in a side-lane, with the plates obscured by a few handfuls of leaves.

As soon as I push the old wooden door and breathe the air through the crack, I know the place isn't used any more. It smells of cloth, and that soft, pulpy smell of old wood, together with something more pungent that I just can't place. My footsteps are gunshot-loud in the nave. Damien, reluctantly, slopes in behind me, shivering, and I tell him to shut the door.

'What are we doing in here?' His voice is no more than a hiss, but he lets the door slam with a boom that shakes the dust, and sends a fountain of pigeons shooting towards the roof. I jump, just for a moment.

We wait, tasting the dusty air, until they have settled, cooing and twittering. And then we continue.

The font is encrusted with splattery pigeon-droppings, white and grey and lumpy like solidified lava or something. It looks strangely bright in the feeble light which struggles through the windows.

I stand in the nave, arms folded, and look around. 'I just want to think for a bit,' I tell him. 'Bring that vodka.'

We sit in one of the back pews. It's quite cold, and we need our coats and gloves as we pour the vodka into the two halves of a blue plastic card-index box which we found in the glove compartment. Well, it's better than drinking from the bottle.

'I'm quite worried about Marcie,' I tell him after a while.

Damien shrugs. 'People are always worried about Marcie. It doesn't seem to improve her life any, does it?'

'Yeah, but come on. You know her better than I do.'

He sighs, and I pass him the bottle for a refill. It seems to have been nicely chilled just by sitting on the stone floor of the church. He takes it and pours, and the glugging, trickling sound echoes through the huge space. Overhead, the pigeons flutter, probably puzzling over these strange creatures who have come to invade their space.

'She's just getting by,' Damien says. 'On the edge, you know? One meal away from being like those creatures in the subways.'

'Does she ever come to you for anything?' I don't know why I'm so curious, now. I've never really asked Damien anything like this before.

'Don't be stupid.' He glances briefly at me. His florid face looks paler in this place, his eyes darker and more intelligent. 'She's too proud.'

'But she does have a job now, right?'

'Am I expected to know that?'

He sounds a bit defensive. I suppose that should worry me, but I don't let it. I shrug. 'Well, I just thought you might.'

He sips his vodka slowly, the blue plastic box obscuring his face for a moment. When he lowers it, he blows a long and visible breath, like a jet of smoke. This seems to remind him that he needs a cigarette, so he starts fumbling for one. As he lights it, his eyes narrow. He's obviously thinking hard about something. 'You're suddenly very interested in Marcie.'

I look down, not meeting his eye. I gulp back the last of my vodka and it burns my throat, filling me inside with a prickly, acidic warmth. 'Oh, I just . . . worry.'

'You shouldn't,' says Damien with surprising sharpness. 'She gets by.'

'Yeah, I know – '

'You know she's bulimic?'

Well, I didn't. But it doesn't exactly come as a surprise. I shrug.

'Terrible for your teeth,' he adds with a kind of morbid glee. 'All that acid vomit.'

'Yeah. Thanks for, er, bringing that up.' There's a silence, broken only by the eternal twittering of the pigeons. 'Look, she . . . did mention some kind of job. Maybe things are better for her now?'

Damien sighs. Serpents of smoke bite at the rafters.

I'm looking at the pew in front of us and I realize that many have been here before us. 'DAZ, April 1995', is carved into the wood, engraved with firm down-strokes. Next to that, in fresh-looking black marker-pen, is a jaunty little poem:

Sex is evil
Sex is sin
Sin's forgiven
So get stuck in!

I remember something similar from the bogs at school. Very original, I'm sure.

'I don't ask too much,' says Damien. He's looking around for something to tap his cigarette on. 'She goes off sometimes, won't tell me where she's going. Sometimes she won't answer the phone for a day or two. I don't usually worry. It's the way she is.'

'She seems to have money.'

I realize what I've said, now. That there is something hanging between us, between the lines, between the pews. Hazing the air like Damien's smoke. I wonder if he will pursue it.

'I said, she seems to have money.'

He tilts his cigarette back, sucking the worst out of it in that way of his. He lowers his head again, sighs deeply. Shrugs. 'Not my problem,' he says quietly.

I don't really notice how long we are in the church, but the light is starting to fade by the time we stagger out, feeling our way like the blind.

The air tastes of a damp autumn evening, mulchy and peaty. The sun is sinking, scattering orange light through a lattice of clouds.

Damien exhales deeply and leans on a gravestone. Below us, the slope down into the valley is thronged with the dark outlines of graves, like a watchful army.

'Fuck,' Damien mutters. 'I can't remember where we . . .' He waves his hand absently in the air. 'Left. Left it.'

'Left the car?' I offer. My head's swimming, but I'm aware that my mouth is so dry it's difficult to speak. 'Best thing. C'mon.'

'Jus' minute.' Damien lurches away into the shadows and I hear the sound of a zip. Giggling and vaguely intrigued, I suppose, I lean on a couple of gravestones – my arms round them as if they're a pair of drunken mates – and peer at him. He's unleashing a steaming jet of piss against one of the newer, smoother stones. I sigh in resignation and slide against the nearest resident, slumping there in the place of rest, my back against the stone, till he's finished.

He comes lumbering over to me, grabbing the gravestones for stability. I wrinkle my nose as I catch sight of something unpleasant and pink poking out from a still half-opened zip.

'You know . . . what I don't understand?' Damien begins.

'Usually, yes. Come on.'

I can hardly remember asking him about Marcie. I'm sure he said something important, but I can't remember what it was.

We move on. Time seems to come in fits and starts.

I'm with Damien. Our legs dangle over nothingness. The wind from far across the planet hurtles into the pier at the End of the World and makes its phantoms sing, freezes our bones. I shiver, and my eyes prowl the glittering coastline for the future-ghost in her silver cloak and her shades.

Several fathoms below us – I estimate it, the thought whizzing through my head and bouncing off the insides like a pinball – is the angry sea. High above us, a few stars peer out from behind the clouds.

'Church,' Damien mutters. 'Why were we in a church?'

' . . . phhwwwhhh . . .'

'What?'

I wasn't aware I'd made a sound. I think back a bit. I hear myself making a strange noise. 'Aaah. Nothing. You should've seen last time.'

'Last time?' He turns his head quite slowly, but I sense a twitch of suspicion – of envy?

'Oh . . . forget it.'

'What did you do in a church? Get married?'

'Yeah, 'course . . . Christ, imagine getting married drunk.'

'Mm.' Damien muses upon this for a while. 'And imagine waking up . . .'

'With your nuptials toasted.'

'Bad enough waking up next to a stumper.' He exhales deeply.

I roll the word around in my head for a second or two, listening to the static hiss of the sea, the water communicating with the sky. Behind us, salt air rusts and rusts the pier as it has done for year upon year. You can almost hear the metal creaking under the strain.

'Stumper?' I eventually repeat.

'Well . . . you know, women . . . Sorry,' he says, wiping his mouth, 'but you're not, like, well – '

'Just get on with it, Damien.'

'Well, you know how some are two-pinters, and three-pinters.'

'I'm familiar with the term.' I'm putting myself into Damien's head-space for a minute or two. And what a filthy and lonely place it is. 'You see a girl across a room and think what a dog she is. One pint later, you think she's not too bad. Two pints later, you'll have her. Right?'

'Right. Very sick-sunct . . . Sinc-suct. Anyway. A stumper, righ'?

. . . It's when you wake up next to her and she 'sleep on your arm, righ'? And you'd, like, rather gnaw your own sodding arm off . . . than wake her up.'

I should never have hoped for more, really.

A bit later, Damien says, 'How did we get here?'

'We got a bus back to town and . . . we walked down here.'

'Ah.'

Silence, but for the sea. Behind us, the town does not sleep. The babble and the clink of the pubs and arcades comes skimming across the water.

I don't know what it is that makes me turn, but when I do, something skitters from the shadows, rattling on the latticed door to the arcades.

'Damien! Someone's there!'

His reactions are dulled, but I haul him to his feet. He immediately slumps back again, but I can't be bothered with him. I race to the other side and in the glimmer from the shore I glimpse a figure scuttling along the pier.

Seawards.

Strange, that. Me, I'd run back towards the shore.

So I give chase. My feet are thudding on the old wood. It's almost like the whole bloody thing's shaking under me. My throat's acid and burning with that hot-cold sensation of running in winter air. I skid to a halt beside another of the arcade entrances. My own breathing is headphone-loud, my heart a bass boom in tune with the sea.

Behind me, great lumbering footsteps shake the wooden floor again.

I turn, going instinctively for my knife. A dark, broad shadow is coming towards me, the coastal lights picking out his hugeness.

It's only Damien. A very unfit and sweating Damien, his coat making him look bigger, bulkier, more threatening. Inside my pocket, I relax the grip on my knife.

He stands there, blinking stupidly at me.

'Someone was watching us, Dame. I don't like people watching me, especially not when I haven't been consulted.'

'Maybe . . . they . . . were fishing.' He slumps against the latticed iron gate to the amusements, and it rattles like gunfire as he slumps, exhausted, to the floor.

'You ever thought of getting in shape?'

'I walk to work. It's enough.'

He's a bloody liar, too. Damien's idea of exercise is to chew his sandwiches a bit more vigorously.

I notice that the latticed gate is loose. I kick it, and the metallic rattle bounces across the pier, across the endless sea. I prod at the lock and it practically crumbles in my hand, smearing my palm with rust.

'Dame,' I mutter to him. 'Look.' I kick him and he moves aside. When he looks up and sees what I'm doing, he heaves himself to his feet.

'It's never used any more,' he growls, gesturing vaguely at it. 'None of it. They closed it down and forgot about it.'

I pull at the gate and it opens with a hellishly loud creak. I turn to Damien and grin. 'Just a little look?'

He doesn't look happy. 'You said you saw someone – '

'Yeah, and I'd like to know what they want.' I raise my eyebrows at him. 'Wouldn't you?'

Damien, breathing heavily, pushes his hair back. His big, burly body's swaying from side to side. 'You asked about you and JJ. Didn't you?'

'What?' He's irritated me, now.

A big, wonky grin steals across his face. 'When you phoned me on the way back from Canterbury. You asked me if they could have found out about you and JJ. Now I wonder why?' He leans forward in a half-drunken leer, a mixture of lechery and delight at my discomfort – I haven't got time for this.

'I'll tell you. Sometime, maybe.'

I kick open the gate to the arcade. We're in what is effectively the central strip of the pier, where all the amusements are housed. It's covered with a glass roof. I look up and see that it's spattered with dirt and pigeon shit.

Light scatters in diamonds over ancient, still machines. It's a museum in here, and it smells of old wood, oil and the sea. Machines stand guard. A row of old one-armed bandits like chunky, oblong robots. A little further on, in the centre of the pier, there seems to be a tank of dead tropical fish, frozen in time. The whole place is washed with a greenish half-light, as if the sea is reaching out to reclaim the place. It's like being at the bottom of a swimming-pool.

I move closer, my breath echoing through the hall, conscious of Damien just behind me. The shadows shift as I move round the tank, and I see what it actually is – one of those cabinets filled with multi-coloured soft toys. They lie there, silent and still, a metal grabber suspended above them.

'Sad-uh,' says Damien, and his hiccup at the end of the syllable reverberates around the hall.

I peer over the tank full of soft toys, wondering how long they have been here. They're not especially attractive, any of them – they've all got garish pink or green fur, and they're of indeterminate species.

'Lovely,' says Damien scornfully. 'What are we doing here?'

'I don't know.' I'm looking into the shadows, and I'm listening. All I can hear is Damien's harsh, alcoholic breathing and the soft wash of the sea. 'Come on, let's have a look round.'

'Why?' Damien sounds bored.

'Various reasons.' I'm whispering, but it sounds amplified. 'Because we shouldn't be here.' I lift my head, taste the musty air of this decayed paradise. 'And because – '

Laughter. From hell.

Demonic, cackling laughter filling the dim space, reaching out from the shadows to ensnare us. It cackles on and on, and it won't stop.

After my initial terror, it dawns on me that the noise is repeating in a loop. It's not natural, it's mechanical.

I see a flash of movement over to my left, and I leave Damien's side to go and look at it. He shambles after me and finds me with hands on hips, nodding at the bouncing figure of a laughing-policeman puppet in a glass booth. This thing must be ancient. It bobs there, its horrible plastic face bouncing in the dimness, a ghoul guarding this lair.

Damien wrinkles his nose in disgust. 'How does this thing work?'

'You put money in the slot, stupid. Same as anything.'

There's a crash behind us.

I whirl round, just in time to see a flash of dark-green slipping back out into the night.

I'm there, right behind it.

The figure's got a long way by the time I get out, but I can see him running back along the pier now, towards the shore.

I nod to myself.

Night is starting to envelop the town now, and I'm conscious of a harsh dryness in my throat accompanying the aches in my chest. My face feels red and tingling as I turn to Damien, who's half-heartedly followed me out.

'So,' he says, 'what was it?'

'Just some old codger. I think we frightened him off.'

I don't know what makes me say that.

We head back to land and wait for the tram, ready to ride it ticketless, as we know there won't be any inspectors at this time of night. Damien's prattling. The town's struggling into what passes for nightlife, with taxis crawling like beetles along the prom. I'm not really bothered about any of it.

Bel Archard is thinking, you see.

Something made her keep stuff back from Damien, even in her current befuddled state. Unusual, that. She'll analyse it when she's more sober. Almost as if that beach-ghost from the future was watching from out on the grey waves, protecting her from . . . something. Or maybe it was just an instinct, just her edginess around him when he's had a bit to drink.

Whatever the reason, I didn't tell Damien what I'd actually seen legging it back towards the shore. A gawky, long-limbed figure in an unmistakable snot-green combat jacket, and a harshly pruned set of dreadlocks.

So they are watching me.

They might be watching JJ, too.

I've no way of knowing.

23 *Truth or Dare*

JJ's Aunt Imelda silently offers me her joint and I take it with the lightest of touches.

The CD's playing *So Tough* by Saint Etienne, great music for this sort of thing. (I always wondered about that title. Is it an assertion of willingness to face the trials of the world: 'I'm so tough'? Or a get-lost tail-end of a playground fight: 'You ain't 'aving none, so tough'?) I always liked them when I was in school, and furthermore, I think 'Sarah Cracknell' is a deeply cool name. Like one of those chocolates you have at Christmas with a smooth coating and a no-nonsense nutty interior.

'I couldn't believe that about the pub table,' I tell her, 'even from my dad. What the fuck is this, the acceptable face of middle-class vandalism? I mean, just what do I have to do to get noticed these days?'

Imelda giggles, and takes another swig of water. 'Kill someone, I suppose,' she offers with a shrug and a jangle of bangles.

I glance at her sideways; but her expression and tone are just the same as normal. Just a meaningless comment.

Jesus Christ, it's like walking on the edge of my own knife. If I ever thought that he'd told her . . . I mean, she's like his mum or whatever. Or big sister, or both. I want to tell her about being at the pier, about being watched by someone who had to be Dreads. But that would mean spilling the whole sorry story, throwing it up over her like a bad meal.

I take a big gulp of air and draw in the smoke, watching the glowing ash, and then I sink into the cushions, handing the roll-up back to Imelda.

The room's foggy, like some period film set, Sherlock Holmes or something. Yeah, well, he enjoyed the odd number too, although he went for stronger stuff. Like Marcie does.

I don't know why I called Imelda. It must be 'cos she cared about me, that time in the cathedral. And she was so good to me that night in the Arcade. I snigger, remembering how JJ was going to leave them there, unpunished. Even then, Damien and I were united in something, as were Imelda and I.

She was happy for me to come right over, but I said I wanted to talk to her, and her alone, and asked if she could ring me when JJ was out of the house. Half an hour later, I was very grateful to get her call. JJ had said he was going down to his flat and that she shouldn't expect him back until the morning.

I felt a chill, of course, at the words, thinking of him there with some bimby, using the little packet I saw him steal. Or maybe even another, by now, using them up. One, two, three.

Imelda. I almost forgot to number her among my friends, and I really should. She stares at me – her eyes rich and full, chocolatey – and I lean back and let the pleasant, swimmy tiredness carry me.

She grins. 'He always talked about you, yeah? In the early days.'

I'm confused. 'My dad?'

'No, stupid. JJ.'

'Ah, right, him. We're talking . . . about him.'

'Yeah. He went on and on about how he'd met you in that bar, and how you took him to a church and shagged his brains out – '

'Oh . . . Jesus, I never thought – '

I hear myself emit something that's half a laugh and half a hiccup. The joint's wafting in front of me again, so I take another deep drag before handing it back to Imelda. Actually, I realize, as her fingers brush my face, warm and soft, it never left her hand. I'm useless now and she has to guide it into my mouth.

'He likes you, yeah? Says nice things.'

'Pah, nice things, niceings. What kinda word is *nice*, huh?'

'A nice word,' says Imelda, and when I catch her eye, we both fall back on the cushions, giggling.

Something's pushed the question up, out of my alien mouth. 'Do you know her, huh? Do you know who she is?'

She shrugs, leaving an orange trail in front of my eyes. I try to follow it, but it's all over the place now, a big cloud with a burning tail, same shape as the *Challenger* explosion (hey, I know some jokes, some really sick jokes about . . . never mind).

It seems like half an hour before she answers. I think the question's still booming like a hovercraft in my head, because I hear a fragment –

'Who she is, huh?'

And then I realize I have asked it again, and Imelda was just getting her mouth into gear to tell me. She takes another ruminative sip of water.

'Look,' she says, 'far as I know, it means nothing, right? She's some little tart.'

'Tart?'

'Well, some girl he picked up in a bar. Cheap little thing.'

'Like he picked me up in a bar. Yeah, cheers.'

'Didn't mean. Y' know I didn't mean that.' I think her hand rests for a moment on my shoulder, but it could have been the hand of a ghost. I don't know. 'He didn't tell me much about what happened with you two, where it all went wrong. I didn't ask, yeah?' Imelda raises her perfect eyebrows at me, runs a hash-smeared hand through her gamine hair.

Just then, the phone starts to ring. Imelda shrugs and smiles an apology, then, all in one smooth movement, flips herself back on to the cushions and scoops up the receiver.

'Yeah? . . . No, of course I'm not alone.' She raises her eyebrows at me again, and I feel myself blush slightly. 'As planned, darling . . . No, of course not . . . Right, then . . . right, then. Yes, my love. Bye . . . Right, bye, then. Yes, I will. Bye.' She sighs and chucks the receiver aside, not bothering to hang it back up. I suppose I ought to be flattered by that.

'Who was that?' I ask casually.

She smiles, and spreads her arms across the sofa. 'One of my Italian babes. Raffaella, she's called. Always worrying her pretty head about something.'

I grin. 'Just how many women have you got on the go, Imelda?'

She does a very Gallic 'pfouilh', with a pout and a shrug. 'Enough! Doesn't do to put all your eggs in one basket.'

'Yeah, well . . . Don't get salmonella.'

'I won't. I always boil them for ten minutes at least.' She gives me one of her flash-frame grins.

I'm sure that's possibly obscene – she's got quite an oo-er-missus, *Carry On* sense of humour at times – but I don't pursue it. 'You were saying about JJ, and me. . .'

'Well, as I say . . . Never did ask. He doesn't tell me everything.'

I nod, and my head is weighted with tiredness. 'Yeah. Yeah. Oh, well.'

'Hey, don't feel too bad.' She grins. 'It's not as if he went off and fell in love with someone new, after all.'

'I don't think he was ever in *love* with me,' I tell her, and I'm haunted by the truth that hangs around those words like the smoke from the spliff.

There's a comfortable, warm silence. I want to kiss Imelda, kind of, but she might get totally the wrong idea. Some sort of cut-out circuit deep inside me tells me that. Like it's reminding me to be straight, in both senses. (Well, I think that's pretty good for this time of night.)

Something takes my mind back to the church – the churches, merging in my mind – and the pier, via Ashwell Heights.

'Imelda?' I hear myself asking, from a soft black cloud where she may also be lying.

Lying. No lying. Only truth here.

'Yeah?'

'Did JJ . . . say . . . much about that night? You know . . . after the Arcade, after you left?'

She blows a long, warm breath. I feel it against my neck. 'Nn-o-pe,' she says – managing to make it four syllables, or three with a little hiccup on the end.

'You didn't ask him?'

'I never ask him.' Her voice is softly reproachful. 'I'm not his mother, thank God.'

I grin, and there is another soft silence. I think she puts the joint to my mouth again, but this time I barely have the energy to inhale.

'Want to show you something,' I hear myself saying.

Before I know it, I have lifted the blade high and it's slicing the smoky light. My knife, jutting towards her ceiling.

Imelda nestles close to me and she looks up and down the blade, eyes wide.

'Can I touch it?' she asks.

'Yeah, sure.'

Her slim fingers stroke the flat side, leaving steamy imprints. 'It's beautiful,' she says.

'It's waiting,' I tell her softly. 'Waiting for the Cut.'

'The Cut?'

'It's kind of something that I'll know. The right moment, some time when I have to take a big decision and this is gonna save me.'

I nod, gripping the handle with both hands. I close my eyes and imagine myself licking the ropes that chafe the wrists of Christ, slicing them to fraying cords, gashing his wrists and going down on them, my mouth red with desire. Taste of rust and roses.

Shit, my head's spinning with pictures. Like technicolor video. I should get stoned more often.

'The Cut's an action . . . the Cut's a state of mind, an assertion. The Cut's going to be the moment when it all comes out, what I'm really like.'

What I am really like. My God. I am millimetres away – just a cut away – from telling her. From spilling the beans (in their slimy sauce) and the blood and the tears –

I open my mouth, aware of the strange loudness of my clicking lips. Imelda parts her own lips slightly, as if to say that she is ready to receive whatever I have to offer.

'How will you know?'

The voice echoes around the church.

It's not a church, it's Imelda's lounge. I blink myself back into the world. My face shimmers in the blade.

'I'll know,' I tell her.

I snick the knife shut and put it back in my pocket.

'Hey,' she says with a grin, 'don't bring it to the party. Might cause some problems.'

'Do you really . . . I mean, want to do this party for me?'

Imelda, taking a gulp of water, giggles and splutters. 'Well, of course, darling. If you're happy with it.'

'Yeah. Yeah, I think so.' I grin at Imelda, but she's already a blur.

I don't even remember getting home the next day. I must do, though, because I'm smashed out of a dream and my hand slams the jabbering clock radio.

I haul myself downstairs. In the kitchen, Jon is cooking scrambled eggs in his new, ultra-non-stick frying-pan. Kate's setting out elaborate cake-sculptures in the lounge. I exchange brief, hostile glances with Kate before slouching over to the cooker to annoy my father.

'What is it this week?' I ask him, dipping a finger in the semi-soft eggs.

'What is what?' he asks breezily, tutting and knocking my hand aside as if I were a fly.

'Kate's coffee-morning. Church, Oxfam or Parish Council?'

'Try again. It's (d), none of the above.' Jon catches my eye for a second and grins, his whole body agitated as he gives his eggs a vigorous stir. 'She's doing a recipe exchange.'

Get the cauldron out, I think. Wisely, I keep this thought in my head. I'm in need of something cold and wet in my dry throat, so I go to the fridge and open one of the six bottles of lemonade which are sitting on top of it.

'Careful with – ' says Jon, just as I've tipped my glass back and the drink reaches my taste-buds.

It's refreshing, for a moment. Then it hits me, the uncanny, cloying mixture of sugar-sweetness and brine. I spit, and a glutinous arc spatters across the kitchen tiles.

'Ugh! Fuckity-yuck!' I lift the glass up to the light. 'What the hell – '

He looks sheepish as he serves up his eggs on to his toast. He clears his throat and tries to unfold his morning newspaper. I'm there, my hand slamming down on the scrubbed pine, pinning the paper so he has to look at me.

He shrugs. 'I made you up some drinks for the party,' he says, eyes flicking down and up and down again. He can't look at me directly. I've never seen him so shifty. 'You have to be sure to get enough fluids and salts.'

'Fluids and salts? What are you on about?'

'Well, I . . .' He shrugs. 'I just assumed you'd be taking . . . stuff, at this party. You know. Ecstasy. I was going to give you a talk tonight about using it responsibly. All the guidelines say you need soft drinks with plenty of sugar and a spoonful of salt added.' He looks up at me like a little boy. He tries to smile, but it's helpless, half-hearted.

'Yeah, I think they mean a teaspoon, not a frigging ladle.' I look over at the six bottles of lemonade. I'm trying to get my head round this. 'Are they all . . .?'

He nods, and shrugs. He picks up a forkful of scrambled egg and chews it methodically. 'Just being realistic,' he says, shrugging again. 'Sorry if I offended you.'

I mean, can you credit it? What is this overwhelming desire to be so accommodating and liberal? Are they trying to erode every single rebellious idea we can possibly think up for ourselves? (I'm still getting used to the idea of free condoms in schools, for Christ's sake.)

Whatever happened to, 'Now listen, kids, all drugs are evil, you take them and you'll die and go to hell for eternity'? I mean, I expected that, I was comfortable with that!

Sometimes I despair. What on earth is the matter with the older generation? Haven't they got *any* sense of responsibility?

Okay. Last night. I drifted.

I wanted to say to her: let me tell you about my childhood, let me tell you how sad I was. Lost among the goosegrass smart-bombs and the rose explosions and the pungent, laughing beefsteak fungi on the trees.

I don't feel myself falling asleep, but two hours later, I'm there with my head on Imelda's shoulder and my eyes are hot as if from tears. It must have been the smoke, getting into my eyes.

24   *Unravelling*

It was them.

All the time. Knowing, watching.

I have been known in too many senses, and I have been watched. I've been totally fucked. I've been unsafely penetrated by future-history.

I'm feeling my way down the top stairs like a mad, blind woman, like a Mrs Rochester come to join in the party. I can feel it throbbing through the banisters.

It was them. Jesus Christ. Stupid Bel.

Take time back.

Give me a chance to think about this thing.

The house vibrates to its loudest-ever party. Just at the moment, the soundtrack is 'Where I Find My Heaven' by the Gigolo Aunts, and the sound blurs, thumping like fists from the speakers. I slip past the crowds of extras, through a haze of smoke, heading through the patio doors into the fresh air of an exterior.

I'm fairly well-oiled on several glasses of Australian Riesling (twelve per cent, not bad) and happy that all these people are here because I asked them, here because of me. Imelda helped me to get it all ready, and then disappeared on some secret mission – I think she went off to fetch her latest flame from St Mary's RC Sixth-Form College. Yeah, I gather she goes for them young these days.

Damien's there, stage left in the corner by the doors. He's got booze on one side and an army of leggy schoolgirls on the other, so he's happy.

'Some things in life,' Damien's saying loudly, to the adoring young floozies, 'you should never leave too late, you know? Like getting really, paralytically smashed. Like travelling round the world.'

He catches my eye across the pulsating room, and seems even more pleased that I have joined his audience. I watch the girls' bright lipsticks floating under the lights like little piranha fish ready to nip Damien's flesh. Glossy A-lines caress their thighs, shimmery with hues of Ribena purple, jelly green, lemon yellow.

'But there's one thing,' says Damien, wagging a finger, 'that you should never, ever leave too late. Know what that is?'

The liquid-skirted girls shake their heads and flick their hair back. They watch him, waiting for his wisdom. I watch Damien getting his beer can ready, so that he can go for the slurp straight after the punch-line, just like he always does.

'Sleeping with a woman,' he says, 'who's old enough to be your mother.'

There's a silence. Then one of the girls giggles, while another snorts her laugh up the wrong way and collapses into an armchair, frantically wiping her nose. The others start to snigger as they get it. Maybe.

As I squeeze my way through to the doors, Damien starts to tell one of his disgusting jokes – it's something to do with a nun and a Doberman.

'Ooh,' says one of the airbrushed babes, 'I hate fuckin' dogs.'

'Stop fucking them, then,' says Damien, and this time, the little group explodes into ribald, screeching laughter straight away.

I get out – I've heard the 'joke' before (and also Damien's disclaimer about it being true and 'not just a doggy-shag story').

The place is buzzing now, full of extras in various states of dress and undress. There's already a couple playing tonsil-hockey over behind the rubber-plant. I've no idea who they are.

There was never a serious intention, luckily, of scripting a 'theme'. I had worried, because Imelda mentioned at one point about introducing some camp retro element. As far as I'm concerned, people in the seventies didn't look cool, they just looked bloody stupid with their Afros or centre partings, their flowered shirts and their sad oval glasses.

I don't think I could have coped with a room full of people looking like newspaper photos of people missing for twenty years whose bodies have just been found. Or a bunch of really crap eighties footballer haircuts, all feathery on top with scraggy long bits over the collar – technically known, I've just found out, as a 'mullet'.

But here we are, anyway – Imelda seems to have ordered stacks of drink, and Jon's taken Kate to a show in London, to be followed by a night in a plush hotel. People are here, and it's all going well.

I get out on the patio, just in time to see an unfamiliar boy plunge head first into the pool with an enormous splash. He emerges, sputtering but laughing. A blonde girl gets the idea of throwing his drink in after him, which her friends find hilarious.

There's a new, small figure coming on set, threading her way through a sea of plastic cups and floating plates and gesticulating hands. Marcie, her eyes thickly-kohled as usual, lifts a hand in greeting and slips over to me.

'Nice do,' she says, flipping out a cigarette from nowhere and looking around. Not looking at me, you see. Looking everywhere else. No problem with that. I find Marcie's eyes unsettling enough without having to watch them for too long. Christ, have I admitted that before? Me, frightened of –

All the same, I can't hide my surprise – first, that she's here at all, and then because of how good she looks tonight. She's had her hair trimmed into a neat bob (tapered at the back) with sculpted blonde bangs, almost albino-white against her dark eyes. (Not exactly come-to-bed eyes, but come-in-the-back-seat, certainly.) Her earrings are a pair of gold dolphins, and she's wearing a chocolate raw-silk blouse, set off by a leather belt and an oyster tulip-skirt of sleek satin. The ensemble can't have been cheap, and it gives Marcie's baby-doll prettiness some unwarranted style. Something's not quite right with that. So, what's brought it on, and what's behind it?

'Damien here?' she asks casually, with a deep drag of smoke.

'Inside. You'll have to drag him away from his coven.'

She smiles. Again, as if she knows something. I don't like this at all. Just what is Marcie up to?

'You look . . . nice,' I tell her, to fill a gap in the conversation.

She blinks in a slow, artificial way, as if to show me that she knows it and she was just waiting for me to say it. 'I know I can look good when I try. Class, innit?'

'A sub-species of some sort, certainly,' I mutter into my beer, but luckily Marcie is too busy being noticed to hear, and I'm confident enough that she'd be too stupid to understand anyway.

'I wannid to show my figure off,' she adds. I'm thinking, I know what she's going to say, please don't let her say how tiny she is. 'It's to do with being tiny,' she says, fluttering her eyelashes and blowing smoke up at me. 'I'm so tiny. I'm a ten.'

'Brilliant,' I tell her, with bile in every syllable. 'A ten? Isn't that just a fat eight?'

It's lost on Marcie. Taking the piss is no fun when your target's someone whose last brain cell is so lonely it's suffering from solipsistic dementia.

She slides even closer to me and jabs her cigarette into the air. She lowers her voice, so that I have to strain to hear it above the babble and the thud of the speakers from the lounge.

'I'll need the next payment by Thursday,' she says casually.

I have to stop myself from spitting my drink across the nearest shoulder. 'You bloody *what*?'

'Thursday,' says Marcie coolly. 'Another hundred, I need.'

'I don't fucking *care* what you need, you little whore!' I hiss at her, grabbing her silken arm as she tries to slip from the scene. Marcie raises her eyebrows at me and very pointedly looks down at my grasping hand. I let go of her, but not without another low expletive.

My legs have gone weak and my heart's pounding. I can see what's coming – clear, ominous, unstoppable.

'Sorry,' she says, in a voice of cold steel. Anything but sorry. 'But I need to pay off the gas.' Her eyes narrow, and she calmly blows a jet of smoke past my right ear. 'I mean, it would be awful if anyone found out you was driving at Ashwell Heights.'

Fury grips me. I cannot let this go on, not now. This little bitch has walked into a party to which I invited her, simply to carry on her sordid little blackmail enterprise.

'Marcie, you can do what you like. For your information, it bloody well wasn't me, it was him. It was JJ, right? Fucking JJ!' I'm aware that my face is flaming with anger, and one or two people are looking over their shoulders.

Marcie's eyes are wide, challenging. Hands on hips, she says, 'You know it was you. We smashed the back window, and you drove us there.'

Shit. In the aftermath of what happened – when she and Damien had gone – I'd forgotten that. And subconsciously, defending myself, I had been talking only about that time after, with Birthmark in the car, with JJ in the quarry.

And there's a twitchy poltergeist of a smile on her pert little face, almost as if she was aware of this.

'See you later,' Marcie murmurs, and slips into the crowd on the patio.

In one smooth movement, with a subtle lighting adjustment, I'm back in the lounge. Damien and his admirers have gone, and Marcie's vanished already. I pan across the room, but I can't see any of them. I start to panic. Someone turns the music up for 'Blue Monday'. I start to head across the room, nervously smiling and nodding at people, and trying to ignore the way the beat's hammering like a pile-driver in my head. The room's atmosphere seems entirely composed of smoke and sweat.

I finally make it through and emerge, gasping, into the kitchen, where I grab a much-needed bottle of beer from the fridge. The floor's already sticky with drink and there's a bunch of long-haired reprobates huddled round an ashtray under the kitchen table. One of the glossy-skirted tarts is getting it on with a stubbly bloke in the corner by Kate's precious Aga. Two stupid-looking girls with fiercely-pierced noses – who the hell invited them? – are having an argument next to the fridge.

'Do you hate your own stomach linin' or what? It's salt, tequila, lemon, that's the order.'

'Piss off, you know nothin'. I'm telling you, it's lemon, salt, tequila.'

I poke my head between them for a moment. 'Actually,' I tell them, 'it's salt, lemon, tequila. Right? Lick, suck, drink.'

I have this mental image of Imelda, raising her eyebrows at the comment, saying, 'My dear, that's the way I always do it.'

Imelda. Where is she tonight?

I leave the two girls to enjoy their tequila in the correct way – at least, I hope it was theirs, otherwise Jon's drinks cabinet has already been broken into, and that wasn't meant to happen until later.

'Darling! I've found you!' The voice is unmistakable, and I turn around in relief for a hug from Imelda. She's glossy and smooth, her body swathed in some white silk wraparound thing. Above a wood-brown face, her hair's adorned with a crown of leaves. She smells of sandalwood and pine. 'How are you?' she asks.

'Pretty stressed, actually. Thought you weren't coming,' I tell her with a half-hearted grin.

'Heavens,' she says, readjusting her wreath with a wiggle of her eyebrows. 'Have another beer, love. Start drinking, stop thinking, that's what I always say in these circumstances.'

'Is . . . JJ here?'

She's rolling a cigarette, but she waves a hand into the throng. 'He's around, somewhere.' Her eyes meet mine for a moment as her tongue pauses, mid-Rizla. She looks for a moment like some demented parallel-universe Roman getting a fix before taking her place in the Interactive Colosseum. 'Do you want to talk to him?' she says (in the tone of voice normally reserved for questions like 'Are you *sure* it's syphilis?').

I shrug. 'Well, I wouldn't mind.'

Imelda nods, gives me a reassuring smile as she peers over my shoulder. 'All right. I'll try and find him.'

Now Imelda's arrived, I start to lighten up a bit. She gives me something to smoke and I lighten up even more. I'm conscious that I keep pushing my hair back with sweaty hands, so that after a couple of hours it's become a tangled mess, a forest filled with latent pockets of smoke and alcohol.

At one point, I push past a queue to get to the nearest bathroom. Leaving my beer can on the top banister – and not really caring whether it stays or falls – I blunder straight in. I have a long, warm, contented piss, and just as I'm putting everything back together again I hear noises behind the shower curtain.

I frown, and, pulling the flush to hide the sound of my moves, I go over to the bath and jerk the brightly coloured curtain back. A dishevelled Marcie's blinking at me in the harsh cutting light. There's a bloke next to her, not bad, with blond, shoulder-length hair and a big nose, but sort of ungainly-looking. He's embarrassed, frantically tugging at the stuck fly-zip on his jeans.

I stare at the tableau, and I'm about to go away and let them get on with it, but something just doesn't feel right.

The way Marcie's looking at me, cowering against the tiles in her classy gear, the satin skirt not quite pulled up to her rump, the chocolate blouse half unbuttoned. With a middle button missing, I notice. And her eyes are big and glossy, tuned-out. She was fine a couple of hours ago.

'Am I interrupting anything?'

'Leave it, Bel,' says Marcie in a small voice.

'Yeah,' says the bloke, pulling on a check shirt, his embarrassment turning to anger. 'Why don't you let us get on, eh?'

'How much, Marcie?' I ask wryly.

She shakes her head, rubbing angrily at the satin skirt. I wasn't wrong. I knew the clothes weren't Marcie's style at all. Someone's dolled her up for the evening. Someone's got her stitched-up, up and running, hot and runny. Ready for the off. I don't believe it. So how much is the little bitch taking home these days?

'Look,' the guy says, half stepping out of the shower. Hands on hips, I look down at his groin in contempt. He pushes his hair from out of his eyes, and jabs a finger at me. 'Just don't spoil this. Who the hell are you anyway?'

I grab the tap and spin it round, soaking the pair of them in scalding water. He swears at me and jumps out of the way, but Marcie just slides down the tiles – scattering soap, shampoo and shower-gel on the way – and slumps there, staring vacantly. I hear the guy storm out behind me.

When it becomes obvious that Marcie isn't going to move, despite the water cooking her exposed flesh to a lobster red, I grudgingly twist some cold into the mixture and leave her there to soak. She lifts her head to look at me – hair heavy and lank, that careful fringe destroyed – and there is defeat in her eyes.

'I knew, Marcie,' I tell her as I turn to leave. 'I knew you had to be back on the game. All that money you'd be earning. It was just too tempting. You wanted it for your drugs, didn't you? That's why you needed all that money from me as well. All your fucking little blackmail payments.'

She draws her knees up to her chin and doesn't answer. The blouse is now thick and wet like chocolate mousse, sticky round her little cleavage. I take her silence as assent.

'You're just a stupid Fally girl, Marcie,' I tell her. 'People like you will never come to anything. You'll always be dragged back by something.' I see that I never did have anything to fear from Marcie and her little rebellion. This isn't France in 1789. You can't cart the moneyed classes off to the guillotines in barrows.

I fling the door open, confronting a very surprised queue with a wall of steam. I march out like the queen of the battlefield, grabbing my beer can on the way. It has stayed there all this time, balanced on the banister, untouched.

I corner JJ by the drinks in the vibrating lounge. He yanks the top off a bottle of red wine. He looks very uncomfortable to see me.

'Aren't you going to say hello?' I ask him, sipping my beer and surveying the throbbing throng through the mists of smoke.

'Hello,' he offers grudgingly.

'So, did you bring her, then?'

He laughs emptily. 'What do you think?' The cork comes out of the bottle with a satisfying pop, and he fills a plastic beaker to the brim. (For a brief instant, I see a chalice ... bread and wine in a desolate church ...)

'And Imelda's latest? She here?'

'Possibly.' He's not making eye contact with me even. 'You seem to be friendly enough with her yourself.'

I'm not quite sure what's intended by that. Still, at least we have exchanged a few words.

This all happened hours ago, back in sobriety. The world has mutated since. Raw energy from another universe – its colours bright, cartoon-alien, its sounds demonic and raucous – has permeated this reality.

I must recall it as it was.

We are standing there, on the fringes of the party. At least we are talking. We are leaning against the same bit of wall. People dance, white trousers and blouses looking purple under the strobes (no expense spared here, you know).

In the corner, Damien's glossy-skirted harem sit in a tight circle. One of them is slicing a plastic lemonade bottle in two. She hands half the bottle to another of the indistinguishable party-girls, who shoves a makeshift foil tray into the plastic cylinder. Then they make a small hole in the side of the bottle and stick a straw into it at right angles. One of them lights a match, with great, unnecessary ceremony, and they set fire to the contents of the foil tray.

'We haven't ... really talked about what happened.'

'No,' agrees JJ. 'Is it necessary?'

The girls in the corner are bubbling with giggles as they ease a plastic bag over the opened lemonade bottle. (Just like putting on a condom, I think ruefully.) I know what happens then – seen it before. The fumes rise up and fill the bag, and as the dope burns it produces hot, raw fumes which are sucked through the straw. The bag squashes and re-inflates, like a lung. A lungful of purest hash.

I glance up at JJ, and there's that touch of little-boy naivety again, that innocence which first drew me to him.

'As necessary as anything ever is,' I mutter into my drink.

He seems to like the fact that he's annoyed me again. 'Now you're just being petulant,' he claims.

'Oh, am I?' I knock back the rest of my drink and sling the can across the room into the melee of dancers. 'Great. Well, that's just great. See this?' I pick up the brimming ashtray, a hideous thing in elephant-grey, shaped like a shell. One of Kate's little bargains. I tip it up and hurl it to the floor, scattering the fag ash and stubs all over his shoes. 'Now *that*'s petulant,' I tell him with satisfaction.

The girls are laughing and pointing as they pass the plastic lung between them.

He sighs, slams his glass down. 'Come back when you're feeling more adult,' he snaps at me. He barges through the wobbling dancers, heading for the hallway and leaving me slumped here by the drinks.

Immediately, I regret it. I grab a bottle of brandy and slurp down a couple of hard shots. I've got this vague memory of having imbibed Buckfast at some point this evening, too – shit, I can't have been that desperate. Someone told me once that it's the most popular drug in Glasgow.

The room is red and smoky, filled with shadows flitting their fingers and gyrating their arms. This party has suddenly turned into the outer vestibule of hell. Expect the wasps any minute. But I don't imagine any bright, gleaming Virgil is going to step through the door and offer me his hand.

Cranes are on the stereo. 'Shining Road'. You can usually judge my mood by Cranes. If I think that the woman's got a lovely, ethereal, angelic voice then things are going great. If I think she sounds like a whiny schoolgirl, it's time to smash something. Right now, my needle is hovering dangerously close to 'remove crockery'.

I want to find Imelda and see if she can patch things up between us, but right now it's hard to get up off the floor. How long has elapsed since JJ stormed out? Ten minutes? Fifteen? Does it matter?

Someone steps up the music to full wall-shattering, bone-cracking intensity for the opening chords of Therapy?'s 'Screamager'. My head is not happy. It's asking for something from one of those Pan Pipes

Moods albums ('the haunting *woo-woo-woo-woo-woooo-woo*, the memorable *wooo-wooo*!' . . .)

'You all right down there, Bel?'

It's Damien. He's grinning cheerfully as he pours himself something. I'm not too drunk to notice that his neck is decorated with a glistening, vampiric love-bite.

'Yeah. Yeah, I'm fine. You . . . getting on well? Or getting off well, I should say, huh?'

He shrugs. 'Not bad. See you later.'

'Don't forget the garlic,' I mutter, and heave myself to my feet. Still clutching my bottle – no one's having that, I can tell you – I stagger upstairs, pausing on the way to shake various people by the shoulder and ask if they have seen Imelda. Someone vaguely points to the next floor up. Oh, hell. I'm going to have to interrupt something. Well, tough.

Slowly, I haul myself up, pausing for a brief shot of brandy on the way. It burns my throat but I'm getting there step by step, steadying myself on each creaking section of the white handrail.

I get to Jon and Kate's room, where various swathes of flesh are making out. I momentarily startle them by flashing the light on and off, but there's no sign of Imelda.

The only place she can be is the spare room.

I knock over the linen basket on my way there. A week's fetid washing – a description of all our lives scrawled in the hieroglyphics of clothes – spews on the landing and the stairs. My black dress is there, and the underwear I wore when I went with that guy. One of Kate's double-D bras. A shirt of Jon's.

I kick it all aside and reach the door. I listen up against it. I hear a giggle, definitely Imelda's, and the sound of a glass being clinked.

Briefly, I consider knocking, but I throw the idea aside. I go in, not looking up just in case it's an awkward moment.

'Imelda?' I call into the dimness. 'Imelda, can I see you for a bit?'

The noises seem to have stopped. I am conscious of various things. Of the thud of the party below. Of two people in the room trying to breathe very, very quietly. And of the pungent, scampi-and-lemon scent of sex in the room.

I swallow hard. I reach for the light, which is a dimmer-switch, and tease just a small glow out of it.

Imelda McCann, tousle-haired, breathing hard, is sitting on the edge of the big double bed, where it looks like she's just sat up in something of a hurry. She's pulled the flower-print quilt over her breasts with her right hand. The wrist of her left hand is tied firmly to the bedpost with her own belt. There's a glass of white wine on the bedside table. Her body glistens from hair to cleavage with something which is also probably wine, mingled with sweat.

Crouching next to her, red-faced, dressed only in an unbuttoned shirt, is her nephew Joshua James McCann, known to me as JJ.

In my wobbly fury, I push past several couples. I hurtle down the stairs, knocking against shoulder-blades. I am dimly conscious of shouts pursuing me along the landing. Damien is there, can in hand, propping up the wall. He's trying to talk to a Gothic-looking creature who's festooned with chains between her nose and ears and eyebrows.

'Nah,' he says, 'no idea what attracted them all. I mean, there I was just minding my business, having a quiet drink, and licking my eyebrows. Bizarre, really . . . All right, Bel, everything OK?'

'No. Everything is not fucking OK.'

'Ah. Well, nevermin', have a drink. This is, ah, this is.' He waves at the girl with the wild black hair.

'Ellie?' she offers with a long-suffering look.

'Yeah. Ellie,' says Damien with a lopsided grin, and tries to fondle her hair.

I've already given him a shove that sends him sprawling against the door, accompanied by a shriek from the Ellie creature.

I blunder down to the lounge. Various people are sprawled about in states of drunkenness or dopiness. Red and blue lights illuminate my arrival. Portishead reverberates through the lounge. Someone raises a hand in greeting as I wade through piles of paper plates and cigarette packets. I feel like they are the floor, and that it's going to collapse, dragging me down into the mud. I open my mouth to say something, but I'm aware that there is a firm, reverberating beat outside. Some- one has put another record on, in the hall. It's echoing through the house.

I spin towards the door. One or two of the lost souls slumped around me start to stir, and one of them, a spindly blond guy called Joe, staggers to the window.

'Shit,' he says. 'Bel – there's some guys – '

I'm out in the hall.

There are two bodies stirring at the foot of the stairs, but I'm not concerned with them.

My eyes are fixed on the thick red carpet of the hall, where the pieces of the smashed fanlight lie in a random pattern.

The door is *shaking*.

I stand there, as if the carpet really has grabbed my shoes with furry arms and won't let go.

A stupid girl called Emma is there behind me, gripping my elbow. 'Shit, Bel, should we . . . call the police or something?'

With my eyes still fixed on the door, I shake my head briefly.

'Bel – '

'Get lost, Emma.'

The wood around the lock splinters and cracks. They're through.

A dart of cold air pierces the sweaty warmth of the house, as the door swings back and hits the wall. A pair of DMs kicks aside the hall table, smashing Kate's favourite vase.

I back away as porcelain crunches underfoot. The vase is the least of my worries.

The sixteen-stone chunk of meat standing in the door is wrapped in a grubby patchwork jacket and adorned with a face full of jewellery, including three rings through its piggy nose. The beats and howls continue to haunt the lounge, as no one has yet smashed or turned off the CD player. One or two people are grabbing their jumpers, bottles or partners and heading for the exits. A realistic ap- proach.

He swaggers forward. His arm's up inside his jacket but his right hand is firmly gripping a dark, oily wrench, protruding from the sleeve like some cyborg attachment, ready to dispense lethal justice. There are other large shadows in the doorway behind him.

'Belinda Archard?' he says in a deep-down, substantially abused voice.

'I'll . . . get her for you,' I manage to croak.

The hall's being wrecked behind me. Shouts and screams fill the house as people realize what's happening, and disperse, either out through the kitchen or through various windows. I notice some of Kate's ornaments – the shepherdess, the gilded violinist – being trampled underfoot. I'm trapped in the middle, whirling this way and that.

There's an explosion of glass from the lounge. I rush in and see the patio doors shattered, and a familiar figure standing there with a vicious fire-axe in his hand. Camouflage jacket, ripped jeans, twisted and stumpy hair. It's Dreads. He stares at me and twirls the axe between his grubby fingers.

I back away from him.

'Look,' I say to Dreads, 'I really don't know what you want. We don't need any trouble.'

'Tell me where Cassie is.' His voice is low, deliberately not threatening. It's so matter-of-fact that it chills me. I recognize Grinner and Chewer, his mates from Ashwell Heights, coming in behind him. 'We're going to turn this place over until you tell me.'

'Cassie?'

'She left with you that night!' he snarls.

Birthmark. Right. So he doesn't know.

'Look, I wasn't driving,' I say to him. 'You'll have to talk to JJ about it, won't you?'

Dreads tilts his head slightly. 'JJ?' he asks.

I nod furiously. 'He's upstairs. Shall I go and get him?' I edge towards the portable phone on the coffee-table.

Dreads sees me. 'Leave that!' he snaps, but I've scooped it up and I've pressed the 9 button once.

'Get out, or I'm calling the police.'

Chewer and Grinner – still performing their eponymous habits – seem to find this amusing.

From the noises behind me, it sounds as if the heavies have gone upstairs to scour the rest of the house.

'I mean it,' I say to them. I realize I must look pretty stupid – my hair a wreck, my teeth bared, gripping the phone with both hands like a weapon. 'You get out now, or I dial another nine.' My finger hovers over the button. 'And then another. Who wants to take the risk?'

His reactions are fast. Dreads smashes his axe into the top of the TV. I wince, expecting an explosion, but there's just a scattering of wood and plastic.

He steps slowly towards me. 'She's frightened,' he mutters to his henchmen. 'She must be lying. It's her we want.'

I raise my eyebrows, gesturing with the phone, jabbing the aerial at him.

Dreads makes a contemptuous sound by blowing air from between his lips. He edges forward again and I see his foot nudge something. An upturned pottery ashtray in the shape of a shell. I suddenly remember how that got there and I feel too bloody stupid and wrecked to care.

The ashtray spins towards me. I jump aside and it cuts the air just beside my ear, before smashing into chunks against the wall.

My finger contacts the 9 button again. The bleep is as loud as a gunshot in the lounge.

From upstairs, there is the echo of walls being thumped and various other breakable objects meeting their end. I wonder briefly if they've got as far as the top bedroom.

'All right,' I say to the Fallies. 'Who feels lucky?'

There's a commotion behind me and I whirl around. One of the heavies pushes a snivelling wretch into the room.

'I found this in the bathroom,' he says, hefting his crowbar with evident lascivious delight.

Red-nosed, damp-haired, sniffing, wrapped in a fluffy red towel, it's the delightful Marcie herself.

'Tell her, bitch,' says the heavy, and gives Marcie a slap round the head (sending droplets of water flying).

Marcie, rubbing her head, lifts her eyes to look at me. 'Sorry,' she says. 'They came looking for me. I told them.'

'Told them?' My finger hovers over the 9.

'Where to find you. I said to come tonight.'

Lights smudge. I sink back into the taxi seat, hoping it will all go away, trying to remember how it all got so out of control.

I stare at Marcie in horror.

'*You?*' I eventually manage to gasp.

So she has betrayed me as well.

'Yeah.' She huddles herself into the towel, not daring to look at me. 'Pretty good for a stupid Fally girl who's never going to come to anything, wouldn't you say?'

I'm shaking with fury. I slam the phone to the ground. Dreads and his friends move in.

'Come on,' says Chewer, his mouth thick with saliva and chewing-gum. 'Let's finish it off.'

I'm not quite sure how it happens, but he doesn't get further than reaching for me before he bends double, screaming, clutching at the red gash on his arm.

I whirl around, the knife held out in front of me. Marcie gives a satisfyingly melodramatic scream. I'm seized with the urge to cut right down her red towel and let the blood come pouring out.

'Back off her,' Dreads mutters. 'Now.'

The coffee-table rolls on its castors, right in Dreads' path. I hurl the bottle, and hear it smash, then I hit the hall running, leaving chaos behind me.

I'm dimly aware of shouts and screams from up above me in the house. Heavy footsteps shake the stairs. Time to leave.

Cold air is punching through the smashed door. I've got the presence of mind to grab something warm – it's a midnight-blue cloak of Kate's. I'm out in the drive, and without looking back I run for the main road.

The night is clear and still, speckled with the phantoms of sodium-light. It's just cold enough to crisp my breath to little jets as I run towards the lights of the town, far below me. Everything looms from the darkness as if trying to intercept me – a post box, lampposts, a jutting branch. My heart's trying to beat a way out of my chest, but I hurry on.

I've no way of knowing whether the Fallies came in a car. If I can't outrun them, I'm probably dead.

I make it to the roundabout, where cars are zooming off to the motorway in their hundreds. I stick my arm out and jump up and down, all the time keeping an eye on the dark, tree-covered road up to the house, expecting them to come down it at any minute.

I almost miss the taxi, its bright orange sign lit and ready, as if especially for me. I leap inside in relief. It's warm and soft and smells of pine air-freshener.

'All right, love,' says the driver, a fat Indian bloke with a little moustache. He leans round and gives me a friendly grin full of well-kept ivory. 'Cold night, eh? Where to, then?'

I think hard. I've got no money, so it's got to be somewhere I can get out easily.

'Westonbourne,' I tell him. 'The seafront arcade.'

And I sink back into the seat, my head buzzing with betrayal, my mouth clogged with old and angry drink, and watch the lights whizzing past like carefree, blitzed-out ghosts on their way to a haunted rave.

Imelda is calling me from the room, shouting my name in desperation. I don't want to go back.

It was them.

All the time. Knowing, watching.

I have been known in too many senses, and I have been watched. I have been unsafely penetrated by future-history.

I'm feeling my way down the top stairs like a mad, blind woman, like a Mrs Rochester come to join in the party. I can feel it throbbing through the banisters.

It was them. Jesus Christ. Stupid Bel.
Take time back.
Give me a chance to *think* about this thing.

25 *Final Cut?*

One by one, they all turned the tables on me. When I thought I was ahead, I was behind.

Of course, it all fits now. Isn't that what the hopeless police inspector says, when Miss Marple or Sherlock Holmes has shown them the pieces of the puzzle, dazzled them with the truth? It all fits now. And you were the bumbling idiot all along, shown up by amateurs. I guessed the end. Yeah, like hell you did.

Little things slide into place and begin to make sense. Suddenly, harshly illuminated. Like Damien at Ashwell Heights, sneering at JJ. 'We know why *you*'re so moody tonight.' Just after Imelda had gone.

My stomach tightens as I imagine what he must have been thinking that night. Waiting to get back to her, waiting to slip into bed beside her.

And then there's the whole lesbian thing. It's always seemed quite real for Imelda, not just a pseudo-cool, chic adornment as it was for some of the girls I knew in the sixth form. For all I know, she might really have all these babes on the go. But she also had a little sideline. Her cute little nephew. For the first time, I think properly about the way JJ looks like a girl. Perhaps that's what she likes.

My life skims past like the misty orange street lamps above the taxi, scene after scene unfolding in my head, shot on a jerky, hand-held camera. Faces loom and leer, their eyes fishy and glistening, their mouths obscenely huge, licking the lenses.

If I can only outrun the Fallies, I can perhaps escape it all.

Some headlights have been tailing us for a while.

*

After about ten minutes, we come to Westonbourne. It seems late, as so much has happened, but this place is still alive, and it's just getting going for the night.

This is a town which has respect and quality. Maybe it had a few more riots than us in the eighties and so earned more money. This town, unlike mine, has not only seen it all, it's got it taped and boxed and ready to sell to eager punters.

'Where you want dropping, love?' asks the taxi driver.

It's a bright night in this far-from-last resort. It looks like a place where the fish would be smooth and flaky when the chips are down. A seaside you like to be beside. Streets with more wine bars than winos. A glittering pier, festooned with colour, trips like a gaudy puppet show out into the backcloth of the night sea. Great searchlight-cones of illumination fill the sky with a V, announcing that this is a winning town, crisply spoofing the two-fingered salute of the chimney smoke at the End of the World.

And those headlights behind us are definitely matching our pace.

'Where you want dropping, love?' asks the driver.

Well-kept bright young things throng the Parade. They flit between designer lamps which look like gob-stopper globes on sticks of humbug. Or limbless matchstick-men with glowing heads, marching in single file down the Parade. (Shit, I knew I shouldn't have mixed those drinks.) Even now, with the nights getting colder, the princes and princesses are in their clubbing gear: the girls shivering in lemon satin mini-dresses and Cathy Gale boots, the boys in Blur-chic of Fred Perry T-shirts and pressed black jeans. They jostle, they laugh, they push each other along the Parade, light each other's cigarettes. This town will smell of perfume and Lynx aftershave and steaks and soft sand.

'Where you want dropping, love?' asks the driver.

'Just here,' I tell him. He pulls in next to the Parade. Opposite, there's a cliff-face of magnificent hotels, palaces carved from white stone, adorned with flags and rounded lawns. There's about a five-metre run for me across the Parade to the rails above the beach.

I leap out, and run for it, ignoring the invective – first in English, then in Gujarati – which skims down the Parade after me. I'm more worried about other pursuers. There are voices babbling. As I hoist myself over the rail above the beach – grateful I opted for leggings tonight – I risk a look over my shoulder.

Dreads is racing along the Parade towards me, flanked by two thugs. He pushes aside a necking couple, but I haven't stopped to see any more. Air is under my feet and I drop like a cat on to the sand. The first thing I do is take a minute to remove my shoes and fling them aside. Then I run. Fast, barefoot, the sand soft under my feet. Thud-thud, thud-thud.

I get closer to the sounds of the all-night funfair, and I risk a look over my shoulder as I scramble up the slope. As I'd thought, they were stupid enough to follow me on to the beach, and they're lolloping along in their ungainly DMs, but still gaining on me.

There's suddenly grass and earth beneath my feet, and the spaces around me have shrunk, become thronged with unnatural light and colour, bright gaudiness and whirls of movement, all permeated by a sweet toffee-and-cinnamon smell from a stall nearby.

I'm up, running, losing myself in a crowd now. Some of them give my wild hair and bare feet a glance, but generally they're too taken up with themselves. Mostly teenagers, some leather-jacketed twenty-somethings out for a last bit of fun before the winter sets in.

On my left, a carousel spins, plastic horses undulating in mechanized rhythm to that Simply Red song with the crashing drums sampled from the Good Men. (Thanks, Damien.) People are queuing, waiting to get on.

I push my way through denim, leather, velvet, hating the sight and the sound and the sweaty smell of people. The light smears behind me in the darkness.

I keep looking over my shoulder. Dreads, Chewer and Grinner have just got to the entrance of the fairground. They're looking round in all directions. Dreads points one way and Chewer slips off. He points the other way and Grinner moves into the crowd. Then he starts to move forward himself, scanning every face.

I move as fast as I can. I almost crash into a pair of albino-blonde girls who are shooting at two-dimensional animals. I push past them, and find myself right up against a crowd of people thronging the dodgem cars. People all around me are laughing, joking. I'm frantically searching the crowd for signs of my pursuers. Behind me, the dodgems swish and collide to the sound of 'She Drives Me Crazy'. Hysterical laughter echoes across the little arena.

I push my way through the crowds. My eyes are watching the people on the other side. The music comes to an abrupt end as the dodgems all slide to a halt.

Then, I just glance behind me for a second – and there's Chewer, shoving people out of the way, his eyes just a fragment of a flick away from seeing me.

I try to pull the cloak up round my face. People around me are jostling, pushing their way to the front of the dodgem queue. Couples, kids and teenagers are piling into the sleek little bubble cars, testing the steering-wheels.

Before I know what's happened, I've been carried right to the front of the queue. The bloke helping people on, a fat guy in an old leather jacket and a cap, holds out his hand for my money.

I hesitate. Then I look across the arena and see Dreads.

He tenses, shouts something. He's seen me.

I duck past the dodgem guy, slipping round him, but that's no good as I'm heading towards Chewer. He stands there, feet apart in the mud, the sky behind him bright with the monstrous, swirling light of the helter-skelter. I gasp. He nods, silently, and smiles to himself as he starts to walk towards me. Behind me, the music has started up again and the whine of the dodgems is getting higher.

Chewer lunges at me. I hop over the barrier, ignoring the shouts of the bloke in the cap.

Someone screams, and an orange dodgem swerves to avoid me. Feeling as if I'm stuck in a pinball machine, I stagger forward, heading for the other side.

Dreads has jumped in, too, and narrowly avoids being hit by a boy and girl in a yellow dodgem. They're whirling round and round, because they can't stop, they all have to go in the same direction, like an unending river of little plastic cars.

I spin round, then round again. The man in the cap, furious, is standing on the barrier and yelling something.

Dreads makes a lunge for a teenage boy in the nearest car, trying to haul him out of the vehicle. Another car skims past, and its front protective bars catch my knee. Knife-sharp pain sears my leg and I hit the floor of the arena. Someone screams, and it might be me.

The music growls and stops, and the cars all gradually slow down, spinning out the last of their momentum.

Dreads shouts, 'Get her!'

Chewer leaps over the barrier, then over two cars, heading for me. I pick myself up and run. With every step it feels like my kneecap's grinding itself into a powder.

I make it to the barrier on the other side and Dreads' hand is there. He grabs at the velvet cloak, which rips off me. The clasp pings undone. I leave him staggering with it as I dodge through the stalls, hobbling, in agony.

I reach the shooting range. A little girl is tottering away from it with her father, beaming happily as she clasps an enormous white teddy-bear. The bear blocks my line of vision for a second or two. When I can see again, Grinner is standing just two metres in front of me.

I spin around, my breath like acid in my throat. I think some of the night's alcohol is about to come back up.

It's no good. Behind me, Chewer and Dreads are pushing their way through the crowd. Under the artificial light, their faces are purple, livid with fury. Just then, my knee gives way and I flop on my right calf into the mud.

Three lots of DMs surround me. Hands haul me up. Then, before I've even realized who is where, a fist slams into my stomach and I'm consumed with agony, nothing in this world but red-hot pain in my stomach, and trying to find a breath and it's like it's all been vacuum-pumped out of my body. Christ, my feet are floating. The mud's rushing by underneath them.

– dimly realize that I'm being carried somewhere, try to struggle, but one of them's got my arm pinned right behind my back and starts to bend my fingers until I scream –

Try to focus on the faces floating past. Try to open my mouth to shout something. Mouth dry and coarse. Nothing comes out.

I hear one of them saying that I've had too much to drink and they're taking me home.

The next five minutes are a blur of light and colour, and then the smells change, becoming saltier and harsher, and that's how I know, when my lolling head is finally allowed to rest, that we're down on the beach.

They drop me. I hit the sand with a smack.

Waves wash in, white and soft in the night, licking at my thighs. I can smell the salt and the seaweed, spunky in its sharp fishiness, and over it there's the doggy, sweaty, veggie-curry odours of their disgusting bodies as they circle me, their boots sinking deep into the sand and the water.

A memory flits across my mind, of seeing anti-bypass protesters on the telly a couple of years ago, and thinking – you want to clean up the environment, start by getting yourselves a wash and a haircut. And how did you get down to Newbury, anyway? Would it have been on the *roads*, by any chance?

I lift my head. The pain in my stomach has started to recede a little, but my head is throbbing now, and I really wish I hadn't drunk so much. Also, needless to say, I'm practically shitting myself with fear.

For some reason, I can't move my hands. Someone's tied them behind my back with something. I don't remember them doing it, but they seem to have done a pretty good job of it as there's no give at all, and it's horribly tight and numb around my wrists.

It's quiet down here. The beat of the fairground is distant. There's nothing to hear except the gentle hiss of the sea, and their heavy breathing as they circle me in the sand. I'm crouched there like some animal, tensing myself for the kick.

It doesn't come. Instead, my hair is grabbed from behind, my face forced up with a pain like a thousand needles on my scalp. Dreads lowers his face to mine. His breath stinks like dog meat soaked in meths.

'All right,' he says. 'You did something to Cassie, didn't you, bitch? You and your nice little friends.'

I meet Dreads' gaze, trying not to gag on the stench. It must be ignorance of what he's going to do that gives me my false bravura. I stare insolently into his unwashed, stinking, scrounging Fally face, thinking how I need to get my hands free, need to get to the knife and Cut right into his trendy, I'm-all-fucking-right-Jack, welfare-state world.

JJ and his utopian, tolerant bollocks. He's got no idea. These people are shit. They need to be treated like shit.

'I don't know what you're talking about,' I tell him calmly.

'That won't do,' he says quietly, and opens his animal eyes at me, shows his yellow teeth.

'Sorry. I don't know what you're talking about, *shit-face*.'

I'm expecting pain, but nothing quite like what I get. It's a full, in-the-face punch, dislodging a tooth, *whackinggreattidesofPAIN*, *hotredAGONY* through my skull. My head's held steady by Chewer from behind so I can't even turn to absorb any of it.

I will not cry out. I can feel the bruise growing on my face.

Something's got to stop me thinking about it. I picture my dad, and Jeff. I think of them screwing these bastards by blowing up their nice little squatty flats. That makes me start to smile. I think of the Criminal Justice Act, the only law stopping smelly acid-fried hippies and their scabby pooches from camping in my back garden and dropping shit and needles for kids to fall into. I get this mental picture of a police truncheon whacking Dreads right across his crusty skull, while another dozen coppers in riot gear up-end their rusting Transit into a ditch.

Now I'm smiling broadly. And I don't care. I really don't care. Whatever they do to me, I've won. We've won. Society, civilization, call it what you will.

Fix on that.

Now, Chewer and Grinner hold my head back. One is tugging my hair, the other has a filthy hand clamped under my chin. Dreads gets a flask out of his pocket. It's black and sleek and gives no indication of what might be in it. He uncorks it. I clamp my mouth shut but they try to prise it open. They try to force the bottle's pungent neck between my teeth.

Eventually I just cannot fight against the three hands pulling my jaw down and the cold bottle bursts into my mouth, scraping my teeth, sending a hot, harsh liquid down into my throat.

Shit, I can't gulp it fast enough to keep up. It's hotter and headier than whisky. I try blowing it back. I splutter, gobbing treacly, alcoholic phlegm everywhere, and the bottle's withdrawn.

My body sways. The lights out on the breakwater are starting to smudge. And the cold sea water's got deeper, too, rising around my thighs, wetting my knickers. I'm coughing uncontrollably, the stuff has turned to acidy bile and I feel it hurtling up my nose, spurting from my nostrils.

Dreads is beside me. His face is spectral.

'You'll tell us,' he says. 'However long it takes.'

The sea comes up to meet me. Cold, stinging, smelling of old salt. Without warning he's shoved my face into it, and I fight, splutter, gag on the briny taste. I'm thrashing my head from side to side, trying to break out from under his hand, trying not to get submerged in the water.

Then he pulls me up. My face is cold and soaking, and the salt stings. I can't see a thing. The pungent smell and the cold glass return to my mouth and I try to force it away with my teeth, but Dreads just rams the bottle in and pours more of the stuff into me. It's got to be stronger than Thunderbird. Vile, sticky aftertaste, like sherry. No more. Gulp, gulp, gag. *No more.*

He pulls it out and I spit the mouthful into the sea. It describes its own path in phlegm, sticking in a long string between my mouth and the water, tensing and breaking only after a second or two. Detail. Got to keep on top of it. Got to know what I'm doing.

Legs and arms going weak now. Getting drunk. Getting too drunk.

'You little slut,' his voice says from far, far above me. 'Drink that.' And my face is in the water again, this time right inside it and I can taste the sand and the seaweed and it's cold in my mouth and I can't hold my bre–

Air. Coughing, choking, just have time to grab a breath out of nowhere and he's yelling in my face again. Hot breath on my skin.

'*Where is she? I want to know!*'

The bottle. Nearly half empty now. Again and again the treacly stuff glugglugglugs into my throat, filling up, no air, no space to breathe, drowning in the stuff, *drowning* –

This time, my coughing goes on for at least a minute, I think. I'm losing all sense of time.

'Where is she?' This time, it's just a whisper.

I try to speak. I can't focus my mind properly. I'm struggling for a word and trying not to keel over on to the sand.

I'm up again. Somehow, they have lifted me to my feet. Three faces, now no more than blobs. Harsh hands, clamping all over my numb body. They're saying things to each other, laughing, and I can't hear. Can't hear.

Legs won't work. Being carried now. Carried away.

Time has passed, but I don't know how long. They brought me here in a blindfold, and I think I must have been sick because my mouth and nostrils are full of a foul, acidy taste and smell. I'm kneeling, hands still tied, and there's what feels like smooth stone or concrete under my feet.

Someone rips the blindfold off. I get ready to blink against the light, but there's hardly any. For a moment, I can't see anything except the dark, stone floor that I'm kneeling on. Then I realize I am in a big, empty hall with a low ceiling, and no illumination apart from the street lamps glowing through a couple of old windows. It smells of shit, piss and decay.

There is breathing in here other than mine, and I sense more odours. Wet clothes and mud. They must be here, and not too far away.

As my eyes get used to the darkness, I can see their black outlines, standing a few metres away. Dreads' face suddenly flares out of nowhere, disembodied and hallowe'en-orange, as he lights a cigarette.

'Do you know where you are?' he asks. His voice echoes as if we're in a church or something.

'Tell me.' My voice is cracked, shattered with booze and sick and salt water. I'm still drunk, and I'm so exhausted that I feel like crying. They'd be those hot, treacly tears that an alcoholic weakness always produces. I can feel them welling but I won't let them come.

He steps forward, each footstep crisp and precise in the dimness. 'You're where you never thought you'd be. The top floor of Ferris Court flats. Fallowdale.'

He lets me take this in for a moment or two.

'Yeah, that's right,' Dreads sneers, crouching down opposite me. I try to focus on him with exhausted eyes. My face feels as if there's a football shoved into it and my throat feels lined with burning acid. What I really need is a drink of water. 'Fallowdale. Not your favourite place, is it, Bel?'

I look up at him, daring him to use my name again. No one uses it unless I let them. You don't do that.

'Oh, yeah, know your name, like. Friend Marcie told us ... The very flats your precious daddy wants to blow up so he can build his lovely new shops. Well.' Dreads straightens up. 'We're out of here. We loaded all the stuff up days ago. Nobody lives here any more. So your dad'll be pleased to know he's won, won't he?'

My mouth chews around some words, and eventually I manage to croak something out. 'It isn't a question ... of winning. It's change. Things ... change. You don't belong here. It's not your home. Is it?'

'Nah,' Dreads says. 'To you, I don't s'pose it seems that way. But then our home is everywhere. Don't know where we're supposed to go, like. Sure we'll find somewhere.'

'Oh, yeah, there must be some lovely fields around for you. Where your dogs can crap in peace.'

Dreads half spits a laugh at me. 'You people have no idea.'

'Hey, if you take a few months over getting there, you can crash at Glastonbury. No doubt the Levellers will be playing. Again.'

There are some worrying rustles from Chewer and Grinner, but I see Dreads' palm, held up high and open and white.

'What about Cassie?' Chewer snarls.

'Oh, yeah,' says Dreads. 'Cassie. She's dead, ain't she, Bel?'

I look up at them, trying to focus. This is obviously news to Chewer, whose pinched features have gone pale and angry.

Behind them, Grinner steps forward and pushes Dreads hard, almost sending him staggering. 'You knew all along, didn' you? You fucker, you *knew* she w's dead! How?'

'How'd I know?' He spits on to the floor, takes a deep drag on his cigarette. 'I was told.' He looks down at me. 'Some people found her weeks ago. I just wanted to see if you'd admit it.'

I meet his gaze, trying not to show any emotion. Especially not surprise. No way, not surprise.

Dreads nods thoughtfully. 'Found her in the forest, near where the bloke said. She'd been dead for days by then. We all buried her at night. Deep. Deep in the ground.' He sighs.

'Go on.' My voice is alien, lizard-skin rough. It's only now that it's really starting to hit me. I'm under their control here. I'm in their power. They can do anything they want with me.

'I'd seen before what happened whenever Cassie went mental. That night at Ashwell, she was out of it on acid. I watched her run out in front of your car with the fire extinguisher and I shouted at her. But she didn't want to know. She *wanted* to die.'

He prods me in the ribs with his booted foot. I try not to react. He continues.

'Bet you never knew that. Cassie always said she was goin' to die in style. The only surprise to me was that you picked her up and took her. I thought you'd scarper as fast as you could.'

'We . . . had to let her go,' I tell him uncertainly.

'Yeah. Didn't think to check she was all right, I suppose?'

'I . . . think she was dead by then,' I say to him. Well, why not? Might as well come out with the whole lot, now. 'We just had to get away. We took the car to the quarry and burnt it out. I don't think it's been found.'

Dreads shrugs. 'Couldn't give a toss about the car,' he points out. He drops his cigarette and grinds it underfoot. 'I really thought y' might lead me to where she was, if we kept watchin' you enough. In the end, we had to let the other ones do it.'

'Other . . .?'

'She's laughin' at us,' Chewer's saying, and he tries to push past Dreads to get to me.

But Dreads is bigger and stronger, and he holds the little man back.

'Yeah,' he says. 'She's having a taste of what it's like to be scared. Always wonderin' who's gonna kick you in the teeth next. Right, Bel?'

I try to get my voice around an answer, but my dry throat can only produce clicking sounds. My stomach aches, and there's that aching looseness around my oesophagus which tells me I'm very likely to be sick soon.

Dreads taps me under the chin. 'As I say, we're leaving soon. And you're all we have to take care of before we go.'

'Let me do it,' says Chewer, moving to his side. He narrows his little eyes as he looks down at me. I'm convinced he's going to spit in my face, and I get ready to flinch, but no, he just keeps chewing, round and round with a slurpy chomping sound, like a cement-mixer. I wonder to myself if he's got the same bit in his mouth, if he's always had it there. It must be wet and flavourless by now, grey plasticine travelling round the contours of his mouth.

Grinner just stands there, smirking more than grinning now, arms folded, watching the pair of them. No. Not that. He's got his wits about him. He's listening. Why? What's he heard?

'This girl,' Dreads says, squatting in front of me, 'is interestin', yeah? Thinks she's got one over on us for some reason.'

His eyes are acid-bright, burning in the darkness with reflected street lights and anger. My bowels have gone sloppy with the realization that he truly is ready for retribution.

'I know why,' says Grinner quietly.

Chewer rounds on him, aggressively. 'What?'

'I know why,' he says. 'She's got a knife. Thinks that means something, carryin' a knife.'

And all the time, I thought Dreads was the clever one and they were just a couple of heavies. But no, Grinner's the one. He's got me sussed.

'That's right,' says Dreads softly. 'And we know where it is, don't we?'

There is a fragile silence in the empty flat. The air tastes of decay. Or is that my mouth? I am shaking with cold and fear. I feel like the most disgusting object on this planet. My knee and my face both pulsate with pain. This hazy thought about a wrecked house surges into my mind, too.

And now, Dreads is sliding his hand into my pocket.

The silence bursts.

It's a snick, a click, a brief and angry sound which has been my friend in the past. I am looking at my own blade.

I am looking at it.

I am looking at nothing but the blade of my own knife. I can almost see my breath misting on its surface.

'Kill her,' murmurs Chewer.

'No,' says Dreads, 'we're not going to kill her.'

He rests the blade against my cheek. It is furiously cold. It seems larger than it ever has before.

'I just want an eye for an eye,' says Dreads.

My eyes are big and bright and bulging. My body shifts and slurps on top of the altar. I remember the brightness of the cross behind us as we took our angry, wine-stained love.

We move towards the finish, sweaty but comfortable, ready to hurtle over the edge now, my cries fluttering up to the roof like pigeons, curling round the rafters. My eyes are big and bright and wide. JJ's eyes are big and bright and wide. JC's eyes are big and bright and wide.

The cross gleams.

My face contorts in painful pleasure.

His face contorts in painful pleasure.

*

'Just an eye,' he says. 'Just so she has something to look at for the rest of her life. To remember what she did. Remember Cassie.'

The cross gleams. My knife gleams. I cut him free. I slice the ropes that bind him to the Church and history. I slice the multi-coloured threads of Birthmark's jacket, the scar blazes on her face, the car blazes in her face, a big flame-mark on her cheek. My knife shines. My knife gleams. My knife is cold against the eye which I'm about to lose.

I am about to lose.

And he moves the blade up to my eyebrow. I'm shaking so much that I can feel my face knocking against the metal.

My body is a corpse, swimming with hideous fluids which will all come spurting out when he makes the incision.

You always think of the worst. The very worst. I remember reading somewhere about the importance of eyes for absolute precision in torture. If you remove one eyelid, dig the eye out but leave the optic nerve attached, then the eye is there, dangling, and has to watch as well as feel the channels of blood being carved in the arms legs toes breasts oh shit oh shit oh shit and be unable to blink or look away.

Light cuts in through the windows.

It is a firm, bright, celestial bar of light. It spills across the floor with the whiteness of milk.

And from outside, down there in the world, the sound of voices, shouting.

Unbelievably, the pressure has gone from my face. I think there is sweat pouring from above my eyes, and then I realize that it's blood, leaking into my eye from where he must have cut me. Just above the eye.

There is a clatter as the knife falls.

I see them, through a haze of blood, frantically gabbling to each other. Chewer seems very reluctant to go, but Dreads grips his arm and pulls him. They're already disappearing down the stairs.

Seconds pass in silence. I wonder what to do. I'm filthy, muddy, sweaty, exhausted.

I've realized, now, that the floor is vibrating. There is a sound echoing from deep within the building. A clunking and whining. It grows louder, and it's obviously getting closer.

It takes me a second or two to work out what's happening. Somewhere in the building there is still a functioning lift. And the lift is coming up. It churns and clunks and whines.

Someone is coming up in the lift. Someone's coming closer and closer, up in the lift towards me.

My hands are still tied, and I try to ease them out of their bonds but they won't come.

The lift climbs higher and higher up the building.

It whirrs and judders to a halt, sending a tremor through the floor. And then light pours on to the stone floor as the lift doors start to open.

26　*Shown Up and Down*

I see my father's face.

I recall the way he looked at me after I asked him if he would stand by me. When I almost gave it all away, almost told him what I had done.

There was something about him, then, in that afternoon winter light, something I should have seen.

I have been believing, all along, that he knows nothing.

Remember.

The darkness gathers around me, here with the concrete under my calves, here in the stinking hole of the Ferris Court flats. I'm sure that the walls were marked by orange frames of light before, and the ceiling by a lighter patch of darkness. Now, it all seems to have receded. There is nothing. Nothing but me and this blackness and the clunking and whirring of the lift.

In dream or in reality, I am here, I am there, I am back again in front of the groaning lift as it comes to a halt.

The light begins, needle-thin, then pencil-thin, and then whiteness is fanning out into my dark world. It moves up like a saw, hacking through the black. It cuts into me, making me screw my eyes up and turn my head away.

For some reason I remember the evening visit to the estate, that time when my dad and Jeff first told me about their plans for these flats.

That sunset in Jon's glasses, like a zealous fire, like the fire of destruction. Burning like an abandoned car. He turns away from the shadows of Ferris Court, shrugs and grins, looks forward into the sunrise of the future and his new complex, his dream.

'When they built these things in the sixties,' he says, gesturing vaguely towards the squat concrete carbuncles, 'they thought they were the best things ever. Build up rather than along. Build into the sky. Use up those ninety-three million miles between here and the sun.' He pauses, nodding, gazing at the sinking sun itself, and draws a long breath as he pushes his sunglasses higher up on his face. 'But now? Here we go, tearing them down again. Like the tower of Babel, isn't it?'

While he speaks, what am I doing? Still leaning against the car, I suppose, watching Jeff Ash rolling up his plans and putting them on the back seat.

'Yeah, well,' I hear myself say, 'there's a thin line between beauty and ugliness.'

'That's very good, Bel, very good indeed.' Jon nods to himself, still staring at the sun. 'I ought to bring that up at the next meeting with the backers.' He sighs, looks down at his feet, now, and turns away, unlocks the car. 'It took us a long time to realize that no one really *wanted* to get nearer the sun. I mean, it's there, it's useful. We need it.' He flips up the back seat and gestures for me to get in. 'But we're sort of comfortable with that ninety-three million miles.'

He is there.

His warmth is next to me, and his long, dark arm stretches out to me, reaches for my hand.

I look up into his face.

And we are falling towards the darkening town, dropping on the high Fallowdale road. I can see myself and my dad's eyes in the rear-view mirror.

'Why are you wasting money on them?' I ask my dad and Jeff.

Jeff turns round in the passenger seat. His grin is unwavering. 'Pleased to see nothing changes. Right fucking little fascist you're raising here, Jon.' He chuckles, as if I'm a freak to be stared at.

249

I scowl at him. 'I'm just a realist.'

Jon's eyes meet mine in the rear-view mirror again and he can see that I'm serious. 'You think we shouldn't invest in Fallowdale, Bel?'

'They don't need it. They don't deserve it.' I'm remembering what Jeff said about the special houses for troublemakers. 'These places only get money thrown at them when they shit on their own floor. If you need the place rebuilt, you have a nice little riot. Get a name for yourself. No one's going to invest in somewhere not too obviously run-down, are they?'

Jeff whistles quietly to himself. 'Got a point. She's got a point, you know.'

I'm warming to my theme now. 'No one cares. And if they have a Labour council, it's in the council's interest to *keep* them poor. Otherwise they might defect.'

Jon seems amused. 'So the affluent automatically become Tories, Bel?'

'No, I didn't say that. Don't turn it round. I'm just saying people do lose their unrealistic ideals when they start to earn a bit of money. Christ, look at the students. They go on leftie, tree-hugging, nut-eating, support-the-workers marches one year, and the next year they're earning a packet in the City. Smart suit, smart car, smart life.'

I sit back, smug. Jon can't argue against any of that, because he's said it so many times himself, hasn't he?

I look up into his face.

'It's you,' I say.

'Of course it's me,' says JJ indignantly. 'What have they done to you?'

We're coming back into civilization now, and the seafront skims along beside us.

'You'll see,' says my father, full of confidence. 'It'll all be for the best. Once the new complex gets going, hundreds of locals will have jobs. Worth losing a few decaying flats for, don't you think?'

I smile. I say nothing.   *

JJ says it again. This time we are no longer in Ferris Court flats. We are in the back of a police car, and I have a warm, thick blanket around my shoulders and a soft pad stuck to my eyebrow.

'Bel?' he says. 'What have they done?'

'Nothing. How's the little Dutch boy?'

'Eh?'

'The one who put his finger in the dyke.'

'Very funny,' he says.

There is a brief silence. He fidgets. Outside, it has started to rain. The clearly outlined block of flats, the bustling police in their yellow jerkins, all smudge through water.

'You got me out,' I say to him, rather unnecessarily.

He smiles. 'You wouldn't believe me, would you? When I said it would get you into trouble.'

'I haven't changed my mind about anything.'

'Well, I hadn't expected you to.' He sighs, taps his knee as if he's embarrassed to be here.

'Look, I'm not in the mood.' My voice is cracking now. I keep losing syllables here and there, and my head is pounding. 'I'm not going to ask you why you're doing . . . it . . .'

'Aren't you? Don't you want to know if Imelda and I are in love?'

I try to laugh, but it comes out as a kind of choking noise.

'No, seriously. Why won't you ask?'

'She's your fucking *aunt*, for Christ's sake.'

He shrugs, grins. 'She's still a fantastic woman.'

'Oh, please. This is sick. This is just not what I envisaged being put on this earth for.'

'Ah. So you're powerless for once. The blade can't solve it for you. How long have you been carrying that thing around, Bel?'

'Long enough.' Well, why does he have to know any more?

'And has it ever solved anything for you? Anything at all?'

'It's made me feel better. Like looking up girls' gussets and shagging your auntie makes you feel better.'

'Ah. Right. You know that two-thirds of murdered police in America are killed by their own guns?'

'Oh, fuck off.'

'It's not nice, is it? Being analysed.' He folds his arms and smiles at me in a superior way. 'Your problem is you think the world revolves around you, and it's OK to put the boot into people who don't live the way you do.'

'Like Fallies? JJ, they did *this* to me. They are not worth *dogshit*.'

'I don't suppose,' he says quietly, 'that you've given any thought to the house, at all, for example?'

Oh, Christ, he's really got a good idea about my priorities, hasn't he? 'They'll get it all back on the insurance. Kate'll have major babies about it for weeks, but nothing a course of uppers won't cure.'

'Oh. Right. Insurance and Prozac. The great middle-class panaceas. They'll solve everything, of course.'

We're moving, now, carried through the town in style beneath a whirling blue light. The bright blueness strobes against the land, catching the waves in slow-motion, trapping the late-night staggerers.

Up ahead, there's another, similar craft, and the Fallies are in it. Thanks to JJ, the authorities got to us in time. They are going to have some questions to ask us.

'How did you know?' I ask him at one point.

'Marcie,' he says. 'She knew. She got a call, saying that was where we'd find you.' He breathes deeply. 'They said we'd find you with one eye,' he adds apologetically.

I don't ask him the more important question, of course. I don't ask why he bothered to find out.

Maybe I'll find out the answer to that one some time soon.

I scooped my knife up before they got us out. It's still there. It's still in my pocket.

27 *Tricks of the Light*

The knife glows in the snow-filled park.

I only ever met Marcie Hales once again in my life, in the precincts of Canterbury Cathedral.

I can see her now, walking towards me, black and red against the snow. On my left, the great honey-brown building, clasped by attentive scaffolding as ever, hits a steel-grey sky which has shed its snow no more than an hour ago.

There are few footprints in the precincts. The air is still crisp, still finding its chilly way beneath the heaviest layers of clothes.

At first, I think I'm going to ignore her, but now we're getting so close that we can hear one another's footprints on the virgin snow. We're away from the traffic here, and the only other sounds are from above, the hammering of workmen on the cathedral and the cawing of rooks. I don't have time to pull my scarf over my face.

We both slow down. We hover, circling, eyeing each other up. She's spindly underneath a black, fake-fur coat and red leggings. I'm bulky in my leather jacket and woollen scarf, and I'm peeking out from under a black trilby. I don't wear gloves.

Both my hands are in my pockets. Hi, my name's Bel. My hands are in my pockets.

'I didn't want to tell them, you know,' she says, as if restarting a conversation from just half an hour ago.

I shrug. 'I don't think it really makes any difference now. Do you?'

She eyes me warily. 'I suppose . . . your dad got it back on the insurance.'

I look coldly away from her. 'Most of it.' There is an uncomfortable silence, and Marcie pivots on her heel, carving a crescent into the snow. 'So,' I ask her, 'what are you doing here?'

She sighs, starts fumbling in her pocket for a cigarette. 'Just been up the council offices on Military Road. Job interview.'

'Another one?' The last I heard of Marcie after the disastrous party, she'd been taken on at a factory near Maidstone. 'What happened to the last place?'

She looks quickly away from me as she lights her cigarette. Smoke mixes with crisp breath. Her voice sounds clear and sharp, punching holes in the air. I start to realize again how much I hate her.

'Well, we had these targets, right? For each week. And we had to fill in these self-cerstifficut forms to say we done it all.'

'Yes,' I say uneasily. I do hope she isn't going to give me a dull, first-hand account of shop-floor life. I can quite happily get through the rest of my days without knowing such things.

'Well, supervisor came round, di'n' she?'

'Did she?' I'm always amazed by the way people like Marcie shove in their belligerent question-tags as if they already expect me to know the fucking story off by heart.

'Talkin' about extra hours. Said if we didn't meet our targets for the week, we'd have to make 'em up.'

'And that was a problem?' (Don't tell me the little cow was sacked for refusing to do a bit of overtime?)

'Well, I was quite relieved she knew about it. I told her I sometimes do make 'em up.'

Her face is earnest, her eyes bright. It is obvious that she still hasn't managed to work out the reason she was given the boot, and I have to bite the insides of my cheeks to stop myself from laughing.

'What about you?' she asks tentatively. 'I heard about . . . I mean, I'm sorry they . . .'

'Yeah,' I say quickly. 'I'm sure you are.'

Her curiosity gets the better of her, naturally. 'Why . . . why did they . . . do it, d'you think?'

I shrug, blow a cold jet of smoke and kick at the snow like an impatient horse. I don't want to stand here arguing things with Marcie. I've left her kind behind now. I don't need any of them any more. 'Because they were complete bastards, Marcie. What other reason do you want?'

She looks uncomfortable. That's something, at least.

'Are you . . . staying round here?' she asks.

'For the moment.' I sigh. I want to get away from her. 'What about you? Got enough money for your drugs these days, have you?'

'It didn't go on drugs,' she snaps, and has to have an extra-long taste of her favourite drug, tobacco, to remind herself of the fact. 'Not directly, anyway,' she adds, under her breath.

'Yeah, right . . . I'm sure a few good honest stereos and cars acted as middlemen. He was good at that, wasn't he? Damien?'

Her ciggie wobbles at her gnawed red mouth. She glances briefly at me, sees my face and looks away.

'Yes, Marcie, I know lots of things I'm not supposed to know. I have a habit of finding them out. Sometimes later than I should – like with JJ and that incestuous bitch of an aunt of his. But even that was sooner than it should have been. They'd have carried on with me, wouldn't they? Being my friend, getting JJ back together with me to hide the whole sordid truth from whoever might want to know it.'

My teeth hurt, but I've stepped closer to Marcie now. My hand tightens over the handle of the knife in my pocket.

'Look, Bel, I didn't know nothin' – '

'Oh, I don't find that hard to believe, surprisingly. I can go along with that, because I don't think you'd have known it even if you'd found it out. But you knew where your money was going, that money you scammed off me all those times. Didn't you?'

She looks down. Ashamed. She nods. She drops her cigarette and it fizzes as its heat burrows through a tiny cylinder of snow.

'I trusted him too,' I murmur. 'Don't worry.'

I suppose I'm quite embarrassed, especially knowing what I do about how Dreads and friends got the information from her. That bit makes me feel like wincing.

I hoist my bag on to my shoulder and hurry away from her. I don't look back.

The knife shines in the abrasive, white cold-heat of the snow. It would be easy.

A few metres away, under one of the stripped trees in the park, a girl in a long green coat and a red scarf has her arms around the waist of a big blond guy. They are wrapped up in each other. There's no one else around.

How it began. I know that much.

Damien asked Marcie, some time before that first time we all went out together, if she would sleep with one of his mates, just as a kind of joke, and that he would reward her. He'd give her a hundred quid to do whatever the hell she wanted with. He hoped that she wouldn't be clever enough to associate the activity with her past profession, and he was right.

Then he asked her to do it a second time, when he knew she was gasping for a fix. Absolutely desperate. And then a third time, this time with a total stranger. That was just before Ashwell Heights, as far as I know. The tension between them, the meaningful looks – under all of that, he was her pimp. And he took the money and ran, because Damien loved money. Damien loved having as much money as possible to buy things and to hoard things and, naturally, to score a few times himself.

Of course, he didn't need to share any of this with me. As far as I was concerned, he was working in the record shop, and that was where all his money came from.

And every time Marcie came back to me – shifty, begging, blackmailing – it was *Damien* who had sent her, and *Damien* who was using me, and *Damien* who didn't care what he said as long as I kept giving him a hundred, and another hundred.

I found all this out later. JJ knew, of course, and Imelda too. They just decided it was best not to say anything, hoping that the whole thing would blow over. And that if any of it ever came out, the blame would fall on me.

They hadn't banked on Dreads and his friends, though, and their dogged pursuit.

Dreads and his bunch of thugs got Marcie in a club one night, I found out. Dragged her into the Gents. Barred the door. She told them who had been driving and where they lived.

So they showed a kind of irony, I suppose, in calling Marcie – on my mobile – to tell her to get to Ferris Court and pick up a bleeding one-eyed victim.

Of course, in the end, it didn't happen like that. But still, it's all come full circle. There is no one left to betray me.

Only myself.

The girl and her boyfriend are hugging as they look up at the distant cathedral. He adjusts her thick, red scarf, pulling it up across her chin against the biting wind. They are paying little attention to me, here, on the park bench.

The light of the world reflects in the blade as I touch my exposed arm, and the cathedral bells are sounding twelve. I've never been squeamish, never at all.

Coldness above the coldness.

Skin sinks and tautens.

Surface tension –

This will make people sit up and listen, make them realize what happens when they try to knock me down.

– breaks.

I slice.

Is it more to see what happens than anything else? I see the Cut, here and now, before I feel it. A beautiful rush of red on the white snow. My God, it's so clear and fresh.

It's dripping on the snow. The blade tumbles and falls, losing itself in the thick whiteness.

The girl and her boyfriend are slo-mo *t-u-r-n-ing* to look at me.

257

Her face is the face of a snow queen, sculpted long and thin below a crown of icicles. Or is it just that her jaw drops as she screams?

Something is streaming out from her neck. It looks like a big thick bloodstreak against the sky. I laugh, try to lift my weakening arm, to point at her and tell her that her neck is opening and gushing blood. She seems to be running towards me over the snow, her long coat like batwings behind her.

My calves are wet on the snow. I have fallen from the bench. I suddenly feel weak, and my wrist is still erupting. Unstoppable.

Up in the skies, the rooks are laughing. Because they are closer to the sun than I am?

I see my father's face, and then everything is snow white, blood red.

28 *Not So Manic Now*

It's quiet in the church.

I walk up the nave, breathing in the smells of wood and cloth. Hearing my footsteps resounding behind me, as if recorded, looped into headphones. I'm like a morsel in the whale's belly, picking through the swallowed treasures – crosses and candles and colour-by-number pictures of saints and apostles. I walk alone through scatterings of colour.

I stop at the altar, turn around to look behind me. There is no one here. The stone and glass are silent. The stone must be breathing, soaking up footsteps and memories. Not letting any of them out.

I walk forward. I look at the big gold cross.

I peer closely at the altar cloth. There is the smallest hint of a pinkish stain, the size and shape of an autumn leaf.

With a rueful grin, I realize that they haven't been able to get it out of the cloth. Fantastic. I've left my mark. Like a birthmark on the face of Christ.

A week ago. The radio plays 'Wonderwall', the gentle strumming of the original version, as the winter landscape hardens. It is December. In ten days it will be Christmas, and the ward is festooned with glittery patterns. I could do without them. Above my bed, there's a string of cards – the usual mix of ridiculous badgers in Santa gear, pirouetting reindeers and pious-looking scenes in stables. Hideous. And around my wrist, in snowy Christmas white, my bandage.

Just above the room, there must be a vent, because I can see the occasional cloud of steam gushing out and dispersing into the air. They look like bungee-jumping wraiths.

I am back in the land of the living.

And this, from now. I sit at the brand-new table in the lounge and write a letter. My wrist is healing, and I will always have a big, ugly scar there to remind me of it all. There is another, a small one just above my eye, but that will fade in time, I've been told.

Around me, an empire of wood, glass and elegant wallpaper has grown back, almost organically. The carpets, left scorched and ripped after the party, are soft and lush again.

I hear Kate in the kitchen. These days, we hardly speak. Well, I don't need to worry about that any more, as I shan't be trapped here much longer. Before, I was condemned to hanging round here, but I've got plans now – Thailand and Malaysia, and then university and a whole new set of lives. One thing I know for certain. The knife won't come with me when I go abroad. It's tempting, but I have to leave it some time.

I am trying to write to JJ, a letter that gets everything straight and tells him where we can go from here.

My feelings towards Imelda have to come into it somewhere. She used me, all along. You can't ever be a friend while you're keeping something from someone, can you?

They are bound together now. Bound on a tram trundling into a big white nowhere, kissing and shagging as it rattles away into no-man's-land. Gasping and squelching. Passing friendly, family DNA back and forth and making something hideous.

I don't think I ever want to see either of them again.

I walk into town, wearing my thick coat and my favourite jeans with the purple stain which Kate finds impossible to get out in the wash. She's always complaining about it. She doesn't know where it comes from, of course. I imagine that one day she will read in the newspaper about the big London shop whose security tags are filled with an indelible purple dye, which stains if you try to de-tag the jeans illegally.

People are carrying umbrellas loaded with slushy snow. The streets are clean of the stuff, stripped bare, exposed like big, glistening grey wounds, but the kerbs are clogged with the dark remnants of it, the underside of winter, the anti-snow that only the devil's children play with. I wonder why no one ever makes an ugly, gun-black snowman out of the mush, stark and scarecrow-frightening against the brilliant white. Maybe it's something I should do.

For some reason I find myself taking a tram, heading high above the town. As the machine groans, I look out over this scraggy patch of land and sea and think of the tortured souls who will never escape it. When I made the Cut, I thought I was escaping, but there must have been something there, deep down inside my black-blooded heart, which hauled me up into the chill of the snow, kicked me back to consciousness.

I was never the type, not a Little Miss Suicide. Don't know why I did it. Guilt?

For everyone, it still goes on. Somewhere, down there, in the seething mass of the seaside town they forgot to bomb, there are still cars smashing into windows, and syringes pumping like blood, and monsters being made with incestuous genes. It's a wilderness, a waste-land where entropy rules. Hey, entropy increases. Did you know that? Two indisputable little words. I like them. I like the certainty of the Second Law of Thermodynamics. I like them because there's fuck all anybody can do about them.

The place hibernates when entropy takes over. In the summer, it's different. In the summer the carousels, lurid in colour, are supple as flesh. Everything is a glossy, dripping organ of the town's great stinking body, from the foaming ice-creams leaving trails on the pavement to the hot dogs with their gangrenous dribbles of mustard. Everything, from the sweaty handles of the fruit machines to the floors of the sharp-smelling bogs, gluey with piss and beer.

In the summer, this town drowns in money, it's flooded with honey. Sun-splodges uncover lovers on the beaches and cliffs. The night-walkers suck neon-bright lollies on the promenade. It smells of candyfloss, of pungent petrol and hot, angry curries. It all seems great, for a few weeks in July and August.

But then the deep-frozen rains crash in, and it's as if someone's turned off the force-barriers out by the breakwater. The demons break through, crushing and crisping all in their path.

Two months on and it's worse still. The place is a splintered winter underworld. The great wheel of the fairground looks frozen still, an alien sculpture of black steel and white ice. And all around, nature gets on with the business of destroying herself. She does a better job than we could ever hope to do. Slicing, biting, snapping. Ponds become cracked mirrors, trees become charcoal, the beach is a moonscape. All ready to be crunched and smashed by her own hands. And the air itself is freezing. Tasting it is like licking cold glass.

I get off at the sub-urban zone, the pot-black heartland of Fallytown. In streets where shadows lurk. Devon Road. I know the name. Somewhere nearby is the infamous Towndale crossing, where the teenage thugs lurk at night. I've heard what they do. They press the button again and again, writing WAIT in orange against the night, and sending ghost warbles across the rooftops. And they do what the letters say. They wait, for the sharp slice of lights through the night, and they keep pressing the button, pressing the button, trapping the car at the crossing, and if it's a lone woman, they get the crowbar out and shatter the windows, ignore her screams, get in the car. They shove her out, pocked with glass, shove her on to the pavement and take the car for a ride before stripping it of the radio and anything else they can sell. This happens just three streets from here.

I can see down to the town. Beyond, the sea is almost visible, under its cloud of ghosts. Just past a passage filled with overflowing bins, I find myself on a patch of grass surrounded by high flats. Even in the snow, it smells of smoke and shit. Somewhere, deep in the Fally heartland, a dog is barking, echoing so that it sounds like it's deep in a pit of corrugated iron. There's clattering and shouting from the other side of the open space. Signs of life – two kids, dressed in bright jumpers, scamper down a fire escape, running after something I can't see.

A young mother struggles from the hallway of one of the flats. She's pushing a buggy containing a toddler in a thick red coat. The pushchair is decorated with lurid carrier bags from Netto and Lidl.

They stop on the grass and the woman crouches down beside the little girl, gets her to stand up so she can adjust her coat. She checks the girl's top button, fusses with her scarf. The girl says something, which sounds shrill and incomprehensible to me, but the woman murmurs to her, ruffles her hair. Then she checks the girl's mittens.

The mother starts redistributing the carrier bags while the girl scampers off to play in the snow. Her red coat is the brightest splash of colour in the whole place.

I slide down the slope and head back the way I came. But in slipping past them across the grass, I have to catch her eye.

'Cold day,' she says, straightening up.

Usually, anyone who states the suppurating obvious at me gets an earful. She intrigues me, though, 'cos up close, she doesn't look or sound like a Fally. Sure, her clothes are the usual stuff – shabby greatcoat, tatty red pullover and rubbed jeans, with an awful pink woollen hat. But her face has a scrubbed, bright-eyed look. It's a lean face, with high cheekbones, but quite smooth, rounded cheeks. The strands of hair which I can see look clean and cared-for. Her lipstick's careful, a claret hue and not the lurid shade usually so beloved in these parts. When she smiles, I can see that she's taken care of her teeth.

I look over at the little girl, who's happily piling snow up into heaps. I can only see her back view, and the hooded red coat makes her look like some busy pixie getting a grotto ready.

'Entertains them, doesn't it?' says the woman.

'What? Oh, yeah.' I nod, rather too much, and I stop when I realize how stupid I look. I was just so taken aback by her voice. It's gentle, educated, with an attractive Borders-sounding accent. Not your usual Fally whine.

'Kirsty won't have much for Christmas. Hope she realizes that.'

'Mmm.' I'm not quite sure what to say. I watch the little girl, who is standing back and admiring the lumpy beginnings of her snowman. 'Do you . . . live up here, then?'

'Unfortunately, yes,' she says with a grin. And when I look into her face, her eyes haven't lost any of their sparkle. There's a sort of complicity there. 'Kirsty,' she says. 'Come on.' She holds out a hand, but the girl won't be dragged away yet.

'Looks like she's busy,' I suggest.

'Oh, yeah. She's very creative. She's always loved the snow.' The woman sighs. 'Last year was so much better, you know.'

I'm curious, now. 'How was it better?'

'We had our own house in High Down,' she says. 'Me and my husband.'

I try to stop myself from softly whistling in awe. High Down's rural, about four miles up the road from me. A mixture of timbered cottages and brand-new, four-bed semis. A far cry from Fallowdale.

'What . . . happened?' I ask her gently, trying not to look around at the desolation.

She shrugs, and turns down the corners of her big red mouth. 'My fault. I could have kept quiet, and we would have carried on just as before. But no, I confronted him about shagging his secretary.'

I pull a face. 'That must have been terrible for you. What a cliché, too.'

She blinks at me. 'Well – not really.' She raises her eyebrows, and her face creases in a smile as she gradually realizes she's given me the wrong idea. 'Such an athletic young man. Fancied him as soon as I saw him at the desk. I couldn't help it.'

Right. I see. 'And . . . your husband?'

'Well, he went up the wall. Demanded a divorce, which he got, naturally. I had to fight tooth and nail for Kirsty, but I got her.' She smiles proudly. 'The courts don't seem to mind adulterers. I needn't have fought so hard, I found out later. Brendan would only have got her if I'd been a suicidal, alcoholic nympho, and even then he'd have had to be exemplary himself.' She sighs. 'You live up here?'

'Oh, no,' I say quickly. 'I'm . . .' (What am I? Think of something, Bel.) 'Voluntary work. Visiting the elderly.'

'Oh, right. Rather you than me, girl. Don't they all stink of piss?'

'Yeah,' I tell her with a grin, and we laugh together, out loud, cleanly, happily, a good sound in this bad place, sending ghosts of breath up into the sky. Punching a hole in winter.

The little girl slaps a tiny head on to her snowman.

'Sorry to tell you my life-history,' she says, and repositions herself behind the pushchair. 'Kirsty, love, c'mon now . . . But I always feel I have to justify being in this dump. I mean . . . I can't imagine anyone would live up here by choice, can you?'

And now I'm standing in the snow, hands in pockets, knifeless for the first time.

There is more snow drifting down from the grey dome of sky above Fallowdale, and I have to close my eyes as I remember what I have lost.

And they're moving away from me, now, mother and child, clattering across the hard ground, heading for the road and the bus-stop. The woman has the pushchair held in one hand and Kirsty's little hand in the other, and she's murmuring to the girl, words of tenderness and comfort in this terrible place, saying, maybe, that there is a way out, there will be a way out. Room at the inn. One day.

The little girl twists her head round to look back at her lumpy snowman, and she sees me, and she smiles at me, and I raise a hand in return.

I see something, very briefly, before she turns back. I've got no way of telling if I'm right. I glimpse the redness on one side of her little face. It might be a trick of the light, or it might be just from the cold. Or it might be that she really does have a bright red birthmark on her soft cheek.

But she's gone, now, and there's no way I will ever know.

READ MORE IN PENGUIN

In every corner of the world, on every subject under the sun, Penguin represents quality and variety – the very best in publishing today.

For complete information about books available from Penguin – including Puffins, Penguin Classics and Arkana – and how to order them, write to us at the appropriate address below. Please note that for copyright reasons the selection of books varies from country to country.

In the United Kingdom: Please write to *Dept. EP, Penguin Books Ltd, Bath Road, Harmondsworth, West Drayton, Middlesex UB7 ODA*

In the United States: Please write to *Consumer Sales, Penguin USA, P.O. Box 999, Dept. 17109, Bergenfield, New Jersey 07621-0120.* VISA and MasterCard holders call 1-800-253-6476 to order Penguin titles

In Canada: Please write to *Penguin Books Canada Ltd, 10 Alcorn Avenue, Suite 300, Toronto, Ontario M4V 3B2*

In Australia: Please write to *Penguin Books Australia Ltd, P.O. Box 257, Ringwood, Victoria 3134*

In New Zealand: Please write to *Penguin Books (NZ) Ltd, Private Bag 102902, North Shore Mail Centre, Auckland 10*

In India: Please write to *Penguin Books India Pvt Ltd, 706 Eros Apartments, 56 Nehru Place, New Delhi 110 019*

In the Netherlands: Please write to *Penguin Books Netherlands bv, Postbus 3507, NL-1001 AH Amsterdam*

In Germany: Please write to *Penguin Books Deutschland GmbH, Metzlerstrasse 26, 60594 Frankfurt am Main*

In Spain: Please write to *Penguin Books S. A., Bravo Murillo 19, 1° B, 28015 Madrid*

In Italy: Please write to *Penguin Italia s.r.l., Via Felice Casati 20, I–20124 Milano*

In France: Please write to *Penguin France S. A., 17 rue Lejeune, F–31000 Toulouse*

In Japan: Please write to *Penguin Books Japan, Ishikiribashi Building, 2–5–4, Suido, Bunkyo-ku, Tokyo 112*

In South Africa: Please write to *Longman Penguin Southern Africa (Pty) Ltd, Private Bag X08, Bertsham 2013*

READ MORE IN PENGUIN

A CHOICE OF FICTION

Grey Area Will Self

'A demon lover, a model village and office paraphernalia are springboards for Self's bizarre flights of fancy . . . his collection of short stories explores strange worlds which have mutated out of our own – *Financial Times*

A Frolic of His Own William Gaddis

'Everybody is suing somebody in *A Frolic of His Own* . . . Among the suits and counter-suits, judgements and appeals, the central character, Oscar Crease, scion of a distinguished legal family, is even suing himself for personal injury after his aptly named Sosumi car runs over him as he hot-wires the ignition . . . Like all satire this is a very funny but also a very serious book' – *Independent on Sunday*

The Children of Men P. D. James

'As taut, terrifying and ultimately convincing as anything in the dystopian genre. It is at once a piercing satire on our cosseted, faithless and trivially self-indulgent society and a most tender love story' – *Daily Mail*

The Only Problem Muriel Spark

Harvey Gotham had abandoned his beautiful wife Effie on the *autostrada* in Italy. Now, nearly a year later, ensconced in France where he is writing a monograph on the Book of Job, his solitude is interrupted by Effie's sister. Suddenly Harvey finds himself longing for the unpredictable pleasure's of Effie's company. But she has other ideas. 'One of this century's finest creators of the comic-metaphysical entertainment' – *The New York Times*

Small g: a Summer Idyll Patricia Highsmith

At the 'small g', a Zurich bar known for its not exclusively gay clientele, the lives of a small community are played out one summer. 'From the first page it is recognisably authentic Highsmith. Perhaps approaching her lesbian novel *Carol* in tenderness and theme, it has a serenity rarely found in Highsmith's world' – *Guardian*